M000033272

The Drummond Tale

Seth O'Connell

To Josh,
Thanks for the support!
Merry Christmas.

Seth O

Dec. 2016

RED ARROW
PUBLISHING

For my father,
without whose love, I may have turned out a Drummond

Acknowledgements

I would like to thank Dr. Lawrence Pettit and Ms. Paulette Kohman for their time, advice and encouragement through the editing process.
I would also like to thank Richard Germinaro (www.logo-doctor.net) for his artistic excellence in all graphic design work. He is a true professional.
Last, I want to thank my wife for her patience and support in all my passions.

Chapter 1

Dawn was still a half-hour off as the boys navigated their way slowly through the dark timber. The stirring light of the eastern horizon was almost visible through the tops of the dense pines. The wind whistled and howled all around them, swaying the boughs of century old conifers and they felt it on the exposed flesh of their faces as it continuously shifted directions. Subtle changes in a world so vast and seemingly empty. Their noses were numb and starting to run as they crept along the worn game trail. The night had been cold and froze the thin crust of two day old snow. It crunched beneath their feet.

Shannon was in front and he chose his steps quickly but carefully, doing his best to avoid branches and unnecessary obstacles and keeping his eyes on what lay ahead. His younger brother Edgar followed some twenty feet behind. Four eyes scanning back and forth through the waning darkness that surrounded them. The dim grey played tricks on Edgar's imagination. He saw shapes and light shades that his mind thought to be elk, deer, or something entirely new and exotic.

Shannon was a practical boy. He knew better. The elk shouldn't be in the timber yet; they would still be on the parks feeding under the glow of the moon. It was on a park's edge that the boys would greet the arrival of dawn. Still the elder brother's eyes scanned their environment constantly, partly for the trail and partly from habit. There was always that chance a bull would be standing out there looking back; standing out there exactly where it shouldn't be. With elk, no one ever knew. There were no certainties.

He had walked this path dozens of times. One of the first hunts the boys' father had taken him on, way back when he was just old enough to hunt, barely big enough to carry a rifle. He had worn huge packs and over dressed back then, carrying the .300 Savage that had been handed down across generations. That gun had killed a lot of elk and a lot of deer in its time. Shannon had killed two bulls himself with it. Now Edgar carried it. He wore it this morning slung over his right shoulder as he maneuvered along behind the orange glow of his brother's hunting jacket.

Shannon stopped a moment. The crunch of his brother's boots stopped simultaneously. No signal was needed. Stopping never hurt. They were close now and it was still a bit early to shoot. There was no hurry. Out here, hurrying never helped. Shannon scanned the surrounding timber slowly, listening for nothing in particular. He just listened and waited. The first hint of predawn light began to break somewhere far away beyond the mountains that rippled off toward the east and west and north and south. Details slowly became familiar. Details of tree and shrub, mountain grass, rock and earth; details that cared not of man's desires but behaved according to a much older order, where life was growth and offspring, and death was not an end but a new beginning in a cycle which the world had accepted and only humans cared to change.

He had taken this hunt with his father, with his grandfather, and by himself. Now, Shannon was leading his brother. He knew it by heart. First, down through the thick pines to the gnarly old spruce that seemed so out of place. Then, avoiding the stunted willows and buck brush to the outcropping of broken granite that marked a slight right turn before you found yourself down in the thick, nasty mess of deadfall that covered the southern face of the ridge, falling off steep into Pickett's Gulch.

Moving northwest from the rock pile, a blazed trail led just down off the ridge's spine and onto a park in the head of Six-Point Gulch. The park was about the size of a football field and ran down into the short, narrow gulch at a forty-five degree angle to the ridge. Years ago, a blind had been built out of old stumps and broken limbs along the top of the park where the timberline met the meadow of lush feed. It allowed for a view of almost the entire park and that's where the boys were headed.

Most of the names the boys knew for geographic locations weren't official in any way. They knew the area with little reference to or use of maps. They knew the land by habit and word of mouth and spatial relation to major landmarks. The topographic maps that hung in the garage back home were old, torn and outdated and only named the major ridges, gulches and drainages. Still, Shannon had studied them constantly growing up. Edgar could hardly make sense of them. The names the boys knew for places had simply been made up over the years for the sake of

2

navigational purposes and the telling of stories around the fires at camp. Most of these descriptions had been passed down to the boys from their father; many had been passed down to him from his father or one of the other old vets that had stayed in the original Drummond elk camp and long since taken his last hunt. It was a system that had worked fine over the years and change had never come quickly or easily in the Drummond family. Eventually this system had come to label even obscure honey-holes, benches and wallows, and allowed camp members to quickly pinpoint exact locations where elk might be without consulting a map of any kind. It became second nature. But because the majority of titles were referred to in relation to another obscurity to begin with, to outsiders the labyrinth of names was mostly useless. Another reason this knowledge became sacred.

The boys' grandfather, Earl, had first started the camp in the fifties and some member of the immediate family had been hunting the area every fall since. But the days of a large, drunk and mostly joyous camp were long gone. Only the two young boys remained of the once great Drummond camp. At twenty, Shannon knew these mountains as well as any man left alive. From the hayfields south of camp to Black Bear Mountain, he had hunted nearly every drainage from mountain top to creek bottom. The terrain was remote, steep, heavily timbered and inaccessible to trucks. It could be hunted and explored only by foot, motorcycle or horse which made it too much of a bother for the average outdoorsman, who felt the bulls weren't big enough to be trophies anyway, and it was this adversity that had long kept the country as vacant of competition as it was vast and uncompromising.

Earl had been a tough, quiet man who never found much use for school. After the fifth grade, he had quit his education and followed in his father's footsteps as a miner by becoming a prospector's assistant. After his father died in a mining accident, the son married and began his own family, moving back into the house of his childhood where his mother and wife shared in the housework and raising of the couple's two sons. Earl had little to do with the boys as children and spent the majority of his free time at the saloon, gambling. Officially, he made his way as a small time prospector, buying and selling claims, but he fed the family mostly as a card player and problem solver. Like his own father he

3

was known for his stubborn grit and willingness to spill blood in solving disputes. Grandpa Earl had been killed in bar fight by a man he had called a friend all his life, stabbed to death over a minor gambling debt. He was just shy of sixty years old.

The boys slowed their pace to a crawl as they noticed the light begin to breach the crest of First Ridge at their backs. The timber had thinned and stopped sixty yards before them. Sparse patches of sedge jutted from the crusted cover of remaining snow and were just becoming visible in the pale blue rising along the steep, jagged razorbacks across the gulch. The ridge they were leaving, which they called the Split, was actually more of a knob that fell from the Main Ridge perpendicular to the four ridges running off it. The Split was a narrow finger ridge that divided Pickett's Gulch from Six-Point, though the two eventually ran together and continued the steep fall between the more prominent ridges into Fir Creek. It was as if Windy Ridge and Camp Ridge had been so violent in their forming that a wave had been raised between them to ensure the spines didn't collide. That wave was eventually shaped and sharpened by millennia of moving, melting snow. Yet the sharpness of the divide made it great transition country for bachelor bulls, and the boys' hearts thumped with anticipation as the chance of encountering elk increased with every step; their optimism shaping their outlook.

The moon, still visible to the northwest, cast added light upon long shooting lanes as it prepared for the celestial changing of the guard. Silence was impossible, but the wind worked in the boys' favor. Light gusts kissed their dry lips. They stood side by side now and each of them found a tree and peered out as the cold blue above poured soft light down upon the earth. They were overtly careful. In the absence of their movements the world fell silent, patiently awaiting the commencement of morning. The opening morning of Montana's favorite season.

Edgar quietly slipped off his right glove and rested the cold steel of the rifle's action in his palm. His fingertips were still thawing, but the ache didn't bother him. It was cold but not unbearable. A crisp fall morning. The last Sunday in October. His brother stood beside him motionless, his eyes fixated on the vast world suddenly stretched out before them. From their vantage

4

point the majority of the park became visible and the horizon glowed like distant war. It was light enough to shoot.

Only after being convinced that the park was indeed empty did the boys creep over and slide down into the blind. Behind its cover they sat while the sun rose behind them. A high and cloudless sky received the rising torch in majestic splendor and with it, instant radiant heat. Shannon closed his eyes a moment and smiled to himself for the first time in twenty-four hours. All the packing and planning, the navigating of the bikes through the snow and the struggles in setting up camp. It had left him distracted. Now, the warm rays felt delightful on his cold skin. Hunkered back on his elbows he wiggled his toes in his boots and felt awake, alive.

Edgar squatted on his haunches against the cover of the bleached, sagging blind peeking over the horizontal limbs and anxiously scanning his surroundings. His mind raced as he carried on an internal dialogue. In his imagination, they were no longer hunting. They were outlaw fugitives on the run in the days of the wild frontier, all alone in this world. The lonesome solitude was no vast stretch. The waiting made him bored and he grew tired. He continuously checked his brother for signs that it was time to move on.

About thirty minutes after dawn, the morning hit full bloom. The Hunter's Moon had vanished. Birds chirped, sang and squawked. The landscape itself seemed restless. Finally, Shannon stood to his feet with an audible, relaxed sigh, and the boys moved back into the cover of the timber and started down into the shadow of the gulch. As they walked, Shannon guided the brothers along the ridge keeping at a middle elevation with Six-Point Gulch below them to their right. Whenever the timber opened up enough to allow it, he would stop to scan the ravine below and peer across to the adjacent spine of Windy Ridge so steep and inhospitable and partially veiled by a rising mist.

They continued on as the ridge rounded and morning warmed and the gulch broadened into a small valley before them. Reaching the ridge's gentle conclusion the boys stopped again. They sat down atop a loose rock ledge with the sunshine on their faces, drank juice-boxes and ate crackers. They spoke in low whispers and fought to hold back laughter at each others' jokes.

5

Shannon leaned his Winchester Magnum against the trunk of a nearby tree and removed his boots and adjusted his wool socks in the warmth of the low hanging sun.

The Leupold scope that rode above the action of his mighty canon was less than a year old. Top of the line. It was a Christmas gift from their father. The last gift given to an eldest son.

Tom Drummond, the boys' father, passed away shortly after the New Year. His life cut short by the usual tragedy of the Drummond family, he had fallen off a ladder drunk while taking down Christmas lights and died less than a month later from the injuries he sustained. He had been a drunk the majority of his life. But he was functional and the boys never saw him as an alcoholic growing up. To them, he had always been tough, wise and stoic, even when he was at his worst. Except for the occasional spanking, Tom had never struck his sons. Nor had he struck their mother as far as they knew. Yet he was often cold, brooding or absent for long stretches at a time. And although he was a quiet man, he could be psychologically and emotionally abusive. But this was all the boys had ever known and they idolized the man. Shannon especially was forgiving of his father's faults, and it wasn't until their mother left that this erroneous image had been broken.

The spring semester of his sophomore year at college was just getting underway when his father had his accident. He drove home the following morning, leaving school and his youth behind. After Tom's death, Shannon sold most of the meager possessions their father had owned to make ends meet. But he wouldn't hock the guns, the bikes, or the tent. He just couldn't bring himself to do it. No matter how much they needed the money. He figured his father would understand.

After the funeral, he went to work on settling his family's estate. There was a life insurance policy, but it was hardly enough to cover the hospice care and family debts. Shannon spent the boys' modest inheritance to keep the little house out on Weekender Lane, the house his parents had bought after their honeymoon; long before a fork-tongued preacher man stole their mother away, or saved her, depending on one's point of view. She had never called or wrote after she left, and even after their father's death, neither of her sons tried to reach her.

6

Shannon never found time to grieve. He went to work as a clerk's assistant at the county courthouse then took on a second job on the weekends as a custodian to keep up with the bills that seemed never ending. Edgar was just a freshman in high school. Two months shy of fifteen. He had just finished driver's training. Tom had promised to buy him his first car. The blow was crushing to both boys, yet visibly hardest on young Edgar. For the next six months he hardly uttered a peep. His grades, which were never high, became horrid. Teachers took pity on him though, and he managed to make it through the year mostly on their leniency. Something hard and angry smoldered and spread within his soul.

Shannon looked out for his brother the best he could, but his efforts were mostly in vain. Shannon had always been a good brother, but Edgar needed a parent. Besides, Shannon was coping with his own loss and struggling with his own pain. Neither of them ever spoke openly of their feelings or sought counseling. It was the Drummond way; the way they had learned from their father and him from his father before.

It was easier for Shannon though. In his rare moments between jobs the elder Drummond rarely slowed down. He spent what free time could be found caring for his brother and studying, trying best he could to get back to school and finish his degree. He simply blocked the questions and despair from his mind and chose instead to rise above such a fate. He tried to erase the memories of his family. He doused his insecurities and fears in the flames of ambition in an attempt to stay one step ahead of his bleeding wound. A seed of exceptionalism took root in his heart - his life had been unfair, those he had loved had failed him. But he didn't need anybody. He would get by on his own. Hunting was the one area his father's status remained heroic and unblemished.

His brother dealt with the grief more openly. Edgar drank and tried drugs. He had violent mood swings, fought and lashed out without warning or fell back into his detached silence. There were entire weekends where he failed to rise out of bed. Wrestling was the only thing that kept him in school. Already a two time state champion grappler by the time he reached high school, he only became fiercer, more intimidating and more unpredictable with each passing year. He was an animal, but the praise of success

7

kept him somewhat stable amidst the world. That and his brother's love.

The younger Drummond was riding a rare high at that moment – opening day, hunting with his last remaining hero. He was smiling, and hope seemed to find the boys as the wind vanished completely and the morning sun beat down, inching toward its midday zenith. The snow softened as it melted, and he wore his heavy jacket unzipped.

The forest changed as a game trail led the boys down off the ridge. The dense pine was replaced by spruce and ancient fir spaciously distributed and covered in moss. The open giants had always been their father's favorite environment to hunt. Their sturdy trunks and long, stout limbs cast shade and shelter perfect for afternoon bedding and their ample spacing provided endless lanes to shoot.

Both boys carried their rifles in one hand now. Snaking along through the transitioning timber, they abandoned the trail and worked their way in a diagonal fashion from side to side covering the deep gulch as they moved down toward the creek bottom. Occasionally a patch of deadfall or cluster of new pines altered their path. Otherwise they moved as they pleased. It wasn't long before they heard the creek running. The hike downhill had been effortless. Shannon checked his watch. Five minutes to ten. It had been a great hunt so far. Unfortunately even perfect hunts don't guarantee elk. There were some years when three weeks of great hunting might not lead to so much as a shot. With elk, nobody knew for sure. You just had to keep out amongst them, keep trying, and never under any circumstances give up. Shannon knew all of this and without word or effort he was passing this knowledge down to his brother as Drummond's had always passed knowledge.

The boys hit the creek and followed it upstream. The mid-morning sun reflected brightly off the retreating snow, casting a hard glare. It was like a different world from the dark, frosty dawn only a few hours gone. They moved quickly now heeding less attention to stealth and sharing their thoughts in muffled whispers. Edgar's mind wandered as he daydreamed more and hunted less. Both boys wore their guns slung over a shoulder. But Shannon remained committed. He knew that a lone bull fresh out of rut

8

could be anywhere still feeding, and it seemed like they always showed up when they were least expected.

A half mile ahead the valley opened up on a vast plain scattered with rolling foothills separating two adjacent mountain ranges. It was ranchland, pasture for cattle and it was no easy place to make a living. The snow had all but melted off around them and much of the moisture had fallen as rain at this elevation where the knee high grass grew the same color as the sun, hunched over from the first hint of the winter cold. The creek bed they followed spilled into Fir Creek across the fence and vanished down a hill toward the boys' right where the highway was visible a mile off. They headed in the other direction creeping through the aspens that surrounded the marshy fork where the creeks ran together back toward the evergreen timberline to the north and east and circling the base of the bluff that ran back up onto Camp Ridge. As the meadow began to climb toward drier earth, three small parks became visible atop the knobby foothills across from them. Shannon couldn't help but stop and inspect them through his binoculars even though the morning was nearly gone. A red-headed woodpecker caught Edgar's attention as it hammered away at invisible grubs in a tall rotted cottonwood. He wondered how the creature could move its head so violently without harming itself. The raw bluntness of the movement fascinated him.

From the meadow a blazed trail wound up a third hillside climbing toward the timbered ridge that ran parallel to the creek they had been following. This ridge ran steep and narrow for about a half mile before it dented into a series of benches. It was on the second of these benches that the boys had set up their tent, in the same spot they had camped for the first week of rifle season since either could remember. It was a long hike back up to camp, but the boys had left Edgar's Kawasaki at the top of the ridge where the blazed trail came out. They had parked it there in the dark, long before dawn and together rode out the trail on Shannon's bike. They were less than a thousand yards from the bike when Edgar couldn't help himself any longer.

Shannon was walking with his head down, planning out his first big breakfast as camp cook when the shot rang out behind him. The surprise nearly ruined his trousers. He ducked and spun quickly and his brows narrowed just as fast. Edgar was headed off

9

to their left and didn't notice his brother's irritation. A moment later he reappeared holding a fat grouse by the head and grinned widely at his brother. Shannon shook his head, angry, but said nothing. He ran a hand through his sweat dampened hair. He was hungry and his thoughts returned to the bacon, eggs, and hash browns waiting to be cooked back at camp.

Edgar twisted the still quivering bird's head off, spraying blots of blood black on the dirty snow. His smile disappeared. Short grey feathers covered his hands and fell gently toward the ground. He watched the feathers touch down silently upon the dirty, needle covered snow, lost in thought a moment. Then he trudged along behind his brother clutching the bird's sinewy legs loosely in one hand.

Chapter 2

The cold nipped at Edgar's ears as the men waited for the mixer to finish pouring. As the truck backed up, they went to work with their shovels, distributing the fresh cement evenly and then leveling it off. They worked quickly, with a sense of urgency. It was a clear morning, and their breath rolled into the air thick as the exhaled smoke from a cigarette. Rising and setting in under nine hours, the sun provided little heat this late in the fall. Although there were only skiffs of white visible upon the highest mountain peaks surrounding the valley, winter was near.

His knees trembled from lack of sleep but he worked with determination. The job was nearing an end. He knew the snow would bring layoffs with it. He had been on the crew just two months, and the unskilled labor was always the first to go. Construction was slowing down. There wouldn't be many job openings until spring.

The job was already his third since returning home. It wasn't that he was a terrible worker. In fact, he worked great when he was sober. His biggest problem was showing up. Once he was on the job everything was fine. Staying busy kept him together. The mornings were easy and the afternoons weren't bad if there

10

was work to be done. It was the nights that were hell. His demons waited for the darkness.

At ten the men took a break. The crew gathered along the rear wall of a nearby salon. Sitting on lunch boxes or the curb, they smoked cigarettes and drank coffee from metal thermoses and Styrofoam cups. A few snacked on pretzels or chips from their lunches. Edgar crouched against the wall a dozen feet beyond the group. His head swayed. He rested his eyes fighting to stay awake. His stomach growled. One of the others approached him.

"What's up Eddy?" He asked in a strident tone. Edgar pulled his thoughts together and focused on the face above him. Only his nieces were allowed to call him Eddy.

"Nothing." He answered, climbing to his feet. Then, almost against his will he added, "And how's Zack?"

"Not too bad. I was hoping for a little fresh snow this weekend, but it doesn't look like we're gonna get any. You been out hunting at all?" Zack fired back. His hands were dug into the pockets of a worn, navy-blue Carhart jacket and his chin protruded outward due to an under-bite which made his thin lips almost invisible behind his untrimmed beard.

"No." Edgar answered firmly, hoping it would end the conversation.

"You and your brother still hunt up there in the Medicine Mountains?" Zack went on without catching the hint. Edgar didn't answer. Something about Zack's face began to bother him. There was an urge to deck him. He turned away. The block had been coned off and he gazed down it to where traffic was being detoured. It was sparse now, but a few cars waited at the manned intersection.

"I guess you haven't really been around to hunt much the last couple years," Zack speculated, "But I figured your brother would still be getting out after em. He's a hunting son of a bitch that brother of yours... I hear he might be running for attorney general huh?"

"Don't know." Edgar said without making eye contact.

"Gonna be pretty tough to beat old Berkman...Course it'll probably help having a big war hero for a brother." He laughed and slapped Edgar on the shoulder of his insulated work jacket. Edgar spit and walked away without so much as a smile.

11

He put his gloves on and went back to work. He wore no watch and paid no attention to the time. He just worked. When everyone else broke for lunch he sat against the wall and chewed at the calluses on his rough hands. The other guys were used to it and nobody bothered him much. At first they'd felt bad for him. Some tried to share their food, but he never took anything they offered aside from a chew or a smoke. Once in a while he brought some candy or a bag of chips. Usually he ate nothing.

They knew about his drinking. Nobody said anything. Nobody offered help. But they all knew. They talked about him behind his back, called him crazy. 'He's crazy from the war' they assumed. 'Something terrible must have happened to him over there' they speculated. 'He suffers from Post Traumatic Stress Disorder' they diagnosed. They talked a lot but did nothing.

After work, he walked home. His coworkers offered him rides, but he liked to walk. The trip was less than two miles. He walked it twice a day. It took him about twenty minutes each way. Those walks were his favorite part of the day. He had a destination, so he had a purpose and he could just get lost in thought. Unfortunately, he always made it home and the walk ended. Some days, if the weather was nice and his outlook was positive he took new routes, digressing as long as possible to make the trip last.

Entering his lonely, cramped apartment, he made himself a small dinner and sat in the kitchen while the sun set. Then, he turned on the single-bulb lamp that lit the living room and paced amidst the shadows as they climbed up on the sparse furniture. Like the rest of the shabby apartment, there wasn't much to the room. There was an antique desk in the front corner beside the window, a couch halfway to the bathroom door, and a small, stiff armchair beside it. Both the couch and the chair were directed toward an old television that sat on an oak end table against the far wall.

The path he paced ran behind the couch from the front door to the kitchen. The space was about twelve feet by four feet. Smaller than his neighbor's dog run. He paced it back and forth, sometimes for hours on end. Some nights the pacing would suffice. The storm would threaten but pass, and he would sit down and read the newspaper or absently watch one of the three channels that came in on his TV's fuzzy reception. Then he would fall asleep.

Those nights were the good nights. More often than not, the pacing would only lead to agitation and the sort of gut-wrenching anxiety that drove restless souls to form sinful habits. Thus, he would throw his jacket on, walk five blocks to the small corner grocer and purchase cheap, venomous poison. Returning home, he would sit himself down at the kitchen table or in the stiff, uncomfortable armchair and self-medicate. At first, the drink brought relief. The first few pulls built a warming sensation in his stomach and eased the tension of the vice grip in his head.

It never solved the problem though and he always overdid it. The calming reprieve became an intensifying agent. He would laugh and whisper to himself before his more primal emotions showed themselves in violent extremes. On a good night, he passed out. On a bad night, he ran out of drink visiting and revisiting the fridge and the cupboards certain that if he only had one more pull or one more beer it would prove to be the solution he needed. Ten o'clock would turn to two in the morning and he would find himself unnerved in the agonizing darkness of his cramped bedroom. It was not unusual for him to sleep ten or fewer hours in a week. The screaming, doubtful voices in his own mind only found strength in his body's fatigue. A man forged on toughness, suddenly so weak.

Tonight, he ate macaroni. There was no milk and the pasta was dry. He ate only a few bites despite it being his first meal all day. Then he paced for twenty minutes before reaching a decision. He didn't know what he should do. But he knew he must do something. Grabbing his jacket he walked out into the failing colors of twilight. The last scarlet blaze of a sunken sun disappearing behind the immense ranges to the west cast the same long shadows as his living room lamp, except now they were beginning to blend with general darkness all around. He walked quickly along the sidewalk with a determined stride. His cheeks numbed in the chill evening air, its thin crispness piercing his lungs with each vibrant inhale. It was dark when he crossed the final four-way-stop to his destination. His body had become accustomed to the temperature and his heart rate slowed.

13

It was still early evening and the quiet outside brought him doubt. He stopped beside the entrance and blew into his dirty, cupped palms without looking in through the small rectangular windows set to either side of the heavy oak door. He didn't have to look for the door's brass handle. He knew where it was. Balling his hands into fists he squeezed them hard a few times to check their condition. Satisfied, he swung the door open and stepped inside the pub with forced resilience. At first his entrance went unnoticed and he walked swiftly. However, by the time he reached the end of the bar and found himself half-way across the dimly-lit room beyond it, a dozen eyes watched his every move.

The pub was half empty. A typical early weekday evening crowd conversed sparingly in a few clustered groups, and two of the three pool tables were occupied. Edgar could tell all of this without glancing around. He had been trained to catch every detail of his surroundings. He figured looking around would provide no help so he hid the shame of his purpose behind a stern grimace that was very real. He kept his eyes forward as he walked toward the hallway that led to the office in back. Every noise in the bar was registered and quickly analyzed by his keen ear. From the loud cackle of the old jukebox to the slightest scraping of a barstool. Then heavy footsteps catching up to him. He did not change his pace. The small hairs on his neck stood as his brain prepared for confrontation. A large man appeared before him. Middle-aged and balding, he had the purple tint and large pores of a life spent drinking, a predominant nose, and dry, suspecting eyes that had long since lost any luster. He spoke from a gaping hole that formed amidst a scruffy auburn goatee.

"What the fuck you think you're doing here?"

The man's voice hardened and hollowed like a raspy blues singer's as he spoke. He wore a dingy t-shirt, faded and ruined by sweat. His hairless forearms displayed faded, illegible tattoos.

"I came to see Mr. Grisham." Edgar answered, his face stone and steady. The man before him was about three inches taller and broad shouldered. He had the head of a bison.

"You're not welcome here, you fucking nut-job. Get the fuck out of here before I bust your skull. Or did you forget what happened last time?"

14

Edgar knew this obscene language was a substitute for courage. The man arched his head back slightly and kept his arms out at his sides in an attempt to appear more intimidating. Staring him in the eyes, Edgar caught every subtle quiver of doubt. It was a gift he had. He had been born with it. The man's ear twitched faintly and his eyes unintentionally shifted slightly back toward the bar in search for support. Then his knees shifted his weight. But Edgar remained still, debating his next move a million miles an hour.

"Edgar Drummond," said an unseen voice, saving the big man's face from irreparable damage. "It has been too long."

The voice was strong and smooth like that of a news anchor. There was a slow rhythmic clicking of fine soled shoes on tile. A crisp, taut man in a black suit and navy tie appeared behind Edgar's adversary. The silky voiced man appeared to be in his late fifties or early sixties. He had refined creases in the dark leather of his face. His silver hair still had streaks of a great stallion's jet black. He wore it combed back but not greased. His smile revealed a large set of strong teeth to match his sharp angled jaw. But the thug didn't see the smile. His eyes remained locked on Edgar as he breathed audibly through pulse heightened wheezes.

"You can relax, Austin. Young Edgar appears to be quite sober tonight. I doubt we will have any disorder."

Slowly and against his will, the troll-like bulk of Austin moved away. The last look he gave Edgar was peaked in a confident sneer. Edgar said nothing.

Mr. Grisham came forward and offered Edgar a discreet embrace. Edgar accepted, but the all-encompassing hate in his soul remained hot. He hated himself for what he had come to do. And he wished he had booze in his veins.

"You have the look of a determined man about you tonight, Edgar." Mr. Grisham commented with a confident smile. He bore the grace and worldliness of a man entitled to guess at the emotional state of others.

Edgar began to speak, but Mr. Grisham interrupted him.

"Come. Let us speak in the office."

Once inside the small, tastefully decorated office, Grisham set down in sturdy oak armchair behind a matching desk. He crossed an ankle over his knee and invited his guest to sit. Edgar

15

declined, bringing a crease to the old man's brow. Evidently, the reaction caught him off guard in some way. He uncrossed his leg and leaned forward with his arms laid open across the desk, displeased at being forced to look up at Edgar but unwilling to stand since he had already sat.

"What is it that I can do for you Edgar?" He asked, his voice losing some of its polite charm.

Edgar suddenly had trouble looking him in the eye. Grisham noticed this. Pleased to regain some advantage he remained silent in waiting. He was well-aware of Edgar's intentions in coming and the question was a mere formality.

"I was hoping for some work," Edgar fumbled, his eyes bouncing from Grisham's face to the edge of the polished desk before him. "Nothing permanent. Maybe just something on the side."

The last, he added in the hopes of maintaining a meager level of self-respect. Grisham looked at the young man hard. When Edgar finally managed to hold his eyes, he leaned back in his chair and inhaled slowly. The chair squeaked.

"I would love to help, Edgar, but I already have three bartenders as it is, you see."

"I didn't mean bartending." Edgar retorted quickly, his eyebrows furrowing.

"Well, we no longer serve food and I hardly think you would make it as a swamper." Grisham said faking a degree of confusion.

Edgar appeared to be at an impasse unsure of how to proceed. He had been previously recruited heavily and hadn't expected this misdirection. He began to fidget with his hands. A long moment followed.

"I was thinking I could go to work as an earner." He broke in over the dull hum of the furnace and strangled noises from out in the bar. His voice was low and without confidence. His spirit broken.

Grisham knew he had him and took his time. He put his hands in his laps and rubbed his thumbs, not in a fidgeting twiddle but in a slow methodical pattern – up and down. His demeanor had a fierce canine quality to it despite his smooth etiquette and manners.

"Zeke is dead, Edgar, and those days are gone. I run legitimate businesses. Everything is on the up and up." Then as if it were only an irrelevant after-thought, "Besides, you're in no shape for that racket. You lack moral control."

When Edgar neither replied nor motioned toward leaving Grisham felt obligated to go on.

"Look, I love you like a son, Edgar. Your uncle was practically family. I cut my teeth beside your grandfather. The Drummond's have always been a hardworking, dependable lot. I know you have been through a lot. And it pains me to say this, but you're a drunk, Edgar, and you're a liability."

Edgar took the words without showing anger. He didn't argue or beg. His pride was all he had left. It had taken a great hit just to come here, and he refused to see it further offended. He simply gave a dull nod of understanding and waited momentarily for Grisham to finish. When the older man said nothing more, he turned on his heels and departed without a word. He was half-way across the bar, marching with great haste, when he heard Austin's gruff remark.

"Night princess. And don't come back you little fairy."

Edgar stopped. Every fiber of his being vibrated with rage and he shot a death stare in the comment's direction. The moment he stopped three shady looking thugs tensed and rose from their bar stools. All of them were big men. Austin's ugly skull was visible behind them. He stood at the bar and returned Edgar's violent gaze with a challenging smirk. Then he gave a throaty chuckle. "Wanna play that game again?"

Edgar remained defiant a moment longer. The men at the bar made no advance and only awaited his next decision. He tasted the dry bitterness of blind hate on his tongue. His heart pulsed with the surge of mind-altering adrenaline that he had grown so accustomed to overseas and never learned to live without. He turned and exited the bar without a word.

He zipped his jacket and crossed the street. The craving for war pounded in the front of his overloaded brain, pulsing through his veins with every beat of his heart. He sped along the dimly lit sidewalks but didn't head for home. There was another destination dominating his thoughts. His wounded pride limped along behind him in the shadowy darkness. He was a man of simple principles.

He saw no problem with dying so long as it came before dishonor. As his brooding deepened, the cold no longer affected him, and by the time he reached his destination he was raving like a lunatic.

Quinn O'Leary opened his front door to find this frantic mess standing on his stoop, blue-skinned from the cold. He assumed his old friend was drunk and barely tried to hide his disapproval, yet he had seen the full force of Edgar's fury many times and it only took him a moment to realize this was more than a drunken stupor. His friend was in one of his fatal trances. He felt he had been wronged and would not stop until his lust for vengeance had been satisfied, which usually required the spilling of massive amounts of blood.

"I need a piece." Edgar muttered behind far-away eyes.

"Whoa. Calm down." Quinn said raising his hands. He was already aware the statement was not a request. Edgar had come for a gun and he would leave with one. Quinn was only trying to slow the inevitable in hopes of Edgar's reaching a more logical course of action on his own. He tried to gather details, but his friend was too far gone. Every question received the same answer.

"Sell me a gun. I'll give you a hundred dollars."

"First of all, we both know you don't have a hundred dollars. Second, I won't give you a weapon until you tell me what it is you need it for."

Edgar's patience visibly crumbled, but he managed to refrain and quell his temper limiting his reaction to a violent huffing and silent glare of warning. There would be no compromise. Quinn gave a last feeble effort.

"Why can't you use your rifle?"

"I'll give a hundred dollars on Friday. I swear to God."

Yeah, if you're not dead or in prison by then, Quinn thought.

"Alright. I have a .45 that's not registered." Quinn conceded with dejection. "Just stay right here you crazy bastard."

Quinn turned and moved down a narrow hallway, disappearing into a room on the right. There was a commotion of sliding drawers. Then, Quinn returned holding a black handgun by the barrel and the stock directed toward Edgar. A look of disappointment showed on his face.

"I only got four rounds for it." He said as Edgar examined the weapon.

"You serious?"

Edgar clicked the action open and looked to Quinn with annoyance.

"Yeah, I am." Quinn challenged.

This time it was Edgar that conceded.

"That'll have to do then." He said, returning his eyes to the gun.

Quinn handed him the shells. Edgar loaded them into the magazine and cocked one into the chamber flicking the safety on with his thumb. Then, he lifted his jacket and slid the firearm into the back of his jeans.

"Thanks." He said flatly.

"Yeah. I'm telling the cops you stole that shit."

Edgar swung the door open and left without replying. Quinn followed him out to the concrete steps.

"Don't forget that hundred dollars either, asshole." He half-shouted in frustration.

Edgar didn't look back. He was walking quickly already, his hands dug deep in the pockets of his jacket. Quinn shook his head and swore to himself. He watched Edgar move to the end of the block before stepping back inside. His ears stung from the cold.

"Crazy prick."

By the time Edgar returned to the bar, it was ten o'clock. Inebriation had grown and the sound of pompous voices could be heard over the buzz of music from the sidewalk. This time, he didn't need to stop for confidence. He swung the heavy door open and moved swiftly. The bar was no busier than it had been earlier, but now people were up and moving about. This created a commotion of slight traffic. Still he quickly found his purpose.

Austin was no longer behind the bar. He was leaned over a small table flirting with a couple of tired old witches, their brittle arms propped up by the elbow and absently holding half-smoked cigarettes between tar-stained, hob-knuckled fingers. Austin was smiling disgustingly as he swooned and the withered hags responded with raspy cackles.

Edgar covered the distance between them in a flash. By the time Austin noticed his presence, he was already within six feet.

19

The troll straightened to his full height, his eyes exposing his concern. In a single burst, Edgar swung a pistol filled hand toward the man's giant skull, striking him hard along the temple. Austin didn't even have time to defend himself. The big man crumbled to the floor.

Two other men stood up from a back table where they had been absently playing cards. They started in Edgar's direction but would not make it close. Before they reached him he jammed the barrel of the pistol behind Austin's ear and looked up at them. They stopped dead in their tracks surprised by the fierce calm of his face.

Edgar blew a light spray of snot from one nostril onto Austin's motionless body and kicked him hard in the rips. Then he turned the weapon on the two men, who were now holding their empty hands up about shoulder height in a posture of surrender. Edgar never uttered a word, and the bar was silent except for the sound of Michael Stipe losing his religion. He hesitated a moment longer before backing his way to the door and quickly vanishing into the cold dark of the night.

Chapter 3

Shannon turned off the water and stepped out of the shower. He dried himself then used the towel to wipe steam from the bathroom mirror. He examined his nude form carefully, inspecting it for any unfavorable changes. Satisfied with what he saw, he practiced his smile and moved to the bedroom to dress.

Breakfast was ready when he came downstairs, and the smell of eggs and bacon caused his mouth to salivate. The girls were playing in the living-room. It sounded like they were getting along fine for the moment. But Shannon knew how short-lived such sibling peace could be.

"Melanie, Nicole…come and eat, girls," he directed gently, nurturing the sentiment of the morning.

He kissed Jill and fixed plates for the girls.

"Hun, this looks delicious," he commented, snagging a bite of bacon before sitting.

He poured himself a glass of milk. The sight of six-year-old Nicole attempting to jelly a piece of toast brought a smile to his face. He watched the struggle silently for a moment. She looked up at him with distress as a large gob of grape jelly fell from her knife and landed in a purple pile on the white tablecloth. He laughed, and she giggled.

The couple carried light conversation through the meal. They talked absently about work, travel, and a story Jill had read on climate change in that morning's paper. The girls hummed, fidgeted and asked questions. Their questions stemmed from the fragments they picked out of their parents' conversation or from nowhere at all.

After breakfast the girls returned to the living-room to watch cartoons. Shannon did the dishes then sat down to read the paper. As he read, his mind became a whirl of thought. He fought against these distracting tangents, yet as always was unable to free himself from work. He remembered his promise to Jill. She would support him in his political aspirations, and he would never put his family second. Jill kept her end of the bargain every day. He did his best to do the same.

Finally, when his agitation became too much, he folded the paper up and set it down on the kitchen counter. His hair was dry now, and he adjusted it slightly using the window for a mirror. On his way up to the bedroom he stopped a moment in the living-room and checked in on the girls. They were laid out on their bellies some six feet from the TV. Their chins were propped up in cupped hands supported by their elbows. Melanie, his three-year-old, was almost an identical miniature copy of her older sister except Nicole had her legs arched up at a right angle and crossed just below the knee.

He didn't recognize the cartoon they were watching; he didn't recognize any of the cartoons they watched. This one had creeping little aliens allied alongside kids with dark, pointy hair and big, round eyes. He watched for a few moments but couldn't follow the storyline. It was mostly still shots of action poses with bright flashes of background doing all the moving. He wondered what ever happened to Bugs, Daffy, and Elmer Fudd. He shook his head, grateful for the quality of cartoons he had grown up with, and then made his way upstairs.

21

He threw on a sweatshirt and a pair of sneakers and stuck his phone in his front pocket. He stood in the middle of the room a moment and looked around him trying not to forget anything. The light shifting of tub-water caught his ear and he made his way down the hall to the bathroom.

Jill was in the bath and he couldn't help but sneak a peek at her. She was a good looking woman. Her body had changed from bearing two children but remained tight. She was slender and her skin was still smooth and youthful. The age marks she showed gave her a hue of life experience and only made her appearance more graceful. He needed to show more passion toward her and seeing her so natural in her beauty, he made a quick note of this.

She smiled up at him absently and he was glad to feel a spark of electricity shoot through him. He tried to remember the last time they'd been spontaneously intimate and couldn't recall. For a moment he debated taking a break from his day and taking her right then and there. The water still steamed slightly. He breathed the warm moisture. It smelled of what he guessed was lavender. It would be hot to take her now with the kids downstairs the way things used to be. He returned her smile. But the moment passed, and for whatever reason he made no advance.

"I was going to run up to the game for a little bit. Was there anything we needed?"

She pursed her lips in thought.

"I don't think so. Check and see if we have bread." She didn't even bother trying to make him stay anymore, "Honey, don't forget we are having dinner at my parents' tonight."

He faked a cringe and clicked his tongue in disappointment. "Oh damn, I forgot. What time was that at again?"

Jill rolled her eyes and pinned her right cheek up with a sigh.

"Very funny mister," she said sternly. He laughed.

"I'll be home by three-thirty, four at the latest. I love you."

"Love you too." These were words they both meant. Words that kept a relationship alive when schedules and familiarity left everything feeling tiresome.

He kissed the girls on his way out, and drove uptown. By the time he arrived at the stadium, the parking lot was full. He

22

found a spot on the street less than five minutes walk and locked the Explorer.

The sky was high and of the lightest blue; a true fall sky. Sparse, stretched clouds moved quickly across the heavens. It was brisk, only cold when the wind whipped. But the sun was shining bright white and had given the impression from inside the vehicle that the day was warmer.

He weaved his way through the noise and commotion of various tailgate parties, stopping briefly to say hello at nearly every one. Shannon knew everybody, and he considered most his friends. But acquaintances would be a better term; he had little time to build true relationships. As always though, he was friendly, albeit careful and guarded. He kept the subject away from himself and if it found him, he spoke in loose generalities, avoiding the predicament of taking a position unless it was one the second party was passionate about, in which case he usually agreed. When he was pinned down or questioned, he drew others into the conversation and slipped away as soon as he was no longer required.

Finally, he found Steve Zowiky's pick-up and was able to let his guard down. Zowiky stood under a red and black canopy grilling brats while Mark Getz, Ryan Howlinger and their wives, carried on and drank beer. Shannon considered Zowiky to be one of his only true friends. He was a bit of a numbskull and lazy as a bum, but he was also clever, handy, and a master socialite. He was one of the few people Shannon trusted to always be himself.

Over the years, Zowiky had been in and out of a number of businesses, most of which failed. Still he learned something from each experience and always walked away a better man. The struggles never discouraged him. He had married into money and done well for himself in the long run. He owned several rental properties, a carwash, and a lucrative coffee shop. Shannon was a year younger than Zowiky. The two of them had been basketball teammates in high school and became close friends during Shannon's junior year. Getz and Howlinger were both old classmates of Zowiky's and had attended law school with Shannon.

23

"You sneaky son of bitch," Zowiky called out, greeting him with an extended arm holding a beer. "You told me there was no way you would make it out today."

Shannon flashed a smile and took a short swig off the bottle. The brown glass was cold in his palm.

"Never count me out." He hinted slyly.

"You never cease to amaze me Drummond." Zowiky laughed. Shannon could see the gleam on his friend's eyes and realized his cohorts were getting an early start.

He barely finished a beer and picked at his plate of beans and potato salad. He was pleased when it was time for the game to begin, and he left his second beer alongside the barbeque – half full.

Zowiky was a fixture at the football games and the six of them took seats that were saved in his usual section. Despite the cool temperatures, the stadium was packed by kick-off. It was a great place to be seen. Everyone was bundled up. The bleachers were a sea of red and black. There was an uproar for the opening kickoff, but after a pair of three-and-outs by each team the anticipation was wearing off and conversations picked up again.

"A little surprised you aren't out hunting, Drummond," Getz commented while the Tiger's offense huddled. His legs were covered to the waist by the blanket he and his wife shared.

"Oh, I would be. It would have been a perfect morning," Shannon answered, nodding in agreement; his eyes remaining glued to the field. "But I already bagged my elk."

"Oh, really?"

"Yep. I shot a bull opening morning." Shannon said downplaying his pride. It was his favorite conversation.

"Nice one?" Getz asked, looking quite impressed.

"Uhh, not bad," Shannon shrugged. "I've shot bigger."

"How many points did he have?" Getz asked. He was no hunter and was getting close to the limits of his knowledge on the subject. Shannon, being an expert on hunting talk as well as generalizations, was able to adjust effortlessly.

"He's a decent five." He said simply, though there was so much more to say. "I'll give you a few choice steaks or a roast if you're interested."

"Yeah. Sure. We would love that." Getz said hesitantly. He glanced at his wife and back to Shannon, then back once more.

"I really enjoy lean game." His wife almost whispered. "It's good for you."

On the inside, Shannon laughed, but he didn't allow himself to show it. He nodded.

"Where did you shoot him?" Howlinger chimed in.

"Right behind the shoulder."

"No, I mean where were you at?"

"Out in the woods." Here everyone laughed. Then, without giving a true response, Shannon transitioned smoothly, "We all need to get together for dinner one night. I know Jill would love that."

"Where is Jill today?" Getz's wife asked.

"She is at home with the girls. She's not a big football fan, and even less a cold weather football fan."

"She's smart," the woman said with a smile. "It's freezing out here."

Shannon glanced about him a moment. His lips were dry and he scratched at the bottom one with his index finger. He thought it was a perfect afternoon.

"Yeah, she's sure cooling off. Summer's over."

There was a pleasing note to his voice as if he had been waiting a long time for summer to end. Then he turned his attention back toward the action on the field and spoke more matter-of-factly. "I heard it's supposed to snow tonight."

"That's what it said on the news," Getz agreed. "Sure doesn't look like it yet. Who knows with the weather?"

The conversation fizzled out. Getz tucked his chin and mouth down into his jacket. They fell quiet and overheard the end of an elaborate story Zowiky was relating to Howlinger. He was a talented storyteller; they couldn't help but listen as their eyes awaited a big play on the field. Zowiky was dropping a lot of 'you knows' and apparently Howlinger did know because he was adamantly agreeing with him and supporting his every opinion with short fits of laughter.

The Tiger's quarterback dumped a screen pass off to a running back on the nearside. The play developed slowly, but the back found a crease, squeezed through it, and took off down the sideline for a forty-five yard score. The crowd erupted; their cheers growing exponentially louder as the ball carrier churned closer to the end zone and climaxing around the five-yard line when it was clear he would not be caught.

Shannon and his friends shared in the revelry. They stomped and screamed, slapped high-fives and chest bumped. Zowiky revealed a hidden flask of schnapps and passed it around. It was a glorious moment; a tribute to the greatness of high school football. Shannon felt like a kid again.

The home-team would punch in a second score before the half then add two more in the third quarter. An interception returned nine-yards for another touchdown to start the fourth quarter made it 35-7 and more or less put the game out of reach.

He said his goodbyes and made his way toward the exit, stopping only briefly to politic a little here and there. By the time he reached his car, he had made plans of some sort with nearly a dozen people. None of which would ever likely take place, with the exception of perhaps a stop by Zowiky's for a dinner party the following weekend.

He started the Explorer and rubbed his chilled, bare hands. He was excited from the game, and his knees bounced as he allowed the engine to idle. It wasn't cold enough to see his breath, but it felt like it should be. He shifted the vehicle into gear, flipped a u-turn, and called his wife to tell her he was on his way home.

When he arrived back at the house, Jill was busy getting the girls ready for dinner. She was half dressed herself, her hair dry and waiting to be straightened. He wanted to sit but knew better. He tried to help where he could. Mostly, he just hovered around, showing effort.

After the girls were more-or-less ready, he dressed himself in an olive-colored shirt with a pine and black tie, and khaki slacks. His wife had chosen his wardrobe, and although he questioned whether or not it was too 'Christmasy', he admitted it looked sharp on him and went well with her jade dinner dress. She was a talented wife.

By the time they piled in the car, the air had dropped another five or ten degrees. They were late; nothing unusual. Jill called her mother to tell her they were on their way. Upon arrival they were greeted with hugs and kisses by Jill's parents and barks and prancing by their chubby dachshund.

Jill's parents were both in their sixties. Her mother, Beth, was a bright, lively woman. The years had been kind to Beth. She could easily pass for fifteen years younger than her husband. She was fit and tight-skinned, showing very few marks of age. Her once brown hair had dulled but was not yet gray. She had a shrill youthful voice, and her face – a carbon copy of Jill's – always wore a cheerful smile. Her husband, Conrad, was a large bull of a man, thick shouldered with stout arms and enormous hands. His head was also quite large though the traits of his face were strong and well-proportioned. He had the broad, crooked nose of his generation and a warrior's commanding eyes. Those eyes could control a conversation; a fact Shannon had experienced first hand on countless occasions. But they could also be warm, appreciative, and welcoming.

Conrad Parker was a military man, like Shannon's father and brother, and his household was run accordingly - in an old-fashioned, no-nonsense way. He was a veteran of the Vietnam War, a retired Army general and a well respected name in the community. A great ally in the political world, his support had been crucial to Shannon's victorious bid for county commissioner.

Shannon was well known around town, and despite their reputation for drinking, the Drummond's were still regarded as a historic family by many. The mere fact that he ran as a Democrat proved to be his greatest political obstacle. As with most of Montana, the county was shifted toward the right with the blue fading quickly to red as the polls moved out from the center of the city's population density. Although he was a member of the Catholic Church, he was criticized as being too progressive and too liberal for a slow to change, agriculture rich district. His opponents presented him as over-educated and out of touch with his constituents' values. But with a bit of help from Conrad and his veteran connections, as well as a last minute deal to garner the church's support, Shannon was able to win the election. Two years later, he carried a ninety percent approval rating and was considered a rising star in the realm of state politics.

The success inclined the party to push him to make a run for state senate. The nomination put him in a difficult position.

Democrats had long struggled in the district. In local and county races a candidate could depend on his or her reputation to be regarded as candid and approachable member of the community; partisanship meant little. But the district included parts of two neighboring counties and had been redistricted to include a majority of rural voters. Plus, Republican's would surely hold all the power in the state legislature. Few names carried enough credence to overcome years of ingrained habit. Shannon didn't know if he was ready to spend half a year in Helena laboring behind bills that stood little chance of passing. Compromise had never been his strength.

Yet rumors of the nomination drew a great deal of publicity and became widely known. Everyone wanted to see their favorite local hero march on the state capital and change the way bureaucratic politics were done. If he declined the nomination, it might prove harmful to his reputation, even detrimental to his career. If he did run and ended up winning, he would be pinned against a conservative majority looking to keep things the way they were. It would be difficult for him to stand out and likely take him two terms to build any kind of momentum. It might also change the direction of his career. It could also delay or hurt his chances of running for governor – his greatest dream.

The dilemma was something he planned to discuss with Conrad after dinner. During the meal, work was discussed but only with regards to events of the past two weeks. Conrad was an old hand when it came to dinner conversation. Manners and ethics were of the utmost importance. Shannon had picked up on the subtleties of these expectations over the years and rapidly became well-rehearsed in displaying proper etiquette.

Nothing was too specific. Stresses might be mentioned but never overtly exposed; the emotions involved were always kept in check. While the men spoke business, the women listened intently. They commented freely though sparingly and never pushed or condescended to their men. Otherwise, they spoke amongst themselves quietly until the topic changed. Breaks were constantly taken to appreciate what mattered most – the children. They were always to be included, encouraged, and spoiled by their grandparents.

The meal was large, served all at once from the middle of the table. There were no courses. There was a salad, boiled spuds, green beans, corned beef, and store bought rolls. The kids drank milk. The adults had red wine and water. After dinner, the men cleared the table, showed proper appreciation and excused themselves to the garage for a cigar.

"So Shannon, your future is looking truly bright?" Conrad asked patiently puffing his cigar with evident enjoyment.

"Let's hope so." Shannon said, holding his cigar absently and searching the dim dimensions of the garage for any spare confidence floating around.

"Why, what do you mean hope?" the old man asked, flashing a stern look of bewilderment. "Christ, you're thirty-three years old and already one of the biggest names in the state party. What is there to piss and moan about?"

"I'm a strong member of a weak party. A party whose popularity is shrinking even amongst urban citizens."

"Oh hell," Conrad cackled, waving his hand and spitting on the concrete floor. "That's nothing but a bunch of hooey. You're a conservative Democrat. You support state's rights, moderate government intervention. You're an avid hunter, hard-working, happily married and the church supports you. You'll nearly win this county on the Catholic vote alone. You have the unions. If we sway the veterans, you'll have the blue-collar vote."

"If I have the church... and if I have the veterans. But those are both big buts... and each will come with expectations." Shannon said, turning to look his father-in-law directly in the eyes. He took a long, slow taste of the cigar. The rich smoke rolled around the nooks of his mouth, and conquered his palate. "The truth is I plan to decline the nomination."

The statement caught Conrad off guard. He was stunned and it showed. He regained his composure quickly though. His eyes relaxed as he smoked in silence. Each man simmered in the new turn of events. They were both logical men, rational and experienced. There was no hurry. Nothing was final.

Shannon went on, "I know that turning it down would be detrimental. Even when my term ends, the slight would not be forgotten by the party or my supporters."

Conrad listened intently.

"I might stall out. Like you always taught me, a shark must constantly keep swimming or he's dead...But what if I did run?"

The question confused Conrad. His face hardened with impatience. He was about to break his silence when Shannon finished his thought.

"...Just not for the senate," he said.

Conrad considered the idea. The loose ash of his cigar floated slowly to the cement floor like the lightest of snowflakes. He took a heavy breath.

"I suppose there's auditor." He said unenthusiastically.

"Yes," Shannon conceded. "...I was thinking of attorney general."

Emotion grasped Conrad in a fit of spasm. His posture clenched and he looked deep and hard into his son-in-law's eyes. Was it a joke? The young man's lips remained flat; his eyes awaited response, advice. Conrad couldn't help but cough.

"Well, you'd have to go head to head with Berkman." Conrad said bluntly. "I know damn well you've thought long and hard on this if you're bringing it up, so I also know you're aware of the impossibility of such a feat."

Shannon said nothing. He was hard and unreadable.

"They will slam your age, your inexperience, any liberal stance you've ever taken, and dig more dirt on you than you even knew existed. And that's only before they slander your name and start on the bold face lies. The campaign will age you overnight. You won't eat, you won't sleep, and you won't have quality time for your family or friends." His speech quickened and his tone darkened as he continued, "And then you must consider the job itself. The duties of the attorney general are hardly the four month walk in the park of a state legislator. You will be taxed and overworked to the point of exhaustion." He paused seeing that none of this deterred the vibrant man to whom he spoke.

"Your personal relationships will suffer. And you will bring your work home with you, hung around your neck like a noose."

The men gauged each other after this last statement. The wind could be heard howling beyond the garage door rustling off the aluminum. Shannon brought the cigar to his lips unaware that it had gone out.

30

"So you think it's a good idea then?" He asked solemnly.

A smile broke on the old man's face. Both men relieved themselves with laughter. Conrad set his cigar down on the work bench beside him.

"It's far less partisan and it's the preeminent step toward governor, a step I always imagined you making, just not so soon."

Shannon's handsome face beamed in a lustrous grin. The old soldier couldn't help but shake his head. He laughed again.

"You truly are the most ambitious SOB that ever lived. Come here."

They embraced in a hug, laughing with nervous anticipation.

Chapter 4

It was ten minutes past three on a gorgeous June afternoon years earlier. The sound of organ music vibrated heavily through the cavernous cathedral. In a small, elegant room beneath the sanctuary, Jill waited anxiously while her mother and a close friend finished the last minute details of her make up. Over the steady drone of the organ, she could hear the movement overhead as the nave steadily filled for the four o'clock ceremony. Her heart fluttered all anew, each time she considered the meaning of this day. In less than two hours, she would be Mrs. Shannon Drummond.

She felt the name had unique clout to it; much more defined and Celtic in sound than Jill Parker, the name she had known all her life. Like a grade school girl, she had practiced writing it for weeks and almost had a signature worked out. She loved the name, as she loved the man who would give it to her. Even now, so close to official and holy matrimony, she found herself unable to believe it was all happening to her, that she was marrying Shannon Drummond.

She had known him all her life. Two grades younger, she had harbored a crush on him since middle school, though she would have gladly dated any of the popular upperclassmen jocks. She was shy then, quiet and a little awkward. Her parents were stricter than her friends'. They carried higher expectations too. While her classmates spent weekday nights on the phone and weekends in the back rows of dark movie theaters, Jill wrote and rewrote essays, practiced the piano, played tennis and swam. Her father thought boys were a waste of time and had no place in the life of an adolescent girl. He eased up before her senior year, but by that point she was so busy preparing for college that she hardly had time to develop the passionate infatuations of young love. It wasn't until college, thousands of miles from Montana and her parents' vigilant eyes, at an Ivy League school on the east coast that she met her first boyfriend, drank until she puked and experimented with her sexuality. She cherished those explorative years of growth. She'd met some of her best friends at Brown, and she'd learned so much more in those four years than a Bachelor's in English seemed to imply. But she always missed the mountains, the peace and quiet, the hospitality and the simplicity of the place she had left behind. Montana had a way of drawing its native sons and daughters home with the tranquil song of its vast horizons, daunting heights and the endless possibilities that it inspired.

She met Shannon, officially, at the county courthouse, early one summer morning between her junior and senior year of college. She was home on break and received a citation for an open container at a party that got busted. She was twenty-one years old. Shannon didn't recognize the stylish, green-eyed girl in the short, yellow summer dress that accentuated her bronze skin and tight swimmer's body, but the name looked familiar and so he pretended. Jill saw right through his act, yet she didn't care. She had filled out nicely since high school and though she received a great deal of interest from the boys at Brown, she had never grown comfortable with such attention at home. Besides, whether or not Shannon Drummond truly remembered her, she definitely remembered him. He was fit and handsome and charismatic and when he smiled at her with that clear interest in his eyes, she felt electricity charge beneath her skin and the lustful throbbing of a woman coming of age.

They spent the next two months sneaking off together at every opportunity. Shannon taught Jill how to read topographic maps, sunsets and stars; more about the wilderness than she ever imagined. He became her mountain man. And she taught him to let loose, laugh at himself and have fun. They shared their secrets while outrunning the day's oppressive heat and their insecurities melted beneath the instant downpour of evening thunderstorms. On the weekends they escaped the monotony and gossip of the college bars downtown and awoke in dew covered tents in high mountain meadows. By the end of that summer, the two were intimately involved, and she returned to school in love and suffering from separation anxiety. It was the most difficult year of her life yet also the most fulfilling, as each trip home meant the excitement and anticipation of renewing something magical and intense.

That winter, over the Christmas holiday, Shannon met Jill's parents. Conrad was skeptical at first, so protective of his cherished baby girl that no one would ever be truly good enough. The boy had the name of a scrappy labor family and Conrad had little knowledge or interest in hunting, but when he learned of the hardships of Shannon's past, his drive and ambition despite such tragedy, and the fact that he was going back to school that spring to finish his degree with plans to apply for law school after, he gradually warmed to the dynamic young man. Shannon latched on to Conrad and absorbed his ideology like a sponge. The man was so much different and controlled than his own father and Shannon found in him a role model he could finally emulate. That spring, Jill finished school and moved home to teach high school English. Shannon stayed true to his word. He earned his degree and was accepted to law school the following year.

It was late fall of that same year, around Thanksgiving, at the end of a strenuous hike, high atop Shelton's Peak overlooking the town below when Shannon dropped to his knee and proposed spending the rest of their lives together. Jill remembered it being a brisk but calm afternoon. The first snows had come and gone and it was dry. Many of the deciduous trees along the avenues far below had begun to change color. But the high elevation conifers between his question and the town where she was born and raised remained sturdy, green and silent as ever, never changing or revealing anything. She cried and said yes.

Looking back, it seemed like a strange time to propose, and although she had never asked him why he chose that day or that place, she often wondered about it. She assumed it was because hunting season had ended or because Shannon had found peace and confidence in his recent success.

As the final minutes leading up to the ceremony ticked away, Jill still couldn't believe her luck. She was marrying the kindest, gentlest, most thoughtful man she had ever met, and she knew in heart their love would never give way. Her soon to be husband was so ambitious and hard working. He would find success, and their family would never be wanting. Their family; the phrase had always brought children to mind, yet for some reason, now it reminded her of their guest list on this most special day. So many of today's guests were members of her extended family, and it shamed her slightly to think that only a single guest, Aunt Dotty (whom Jill had never met nor even heard mention of, despite the fact that she lived right here in town), from Shannon's family was in attendance. It was sad to think this great man had no one to watch him soar.

His brother, Edgar, who was in the service somewhere overseas and unable to make it home, was the only immediate family Shannon had left, and Jill wasn't sure how close the two were, for although her fiancé spoke with high regard of his younger sibling whenever his name was mentioned, he rarely brought him up on his own, and the few times Edgar had stayed with them, the two hardly spoke. For some reason, Jill sensed a deep, strained tension between them.

At least Shannon had Steve Zowiky, his best man and best friend. Zowiky was a bit of a knucklehead and a big talker and his personality had taken Jill some getting used to, but he seemed to be a loyal friend to Shannon, and his carefree outlook helped to balance Shannon's rigid austerity. It bothered Jill early on that a man as reliable and agreeable as Shannon would have so few close friends, but her father assured her that all great men were cursed to solitude, and that his position was the result of his determination and ambition, rather than a character flaw. 'He is a leader,' Conrad had said. 'And leaders must often take the lonely path less traveled.' The assessment made perfect sense to Jill, who had been raised to respect and understand the outlook and opinion of the greater social order without succumbing to its impulsive belligerence or emotional wavering. After all, she too had been lonely for many years. Now she had found prince charming and none of that mattered any longer. The perspective promptly eased her concern.

Besides, it wasn't as if Shannon didn't have friends. He had tons of them. They were constantly attending functions and parties and forced to turn down countless others. Shannon knew everyone, and the majority of town spoke of him with admiration and respect. He networked brilliantly and could converse on nearly any subject knowledgably. But there was always a calculated reservation to his interactions, a controlled manipulation to every conversation as if he couldn't fully expose his personality to anyone. He couldn't show vulnerability. It might have been typical Montana bravado but Jill couldn't understand it. She knew the real Shannon Drummond, beyond the facade and aloofness, and this is who she loved. She hoped someday her husband would let others in as well.

The final preparations had been made, and Jill stood before a golden bordered, full length mirror examining her appearance while her mother and friends beamed with tears of joy before her stunning beauty. And she did look beautiful. Her long brown hair was streaked with highlights, coiled and pinned up in faultless detail by white pegs accentuated by glittery sequined tips like a crown. A few loose curls hung stylishly from behind. Her green eyes sparkled beneath her dramatic lashes and complimented the pale youth of her perfect skin. Her limbs and torso were long, made for the refined Mischka gown she wore. Taking it all in, she fought from tearing up and split the meticulous pink of her lips to reveal her immaculate smile. Then the women came together in one final embrace, so careful in nature that contact hardly occurred. No one had the words to speak. Her mother squealed. The others looked away, wiping at their eyes quickly as if tears were contagious.

There was a knock at the door. It was her father, and it was time. His knock went unanswered, and yet he opened the door. One look and he too was forced to turn away momentarily, for the shining glow of his daughter, so elegant and grown before him, knocked the final wind from his guts. He had already been struggling against an unfamiliar amount of emotion for much of the day, and this was more than the old general could take. Gathering himself, he lifted his head and forced his eyes to stare directly into her full glory.

35

"Honey, you look amazing." He understated, using every molecule of a lifetime of practiced discipline. He was staring at her, capturing her image in that moment with all his soul, and yet he wasn't looking through his eyes for the sight of her was too much for him to bear and still make it down the aisle. "Are you ready?"

"Yes, daddy," she said – his tender child still, now and forever.

He offered his arm as she walked carefully toward the door. Then together they moved slowly up the stairs as the organ stopped and the silence became absolute and eternal. They stood arm in arm, eyes forward, before the giant oak doors between them and four hundred waiting guests. Children cried and indistinguishable whispers seeped between the polished marble floor and the heavy wooden barrier. The fabric of space and time pinpointed this place; this moment.

Then the organ rose without words to beckon forth the bride. The doors opened, seemingly by themselves, and the heat of all those eyes fell upon the father and his little girl. A lifetime of lessons reached its pinnacle. There were oohs and ahhs, but Jill saw the masses only in her peripherals as she concentrated on her smile, her steps and the man she loved, so handsome and waiting. She was flushed and felt faint but weightless. They had known each other just two years, and there was much left to learn. But she didn't think of that now. She didn't think of the mysteries surrounding her new family, or that which remained unknown of the man. She didn't think of the past or the future. She was here entirely, and his smiling, loving gaze told her he was here as well. That face assured her of the man's transparency, honesty and protection. Everything would be perfect. Nothing else mattered.

Chapter 5

Shannon stopped. He had been traveling along a narrow trail worn through the trees and brush from years of game traffic when the fresh scar of a young sapling caught his eye. The bark had been stripped in a violent halo that circumvented the trunk

36

some four feet above the ground. The hardened shavings laid about the ravaged sapling's base partially coiled and frozen in the worn snow. The exposed cambium was the off white of a smoker's teeth. Shannon ran his palm along the scar. The sap was still sticky. The rub wasn't a week old.

Shannon guessed it was the work of a young rag-horn bull but couldn't be certain. It might have been a spike or a big, mature six-point for all he knew. Typically, an aged bull rutted early and chose a more intimidating and useful scratching post where his marks ran higher than a man could reach. But there was no hard science that kept an ornery, old critter from demolishing a couple shrubby little pines here and there. Regardless of the culprit, the tree would be dead by spring. Scarred, red-needled saplings could be found all over elk country, especially along beaten game trails; the victims of an annual itch divined by a seemingly malicious nature.

The rub, along with scant droppings and a few crusty tracks were enough to convince Shannon there were elk around despite the fact the Drummond boys weren't seeing any. They had crossed through the head of the gulch and fed through the open timber. The temperatures had risen the past few afternoons and the snow persisted to recede. The earth lay black, wet and bare beneath his feet. He saw no reason to believe they had gone far.

Shannon continued along the trail as it carved safe passage through otherwise thick stands of young lodge-pole where in the summer wildflowers painted the undergrowth. A few huckleberries left by the bears hung shriveled. Shannon could almost imagine that delectable aroma as his path rambled along a side hill above a low saddle where the density of the pines made it impossible to recognize the surrounding topography and the skiffs of snow turned to a steady coat, soft and slushy. He followed the tracks and guessed where they would lead him. His only point of reference was the unmistakable peak of Black Bear Mountain with its open park which remained partially visible through the canopy to his left which he knew to be west. He used the peak as a landmark to orient his position; a skill his father had taught him as a young boy. 'As long as a guy can look up and make out a familiar landmark as a reference point, he's never lost,' he remembered his father preaching. Shannon took pride in what he considered to be a gifted sense of direction.

He checked his watch, though he was more or less without agenda. His final destination was the park atop Haystack Hill. But he didn't see any reason to be there until an hour before dark. Time was on his side. It was only four now, and he had a couple hours to kill. He wore a black turtle neck, leather work gloves and an orange wool cap. His heavy jacket hung from his waist. Despite the warmth of the day, the evening air was cooling off and Shannon felt the change on his skin.

After a morning hunt, the boys had eaten breakfast then taken short naps before setting to work chopping firewood and hauling water up from the spring. The work went quickly and they found themselves sitting in the tent bored stiff by early afternoon. Midday is not an ideal time for elk hunting. Elk prefer to feed in the open parks from late evening until early morning. In the afternoons, they tend to bed down in the timber to rest and hide. Among the most fretful, anxious critters on earth, their entire lives are spent either cautiously eating or watching, listening, and smelling for threats. They don't recognize shapes well, but they are excellent at detecting movement. Their keen, cupped ears hear everything and they have a nose like a bloodhound. It's hard enough to sneak up on them when they are moving around, focused on feeding. Sneaking up on them when they are bedded down, on the lookout and surrounded by crunchy snow and dry tree fall requires as much luck as it does skill.

Shannon knew all this, and Edgar was learning. The behavior of the wily wapiti and the strategies and theories to outsmart the cunning critter had been drilled into their heads since they were old enough to comprehend words – if not before. Their great grandfather had come west with the discovery of gold and immediately found a passion for hunting elk. Their grandfather and his brothers had hunted elk. And their father and his brother had carried on the tradition. In fact, as far back as anyone could remember there were three certainties about the men of the Drummond family; they died young, they died broke and each fall they slipped off into the mountains with an insatiable fever. It began as a necessity to feed the family. But Grandpa Earl took it a step further. His love for the hunt had bordered on obsession. The few who knew him well used to say, only half-jokingly, that Earl's year was divided between hunting season and drinking season – although in Shannon's memory the two had always overlapped and blurred together.

The elder of Earl's two sons, Tom, turned faithful passion into full blown hysteria. From around the age of eight, Shannon and Edgar's father was a hunting machine. He literally lived, breathed, and bled elk hunting. He missed work, weddings, funerals, and much of his children's youth, pretty much anything that came between him and filling his tag. The sickness ruined his marriage, his finances, and his liver. He tried to change a few times in his life. But in those efforts he found neither happiness nor resolve and sooner or later he was out again, for days, sometimes weeks on end. Alone in a tent in the mountains. His knowledge of the country and the animals that lived there was second to none. And he passed it all down to his sons.

Shannon, in particular, caught the infection of elk fever at an early age. A good looking, capable boy, he fell in love with the outdoors, the hunt, and the social life of camp. As a child, he worshipped the hardened, rugged men that hunted the last remnants of deep wilderness, particularly his father. He soaked up their legends, their history and their knowledge. He idolized this austere, masculine way of life but never the ironic solitude, and thus never fell victim to the same hardships. If anything, Shannon grew to feel superior to these men though always with too much shame to define the sentiment. He was too disciplined, calculating and sensible to wholly commit to uncontrolled passion, or so he thought. And perhaps that explained his fascination with men who gave everything and gained little in return. Men that died young and never questioned what life had to offer.

The men he idolized smoked, swore, gambled, lied and often cheated. They were veterans of the armed services. Most were divorced. Several had served time. And Shannon, as a naïve adolescent, secretly feared that despite all they shared, he would always remain an outsider amongst this cast of recluses. The truth was Shannon fell in love with the glory as much as anything else, more so than any Drummond before him. He was ambitious in a way that had never shown through in his ancestral gene pool. People said it came from his mother's side. But his mother had been raised by her sister and never knew her parents. Regardless, Shannon craved greatness. He reveled in the recognition that came with the trophy – not the self-satisfaction of all the hard work but rather the warm light of praise. It was the same end result in his eyes, and he saw neither shame nor irony in his love for it.

Being nearly six years behind, Edgar hadn't received the same opportunities as his brother. The camp was dwindling in numbers by the time Edgar turned twelve and earned the honor of carrying a carbine. Too many lives had been torn or ended by tragedy. It was a hard time, and his father had only had two official years to hunt with his youngest son. There was so much left to be taught, so much left to be said. That sense of incompleteness remained engrained in the withdrawn youth.

As Shannon finally crested the rise, he stopped to catch his breath, gazing back at the country he had tromped through. The exposed batholith between his location and the higher, dark-timbered slopes of Black Bear Mountain caught his eye. The trees atop the peak still held snow. Then as he shifted his look to the south over the camp trail ridge he could just make out the highest point of Windy Ridge running away from him. The jagged razorback was high and narrow, strewed with massive granite boulders and it came to an abrupt conclusion as a sheer cliff, as if it had formed as a rolling, liquid wave before suddenly cooling to solid unplanned rock in a single instant. The snow had long since vanished where the wind and sun had toiled away unchecked. Broken fragments from millennia of erosion scattered down the steep wall. Here and there a few courageous trees, marvels of survival, sprouted out from the dull gray of an otherwise barren slope. The name Windy Ridge was no mystery to anyone who had ever set foot on it. It had been his father's favorite spot on earth. It didn't look inhabitable, yet over the years nearly a dozen elk had been shot there, including a few big bulls, and countless others had been jumped off the end where the boulders faded to earth and grass and more hospitable terrain as the rampart ran down into Fir Creek.

Edgar was there somewhere, or he would be soon. He had told Shannon he had a hunch. Shannon had not argued. A hunch can be a powerful tool to a hunter. Sometimes hunches were all a man had against the epic expanses of wild. Sometimes hunches worked out. Windy Ridge was long and meandering. But the best hunting was up high. The timber down lower was tight-knit and crisscrossed with deadfall. When the Drummonds hunted it they tended to walk out to the high point down into the first saddle and then either drop off east into Six Point Gulch or west and move south down into the meadows and wallows that bordered the transition country. A bowl formed there. It was essentially a short loop, but the basin spread out relatively flat and could be confusing. There was no point in leaving camp early. It would only screw a guy up.

Shannon couldn't wait around. He had to get out there amongst them. 'You won't shoot anything sitting around the tent,' the old timers used to say. He decided to hunt the far end of Prospector's Ridge and be somewhere on Haystack Hill at dark. It was about a twenty-five minute ride on the motorcycle out to the ridge which was on the north side of the trail then an hour walk to the park atop the hill. To burn more time, he had parked the bike back the trail a ways and crept through a little honey-hole in the gulch that only a couple souls knew about.

It was just above this low saddle that Shannon began working his way up onto the ridge. The hike took him about half an hour. Cresting the ridge, the timber opened up and a superhighway of game trails crisscrossed in every direction. He could see them as long lines dipped in the melting snow. He stopped to catch his breath, pulled a water bottle from his pack and drank. A frigid wind came up out of the next gulch and chilled his sweat-laced skin. The clouds overhead were in motion. High, white wisps stretched across the sky were quickly being blocked out by grey billows that raced toward a dark, gathering front. A storm was forming. There would be new snow tonight. The melt was over. He untied the sleeves of his jacket and put it on, zipping it halfway. The approaching storm didn't bother him. In fact, he hoped for snow. There was no better aid when tracking ghosts.

The wind whipped atop the ridge causing the trees to sway and creak in ancient conversation. It was a perfect wind, blowing up out of the gulch. A head wind was a hunter's best friend. He crept along now, mindfully searching for a blazed trail marker. There were several ways to reach Haystack from Prospector's Ridge, but there was one he preferred. A hidden path his father had

41

discovered only a few years earlier, the last secret the father had shared with his elder son. The trailhead was marked by a single blaze carved into an unassuming pine. The mark consisted of a six inch by two inch rectangle beneath a small circle, the shape of a lower case i. It was subtle and easily overlooked. Shannon had missed it before. But he refused to make a more recognizable mark; mostly out of selfish greed. He didn't want anyone else to know his secret. He had never even shown Edgar.

It was a great hunt. The trail edged along below the ridge a ways then veered down onto the open bench. There was a series of small parks along the bench. Through these parks had always been how anyone familiar with the area had hunted their way out to Haystack. It took some familiarity not to miss any. Above and below the bench the timber turned thick and nasty and there was no easy way through it, or so everyone had always thought.

A few years back Tom Drummond had pushed through the mess below the second park while tracking a lone bull. Tom was getting older and admitted later that he had almost said to hell with it, figuring the bull would feed out onto the Haystack at dark anyway. He was as bitterly stubborn in old age as he had been relentlessly stubborn in youth, however, and he hated to abandon a fresh track, especially a big track. It was always a big track.

About three hundred yards into the dense mess of waist high deadfall, tightly knit branches, and impassable buck brush, the old man began to curse himself for his stupidity. Branches snagged his clothes and snapped loudly under his boots, his pant legs were covered with beggar's lice, and he stumbled over dense, fallen logs. But then the new growth vanished gradually and transitioned into midsized open firs. Tom hadn't expected the transition and it confused him. He couldn't pinpoint his whereabouts. The truth was the area below the bench was difficult to see from the adjacent ridge or anywhere else for that matter. The boys' father, as knowledgeable as he was, had unwittingly stepped into uncharted territory.

Over the next half mile, the elk he followed led him along a fertile side trail, never moving up or down hill. The trail was worn by traffic and surrounded by flat, open shooting lanes. A few places he was able to see down into the gulch two hundred yards or more. There were springs where wallows had formed and he found

42

beat down beds and sign all over. Finally, the track headed back up into the thickets and came out on the blazed trail just before it climbed toward the open park above. He couldn't believe a track had never led him to this discovery before. Tom never caught up with that elk, but he cherished the secret it had shared with him. The hunt had given him new information about the land he loved, and he was thankful for it. For Tom Drummond there had always been much more to the hunt than the kill, and the joy that shone in his face when he passed this tale on to Shannon was only one example of an unyielding, unquestioned, and eternal worship of things wild.

In his life, their father had seen brutal blizzards, poverty, depression, and tragic, pointless deaths. Yet he had hunted on through it all. He said 'life didn't always make sense. But elk hunting did.' And now his eldest son followed in his footsteps down that same secret trail. Shannon didn't have to push through the thick stands of brush though. He found the trailhead before the bench and made his way down into the firs a quarter mile back, before the mess. His boots crunched along on crusty snow that had melted and refroze, remaining resiliently present. He walked slowly avoiding the fragile stems of bear grass that filled the timber. The temperature continued to drop with the sun's angle. He had stopped sweating, but he wasn't chilled yet and he still had his gloves off. His mind envisioned the glory of showing off the trophy bull that lurked somewhere before him, yet his eyes saw nothing but small birds and chipmunks on onion grass.

He reached the park earlier than expected. Nearly two hours remained before dark, and it was with a slight damper of disappointment and frustration that he tucked himself back into the brush along the edge of the timber. From his position, he could see two-thirds of the open hillside. The exception was an inlet that formed a corridor to a second large meadow at the hill's peak. He sat in rigid silence, considering his fate and cursing his luck. It was so early in the season, yet already he longed for success.

The yellow-gray shoots of straw moved to the whistle of the wind as much as the frozen snow allowed. As he sat, his mind wandered through a mostly trivial agenda of topics. He had never had much of an imagination and therefore had always struggled with free time. Mostly, his mind focused on the concrete: success,

43

money, the future, and getting back to school. But on occasion his thoughts broadened to include sports, movies, and girls. Tonight, one girl in particular flickered in and out of his head, although he felt guilty about it and tried to stop.

Her name was Holly, and she was Edgar's girlfriend. Shannon knew she was the one girl on this earth that was off limits. At seventeen, she was older than Edgar but too young for Shannon. She was pretty, but not gorgeous. He thought he had surely been with better looking girls. He had been with girls younger than him as well and never cared for them. He didn't know what it was about this girl that wouldn't stop nagging him. Perhaps it was the fact that his brother had found someone to help him through his loss while he remained all alone.

It was after his father's death that they met, before she had been Edgar's girlfriend – at least before Shannon knew. He had been piss drunk at some high school party after the funeral; the type of thing he never did and the type of party he never attended even when he was in high school. He got belligerent and acted a fool. Holly had recognized him as Edgar's brother and offered her condolences and her honesty had touched some vulnerable place in Shannon's heart. Apparently, she had done the same with Edgar, and the two began dating soon after. Now every time she came around the house, Shannon had to excuse himself because he felt something unfamiliar and uncontrollable. He wasn't worried. It was merely his competitive nature. Nothing would come of it, and it would go away. Ignore the feelings long enough and they always go away. Emotions were weaknesses that could always be overcome.

Shannon had never had a steady girlfriend. He had dated a little in high school but never grew too attached. Crushes or flings, whatever they were labeled, they never meant much to him for more than a few weeks. People accused him of being hard and self-centered. It became a defining characteristic of his nature. 'He has no feelings,' the girls said. 'No one will ever be good enough,' they complained. He had never paid much attention. He had seen his parents' marriage crumble first hand, and it was the only weakness his father had ever shone, the only time he had ever given up on something. A crushing shock for an idolizing son and one that had haunted him ever since.

44

As sunset drew near, the sun remained a hidden orb visible to the naked eye behind the congregating clouds to the south. Cold vapors swirled in vertical columns over the shadowed peaks like smoke from a distant volcano. Then the sun appeared momentarily, epically vast and unfathomable in a last gasping flash of scarlet before vanishing in the slow daily brilliance of colorful transitions beyond the western horizon and yielding the heavens to a bright, ivory moon that seemed modest and naked in comparison. It was the hunter's moon, only slightly waning. And it was beautiful, although Shannon gave it little consideration tonight. His father had taught him to find joy in all that came with the hunt, but his father was gone and Shannon wanted the thrill and glory that he had decided in his wounded soul would somehow right the wrongs he had suffered.

The park remained empty. With darkness came total silence as if the two had traveled together across the expanses of time and space. Shannon waited until the clouds were no longer shadows of twilight but illuminators of moonlight. Then he started the long trek back. His butt was numb. His nose was dripping. His toes were cold; his ears stung. He had held out longer than most can alone with only their thoughts to keep them company. He was tough and did well on his own. He had to be. There was no one else around to look out for him. Edgar had him, and now a girlfriend, but he had no one. It wasn't fair. He was a good brother. He knew this, and people told him all the time. 'It's just amazing the way you look out for that boy,' people praised. 'You are so selfless, Shannon, you will go far in life,' they told him. It was another boost that fed his ego and kept him from giving up. People said these things. But they couldn't possibly comprehend the daily hardships and perils this selfless boy faced.

The walk home was always tough after not seeing anything. Shannon flipped on his flashlight and marched swiftly behind its tiny beam. His breath and his boots created a rhythm that inflicted his thoughts. He was somewhere else; older; a hero amongst his peers. It was here, in the darkness of the empty wilderness after all the work was done that he allowed himself to dream. He wanted to be a movie star, or famous author, someone that was respected and never forgotten. He wanted to change the world for the better, to shine like a beacon, so his father would look down upon him with great pride.

Somewhere along his walk it began to snow. Sparse at first. The heavy flakes floated through the quiet timber almost unnoticed until they touched his face and became droplets of water. By the time he reached the open trail, the flakes were beginning to stick, big steady flickers of white reflected in the rays of his flashlight and glow of the moon. At first, they melted as quickly as they reached the earth. Now, they were accumulating and a thin layer of clean white covered the previous snow. The wind whipped across the ridge, howling.

He heard little else, still lost in his thoughts. The uphill trek warmed him, and thirst became his primary want. He wondered how his brother had fared. He knew Edgar hadn't shot. Even with the wind, he would have heard it. But maybe he saw something. If so, Windy Ridge might be a good spot to be in the morning. But he knew he couldn't face that place yet. Somewhere hidden away, he was pleased knowing his brother hadn't shot anything either, especially on his father's favorite ridge. His relief left him feeling guilty.

By the time he reached the bike, the seat had been covered by a half inch of light, fluffy snow, and still the white flakes fell steady. He kick started the engine, and the roar of the two-stroke tore off into the timber, somehow making the stillness around him seem even more silent. The single headlamp flooded the darkness with an alien yellow luminosity that exposed a world freshly coated in the blue-white glow of moonlit snow. Aside from his brother and their camp, he was miles from the nearest beat of a human heart. High atop a lonely peak, surrounded in all directions by ancient mountains and endless trees, it was always an eerie thought. There was something spiritual about the whole experience. Shannon hesitated a moment and glanced around through the crystalline flakes. The view of the mountains was probably the same as it had been for thousands of years. Suddenly, he felt very small. The thought scared him. He turned God, or whatever it was away from his mind, pointed the bike onto the barely visible trail and gunned the throttle.

Chapter 6

Edgar stepped outside and lit the cigarette that hung loosely from his chapped lips. The zigzag tread from his boots accounted for the solitary marks in the quarter inch of fresh snow that carpeted the concrete stairs at the bar's rear exit. The night was still. It must have snowed while he was inside. Darkness had fallen and the industrial florescent light of the exit sign buzzed behind his head. The low clouds formed an undisturbed ocean of vapor overhead that caught the glow from the surrounding streetlamps and refracted it, like dust particles between a projector and the screen.

He sniffed at a running nose, the effects of a cold that he was no longer sure was coming or passing. He spat and it stuck to the brick wall of the building where it began to freeze. He pulled on his gloves and started down the empty sidewalk. At the corner, he hung a left. The smoke he exhaled crept slowly from his mouth in a heavy fog and hung there like soul departed.

He reached the lights of downtown and the night awoke around him. The sounds of entertainment escaping the opening and closing doors of heated pubs and saloons filtered through his distracted mind. His senses detected a familiarity but he had no concept of what this meant. The blues and the reds of neon signs behind foggy glass beckoned him like the whisper of a siren. Fellow smokers shivered and shifted beneath the canopies, pissed they hadn't voted against the ordinance they blamed for their predicament. A homeless man, wrapped in tattered rags, sat beside a shopping cart full of junk holding a sign that said 'Trust in Jesus.'

Edgar flicked his cigarette arbitrarily into the street and considered lighting another one before realizing he had none to begin with. The one he had just smoked had been bummed along with the half dozen before it. He rifled through his pockets but found only a receipt and an empty can of Copenhagen which he discarded into the clean, unmolested snow. His wallet was empty. He didn't have to look.

Through the window at Finn's, he could see there was a crowd. He felt disappointed. Upon entering, the contrast between this place and the one he had just left hit him, and he wondered how such a dark underbelly of crime could exist right in the center of town for so long without being discovered? He realized now that aside from the rare murder that hit the papers, the drugs were the only issue society felt compelled to clean up. And hidden from sight might as well have been 'cleaned up.' Most never made the connection that any drug problem that existed was merely tip of the iceberg. The guns, illegal gambling and prostitution were all below the surface, and it was all connected with the liquor licenses of the bars and casinos.

He shrugged this off amidst all the noise and worked his way through the crowd of jubilant twenty-some-things to find a table near the back. Shortly, a waitress approached him, but not the one he had hoped for. She was a short, thin girl with a young face created by various ovals. Her hair was bleached almost white except where dark roots shone, and her small breasts were shoved together and pushed to the top of the purple tank-top she wore beneath a black blouse, making them her dominant feature. She was quite pretty.

"What can I getcha?" she asked with a high-pitched, impatient snap. She leaned in, anticipating some degree of difficulty in hearing him over the commotion of the bar. The motion further accentuated her cleavage, a fact she was well aware of, and there was a faint glow about her, a glistening of perspiration.

"Is Krystle working tonight?" he asked. Making no effort at eye contact he continued to scan the room.

"Yeah." The girl replied flatly, everything about her turning cold in an attempt to match his indifference. Here she was, oozing sexuality, and this weathered tough wanted Krystle. Apparently, he was wasting her time. She was young – maybe a year or two beyond the drinking age. And her world revolved no more than five feet beyond her person.

"Who are you?"

Edgar peered directly at her for the first time. The look on his face showed both impatience and sudden contempt.

"Tell her to come over here." He said with words that carried great weight without effort.

The waitress's eyes opened wide with disbelief, as if no one had ever spoken to her in such a way. But there was also the impression she enjoyed the emotions he evoked in her. She turned and started away, shaking her head, but after a few steps Edgar called her back.

"I'll have a PBR too."

A few minutes later a tall, hearty woman in her mid thirties approached the table. She was grinning widely; the hard lines of a life well-lived shone through on a face framed by a stringy garden of dark, curly hair. Her face was narrow with high cheekbones and full lips that dominated the organization of her features. She wore too much makeup and her skin was pale. Her body consisted of the broad curves and bubbly proportions of strong genetics overcome by poor posture and diet. She had a small waist that swelled out at the hips and shoulders. She looked sturdy, like a mother, though Edgar knew she had no children. He greeted her with a soft look, inviting her to sit with the casual beckon of his hand.

"This poor girl," She started in a smoky drawl, "still in college, I might add, comes to tell me that some scrub wants to see me and forewarns that the guy is a real asshole," she sighed but kept smiling. It was evident she was glad to see him. "I spose I shoulda known it was you." She said, easing into the chair offered. "I should've seen right through her phony disgust too. The poor thing's probably already fallen head over heels."

Just as she finished speaking, the girl returned and set a beer meekly in front of him.

"See what I mean." Krystle said rolling her eyes. "Darling this is Edgar Drummond. And if you ever see this man again, immediately turn and walk away."

The girl looked at them both. She faked a smile, evidently confused. Her interest had definitely been peaked.

"Oh girl, please." Krystle scolded. "How innocent are you? He will never have money, and will only leave you broke, broken and exhausted both emotionally and physically."

Edgar didn't smile. He kept his eyes on Krystle and never looked up.

"That's three bucks." The girl answered, unable to think of anything else to say.

"I'll take care of it hon."

49

The girl nodded in understanding. Just as she turned to leave Edgar caught her by the elbow. The calluses of his hands pricked her soft skin like sandpaper.

"How bout a couple shots of Irish whiskey on Krystle's tab too." He said, finally breaking down and flashing a true smile. "…thanks…hon."

"Are you serious? I can't drink right now. I'm closing. I have to be here all night."

"Who said anything about you drinking?" Edgar asked with a wink. She laughed. She could tell he was in a good mood. But soon, the magic wore off and Krystle mustered her courage.

"So, you're broke or horny. And I'm guessing you came looking for money?" She asked, her foot tapping and the smile easing into a rehearsed blank expression. There was no anger in her tone and she did a great job of hiding the hurt, yet tiny grains of pain escaped on the last few syllables further drying her already measured drawl.

Edgar flinched slightly with something close to honest shame then his shoulders adjusted to lower his face toward her. He laid his forearms out flat on the table so he had to look up to make eye contact.

"What's that supposed to mean?"

"Well, I'd call it a loan, but we know each other well enough to skip all that bullshit." She shook her head, a bitter smirk revealing itself just beneath the surface.

"Ok, I deserve that." Edgar said with a smirk of his own. Their reunion brought out a genuine happiness in him and in rare strategy he played vulnerable, trying to steer her emotions away from the grudge rather than simply ignoring it, "But, I don't need money. I only came here to see you, ask you to come stay with me tonight."

She held out, cutting him off.

"Why so you can blow a gasket again and throw me against the wall? Or better yet, maybe this time you'll go completely off the reservation and smack me around a little." She turned cold and Edgar hardened in response like cooling steel.

"You know you never even said you were sorry afterward." She continued, "I mean I understand you have issues, but after you shove me and kick me out on the street in the middle of winter,

50

maybe there should be an apology, or an explanation," her voice rose as she grew animated, "or at the very least a phone call."

Edgar said nothing.

Amidst Krystle's ranting, the young waitress returned with the shots but then hurried away from the train wreck that was beginning to draw attention. Edgar threw the first shot back quickly, debating how much he was willing to take. He was lonely. But, he didn't need sex. He could care less about it. She wasn't beautiful by any means, and he worked his tensions out in the shower. Besides, in his line of work, if he wanted sex it was always easy to come by. It wasn't the act but rather the company he craved, the intimacy; a familiar voice telling him that she wanted him. That she needed him.

But this realization never fully occurred to him and he would never admit it if it had, even to himself. Now, here he was and as usual his pride stood in his way like a concrete wall.

"I don't have any issues... I was drunk." He said, pausing to choke back the second shot. He took this one slower, in two separate gulps really letting the fire linger on his tongue and throat. "And I am sorry." He admitted. "But, I didn't *shove* you. I simply grabbed you because you wouldn't calm down. Remember, you were swinging at me, and you got a pretty good right." He spoke the words in a way that neither accepted nor redirected blame but didn't compromise either. There was a detachment from the events that was complete, without choice or second thought. Krystle had fallen victim to this manner of logic before. She wouldn't buy it this time.

"Oh sorry," she flashed, fire blazing in her eyes. "I guess it was all *my* fault. And that's right you didn't shove me, you just restrained me for my own good. Forget about the bruises on my shoulders. No, biggy I spose. Hell, it was just an extra physical hug then right?" Then as if she found something she had said funny, she laughed hysterically. "Oh no wait...that'd be showing too much affection for you, you asshole."

"I said I'm sorry." Edgar said, interrupting her before he lost her. His humor had abandoned him but still he spoke slowly. Cool. Honest and even, "Baby, I'm not perfect, but I'm not gonna sit here and grovel either. I'm sorry I haven't called. I've been

51

busy. And I'm sorry I lost my cool. You were digging pretty deep. Don't bring a shovel to the cemetery if you scare easy."

Krystle was a proud woman, but she was also a realist. She dropped it. She knew his words were heartfelt. Three apologies were more than enough to appease her. Besides, the majority of the emotion fueling her outburst stemmed more from missing him than anger over the situation itself, and she knew it would happen again. It would happen again and again, until one of them eventually moved on or got killed. She didn't care. She loved him. She smiled and dabbed at her eyes with the napkin that served as the coaster for his beer,

"Damn it. Now, you're gonna mess up my eyeliner."

"Who gives a shit," he said. "This place is all frat fags anyhow. These little pricks wouldn't know what to do with a real woman if she walked up and grabbed him by the cock." His eyes narrowed and he popped his knuckles. The battle seemingly won, he searched unknowingly for an outlet to unleash the emotions he had just fought to withhold.

The little blonde hurried by, shooting a look of frustration in Krystle's direction.

"I have to help her out."

"Why is this place so busy tonight?"

"Two dollar shots of Jagermeister," she said rolling her eyes again. "Stick around though. I'll buy you a couple drinks."

He pointed at her, and she smiled.

"PBR?" she shouted moving back toward the crowd gathered around the bar. He nodded.

He watched her for a minute as she fought her way back behind the bar and started taking orders from impatient, inebriated fools in bright matching colors and shiny jewelry. The sight made him sick. He thought back on the afternoon trying to pinpoint what had brought him to his present situation. But he found nothing of use. Reflection was not his strength. Finally, the agitation engulfing him would allow him to sit still no longer. He made his way to the jukebox. He had no money to make a selection, but it was a distraction, and that was better than nothing.

A young man - a young punk in Edgar's mind – stood before the machine, tapping directions on the screen. The kid was only a few years younger than Edgar, but Edgar made no internal recognition of his being a peer. He wore a form fitting red and white striped rugby shirt with the sleeves drawn above the elbow. His jeans were intentionally faded, visibly expensive and worn below the hips.

The mere sight of him standing where Edgar arbitrarily meant to stand caused his blood to boil. Instantly, he became hypersensitive to every microscopic detail in the room and debated busting the kid's jaw just to see if any of his supposed friends would come to his aid. But before he could act on the impulse the kid turned to him with a pie-eyed grin,

"Hey dude," the kid muttered freezing Edgar in place, "I'm so faded." His eyes were barely cracked and his face was flushed. He wore his hair crystallized in a chaotic spike that looked as if he had styled it in an effort to support his claim. Edgar didn't smile. He stared intently at the mess before him trying to recall what it had been like to drink for the sheer joy of inebriation. He wondered where a booze-induced stupor took someone so different from himself. The kid interpreted nothing from his silence.

"I threw on some Tupac," He said, unable to control the volume of his voice. Edgar watched closely as he swayed as if the floor moved beneath him and his head rocking back and forth. "Some a that gangsta shit, my nigga."

He tilted his head back and broke into heavy laughter, leaving the vulnerable flesh of his throat exposed. But Edgar remained indecisive.

"I left a play on there for ya. I am *way* too wasted to concentrate anymore." He said, raising a hand to slap before shouting, "I fucking love Jagerbombs." More hysteric laughter followed.

Edgar left him hanging on the high-five, but the kid didn't seem to notice or take offense. Instead, he belched and stumbled off in the direction of the crowded bar and Edgar was left standing alone. He glanced around without fully realizing what had just transpired or guessing what it meant. It took a moment for the stimulus around him mesh together once more, and when it did he realized he was more out of place here than the oddball he had just interacted with. He couldn't help choking out a few muffled laughs of his own. His tension eased, and he felt more relaxed than he had in recent memory. He was in that rare phase of inebriation where nothing bothered him. He scanned through the digital catalog by pushing indicators on the screen. He enjoyed the new juke boxes and wished Grisham would upgrade the old pile at the bar, or at least add some new songs to it. There was only so much sad country and Bad Company a man could handle. It didn't take him long to find something he liked. He chose Metallica's Master of Puppets and, since there was money left, he used the extra credit to have it played next. Pleased with himself, he smiled and headed for the bar for another beer. But before he could reach the crowd a familiar face appeared out of the mob.

It was Quinn. Edgar's smile snapped off like a light, and he became wooden again. He knew it wouldn't last. Things could never go so easy. He looked at his friend hard and intolerant. But he didn't speak. He waited to be spoken to.

"There's a problem down in the canyon." Quinn said carefully, although he nearly had to shout to be heard.

"And?"

"A couple of out of town big shots got into the early game, business guys from Chicago or something. Italians. They're trying to play it off like tough guy mobsters or something, saying they're connected and using fancy lingo." He was leaned in to Edgar's ear. Edgar made no effort to aid him and showed no reaction to the information provided.

"Why would big shot mobsters ever be in Montana?"

"Don't know."

"So what?" Edgar shot quickly. He was inhuman again.

"So now their down close to three Gs, maybe more since I left. And they are acting like they are being cheated, getting loud and drunk."

"How many of them are there?"

"Just three." Quinn said with obvious shame.

"And who the hell else is out there?" Edgar asked. The agitation in his voice undisguised.

"It was Darnell and me. Stubes was dealing, and there was a full table. I think ten guys."

Edgar pierced his lips and glared hard at his friend.

"Look bro, I know. I'm just saying these are some big old apes, wearing crisp suits and gold rings. I just wanted to run it by you. I called up at the bar and you weren't around, so I thought it was best to come find you. If you got a cell phone, like a normal mother fucking person, we wouldn't have these communication problems." He stopped there seeing it wasn't helping. "It's your call."

Edgar sighed. He looked to his left where Krystle stood washing glasses with an urgent rhythm. She had her hair pulled back now and glistened with sweat, answering the endless swarm around her with short, prompt responses. Her stress was visible, but there was this calmness to her as if nothing they could do or say could reach her. She looked irresistible.

"Alright," Edgar said calmly without taking his eyes off her. "Let's run out there."

"I got the Buick running out front." Quinn said, relieved.

They pushed their way through the crowd and stepped out into the clear, dry winter air. The noise faded behind them as they crossed the street. A focus as cold and pure as the night cleansed Edgar's mind. A tattered, gray sedan waited directly in front of them. The dull idle of the engine rumbled as Edgar made his way around to the passenger's door. This whores and gambling crap wasn't what he wanted, but he couldn't work for Grisham much longer. He couldn't take the shame or the abuse. Sooner or later he was either going to kill himself or everybody else, and no Drummond had ever committed suicide.

"You got a cigarette?" he asked before climbing in.

"I got a chew." Their breath rolled out toward each other over the top of the car and disappeared into the vast nothingness that surrounded them.

"That'll work."

Quinn threw the tin over the roof of the car. Edgar caught it then climbed in the passenger seat and never looked back, for to look back would mean there had been a choice. And he didn't have a choice. His choice had been made for him long ago.

Chapter 7

Melanie played by herself in the hallway. She still wore pajamas and her hair was ratted from sleep. It was Sunday. No one had come to wake her for church and the knowledge of this oversight gave her a rebellious sense of privilege, as if she alone possessed a great secret. She had no plans to point out the error in case it had yet to be discovered. She wasn't convinced she was in the clear just yet. Better safe than sorry. But, that didn't mean she wouldn't flaunt her freedom.

Melanie didn't particularly mind church. She didn't love it like Mommy or Nicole, but she didn't hate it either. She was like Daddy when he actually went; he might sigh or complain in the car, hunched over and pouting on the way there, but once they arrived and were seated, he listened contently, sang quietly and always enjoyed 'peace be with you.' Melanie felt similar. There were things she would rather be doing, and sitting still so long – especially during the hot days of summer – could be torture, but she liked watching all the people come so humble and leave so happy and she knew Jesus, Mary and God enjoyed her visits even if she could never see or hear them.

Nope, she wasn't about to ruin this day. It was like having two Saturdays in a row – like summer vacation. She had peered in on her sister's room after she crawled out of bed to assure she hadn't simply been forgotten. She found Nicole soundly asleep. No one was in Mommy and Daddy's room, which gave her a moment of alarm, until she heard Daddy's voice coming from his office.

After roaming the rest of the house in search of Mommy – the bathroom, kitchen, laundry room and living room, since Mommy never went into the basement – Melanie did exactly what any kid does when getting something by on their parents; she flaunted it. First, she quietly opened the cracked door to Daddy's office far enough for him to see into the hall. Then, she commenced to summersault, crawl and skip back and forth down the hallway, carrying on the pretense of trying to be silent and unnoticeable with all the efforts of a Broadway star. When this failed to garner any attention she grew frustrated and bold, wandering into the office where at least there was a certainty of recognition.

Her father was standing fully dressed and facing the window behind his desk. He looked sleepy. All around, massive elk horns and framed certificates cluttered the walls of the small boxy room. It was not a room that Melanie spent much time in, and she was suddenly fascinated by the man who occupied it, as if he were someone other than her father. Something about him seemed larger or perhaps just more detached from her recognition, like a robot. He spoke in the slow drawn voice that he used when he said Mommy was nagging him. He used that voice a lot lately.

Melanie pictured a mean bad guy on the other end of the line cackling wickedly as he tried to wear Daddy down.

"Jon, I don't know any other way to say it." Daddy said. "There's just no money. The program is broke. Even if I called in favors, pushed and prodded, we couldn't make it work." He turned now, one hand on his hip, his eyes staring at something far away as he nibbled his lip. A void of emotion surrounded him and Melanie's carefree joy abandoned her. "Is he a Republican?" He paced behind the desk concentrating on muffled words from the unseen speaker.

"I'm doing everything I can, Jon. It's not that simple though and you know it. I have a responsibility to try and do what is right." Then, the man on the other end must have said something very important because Daddy looked shocked. Then he looked hurt. "That's old establishment bullshit and you know it, Jon." He said angrily. "Things have changed and…" he stopped there, apparently interrupted. This time he was quiet for several minutes, standing tall and actively listening. Melanie watched carefully. "Ok," he spoke softly again, "I'll do everything in my power to push it through. This is not the way to do business though. It's going to look real bad, Jon. If anybody notices… it will look real bad." More silence followed. "So, then I'll have your support I assume?" As he asked the question, he turned to sit and noticed Melanie on the beige carpet staring up at him with absorbing eyes. Melanie didn't recognize the look she saw. But she knew she didn't like it. It looked too much like embarrassment. "Ok. I got to run Jon. Have your guy call me next week. I need to sit down with him and talk about this bulk plant case."

57

"Ok."

"Ok."

"Will do."

"You too."

"Alright, talk to you later."

He hung up the phone and smiled down at his daughter. Melanie didn't smile back.

"And just what exactly do you think you're doing, crazy?" he asked, in a voice still strained though he tried to conceal it.

"Nuffin, jus playin." Melanie answered shyly.

"Oh you are, are you?" Daddy asked coming around the desk and bending down to her. The color returned to his face and the familiarity eased Melanie's concern. "And what are you playing?"

Melanie shrugged and pouted her bottom lip, "jus playin."

Her dad couldn't help but laugh. She was so adorable. "Well, you know you and your sister aren't supposed to play in Daddy's office right?" He asked. His voice was playful and he looked at her out the corner of his eye with false condescendence. Melanie nodded her head in acknowledgement.

"Sowry." She said slowly, playing her cutest.

"I guess I'll have to spank you." Daddy said, frowning. Melanie's look turned to one of pure fright.

"Or tickle you!" he shouted, reaching out two tentacle like fingers before she could react. Melanie screamed bloody murder. Laughing hysterically, she desperately struggled to free herself from Daddy's clutches. The two of them locked into a ball in front of the doorway, him in his suit without the jacket and her in her white Hello Kitty pajamas.

A tired Nicole appeared only to be quickly swept into the battle. He took turns clutching one then the other. While one of the girls was being held, the other did her best to escape, crawling away as she panted frantically to catch her breath. Just when she reached the hallway, Daddy would grab the escapee's leg and pull her back in. Then, he had them both down. Pinned beneath him and red-faced and crying from laughter, they failed to make recognizable sounds any longer.

This continued until a hard knock on the front door caught Daddy's ear.

In no great rush he straightened himself out, checked his watch and made his way to the entrance room crowded with shoes and coats and other random clutter. He was still slightly out of breath as he opened the door to find his brother standing on the porch in the morning light. A beautiful Sunday surrounded him. The sun was shining bright. Most of the snow had melted and the warm, wet smell of false spring flooded into the house. Shannon was surprised and caught off guard.

"Edgar, how are you?" he smiled. He was about to ask if everything was alright, but he was able to swallow the inquiry before it left his mouth. His brother looked haggard and pale. He had a sparse three or four day beard growing, and the clothes he wore looked as if they had been lived in for some time. None of this prompted Shannon's concern, however, which stemmed from the visit itself. His brother didn't visit regularly and never this early.

"Morning, brother," Edgar greeted with a nod. They didn't hug. They had stopped that habit years ago. "Sorry to stop by so early on a Sunday." He started, fumbling over his words yet maintaining firm eye contact.

"Oh nonsense," His brother said in all seriousness now. "Come in. I was just playing with the girls."

Melanie saw Uncle Eddy pass through the living room from her position in the hall.

"Uncle Eddy," she shrieked, rushing in to hug him. She was about to grab him around the knees, when in a single smooth motion he crouched and scooped her up around his neck. She recognized the musky familiar smells that always accompanied him. The odors were both sour and sweet, and she could taste the chalky, smoke from his cigarettes.

"Where is your fwend?" she asked him, staring deep into his young, hard face. She loved him. She didn't know the name for it yet, but she knew he was her favorite person in the whole world, boy or girl. She knew he was Daddy's brother, but she didn't believe it. Eddy was so much different than Daddy. He was so quiet. Besides, he was so much younger than Daddy, and he played and carried on with kids even when other adults were around. She had told Mommy that when she got bigger she wanted to marry Uncle Eddy just like Mommy married Daddy. Mommy had

59

laughed and told her she couldn't marry her Uncle. But she had not lost hope.

"What friend?" Uncle Eddy asked.

"The girl you were with last time?"

"You mean Krystle?"

"I dunno." Melanie answered with her patented shrug. As usual it worked. Uncle Eddie laughed and kissed her affectionately. The hair on his face scratched at her skin.

"The girl with the big head. I fowgot her name." Edgar laughed again,

"She has a big head?" he asked, still holding Melanie clutched to him. She nodded yes. "Well, she's probably at home I guess. I haven't seen her in a while." This made Melanie happy,

"Good. I don't wike her."

"You don't?" Uncle Eddy asked, holding her out away from him with his arms extended. "Why not?"

"She's dumb."

"She's dumb?" he repeated her words incredulously. She only nodded and laughed as he began bouncing her high above his head.

"She is ugwy too."

"Wow. Dumb and ugly, I better stop hanging out with her then." Uncle Eddy conceded. The two played like this for several minutes before Uncle Eddy put her down and explained that he needed to speak to Daddy. He referred to him as her father. But Melanie did not leave the room. She played in front of the two men while they spoke, continuously trying to recapture her uncle's attention. Nicole sat quietly in the chair across the room.

"Hi Nicole." Edgar greeted her.

"Hi." She smiled politely, always the prim and proper picture of control. Shannon motioned for his brother to follow him into the kitchen.

"Sorry, I didn't warn you about the commercials," Shannon said. The two men faced each other across the island in the center of the well lit room. "That is all PR stuff, and I really wasn't even sure what they were going to do with it. They had only run the idea by me. Nothing had been finalized."

"It's fine." Edgar smiled. "It gives the guys down at the bar something to harass me about… It's no big deal." With that,

Shannon fell quiet. He rubbed at his neck and jaw uncomfortably. Edgar seemed content to wait, and the air hung unsettled as the hardwood floors creaked under their feet. When a tension had built, Edgar coughed,

"You need to go see Aunt Dotty." It was not said as a suggestion but rather one of maybe four or five orders Edgar had given his brother in his entire life. Shannon nodded.

"How is she?"

"Not good." Edgar answered flatly, looking his brother straight on, dry eyed. "She's dying, brother."

"Who's dying, Daddy?"

It was Melanie. She had followed them, and now she stood half hidden by the wall. Nicole stood behind her. Daddy choked up from surprise searching for a gentle answer, but Uncle Eddy never hesitated.

"Your Aunt Dotty is, Sweetie." His words were gentle, honest and loving. He hid nothing in his soul.

"Can we help her, Daddy?" Melanie asked. The question was beautifully spoken. The most beautiful words ever spoken.

"Go play with your sister." Daddy started. His voice was uncertain and unfamiliar. Uncle Eddy cut in again,

"Yes. You and your sister and your father and your mother are going to go visit Aunt Dotty." It was a sentence of possession, spoken with the most earnest of love. All the ugliness that clung to this hardened man, like moss on those old firs in the mountains where they were raised, was canceled out, forgiven by the innocence, beauty, and hope of the child he conversed with in this time of bare-boned emotion.

"Nicole, take Melanie in the other room." The voice had found strength, not from anger, but from fear – the fear that his protection would not be enough, for the world was too rough and the curse too old. When the children had gone they were quiet again. Shannon was angry now, convinced this was his brother's doing. Always the antecedent of loss and hardship. It wasn't Edgar's fault, but it was his curse not Shannon's and not his family's. Certainly not his daughters'. The second hand ticked, and the sun moved a quarter of an inch, its shine suddenly striking Shannon's eyes through the window above the sink. He shaded them with his hand before moving out of the glare. Edgar shook his head,

"You jump to defend every spear-chucking squaw, dike and welfare-abusing whore in town with your fancy talk and lawyer bullshit. Anything to get a vote. But God forbid you should have a flaw in your own family tree… You know we might not be perfect, but we're family. That used to be good enough…Hell, that used to be all that mattered at the end of the day."

He spoke not in anger but in disappointment, and it was like a flashback to that day he found out about Holly, the day that changed their lives more than the departure of their mother or the death of their father. For up until that day, they had each other. No matter how tough life got, they had each other.

The rest happened quickly, like fragments of a dream. The conversation was short. Edgar was leaving now. He knelt and hugged both girls, not playful this time, for they were smart girls and they understood the weight of the moment. They were Drummond girls. No matter how hard Shannon worked to hide them from it. Edgar hid nothing. He stopped before the door to the entrance hallway. It was over his shoulder that he spoke,

"You take these girls and you go see Aunt Dotty. And I'm sure I'll see ya around." And, then he was gone.

Chapter 8

The pub was dim and smelled of mildew and liquor. Edgar sat at his recently acquired place at the end of the bar closest to the back office. There was a glass of cheap bourbon in his left hand and he was hunched over it. His frame looked gaunt, his face swollen, his skin pale. He was almost unrecognizable from the marine he had been only two years earlier. His eyelids were heavy with drink, and he appeased them with sluggish blinks. The reflection in the dirty mirror behind rows of bottles only disgusted him more every time he reopened them, and he would rather leave them shut.

Behind the haggard stranger in the mirror, he could make out the reflection of a banner he had once lived for. Starred and striped, never before had he more longed for anything than he longed to have died for that banner. It wasn't the cloth he had loved. He had loved what he once believed that flag represented, and while somewhere inside he still believed that passion existed, he couldn't recall what it felt like for the life of him.

Edgar had been a great soldier. He had been told so by every superior he had ever served under. Mission after mission he arrived at the rendezvous point to looks of shock and surprise. Then something changed. His commanding officer told him that he would be moved to a standard company; he told him thanks. He had been too good, too indifferent to collateral damage to be used any longer in the role he had known. Two weeks later, he failed repeated psychological screenings. He would never again see combat.

After he had been 'honorably' discharged from the only occupation he had ever been any good at, he had been told that nothing he had done beyond his first tour in Afghanistan had ever occurred. All the classified missions in Asia, the Caucasus and South America were to be sealed. The last three years of his existence were to be dismissed from the pages of history. His thinking, his breathing, his life had never happened. They made up a separate existence for him, false stories and records. He had been given some medals and thanked for his sacrifices then told to sign his name on some forms he never even bothered to read.

He came home to a big parade, wearing the crisp dress uniform that had hung in his closet in Virginia for years while he was living out the nightmares of grown men in the most sinister corners of the globe. People who had never met him cheered him and had their photos taken beside him, ignorant of what it was he had done or the lengths he had gone to do it. The governor shook his hand and told him thanks.

Edgar had never seen Shannon so proud. They both knew why he joined the military in the first place – though neither of them had ever spoken of it. And while such wounds may never heal, they were able to leave the pain unresolved for one day – locked away with all other hardships they had endured in silence. They smiled and gave into the moment. They enjoyed each other's company and pretended a girl had never come between them.

63

The past was unbearable. The future may be unobtainable. But in that moment was their shared glory. It was a moment for the Drummonds.

Edgar didn't dwell on the nostalgia for long. He never dwelt long. He just raised his glass until it was parallel to his chin and stared at the copper-colored poison. He could see the cause and beyond it, the results, unavoidable in the dim, blurred reflection. There was no beating it though. Even if it were the worst possible way out, it was the familiar one. So, he tilted the glass to his lips and washed down another dose of self-loathing.

The warmth swallowed the same, but his state of mind didn't change. After about the second one, it never did. 'One was too many and a thousand was never enough,' he had heard his grandfather tell his father. He smiled at this memory, but it did little to cheer him. He was a young man, but his memories had already been shadowed by hardship, molded together and distorted with jagged edges that were impossible to see yet always cut deep. The Drummond curse was a sorrow that was passed down rather than shared, and it was the isolation that was hardest to stomach. He wondered if it was more honorable to steal or to beg.

He spun the empty glass on the bar's surface, debating whether to fill it again or use it to shatter the mirror. He was distracted when movement from the back hallway caught his eye. Mr. Grisham moved gracefully across the poorly lit space between the hallway and the bar. He wore brown loafers, well polished as always. His movement was quieter than usual. He had been in the office all afternoon, and he looked tired and old, though still wise and aware. His hair was slicked as always, but a few loose ends caught the light close up, and Edgar could tell he had been running his hands through it. Smoothing his hair back was as close as Grisham came to carrying a visible tell.

"I need you and Austin to visit a friend of ours this evening." He said, resting a hand on Edgar's shoulder and breathing heavily through his nose. They were close, and Edgar could smell his aftershave.

As Edgar was about to reply, Grisham's expression fell stern.

"What did I tell you about your drinking?" He asked firmly.

64

His unwavering confidence was something Edgar had always admired.

"That it was a problem." Edgar answered, unapologetically. Grisham nodded, frowning.

"Yes, I also said you are a good for nothing lush Mick. If your fists weren't as hard as your head, I would have no use for you." His words were harsh, but his tone was even and controlled.

It was not unusual for Grisham to speak down at Edgar. Despite the bond that had grown between the old man and his youngest associate, it would always be a business relationship. With Grisham there were only business relationships. Still, he had no children of his own, and he had taken a special interest in Edgar. The boy's uncle, Marvin, had worked for him in the early years before he had accepted the stress and responsibility of being in charge, and the boy reminded the old man of a youthful Marvin more than his own father – who had always been too hard-headed and prideful to be concerned with easy money. Unfortunately, Marvin would eventually succumb to the opposite problem and his debts became too large to ignore. Grisham's predecessor, Zeke Franklin, had handed down the order. It was one of his last.

Marvin had drunk too much. Both of them had drunk too much. They all drank too much. Sooner or later the booze did them all in. If an Irishman had a weakness the bottle would exploit it and then compound it. Grisham knew the same fate would take the boy, and there was nothing that could be done. It was life. It was the grace of God.

He expressed his disappointment in the boy with snide sarcasm and open belittlement, but he only spoke the truth. Sometimes Edgar's ears would burn and he often fell into his silent rages, but Grisham had learned to read him well and knew exactly how far he could push and get away with it. The old man had built his life exploiting the weaknesses of others: pride, lust, gluttony, and envy. He was an expert in human psychology though he had little schooling. He scolded Edgar harshly because he knew it got results.

It was the same when rewarding his young disciple. Grisham paid Edgar no more than anybody else – although he was far more valuable. Instead, he stroked his need for approval and justification, treating him publicly to special favor after a job well done. Through this hot and cold relationship, he was able to control his most dangerous weapon. Grisham was no fool though. He had been around a long time, and he knew – just as the military had known – that such a volatile tool remained useful only for so long before its liability surpassed its value. And despite growing affection toward his introverted, moody young pit-bull, he knew he couldn't keep the kid around much longer. Like his uncle, Edgar's indulgences would eventually surpass his worth.

But Marvin had never been so cold-blooded or so calculating. There was a bluntness to Edgar, a genuine wooden quality that Grisham had never seen in all his years around thieves, thugs, drug addicts and plain psychopaths. He knew that when the time came if he didn't strike swiftly and with all his might, there would be no second chance. Even now, reprimanding him like a child, Grisham felt a quiver in his lower spine that he hadn't felt since he had faced off against Dirk Zaddick at Hilltop Cemetery in the tenth grade.

He had stuck that fat bastard between the ribs with a pocketknife and twisted it until Zaddick's eyes rolled back and he had passed out. A week later Grisham had quit school for the last time and started working for the bootleggers collecting debts. He still played the part of a Catholic, but he had not stepped foot in the Cathedral in over forty years. If there was anything he had learned in his whole life, it was to never ignore a problem; always deal with it immediately and always face it head on.

Edgar was unaware of any of this. Like a wolf, he trusted the pack and hunted by his instincts, learning only what was provided him by his environment. He did not philosophize or stop to worry what his prey thought of him. He saw Grisham for all his flaws, but he had never known any other kind. He respected the fact that he kept to his word. He respected his impartial ruthlessness. He looked to Grisham as a father figure, and he planned to run his fledgling brothel up in the canyon just as Grisham might run it himself. He wanted to make his boss proud, and reveled in the gleam of his affection. He had no idea that Grisham already knew of his disciples other business and watched it carefully.

He slid the glass away with the back of his hand and stood to his feet without replying to the old man's insults. He grabbed his jacket, and as he pulled it on he called Austin over with a nod. Then he turned back to the old man. Grisham only shook his head. He was tired and he suddenly felt his age. When Austin reached the end of the bar, the old man faced him but addressed them both. The sour stench of the fat slob, whose forehead was already beaded in sweat, made Edgar light-headed and distracted him from hearing Grisham's directions. It didn't matter. He wouldn't know where they were going anyway. Austin was the driver. Good thing too since he was never much help once a destination was reached. Edgar watched him as he concentrated on the old man's words, nodding his fat, egg-shaped head repeatedly and wheezing through his gaping mouth. Suddenly, disgust returned to the forefront of Edgar's buzz as he wondered for the hundredth time why he had yet to kill the inbred sloth. The unbearable odor pulled the bourbon from his pores and he fought back vomit when his stomach tightened from the nausea. A memory momentarily flittered through his internal dialogue only to be lost before it fully materialized. The bitter taste of bile clung to the back of his throat.

"Let's go, Edgar." Austin said. His voice was without haste or emotion. He knew better than to taunt his accomplice – both from personal experience and from witnessing his handy work over the past couple months. The big man was already bathed in concern despite his best efforts to disguise his fear. He hated working with Edgar. He didn't care what the job was, for he had seen the transformation, the absolute disconnect, and he knew it was only a matter of time before he found himself in the wrong place at the wrong time.

The men exited the bar, Edgar giving the big man plenty of distance despite the dawdling pace of his awkward gait. The night was cold. Their boots squeaked on the snow-packed ice. Before they reached the car, Edgar had already stopped twice for long pulls off a flask he had stashed in his jacket. When he climbed into the front passenger seat of the dark blue SUV, it was like crawling into a vacuum. The air was dead and noiseless – ten degrees colder than the night. His eyes bounced with inebriation.

It was Austin who broke the silence. He labored in behind the wheel, and the vehicle labored to accommodate him; both machine and man groaning to displace such unnatural mass.

67

Digging the keys from his pocket proved to be another job and it took him a full minute before he turned over the ignition.

The engine sputtered to life. The defrost fan churned cold air against the frosted surface of the windshield. Edgar sat still as a stone. His eyes remained glued to the opaque glass, thankful to have escaped the scrutinizing transparency of his own reflection. Crystals of ice glittered randomly in a million unique locations. Edgar observed the false movement without interest. He would not recall what he saw, for he was already somewhere else.

The whole display was nothing unusual for the man beside him. Austin had seen it all before. At first, he had decided it was all an act, some form of intimidation. It was a tough job and every guy had his own way of dealing with it. Some guys liked loud rock music. Others might prefer gangster rap. Something to psych themselves up. Some talked a lot, others not at all. He had known a few guys that literally slapped themselves.

Edgar preferred hard liquor and total stillness. If Austin spoke of a plan, he might get a grunt or a nod for an answer, but there was never eye contact. The stare remained on the windshield and the road before them at all times. There was no radio and no conversations, only the hums and ticks of the moving vehicle. Each reverberation amplified by the smothering dread of impending violence.

But it wasn't anger. Austin was sure of that. He was still unsure of what exactly it was lurking behind those eyes, but he had braved observation enough to know what it wasn't. He had seen Edgar angry, felt the brazen wrath. His anger was blunt and struck like lightening. This was different. There was a patience to it. He could not describe what it looked like because it wasn't in the expression or the eyes. It wasn't something that was there but rather something that was missing. And whatever it was, Edgar had long since accepted it. There was a mix of guilt and sorrow, and yet there was acceptance, like he knew precisely what was coming, down to the last detail, and the imprint of his actions would not only haunt him for the rest of his life but had already existed within him long before. Whatever it was, Austin didn't want to trade places with the little Mick bastard for all the money in the world. He pulled the vehicle into gear and did his best to keep to himself.

Chapter 9

The cold awoke Shannon from a vivid dream. Even in total darkness, he was immediately aware of his surroundings. He smelled the wood smoke. He heard the rustling of the wind against the canvass walls of the tent. It was a dense, frosty chill. Longing to finish a dream, he pulled his beanie down over his ears and hunkered deep in his sleeping bag, but to no avail. Ten minutes passed and still he was wide awake, shivering.

He searched beside him with his hand until he found his flashlight. Clicking on the beam of light created a whole new world inside the dark walls of the tent. He pulled on a sweatshirt and his slippers and went to the stove. The fire had gone cold, and he opened the rusted hatch with a creak to find nothing but a scatter of glowing coals.

Edgar must have left the flue all the way open. Shannon had reminded him to close it several times. He shined his light around to find his brother sound asleep on the ground a few feet away. He slept on a tarp, with no padding, and his entire upper body was hanging outside of his sleeping bag sprawled about like a strewn corpse. Shannon couldn't help but smile.

He had known for some time that his brother was entirely unique, raw and tough, unlike anything that had ever been created or would likely be matched. Life kept him so busy that he usually took his brother, as a person, for granted. He was too concerned with keeping him fed, out of trouble and in school to fully appreciate all the complexity he had to offer.

Edgar wasn't a cowboy in the definitive sense. He lacked the drawl, the dress, and perhaps the ethics. But he was rugged, independent, and harder than the decades old cast iron stove in front of which Shannon crouched. Despite Shannon's best efforts, his brother already chewed the snuff of a cowboy and had adopted the vulgar mouth of an old western whorehouse. There would be no stopping him. Edgar's toughness came from quiet depths, the result of seemingly endless bad breaks and an unyielding flame within.

Even as a small boy, Edgar had shown an iron will, regardless of whether or not it was in his best interest to do so. In

69

fact, he didn't seem to care much for his best interest – only his pride. He was as determined as any Drummond before him and from the time he was old enough to crawl, he had been adventuring off in search of the unknown. He acted in a way that suggested his decisions were without choice, reacting confidently and rather indifferently regardless of consequence. And he was stubborn and hot-headed as an unbroken mule. If he wanted something, no force on this earth could stand in his way. He would simply out last and out will any adversary or obstacle.

Shannon had always admired and often envied Edgar's instinctive nature. But he also grew frustrated with his brother's recklessness, his total disregard for the future or the family's legacy. In truth, Shannon longed to be more adventurous, but was unable to blindly embrace risk. It wasn't in his makeup; someone had to be responsible. There was nothing he could do to change that. At times it was hard for him to accept. He constantly strove to improve on every aspect of his life, particularly those that he saw as weaknesses or issues of self-consciousness from his youth. He was uncompromising, like all Drummonds. But unlike his brother or his father, he did care what others thought of him, and this became a source of constant second guessing.

Edgar on the other hand seemed to have a profound understanding of individuality based on the environmental constraints of one's given time and place. He had grasped religion from their mother before she abandoned them and had immediately accepted the archaic ideals of fate. It was never why. Things simply were. Why never mattered.

In the years since, Shannon watched Edgar struggle in his relationship with God, a relationship strained by the hardships he had dealt with and the losses they had faced. To Shannon, this was illogical and unproductive. He hated religion, due to its dependence on faith over fact and because of its varying depths of interpretation. Shannon worked in a world of controllable outcomes and changing opinions. Data. Particulars that were known with certainty to those willing to find them and could not be overcome by emotional attachment in matters of disagreement. That's why he wanted to go to law school. He believed in human growth and individual change. He believed a man was not destined to the fate of his forefathers.

Shannon filled the stove with split pine and closed the damper halfway. The coals burned hot, and he sat with the hatch cracked open watching the flames slowly crackle back to life. He checked his watch – it was 4:15. The coldest hour of the night. As the earth turned, dawn approached. The slow burn as the ignition rose through the dry logs mesmerized him and his thoughts returned to his dream.

He had been dreaming about his mother. A strange dream. She had come to him as a well-dressed real estate agent. He had fallen in love with a huge, flashy mansion she had shown him, but she became annoyed when she reviewed his finances and ridiculed him for his poverty and incompetence. Repeatedly, she had threatened to leave if he could not come up with the money on his end. His father had been there. But he sat by silently and did nothing. There had been more, but he couldn't remember.

It was rare that he dreamed of his mother, or even thought of her anymore. She had quite on her family, like a coward. She had found religion, took the cure, and then found a manic, cult pastor that absolved her of all her sins. One morning, she snuck out, moved to some small town in the Midwest – in Kansas maybe, though to Shannon it might has well have been China. He had just turned twelve when she left and Edgar was a mere seven, and their father had shown little emotion upon hearing the news that his wife of eighteen years had fallen in love with another and was leaving him. Shannon remembered standing on Windy Ridge when his father told him. He saw the hurt that balled up in his father's guts and shown on his weary, haggard face over the next few years. But eventually he managed to choke it down into his soul where all the other pain and sorrow lay scarred, festering and unspoken. The weight of the circumstances aged Tom overnight.

Not that his father was innocent in the whole matter. Tom Drummond was no saint. He was an untamed pioneer. A man born far too late for the era to which he belonged, who rarely showed his love yet always showed his anger. He drank too much, spent too much time alone, and he spoke too little. His wife enjoyed the woods more than most women, but the isolation wore on her. When she found God, she decided the obsession that consumed the bulk of her husband's heart was unnatural, and he was unwilling to

71

change even for love. The mountains were his sanctuary. He claimed to be helpless in the matter, and this was probably true.

Edgar had been close with their mother, much closer than Shannon. He had taken it hard when she left. Afterward, he cried without reason or constraint and fell victim to vicious outbursts and tantrums without direction. His father, struggling to hide his own grief, came down hard on his younger son, the son that wore his own face and had been held to a stricter standard since birth – the same as it had been with him and his own father. Tom would taunt Edgar, put him down, and assign him difficult labor as punishment. 'The Drummond family had never seen such a baby,' he used to say.

In an unspoken bond, Edgar turned to Shannon for nurture. In his soft beautiful face, Edgar saw his mother and found the only love he identified as real. He came to his older brother with questions, strange deep questions that were almost metaphysical – questions centered on loss, death, and the hereafter. They were questions far beyond the scope of a seven or eight year old child. Shannon treated such inquiries with patience and answered them honestly to the best of his ability. But he wondered often at the source of these inquiries. When he pried Edgar, the youngster was never able to describe the place from which his thoughts came.

Eventually, Edgar seemed to grow out of his phase. He made friends and Shannon's concern for him eased. Still, the departure of their mother was the source of a fork in the roadway of their lives. The two boys visibly separated when she left and forever lost something they had shared until that day.

Shannon remained ambitious and outgoing. He excelled in football and basketball. Parents and teachers loved him, and by his senior year he was vice president of the student body and the most recognized face in the school. Meanwhile, Edgar became stealthy and stoic. He chose his friends carefully and would not tolerate disloyalty. Even while he remained a fairly well-behaved kid, one most parents approved of, there was something about him that brought unease to all he came in contact with, as if he reminded people of the frailty of their own moral vigor. The majority of the friends he ran with lived on the wrong end of town, where a name meant nothing and only one's actions earned respect.

72

It wasn't until he started wrestling – and excelling at it – that Edgar carved out his own notoriety. At twelve years old, wrestling coaches all over town were already taking notice. No one had ever seen such fierce determination in a boy so young. What he lacked in technique, he more than made up for with instinct and a seemingly endless source of explosive power he kept hidden somewhere in his tiny frame. Soon, he was pinning the best eighth graders in town, wearing them down with his tenacity and quickness. His ability to dish out pain without showing signs of fatigue was unreal. He was an animal in his natural environment.

In seventh grade he went on to beat every challenger in the state, and the following year he was named a champion at the AAU National Free Style Championships in Michigan. He found bravado and began carrying a chip on his shoulder, yet overall he remained the same introspective, disturbed youth despite all the victories and accolades. The only time he changed was in the moment the crowd erupted. He lived for their praise, and Shannon recognized and understood his cravings. He was proud of his little brother. But sometimes he felt envy too.

Now, he sat scratching his head at the past wondering, as he often did, how differently things might have turned out if their mother hadn't abandoned them and their father had not perished, or even if he had died instantly, rather than wasted away slowly before their eyes – first at the hospital for ten days in constant pain, coughing blood and unable to stand for the first time in his life, then in those last few days in and out of that sterile white hospital room and his own bed. The hospice nurse a constant fixture at his side, as if suddenly at the final moments before death somebody took notice of the Drummond family's demise but only to stand by, watch with abject pity and serve witness to the conclusion of a once prolific family. It was hard for the boys to watch. They grew up thinking their father was indestructible. To watch him crumble was a rude awakening to the cruelty and futility of the world around them.

The fire was roaring now. The logs glowed red beneath the yellow-blue flames that hissed and popped, and the tent was warming quickly. But Shannon knew there was no point in trying to return to sleep this morning. He stepped outside to take a piss. Six inches of fresh snow had fallen overnight, but the snow had

73

stopped. The morning had grown calm and still. A few luminous clouds hung tolerably within the restricted scope of sky above camp, detectable by the light of an unseen moon. It glowed somewhere behind the turret peaks that bounded their location in all directions, and he remembered it was still full. Under well-lit, snowy midnight skies, the elk may have fed all night. A few stars dotted around the non-invasive billows, and the mountain silence filled his conscience with an endless familiarity. There were memories unseen, neutral and yet powerful. A true and endless silence can be haunting, and he shivered off the cold once more knowing that light from the east would arrive soon. It was still a few hours away, but it was not too soon to anticipate.

Shannon loved sunrise; the birth of a new day; the conquest of light; the endless possibilities; the hope.

His bare hands grew cold, but he remained standing a moment longer in only a light sweatshirt and long underwear, his slippers buried in the soft, virgin snow. He inhaled the cold tranquility, slow and deep. Why couldn't this be enough? It would be so simple. It seemed so obvious. Finally, the sentimentality wore off – seeping from him along with his body heat. He returned to the tent and crawled into his bag. Pulling a book from his duffle bag, he read by flashlight until his patience diminished and then he rose, lit the lantern and placed the percolator on the stove.

"Rise and shine baby brother." He said, smiling down upon the disheveled heap below him as the scent of coffee filled the tent. Edgar awoke and gave his brother a sour look, squinting toward him with a single unperceptive eye. He rubbed at his sap and smoke stained face awkwardly like a child and sat up without a word. Upon reaching a ninety degree angle, he froze as if he were lost then gave a long yawn.

Shannon moved to the makeshift bench and poured cereal and milk into a paper bowl.

"I was thinking we should go all the way around Camp Ridge and drop down into the valley," he said chomping loudly over his words. "Not down as far as the Utterback Ranch, but at least into the foothills. I have a feeling old Joel's been letting some guys walk the place, and they might push something out. Plus if we jump a track on the ride out, we can always drop off and follow it.

The snow must have just stopped in the past couple hours. Any track can't be more than a few hours old."

His brother listened with patience still half asleep. It was impossible to know what sank in. The respect and love for his elder and provider was visible in his face, yet he remained silent even as Shannon finished speaking and went on slurping the milk from the flimsy bowl. The steady hiss of the lantern was the soundtrack to which the boys dressed.

"Dress warm," Shannon advised his brother, pulling on a second layer before reaching for his jacket. "It might warm up later this morning, but it's cold out there now, and you can always take layers off."

While Shannon followed his flashlight out to start the bikes, Edgar wolfed down two granola bars and slurped most of a half-frozen can of pop. His eyes were still red and swollen from sleep when Shannon found him returning to the tent after taking a leak.

"Ready?" Shannon asked. His rifle was already slung tight across his back, the strap stretched from the bulk of his extra layer. Edgar nodded, the cold waking him from his stupor. He ducked his head in the tent, grabbed his gloves, his hat, and his gun and turned off the lantern and made his way toward the rumbling call of the bikes. Shannon had already wiped the snow off the seats and fenders.

They climbed on the bikes, flipped on their headlights and started out the trail. Shannon in front, Edgar close behind. The two beams of white light bounced, cut and weaved their way through the otherwise black wilderness, visibly and audibly disrupting every molecule of the immediate vicinity, while remaining solitary and unbeknownst to the world at large. In their wake, they left only a haunting recognition to the previous silence of the morning and the woods. The tire tracks were the sole evidence of their existence, but with a gust of wind or a little new snow that memory would be erased and lost forever.

Chapter 10

Oliver Carino was grabbing a sack of groceries from his car when fate intervened. It was already 9:30, and Oliver was irritable. He didn't like to be out after dark when he could help it, especially when it was cold. His joints tightened in the cold and he had a difficult time driving at night. He had stayed late at the gym working with one of the older boys on his chokes. The boy was making his professional debut, and he still finished poorly. Oliver was aggravated about that too.

He didn't know what it was about these kids, but he couldn't find their guts. Maybe, he was losing his touch. Maybe, the toughness he had grown up around didn't exist anymore. Hell, some of the boys he trained were looking for endorsement deals before they had even spilt blood. They were too pretty and too privileged, like the world should bow before them because they had won a couple fist fights in high school and the bouncers at the local discotheque were intimidated by them.

The one that afternoon had been more than he could take. A nagging feeling had followed him since he left the gym. And now, knees aching and struggling to catch his breath, he decided enough was enough. He would retire.

There was no point in it anymore. He trained fighters to get them off the streets, away from drugs, out of gangs and to teach them how to cope without killing. But now these kids just saw some silly old man who taught archaic methods and got confused and forgetful when he let his emotions get away from him. He knew the kids noticed him slipping. It was the damn medication's fault. He would almost rather deal with the vertigo than lose track of his own mind. Hell, it took him almost ten minutes to move around the car, open the back door and grab the damn groceries. He was getting old, and it was time to accept it. There was nothing to look forward to but loneliness, dementia and death.

Sil would never buy the retirement bit. In Sil's upbringing a guy retired when he died. Maybe Oliver would tell his friend he was moving back to Chicago, had the itch again. He didn't want to move though. He had grown to love Montana. The people were finally accepting him as one of their own and achieving that fit had taken nearly a decade. It was a tough place for outsiders to find acceptance, but he knew he had brought out the best in more than a few kids he had trained here. It didn't matter one way or the other though. Without the guts, all the coaching in the world was a waste of time. Like the kid that evening – he was a thoroughbred. His athleticism and potential were endless. He could strike and grapple, had speed and trained hard. Twenty-two years old and he was 8-1 heading into his first pro fight.

And yet Oliver could see right through him. The kid would fold like a cheap card table at the first true test of courage and continue to flop at the hands of every real challenge he faced. He might last for ten or fifteen fights if he was lucky before he hung up the gloves and moved on to become a trainer or fitness instructor – which is probably all he truly wanted in his heart to begin with. The kid was a specimen. But he was soft. He wore hairspray and went to the tanning salon. Not that a fighter couldn't be pretty. Oliver had nothing against pretty. But the vanity had to have a place in the fighter's perception of self. It should be a source of his confidence and not a weakness. This kid was being hyped for his physique, but it was all curls and sit-ups and steamed broccoli and grilled chicken. No flavor. He was gym made. He was a kid from the suburbs. He had never worked a day in his life outside of training. His parents worked in air-conditioned offices, talked problems out and didn't believe in spanking their children. It wasn't the kid's fault he would never be a fighter. He was an athlete and trained accordingly. Toughness is created by environment, not a bench press or sparring partner.

All this was running through Oliver's mind as he reached down carefully and removed the two paper bags filled with low sodium, high fiber foods from the backseat. He was irritated and he was sad, and he worried that maybe there was nothing wrong with the fighters, maybe it was he who had nothing left to offer. He didn't want to believe that, but the nagging doubt wouldn't go away. There was less crowding in his thoughts than even a few years ago, and it was harder than ever to shake a notion once it settled in.

The dilemma remained his solitary concern as he struggled to shut the car door. He held a brown paper sack in the crook of either elbow supporting the weight against his body and tried to

77

push the door with his hip. It closed, but he knew it wasn't shut. He cursed the car. Then he cursed the winter. His ears were cold, but it was his embarrassment at being out of breath from such a menial task that was really bothering him.

"Oh to hell with it," He finally said aloud. He pushed the lock button on his key chain and started the slow journey to his front door. He was still shaking his head at his luck, picturing the pretty kid with the bulging biceps and shaved chest, knowing how unprepared he was for professional fighting, when a commotion startled him and he nearly fell over on the sidewalk.

The gate of the apartment building next door to Oliver's house swung open with a heavy clang that echoed in the dry, cold silence. A big man shot out, leapt the cement stairs, and headed straight at him. The block was mostly unlit and Oliver was unable to make out any details of the man's appearance, but evidently he had left wherever he was coming from in a hurry, for despite visible athleticism, fleeing didn't appear to be a habit. He was large and underdressed, wearing only a t-shirt and sweatpants. The bulky figure moved with unnatural effort like a grease fire, crunching through the frozen snow at a violent sprint. Still, even in the heat of the moment Oliver was impressed with how quickly he moved for a big man.

Oliver wasn't afraid. The man may have been on drugs, but his movements were too rushed to be a mugger. The old man stood his ground. He had always been a stubborn man and some things never changed. Besides, he couldn't outrun a lawn mower and it wasn't this man but rather whatever or whoever had him stampeding that troubled him. Twenty yards from where he stood, the big man turned and veered toward the street. As he passed Oliver had a pretty good look at him. He guessed him at about six foot three and close to two-hundred and sixty pounds.

The big man was cutting between Oliver's car – which still had its dome light on – and the car parked behind it when the gate clanged again and a second figure darted out of the shadows. This guy was smaller; maybe five-ten and slim even in a winter jacket. He ran more naturally with a short quick stride and gained on the big man quickly. The chase presented a strange scene; at first look, one might think they were watching the gazelle giving chase to a lion. But Oliver's keen eye recognized the graceful pursuit of a carnivore. Half-way across the street the big man gave a glance back and realized he wasn't going to outrun his pursuer. He turned to fight, but before he could square his shoulders, the little guy hit him belt high with a shoulder tackle and both men fell out of sight behind the vehicles. Oliver could hear the commotion of close combat on the icy blacktop. He shook his head and looked above him into the night sky. There was no moon. It was a dark night.

"You've got to be kidding me?" he muttered to the heavens. Then he cursed his luck again, wishing he had just stayed home and watched Wheel of Fortune.

Carefully, he set the bags down on the stoop and started back toward the street. The men were still hidden from view, but he could hear the groans of their labored breathing as they struggled. Common sense told him how ignorant his behavior was, and yet his steps continued onward. At the curb, he stopped as the smaller man suddenly rose in the florescent glow of a distant street light. He had climbed to his feet and was kicking his opponent hard in the ribs. The big man was doing little to defend himself. He was lying in a fetal position. The blood pooled around him was black in the dim pink of the street lamp.

"Oh, Hell," Oliver cursed to himself, shuffling into the street. He was about thirty feet away from the violence when the assailant sensed him and spun quickly, wide eyed, fists ready. The sight of the elderly man seemed to catch him off guard. Through the shadows, Oliver sensed a tinge of shame in the wildest eyes he had ever seen.

"I think that boy's had enough." Oliver said. His voice sounded unfamiliar and he was unsure of where the words came from. He cursed himself and God in his head. The man didn't move.

Up close, Oliver could see that the victor was much younger than he had expected. He couldn't have been much older than the kid he had worked with earlier that evening. Couldn't have been thirty, though Oliver could sense there had been some cold, hard years in his past.

Finally, he seemed satisfied Oliver posed no threat and he turned and kicked the man hard in the head; the blow not so much despite Oliver's words as in direct defiance of them. If the big man had been conscious, he gave no sign of it. The kick was ruthless. It may have killed a smaller man. Oliver had been in and around

79

fights his whole life, and still the brutality of such an act against a defenseless man made him woozy.

"Alright son, you kick that boy again and you'll likely kill him. You sure you're ready to have that on your soul?"

The word soul seemed to catch the boy's attention and he looked at Oliver more carefully. The guilt was gone. He inched toward him before he spoke,

"What do you care about my soul, old man?"

Oliver recognized the dead flame in his eyes. He knew the look all too well. Right then, he knew the kid had seen death up close and grown accustomed to it. Over the years, he had seen that cold burning flame and witnessed how it mangled and polluted men's hearts. There was no cure for such indifference. No matter how much time passed, it never burned out, not until it had consumed everything and left nothing. He had lost a few great fighters, a few great kids, to that cold, dead flame.

The excessive atrocity of the kick had mustered courage in the old man, but it abandoned him in the face of such a hardened individual. His voice cracked and nearly failed him as he spoke,

"The fate of your soul is between you and God, son, but I know there is no courage in kicking an unconscious man to death. Whatever it is that boy has done can't be undone by killing him."

The kid turned back to the man lying heaped beside him. The shirt he wore was black with blood as was the snow and ice all around him. He had rolled over in a last ditch effort to protect himself. The kid seemed to be debating the situation. Oliver knew he was trying to visualize the fate of his soul or its existence. Somewhere a dog was barking. Otherwise, all was calm and quiet on the street.

Seconds ticked by like days.

A voice called out from behind Oliver, momentarily easing the tension of the confrontation. Another man appeared in the street out front of the apartment and waddled toward them in sad attempt at haste. This man was bigger than the first man, without the build. He was obese and wheezed as he reached the scene. In the glow of the street lamp, Oliver noticed a pleasant smile flirt his face at the sight of the injured man still lying on the hard ice soaking in the warmth of his own blood. Then he turned to the old man, and the smile was replaced with a stiff grimace. The look lacked the intensity of the smaller man, who now stood and watched them both in rigid silence. Even facing the fat man, Oliver could feel the eyes of the wild one watching.

"What the fuck is this?" The fat man said, panting like a dog. He looked to the kid for answers but received no response. "Run along coon. It's past your bedtime."

A war vet who had seen his share of battle outside the ring, Oliver could spot a fraud a mile away, and this grotesque disgrace to his ancestor's evolution and the advancements of modern hygiene was completely yellow. The fat man came closer and Oliver noticed his left eye was swollen and beginning to bruise. The wound probably explained his satisfaction at the unconscious man's pain.

"I don't want no trouble now. Your friend here has done enough damage for one night. I'm going to head inside and call this poor boy an ambulance. You boys scatter, and no one will be the wiser. Whatever business this is can be settled…" The fat man interrupted him right there,

"Shut the fuck up, you crazy old fuck. I'll put your black ass in the nursing home. Telling me what's gonna happen." He grabbed the old man by the shoulders and shook him. Oliver struggled to keep his balance. Ten years younger, maybe less, and he would have put this fat punk in his place.

"Stop." The kid directed. He hadn't moved. He still stood about thirty feet away and his voice wasn't forceful. It was emotionless almost conversational. He looked down at the big man below him one more time and at last seemed satisfied.

The fat man froze and turned at the sound of the smaller man's voice. But the kid wasn't looking in his direction, and the goon misunderstood the order. He pushed the old man, who surprised him with his strength and coordination. This only seemed to anger the fat bastard, and he pushed the Oliver again, hard this time, sending the old man to the ground.

Oliver fell hard on his hip. The impact disoriented him and a pain shot up his side. He rolled to his butt to defend himself but there was no need. The kid had covered the distance between them in the time it took Oliver to hit the ground. He shoved the fat man into Oliver's car door with a heavy crash as the metal dented.

81

Oliver crab crawled on his palms, keeping one eye on the assailants.

"What the hell is wrong with you, psycho?" The fat man asked in a voice filled with fear and annoyance. He used the support of the car to regain his feet.

The kid didn't answer. He looked at the old man and again, and Oliver stopped moving. The kid seemed satisfied with something he saw.

"Go get the truck." He said to no one in particular. He was looking out into the night now. It was cold and his words leaked out as steam and faded away.

The fat man ran a hand through his coarse, filthy beard several times as if he were debating the orders. Then he gave a childish moan and started down the street without argument.

After he had gone into the darkness, Oliver made a strenuous attempt to stand. He was in pain, and he cursed aloud several times in his efforts. Still, the boy said nothing. He offered the old man no aid and paid him only passive attention.

The big man had regained consciousness. He was sobbing hysterically, begging for help. The boy looked down on him, and in the pink glow Oliver could see it was a look of total detachment: no joy, no guilt, no sorrow. Whatever spell of violence had been provoked in the boy had passed.

Oliver knew better than to speak again – it was his big mouth that had gotten him into this whole mess in the first place – but he couldn't help himself. He was old, mentally and physically drained, and he was stubborn.

"You know you could use your talents in more productive ways, son." He said in slow gasps. It hurt to breath, and the vertigo was setting in. He needed to lie down. The boy looked at him but said nothing, his face wooden.

"I train fighters," Oliver specified. "We could get you in a ring. You could work your problems out in a constructive way." The boy still didn't answer. He seemed to be listening though.

"Whatever's happened, son, God's forgiveness is greater." These words he spoke gently. It was a statement that meant more to him than any other, a statement that someone had told him when he was seventeen years old that had saved his life and he had since told to nearly a dozen outcast youths over the years, many of whom had also been saved by finding God.

"God's forgiveness is greater than any hurt and all the pain." He repeated, nodding his head as if to agree with himself.

The boy looked at him again. He didn't answer, but something told Oliver he was listening. Headlights approached from the north. They blinded Oliver as the vehicle squealed to a stop. He shielded his eyes and squinted. The car engine groaned against the cold. The boy held his ground. The white light silhouetted his figure in an angelic halo. The old man's jaw fell open and something inside him gave way. The boy turned his back starting for the vehicle.

"There's money to be won." Oliver tried, desperate suddenly, driven by a sense of fate. The boy didn't flinch.

"A man can almost scratch an honest living if he has enough talent and the guts to stick it out." The boy was almost to the vehicle's door and the old man had to raise his voice to reach him.

"If you ever change your mind, we train six nights a week at the Church of Christ on Park Avenue," his speech was rushed now as he searched for whatever nerve he had touched earlier. "God loves you son. It's ok to be afraid. I know you've been betrayed. God won't betray you. Let Christ's love into your life."

The boy swung the door open, spat, and stared back at the feeble old man with his tight white curls and worn brown skin. Oliver was shaking slightly, his hand up to shade his eyes from the blinding glare. He couldn't make out the boy's face but knew he was watching him a moment longer. Then the door slammed shut and the Ford tore by leaving the tired old man, a semiconscious victim and a distant barking dog alone in the cold chill of the night. The old man looked heavenward once more as a siren rang out. But Oliver knew it wasn't coming here.

"Sometimes," he whispered. He looked down at the big man who lay crying in the street.

"You just hold on there, son. I'm gonna go fetch you some help, you hear?"

Starting back toward the house, the pain was excruciating and every step was a chore. Damn. Oliver shook his head. He couldn't help but laugh at his luck even as he winced at the hurt.

"Sometimes," he said again, aloud this time. "They be mysterious ways you work, Lord."

Chapter 11

Shannon was running late, and he was still in the process of buttoning his coat as he exited the office and headed for his car. He had a small duffle bag in one hand which doubled as a briefcase and gym bag. He played basketball Tuesday and Thursday afternoons at lunch, and his hair was still damp from a one o'clock shower. He wore his grey twill pea coat over a white shirt, light-blue metallic tie and dark slacks. The addition of a silver wool scarf finished a look that was more J. Crew model than small town attorney, a fact he was aware of and that had often made him self-conscious.

Shannon dressed casual most days. He had never been a trial attorney, and blazers never suited his image. Shirt, tie and slacks were common place, although on Fridays he typically left out the tie and on occasion he would tuck a dress shirt into a pair of blue jeans. Growing up in a family of miners, Shannon had never seen anyone in his family don a suit, and ties had been reserved strictly for weddings and funerals. Professional style had been a learning process.

The scarf and the pea coat had both been purchases made by his wife, upgrades from ski jackets and other outerwear mismatches of a man who had never realized work attire included what one wore on the ride to the office. It only took Jill one time seeing her husband throw a camouflage jacket over suit and tie to force an intervention. Shannon had taken immediately to the light and stylish overcoat, but the mufflers had been met with strong resistance and taken a few years of persuasion.

It was early afternoon and a hazy sheen partially hid the midday sun. The day's temperature had reached a rather pleasant high just above freezing. Shannon had left his sunglasses in the car and the flat light forced him to squint as he marched doggedly toward his parking spot. The downtown area was alive with weekday activity: window shoppers strolling with young children or elderly retirees, office workers out for smoke breaks or rushing back with their afternoon latte and a growing number of transients soaking up the day's short-lived radiant heat.

The snow from the past storm had vanished, except a few stubborn reminders stashed in the hidden nooks of manmade structures where shade allowed it to linger. The sidewalks and streets were filthy with mud from the sand soaked slush. Vehicles too were mostly unwashed, and the harsh, white light of winter exposed everything in a fraudulent manner, like Midwesterners laid out beside a Vegas pool.

Shannon rounded the corner of a four-story brick building and climbed the short flight of stairs to find a white cruiser with 'sheriff' written in bold, brown letters along the door, parked beside his Explorer. He stopped for pause, only momentarily, more annoyed than concerned by what the scene implied. It caught him off guard. His pace slowed. He was in no hurry to speak with the tall, conceited asshole leaned lazily against the rear hatch of his SUV.

Sheriff Brad Gale was a chiseled, sandy-haired lawman straight out of a Hollywood thriller, and he came complete with the dimwit, open prejudice and shoot-first-cover-up-later attitude expected of such a small-town narcissist. Gale built his reputation on image, and he maintained that image meticulously with hours of weight lifting, weekly visits to the tanning salon and sixty dollar haircuts. He was a couple years older than Shannon and had been a local baseball legend growing up. Drafted by the Detroit Tigers out of high school, he chose the road to stardom over a scholarship to the University of Minnesota.

Rumor had it he had buckled at the first signs of adversity. By twenty, he crawled back home where he quickly followed in his father's footsteps as a crooked, albeit charismatic cop. Like Shannon, Gale was ambitious and set his sights high from the start. He proved talented in the art of politics. Well known and handsome, the poster boy for conservative small-town America had risen swiftly to the post of Deputy Sheriff without effort or the entanglement of paper work.

He was Grisham's lawman, just like his father before him. Anyone paying attention knew this to be a fact, but the county still ran on the outdated ideology of frontier justice. People stuck to their own business. Crooked businessmen like Zeke and Grisham were all too often viewed as outlaw heroes, so long as nobody innocent got hurt and the unemployment rate stayed low. Nobody seemed willing or able to do anything about the patterns of corruption. It was all anyone had ever known. Dishonest men ran big business through cutthroat means and maintained power by funneling much of their wealth to community coffers. Occasionally, some bit of dirt would come to light, and if the people decided the deed were dark enough, one tyrant would be replaced by several until another rose to the top. It was democracy in action, the will of the people.

Perhaps no crime lord since the original mining barons had proved as skilled at the art as Grisham. He possessed an unmatched talent for blending masterful political machinist and ruthless capitalist profiteer. Although he inherited his position, he had expanded his empire by creating a Robin Hood image. He dressed, spoke and acted the part of a refined gentleman, always generous and never flashy. He promoted his lack of education and simple Catholic ethics. Grisham controlled the local media and kept the consequences of his business off the boulevards and pictures out of the papers. When the ugly truth of his business ventures was exposed to the public eye, he swiftly surrendered a lackey to appease the town's vigilance.

And of course, Gale was always there to make the big arrests, although whether or not the evidence held up and a conviction was made depended on Grisham's discretion. As county commissioner, Shannon was Gale's boss, and he could have put the cocky bastard away on countless occasions – Gale made little effort to cover the tracks of his imprudence – but each time he swore he would act, only to convince himself Grisham would simply replace Gale with another crony; and Shannon with someone smart enough to keep his mouth shut.

"Afternoon, Shannon," Gale greeted, straightening smugly to his full height. He was about six two and had an angular, blocked jaw that operated with the harsh movement of heavy machinery as he chomped deliberately at something between his molars, presumably gum although Shannon typically imaged it to be a wad of cud. He was clean shaven as always, his uniform tailored tight to his wide chest and bulging arms. His hair was gelled, the tips, frosted and tangled, shining in the yellow light. He had one thumb latched behind a large gold belt buckle and wore a matching ring, although he was not married or dating. Everything about him had been scrupulously considered in an effort to present himself as a man of superior importance. Nothing was accidental.

"Hello, Brad." Shannon said, his words falling somewhere between cordial and bothered. "And what exactly is it I can do for you today?" Shannon asked, dropping the friendly act immediately. He had never gotten along with Gale and had no intention of spending a great deal of time conversing with a crooked cop in the open, particularly now that campaign season was hitting full stride.

"I was just making my rounds through the neighborhood, saw you walking and thought I'd stop to deliver you a message personally." Gale smiled. He spoke with the forced pauses of a man who's never said anything honest in his whole life. He thought himself untouchable and had no concern for what anyone saw him do or heard him say. He knew Shannon's predicament, was aware of his anxiety. It was part of his reason for staging their meeting here, not in a blatantly noticeable place but a place just public enough to make Shannon uneasy and at a disadvantage.

"And just what would that message be?" Shannon cut straight to the chase as he nonchalantly scanned their surroundings.

"Mr. Grisham would like a word with you."

"Well, I'll be sure to give him a call this afternoon then. Thanks for the message."

"You'd better just stop by the bar." Gale cut in sharply. His tone changed to match Shannon's directness. The order turned Shannon defiant.

"When I have time," He simmered, before composing himself, "I will stop in to speak with Mr. Grisham." He paused, suddenly self-conscious of the scarf and his wool coat. "Is there anything else, Brad?"

Gale squared Shannon up. The two men locked eyes. Gale moved in a step, then another. He was a few inches taller than Shannon and clearly enjoyed looking down at him. For a moment there was tense consideration from both men.

"There's a pecking order in this town, Drummond. And for some reason you see yourself higher up it than you actually are."

The two men were nearly chest to chest now. "Here's a history lesson for yah. The Drummonds have always been miners, laboring folk…Drunks mostly…Now, you might envision yourself as the torchbearer of the family's future, but don't you go and forget how things are done round here."

Shannon said nothing. He didn't look away. He didn't back down. He could hear his own breathing. Then Gale smiled and resumed his rhythmic chomp. But it was a different smile; he could no longer sell it as casual.

"Don't forget who the boss is. And don't think you can get where you're going without help."

"Is there anything else, Brad?" Shannon repeated, adding emphasis to the name this time, as if he were addressing a young boy. His veins pulsed with anger, but he revealed nothing. Gale's smile shrunk to a smirk. His chewing raced, but his lips tightened and hid his teeth. He eased back.

"No, sir." He shook his head. "That's all I got."

"Well, I'm glad to learn we have such an efficient courier service here in town, but if you'll excuse me, I'm in a bit of a hurry." This time it was Gale that had nothing to say. He stepped aside. "Thank you, sir." Shannon added and made his way around the vehicle to the driver's side. His hands were shaking as he unlocked the door. He couldn't leave this way. His mind raced. "And Brad…Or uh, Officer Gale?" Gale looked across the hood with perturbed dejection. Their eyes met between the corner of the windshield and the curve of the open door. "Next time you have a message for me, go ahead and pick up the phone. You might have taxpayer time to kill, but some of us are very busy." And for the first time, Shannon found his smile. It felt forced. But it felt good.

"And you tell your family hello," Gale replied quickly, revealing his reaction. He was no longer smiling or chewing, and his teeth were clenched so the rear of his jaw balled outward. "It's a shame that brother of yours can't seem to stay outta trouble…Maybe you should remind him that prostitution, serving liquor without a license and unregulated gambling are all illegal in this county… not just inside city limits…I've been hearing rumors about a brothel up in the canyon, and I'd hate to see him ruin his life. Not to mention big brother's political career." The words marked the first direct threat of the conversation, and Shannon felt a stabbing pain behind his left kidney. "And, Shannon, you have yourself a nice day."

Shannon climbed in the vehicle, started the engine and checked his mirrors, determined to maintain his poise. From the corner of his eye, he could see the tight, brown pants, legs shoulder width apart, hands on hips, standing firm and in place. He couldn't see the face he had always recognized as nothing more than an arrogant bully, arrested in adolescence, willing to bend the rules for collateral gain but incapable of posing any real threat. He tried to move the mirror, but Gale stood in a blind spot, and he couldn't expand his vision above the belt. As he backed out, those shined, black boots only reminded him how deeply the problem was rooted.

He turned his head refusing to look back again even as he was forced to make an awkward three point turn. He could feel the eyes upon him, not the cold blue eyes of Deputy Brad Gale, but the eyes of a community that acted with mob mentality, like naïve sheep, burdened by the bias of their breeding and culture, unwilling or unable to think individually and frequently swayed by the information presented to them without waiting for all the facts. He raced quickly from the parking lot, ripping at the scarf that constricted his breathing even as cold air still bellowed from the dash. The windshield fogged as he dialed the radio to distract his thoughts. A Creedence song hummed to life. Fogerty proclaimed his omission from those born fortunate. The irony wasn't lost on him. In his heart, he had long known that ties and designer scarves couldn't change the fact that he was born a Drummond.

He didn't know exactly what Grisham wanted, but he knew it would involve a favor, and he was beginning to realize that debt would never end. Political aspirations called for money and a cast of powerful supporters. Upsets required a shifting of the mass opinion. This is never easy. Shannon knew early on that defeating Berkman would require Grisham in his corner. It was an ugly truth that he mostly ignored, but that made it no less true. As a self-envisioned utilitarian, he was willing to sacrifice certain concrete principles in order to maximize the ability to create lasting change for the greater good. He was a progressive but a realist. He had worked with Grisham before, and he didn't see these compromises as being any less ethical than closed-door meetings with labor unions or special interest groups. Everybody wrote checks to cause change.

Grisham had never asked for much, and Shannon had needed just that extra little push to get his foot in the door. But he was beginning to realize that the higher he climbed, the more that would be asked of him. His only justification came from the firmly held belief that eventually he could be the one to put an end to Grisham and Gale and all that they represented.

But first, he would have to compromise. He had to play the game. And that meant keeping his brother out of trouble, at least through the election. He had tried talking to Edgar. But that was like talking to the wind. He wished there was more he could do. He wanted to help his brother. He loved his brother. He had never understood him. But hadn't he always tried?

What was this business Gale had mentioned? Was it cause for concern? If Edgar were running a brothel or casino in the canyon, wouldn't he have to be doing so under Grisham's direction? Why would a power player like Grisham ever need Shannon's help to control a single man? Or maybe Grisham let Edgar think he was running something under the old man's nose so he could hold it over Shannon's head.

His mind was a blur with unanswered questions. Only muscle memory and habit kept the vehicle on the road and heading in the right direction. He had a meeting on the north end of town with city planners and hoped to convince them to permit annexation of an eight lot multifamily housing development into city limits. He was a partner in the project with the broker, contractor and a local banker. Getting the annexation and sewage approved was his responsibility. He had been branching out into real estate and other investment ventures for the past couple years, and it's where he saw the bulk of his future income.

It was all part of politics as he viewed it. He never struggled with the moral dilemmas of benefitting personally from his positions in public office. It wasn't what he had originally envisioned, but he worked hard and enjoyed providing for his family. Early on, he went to his father-in-law for advice, and Conrad reassured him that investing in one's community was improving that community as well as putting its people to work. But he knew what Conrad thought about Grisham and his ilk. His father-in-law spoke often and openly of ridding the town of such filth. He planned for Shannon to play a major role in the matter. But he was an idealist. He didn't understand the true scope of Grisham's power. Or that everyone had to play the game to get anywhere. Still it was a sensitive subject for Shannon. Most days he was more afraid that Conrad would discover his relationship with Grisham than all his other constituents.

As Shannon left the downtown area, he passed St. Patrick's Cathedral perched high atop Beacon Hill. Beautiful and ambitious, the church's massive columns stood high above the original boundaries of the town like vigilant eyes. Even after years of near daily passing, the sight of it still brought Shannon emotional reprieve.

Despite economic booms and countless urban renewal projects, the gothic sanctuary remained the city's most awe-inspiring structure. But the town had grown steadily beyond its view and eventually onto the nearby hillsides high above. The population no longer had time for morality or the consequences of the hereafter. There were too many other distractions. The church's presence no longer produced the same obedience in the citizens' hearts. Attendance remained stable on Wednesday nights and Sunday mornings when an aging group of disparaging citizens, far removed from their ancestors' dogmatic faithfulness, gathered mostly to be seen and to cast judgment on those less righteous. They picked and chose the teachings that suited them and lived by the book only when it was convenient. Maybe it was changing mass from Latin to the common dialect, or the continuous concessions the church had made to an ever progressive world. Maybe man had simply grown too intellectual, too logical or too busy. Regardless, the church was slowly losing its hold on the community's soul. But the building itself never ceased to amaze Shannon.

The once white stone had darkened over the years, smoothed out of limestone pulled long ago from deep within the surrounding mountainsides, by strong, steadfast men as unwavering as the rock they chiseled. They were hard men, drawn to a hard land by hard labor. Nothing had been promised them. They had little technology to aid them. They simply followed their own optimistic dream to somewhere new, somewhere unconquered, untainted by the order of man and God.

Those once great quarries had long since closed, along with the mines and mills; victims of the slow grind of progress. And the world was running out of new, untamed and untainted frontiers. Building supplies were shipped in these days from far away, as Shannon's fellow bureaucrats signed bills and fought lawsuits to protect the lumber and rock from desks in office buildings where their hands had long forgotten the fruits of the Lord's labor. They protected the earth with the compassion the church once taught them to share with their brothers and sisters. The environment was replacing religion as man's latest daily dose of guilt.

Men did nothing to stop the change. They lived longer, more leisurely lives. But at some point they lost their optimism and their vision as the cage slowly built around them. They bitched; blamed politicians, schools, union leaders, bosses, foreign powers and the exceptionally wealthy. They blamed everyone and anyone. But they did little more than talk. As with the church, they held dearly to the changes that benefited them and damned the others. And meanwhile, the dwindling explorers, the last men of action, stared out at the distant planets and dreamed of future frontiers.

Shannon glanced up at the remarkable architecture as the stained-glass windows caught the light of the western sky, lustrous in the full majesty of the color spectrum. The scene was imposing in both scope and beauty, though Shannon had always favored it at dawn. The windows, belfries and sculptures were the work of world class artisans, commissioned by one of the semiliterate, overnight millionaires that discovered the surrounding mines. Shannon imagined it as an old man's attempt to absolve his sins and sorrows by building something beautiful enough to forgive for a lifetime of breaking unions' strength, men's backs and families' spirits for an extra dollar a day, year in and year out; a single great and holy act to wash his hands of all it forever.

To Shannon, who secretly detested organized religion and yet married his wife and baptized his daughters in this very building and attended mass here faithfully every Sunday (except during hunting season), the cathedral had always represented homage not to some unseen divinity waiting to cast judgment for

92

mistakes rendered, but rather, to man, his potential and vision in creating something glorious. Religion, in Shannon's mind, represented a clinging to guilt and an effective yet outdated means to control the masses. He had seen what blind faith had done to his mother and associated church closely with the downfall of his family. But he also recognized modern society's failure to create an adequate replacement and respected the principles of a pious and spiritual existence, particularly in a world seemingly gone mad. He believed there must be some balance between the hope and fear that conviction teetered between – a way to have it all without the suffering or the sacrifice. He respected the church. He simply believed it no longer served its useful purpose. Man no longer needed guilt. Man needed hope. Shannon longed for a day when man could gaze at his own reflection and feel pride in the limitless possibility of his logical mind. He wondered if that was so wrong.

As the cathedral disappeared in the rearview, and an existential feeling of powerlessness washed over him, an advertisement came on the radio – a stern, steady voice speaking over a patriotic, brassy tune. The authoritarian muse listed the impressive accomplishments of Edgar Drummond, abroad, and Shannon Drummond, at home, tying the two together with the final line, "The Drummond family has been helping to shape this community for three generations, serving to protect our families and our country with selflessness and patriotism. Vote Shannon Drummond for attorney general."

Shannon turned off the radio. The thought of hearing those ads for another ten months made him sick to his stomach. The scope of his thoughts narrowed from the condition of man back to his own life. His mind continued to grind at a hectic rate, and he felt drained by the long hours of another endless day. Each morning he awoke with childlike enthusiasm, excited to take on the day ahead. But each evening, it seemed, ended in fatigue and a sense of disappointment in failing to improve or fully understand the world around him. He couldn't recall how long it had been this way.

He thought again of the Cathedral, its steep, red-tiled spires and those stain-glassed windows, telling man's fable, from humble, noble beginnings. It was such a simpler existence then. He considered Gale, his flawless appearance and his uniform, and his brother, the quiet, sturdy boy he had once been. He thought of Jill, the love of his life, who lately he had been unable to connect with, and his girls, who he would do anything to protect. He wondered how much say he had in any of it. And somewhere, as he always did, he saw his father, the man he had idolized and yet never understood. He remembered his surrender that morning on Windy Ridge. Then he felt a desperate frustration. Disappointment in his inability to understand any of it, and to have worked this hard and come this far, only to be here.

Chapter 12

The television blared infomercials at full volume, but Edgar heard only the ridicule of unseen voices. The day had been short and particularly cold, and the night's darkness brought with it the heavy burden of shame. The wind howled and the demons were in control. He had been expecting Krystle for hours, and the time was passed alone in the company of a pint of rot-gut whiskey.

There was nothing more than a thin syrup coating the bottom of the clear bottle when he called her for the fourth time in an hour. Again she didn't answer. Tears fell with heavy sobs as the bottle dropped from his idle hands, hit the carpet with a muted thud and came to rest on its side with the last swallow or two swilling toward the neck before pooling patiently along the label. All that he had ever done and never done was with him now in his retched, lonesome sorrow.

Almost as if the bottle's failure to break had served as some final straw, he glanced down at his vice a moment, so clear and simple lying there, and then he climbed to his feet, grabbed his jacket and headed out the door, leaving the lights on behind him and the TV screaming. Whereas the day had been cold, the night was freezing, and the sub-zero temperatures hit his exposed flesh like the sting of death. Breathing in the oxygen of the high, frosty air shook him from his self-pity, which it replaced with a vague determination. Although it was Wednesday, Krystle's night off, he marched directly toward Finn's and arrived shortly before eleven.

The bar was calm, half empty, with patrons sitting at dim lit tables or on barstools while bluesy-rock played at a comfortable volume beneath the conversations. He stood in the entranceway, swaying slightly amidst the shadows, searching their silhouetted faces for the one he hoped could cure all the pain that ailed him. All he found were skeptical glances, fearful of the unknown which he represented or expectant for the entertainment his condition implied. In those hollow faces, his demons lurked and whispered, and he closed his eyes a moment, desperate to remember something he swore he had forgotten though he couldn't imagine what or when or why. As his eyes closed and he absorbed the sounds of the living, his body swayed and he stumbled slightly and bumped a man leaving the bar with a well-dressed, makeup-masked woman. The man was taller than Edgar, broad and bearded, and he shoulder checked him and told him to watch where he was going. There was a challenge there, and although Edgar let it slide, whatever hope of peace that had remained choked at a final gasp of fleeting air. It was as if the bottle back home had broke after all, and those jagged edges of unbearable confusion and loneliness turned to the flat, smooth blame and anger that had become so familiar, so comfortable, so easy. It was as if violence were inescapable.

The bartender noticed the exchange and signaled his bouncers to pay attention – two big lineman types that couldn't have been a day over twenty-one; college boys. He asked Edgar if he could help him, and Edgar mumbled something about Krystle, but it was incomprehensible, and the bartender shook his head in disapproval. He was a young man himself, still ignorant of pain life was capable of inflicting, though no longer so young as to be quite full of promise. He hadn't been working at the bar long, and as bartending was hardly the career he had long envisioned, he carried an air of entitlement about him and made no effort to understand his clientele on any significant level. He had over-served customers on countless occasions and their money was always good, so long as they had some and left a tip. But there was no irony in the disgust he felt for the vagrant before him.

Another worthless drunk, he thought. There was getting to be too many of them. He didn't care to hear their excuses; the stories were all the same. He wished they would close the shelter, and make the sorry sons of bitches fend for themselves. He was certain it would fix the problem, force the lowlifes to take some responsibility.

Edgar kept talking, but the bartender had heard enough. He called for the bouncers, secretly hoping the guy struggled a bit and caught a decent thumping. It might do him some good. Edgar heard the footsteps, and he tried to clear his head, but he was too far gone. Both boys were over six feet tall, the one was closer to six and a half, probably pushing three hundred pounds. They were strong, and they were sober. The bigger kid got a hold of Edgar from the back, raking his left arm tight with a half-nelson. Edgar swung his momentum the other way, but the smaller of the two goons caught his drunken flail and countered with an uppercut to the guts. Trying not to make a scene, the bartender directed them outside, giving Edgar a moment to catch his breath while they dragged him limply to the door. Despite the sobering effect of the uppercut, Edgar remained slow and off balance from the booze, hunger and emotional depletion, and he took a few hard blows to the skull and ribs on the sidewalk before they let him pick himself up off the concrete. He sidestepped the next blow, caught the bigger guy's arm at the elbow and broke it with a grinding snap before knocking the other kid unconscious with a right jab and a single, stiff left-cross.

The big kid fell to the sidewalk beside the curb screaming in agony. It was a piercing, awful wail. His right arm hung limp and bent in the wrong direction. Behind him a pool of blood drained out and spread toward the street from where his coworker's skull cracked against the sidewalk. A crowd was quickly gathering, but the fight was over and only a couple that had been outside smoking had seen anything. The girl cried in helpless hysterics while her boyfriend rushed to aid the unconscious man, using his jacket to slow the blood bubbling from his skull. The newcomers looked nervously at Edgar but made no move to detain him. He said nothing, and as whispered conversations grew amidst the mayhem, Edgar abandoned his jacket, which had been torn off him amidst the struggle, and hurried off up the block where he found an alley and ducked in it and sat down with his back against a dumpster and checked his injuries. A few teeth felt loose but none was lost. His fist ached and was beginning to swell, and his right eye was closing fast. He probably had a concussion. The terrible cold didn't help. The exposed flesh of his arms was turning blue and his teeth grinded. As he panted to catch his breath, police sirens filled the air. He knew he had to move.

He made his way down the alley and hung a left then climbed the gentle rise a dozen blocks to Lewis Street and turned right. He was moving away from home. The cold was unbearable. It numbed the pain of his injuries, but he was in bad shape. Each time he heard tires rolling or saw headlights, he ducked off the sidewalk into yards or behind porches. He was shivering and threw up twice. His eyes wanted to stay closed. Living became a conscious effort.

The Lewis Street 'Hood' was the toughest neighborhood in town. One of the few remaining relics of the city's brutal origins, it had served as the original Irish parish, filled with hardened miners speaking a mishmash of English and Gaelic through thick accents and virtually closed off from the rest of the fledgling municipality. The autonomy, at its largest, once stretched the six blocks from 6th Avenue to 12th and five from Blake to Lewis, in the shadow of the Cathedral, complete with its own shops, newspapers, delis, bakeries, and bars. It had its own law too. Although that 'law' rarely cooperated with the municipal police, particularly in turning over one of their own, they were swift and fair and often harsh in conducting their own internal justice. The last reported vigilante hanging was less than sixty years passed, and the Drummond brothers had been raised on the legendary tales of these rough and tumble days of old.

Over the years, however, the aging population's refusal to trust or work with the city's growing number of non-Irish civil servants, coupled with the decreasing demand and increasing competition for manual labor, led the neighborhood's unemployment levels to soar and its housing values to sag. Crime ran rampant. What had once been revered as place of honor became a haven for impartial distrust. Now, the heyday of immigration from the Emerald Isle was long since gone, and the hood drew only the few impoverished minorities, drifters and down-and-outers desperate enough to come to such a hostile environment.

97

Although the Drummonds had never lived here, as children they had come often to visit Aunt Dotty. Shannon grew to despise such visits, especially if the boys were to stay the night or weekend with their aunt. He was wary of the unkempt people of the decrepit neighborhood, always outside yet never in the act of industrious activity. In his early teens he threw a rare tantrum once, refusing to go. His father had made him go anyway though he said little of the matter. But later, after a night of drinking, Tom had taken his eldest aside and explained to the boy that this was a place of importance to his ancestry and that these were his people and he had nothing to be embarrassed about. Then, even though Edgar was probably only six or seven at the time, he scolded both boys for feeling shame or superiority toward the historic ward, stating that no matter what happened in their lives, they must never forget their family or where they came from.

In the summer, these blocks would be alive with music from stoops and rooftops and devious, opportune eyes would lurk everywhere, but on a night this miserable, all was silent but the cruel wind. Porch-lights were off, and the neighborhood appeared deserted. High above the dark streets, the lights of Saint Patrick's Cathedral shone. Hunched over and utterly defeated, Edgar peered up at the mighty sanctuary where it glowed upon Beacon Hill through narrow slits of the shanty shacks and multifamily dwellings, as a humble peasant may have once looked upon the greatness of Rome at the conclusion of a long pilgrimage. The structure had caused him both awe and unease over the years as he had contemplated fate and what it meant to be saved or forsaken. But tonight, he didn't blame God for his circumstance, nor did he pray for divine aid. He had given up on all that after his father died, along with so many other things he had once believed. Tonight, he saw only a massive and grandiose building high on a hill and nothing more. He gave it only a moment's consideration as he had seen its divine glory and seemingly endless wealth do little in his lifetime to help those living closest to it, those in the direst need of succor and saving. He limped on toward Krystle's apartment.

The hundred year old building where Krystle lived was on the far end of Lewis, where the street climbed toward the hills. Apartments had been converted from the once celebrated mansion

98

of one of the many local tycoons who had made millions in the gold boom of the 1860's. The property had originally been a massive estate with gardens extending the length of the entire block; an aristocratic life a mere block from the commoners and immigrants. But the man's sons or daughters had apparently failed to follow in their father's industrial successes, and the home had been abandoned; the family forgotten by all but a few historical scholars. Eventually, some savvy opportunist bought the property and converted it to rentals, but his efforts had long since become distressed and the structure an eyesore. Almost as if the building were embarrassed of itself, the former servants' door had been converted to its main entryway, and the apartments were now accessible only through the alley.

Beer cans and cigarette butts strewn amongst neglected children's toys lined all sides of the three paths trampled through the snow to and from the building in various directions. The air smelled of wood smoke. The lights were out in Krystle's bedroom window, and Edgar lifted the heavy outer door and turned the knob on the interior one. As usual it was unlocked, and he opened it and entered a small hallway lit brightly by a naked hundred-watt bulb. The hallway was cold but at least sixty degrees warmer than outside. His breath was visible at first but then faded as he moved to the second doorway on the right, no longer sure of his reasons for coming and suddenly apprehensive for the moments ahead. He had all but forgotten how he had acquired his injuries, and his thoughts were obsessed with visions of Krystle and another man. If he found the faceless man behind this door, he would kill him and probably her too.

He rapped softly on the door marked "2". The sight of his battered knuckles served as a reminder to the sad truth of his life's condition. He waited a few seconds. Nothing happened. So he knocked again, slightly harder and longer this time. He told himself that if she didn't answer this time he would leave. But he knew it wasn't true. He had to see her, and he would walk through the fires of hell to find her.

Footsteps squeaked and moaned across the hardwood floors inside. A light clicked and shone beneath the door. Edgar felt relief but also the dread of what he had come to do. He no longer felt drunk. He debated whether he should flee. But his feet wouldn't move. Finally the door opened and Krystle stood behind it in grey sweatpants and a slack white shirt. Her hair was matted on one side and her eyes swollen from sleep. She looked angry and unafraid. Recognizing him made her angrier.

"What the fuck are you doing?" She asked quietly.

Her arms crossed at the chest and she kinked her neck to one side in case the question failed to express her mood. Edgar said nothing. There were no words for him to speak. He simply stood there, exposed and beaten. He was angry now, and he wanted to direct his rage at her but he knew she slept alone, so he had no reason and this revelation stole his words.

She examined him, but his condition brought him no pity. It only made her angrier. It was obvious she had reached some new resolve in her attitude toward Edgar and their relationship and she was determined to maintain it.

"What the fuck happened to you?" She sighed. Again, Edgar said nothing. And so, the two of them stood there in the silence, their love for each other barricaded behind impenetrable walls of so much disappointment, hurt, anger and shame. They were no good for each other. She knew it. They had shared too much pain, too much violence. They had hurt one another too often and been wounded too deeply. Those scars would never heal. They would remain fresh in each other's eyes and words. But they had both grown so accustomed to such misery that they couldn't live without it either. It was like a drug. Neither of them remembered what it was like to feel hopeful or happy. Neither of them knew how to trust. This was the sickness that drew them together in the first place. And so they would go on dancing this perilous dance until the music stopped and the song was over.

"I thought you were coming over?" Edgar asked, his voice meek, hoarse and unfamiliar. In his tortured mind, the only reason the woman he loved wouldn't answer the phone had to be infidelity. But now, he found this to be incorrect, and he had no way to cope.

"No," she answered firmly. "I told you we are done, Edgar. I can't fucking do this anymore." The corners of the cramped hallway echoed her voice back, reaffirming her words. Tears welled in her eyes. She would not lose her resolve. "What the *fuck* happened to you?" she shouted. "Who did this to you? Are they alive?"

Nothing.

"Answer me you son of bitch!" She screamed. She began to sob. But she was a tough woman, and her anger was strong and familiar. Edgar hung his head. "Tell me!" she shrieked, shoving him hard in the chest. Behind him, a door opened but after assessing the situation closed again. *Tell me!*"

"Is there someone else?" Edgar asked, clinging to the scenario that was already cemented in his head.

"Are you that fucking dense?" She asked. Then she almost laughed, but tears formed in her eyes and gave her away. "You wish there was someone else. You won't accept it until there is. You'll never trust me. You'll never trust anyone. That's the whole fucking problem!"

He gave no reply.

"Is that what happened to you tonight? You went out and fought everyone I'm sleeping with in your sick twisted fantasies? Huh?"

Edgar remained wooden.

"Answer me!" She screamed again, her voice cracking.

Again, silence. The weight of it crushed her, but he didn't know and he couldn't help her if he tried.

"Do you think you're tough? Cuz you can take physical pain. Beat up anybody and everybody in the world. Why don't you beat me up? Huh?" She pushed him again. Then she slapped him hard across the face. "Go ahead tough guy! Hit me." At some point in her tirade Edgar had raised his head. He looked her directly in the eyes and listened in shame, taking the slap without a flinch.

Through a wall, a child began to cry.

"You're not tough." She began anew, almost laughing, calmed somewhat by the release of the blow. "Sure you can fight, but you can't fight what's killing you, can yah? You can't learn to live with yourself, can't stand the sight of yourself, and you won't share nothing with nobody. You think you're so fucking tough because you keep it all in, but you're not. You know that? You're not tough. You're a coward because you refuse to fight the one thing tougher than yourself; you refuse to let anyone help you...just another quitter clinging to an excuse... So you had it rough. Who

101

hasn't?" She was wearing herself out. She stopped crying and wiped the tears from her eyes. She regrouped. Still, Edgar stood motionless and silent.

"I hope you find help. I honestly do… But I want you out of my life." She finished with practiced resolution, her voice lowering almost to a whisper as she tried to close the door. He made no effort to stop her, and yet she stopped on her own. She couldn't believe he would stand there and do nothing, and she knew him as well as anyone. Something inside her broke. *"Say something you son of a bitch!"* She shrieked as she lost it all over again. She attacked him, pushing him first with open palms and then closing her fists and striking him with a ferocious barrage of downward punches in a stabbing motion. She drove him back into the middle of the hallway where he stopped their momentum and stood firmly, wearing the bulk of her frantic strikes. She swung hysterically as she cursed him, her face twisted in a violent trance. Only when she hit his swollen right eye did he instinctively raise his hands to defend himself. Slowly, she wore herself out and he brought his arms down around her hugging her elbows to her sides. She continued to struggle a moment or two but then fell limp and sobbed uncontrollably. He held her loosely, yet tender but still spoke not a word. There were no words. There was nothing beyond the sorrowful song of her tears. Eventually, she allowed her cheek to lie against his shoulder, and he could feel those tears soak through his shirt to his flesh. Her untamed hair touched his lips, filling his damaged sinuses with the scent of her cigarettes and shampoo. He felt the quivering of her body. For a moment he closed his eyes, but it gave him the spins and so he reopened them. They stood and clung to each other as everything beyond them washed away.

There were no sirens when the police arrived. The interruption to their tranquility was brief and minimal. The door opened at the end of the hall, and the first of three officers entered rather quietly to find the two of them, like ghosts, intertwined in their tragic embrace below the harsh light of the naked bulb. The baby still cried. But otherwise the night's conclusion was rather anticlimactic. Edgar put up no resistance, and neither of them fought the refusal of a desperate surrender. Edgar was handcuffed and led from the building back into the stark, unforgiving night where red and blue lights flickered quietly against the frozen dark of winter. He heard nothing more than the squeak of their footsteps meeting the cold snow. The officers moved him along at a hurried pace, and he stumbled to keep up. Occasionally, a radio chirped from the officers' chests. Neighbors peered from drawn back curtains, perceptible only as shadowed, judgmental ghouls in the flashing red and blue strobe. Edgar was read his rights and then ducked into the cramped backseat of a squad car where a heater roared and the air was at a pleasant temperature. Krystle's scent lingered; cigarettes and soap; Winston's he remembered. Then there were the tears; he saw them, heard them, felt them etched beneath his skin as he closed his eyes again. Before the car shifted into gear, he had passed out.

Chapter 13

A hazy frozen fog lapped against the earth's contours in the deep ravine below like a ghost tide rising and falling in the fjord of some extinct sea. To the northwest and distant south the highest peaks poked through the mist like jagged spears. Edgar moved along hesitantly, unsure of his bearings amidst the flat light and haze along the ridge. The limited visibility caused flora to appear suddenly and blend together. The fog's grasp had crystallized the trees and the usual morning contrasts were lost. Everything shared in the colorless grey-white that seemed to illuminate from the snow underfoot rather than the unseen sun. Then the timber opened along the high spine of the ridge and the wind rose and the surface definition vanished completely. Edgar could hardly tell up from down, and the distant ridges and peaks were nonexistent. The sun would rise before him at any moment, but there were no signs of it, and he knew the direction only from habit and familiarity.

He felt a slight rush of vertigo and sat down on an exposed rock to catch his breath. The temperature was below freezing, but a light sweat coated his back from the hike. When he sat the moisture cooled on his skin and the slight breeze shivered him to the bone. His butt grew numb and he wished he had worn an extra layer.

Digging around in his pack he pulled out the last can of chew his brother had failed to find and confiscate. It was half empty. He rationed a small pinch by scraping along the edge of the tin. The thick black wad calmed him the moment it touched the soft flesh of his bottom lip yet only increased his growing thirst. He had still been half asleep when he left camp in the dark and packing water had never crossed his mind. It was the type of forgetfulness his father used to ream him for and he found himself wanting more than anything to be reamed. It was a long while before he spit.

The fog crept up the ridge silent and slow. He knew the wind would break the fog and humidity would fall as the temperature rose and he was in no hurry. As he sat he could feel the earth rotating beneath him, and his brain reeled in his imagination from a thousand outlets, and he experienced a moment void of internal dialogue; the kind of total silence he felt before the combat of a match, that primal sense of instinct taking control. The world was so quiet his ears began to ring with a high pitched whine. Then slowly his thoughts returned.

He wasn't afraid of the wild. He knew there was nothing out there that could hurt him. It was the sheer size of it all, the distances, the heights and the emptiness that was overwhelming. As if the meaning behind it all was written out there on the Earth's rugged surfaces taunting the introverted boy in a language long forgotten. The wilderness had a way of making a young man feel special, like he was all alone atop the world. But this morning it reminded him of that familiar and hopeless sorrow that always felt so close and bittersweet. And yet, the sadness seemed unable to penetrate him in this place, and so it was left to hover about him, where he was free to examine it without bias, as if the parameters of solitude itself were different here and the grievances that remained were only those which he brought with him and perhaps those too would evaporate given enough time to process. For a moment he considered his dwindling belief in God and what was real versus perception and the purpose of life and the world, things that had greatly interested him at one point in his youth. It was hard not to think grandiosely at such a wild and untamed height. He was very near to his father's favorite perch, where Drummonds had long come to forget their ailments for a while. A sense of serenity soaked through his lip, and he wondered why his brother stayed away from this sacred place.

Soon his thoughts shifted and returned to the secular and to Holly, and hope surged through his veins. It had been five days since he had last heard her voice. Five days since he had held her, smelled her, felt her frailty. It was the longest they had been apart since the whirlwind romance began with teenage heroics and a four a.m. kiss. There had been no physical rescue, no fight to speak of. He had simply saved her from peer pressure – close friends encouraging her to try smoking marijuana from an aluminum pop can.

There were five of them – three older boys, Holly and her friend. They were huddled along a backyard fence at a house party. Edgar didn't remember how he arrived or why he came. But as he walked through the gate, their faces turned to him. Four of them appeared hesitant through the darkness between them; momentary caution, turning to vague recognition and eventual relief at finding a boy several years younger than themselves. But one face showed a much deeper concern. A look of shame, trimmed with anxiety. Without thought, Edgar found himself drawn to that face. He approached the group without word, ignoring the formalities of high school etiquette and hierarchy. He didn't know the owners of the eyes that tracked his movement; had no concern for them. His eyes never left Holly. The silver and blue slab of aluminum was held in front of her, twisted with thin smoke rising off a crumpled surface like smoldering trash. The boy holding the makeshift device had repeated a prior appeal, but his voice was deflated by Edgar's presence. 'Go on, take a hit…Try it.' He had demanded once, now he pleaded. Holly shook her head gently. 'Oh come on.' Her girlfriend chimed in, trying to recreate a carefree air that was impossible in Edgar's presence. Her forced laughter only increased the tension. 'I did it. Don't be a baby.' Holly never turned her eyes back to Edgar. But he could see her every fiber pleading for help. The walls about to cave.

'She said no.' Edgar had spoken abruptly, his words lacking the doubt and uncertainty expected of an underclassman at odds with the group. The words were neither confrontational nor void of force. Emotional glances turned on him as the older boys found themselves unable to disguise their anger. 'Who are you to say what she wants?' the other girl asked putting words to the question on the boys' minds. 'Why don't you mind your own business?' Edgar said nothing. He simply stood his ground as he had always done. The boys fell quiet too. They didn't know Edgar. But they could sense enough to leave him alone, and so they stood at an impasse, not wanting to escalate the situation yet not knowing how to back away without shame.

Finally, Holly let them off the hook. 'I don't think I want to,' she told her girlfriend directly with a shy shrug. Her friend protested, but the boys were more than satisfied to escape the situation. In the opportunity to retreat, they drew their first signs of courage.

'Your loss,' one hissed as he withdrew the outstretched can. They left amongst a heavy silence, laughing only after a safe distance had been reached. Abandoned by the majority of opinion, her friend blamed Holly, at least momentarily, and then abandoned her. This left Holly and Edgar alone; together. They remained there for the better part of an hour talking sparsely before leaving together.

In exchange for this rescue, Holly had saved Edgar from himself and the growing void of sorrow that was engulfing his life. As the weeks turned to months, she was there for him while he dealt with his loss and the inability to share it. She never made him speak and they often sat in silence for hours in close proximity. His favorite activity in the world was simply holding her.

They quickly grew inseparable and started dating without anyone actually asking or accepting. It was just assumed. And it was real. He hadn't called it love yet, at least not aloud. He knew very little about love or what it meant outside of the allegiance owed to family, but he felt for her an overwhelming sensation of both joy and fear he had lost somewhere. Every moment they spent together was unmatched by anything he had ever experienced. She was immediately perfect in his eyes, without effort, and her mere presence made him a little less molested and a bit more worthy of life. She brought purpose to his days. He knew better than anyone that nothing was forever, but his feelings for her would serve as his definition of eternal.

As the morning grew light and the fog burned off, the clouds above condensed and grayed toward the south refracting glare from the rising sun, and he sat and pictured her in her bedroom, lying on her bed, her scrawny legs turned to the side bent at the knee, dressed in flannel pajamas. Her pale skin tender and longing for the touch of his rough hands. There was a virtue to her that reminded him of his mother before everything had gone to hell. When they ran out of words, he gazed not at her but into her and was reminded of the fulfillment he had once felt when the priest at the Cathedral shared the word of God. He had been with a few girls, yet this one was different. She was smart, well spoken and elegant beyond her seventeen years. She belonged to a family rich in tradition and Catholic values. Perhaps more importantly, she was fragile, sheltered and pure; a virgin still. And yet she saw something in Edgar despite his history, sullen disposition and reputation. She made him feel needed, like a protector, and there was a belief in her eyes that returned to him a purpose he had given up on.

It reminded him often of his former trust in his mother and her church, of the vast, vaulted ceilings, the gold and the stained glass and the priest's words about the Lord's unyielding love, about his forgiveness. He had once given himself unto such wild ideas of faith. The church had been an early sanctuary for him. It had lifted such a heavy burden off the brooding child to learn that God could be depended on, that prayers were heard and answered. But then his mother left, and when he learned that the church had been partly responsible, doubt and darkness polluted his heart. He prayed for her to come home for things to be normal again, and when bad became worse he prayed even more. But when his father died, he quit praying all together and cast away all gentle emotions as weakness. Weakness that would only bring him pain. If God was real he was indifferent, and everyone and everything he had ever come to love would be taken. And so he swore to never care again. He surrendered all fear. Other than the admiration and love for his brother, Edgar's heart became a place affections went to die. And yet, Holly had penetrated that place without force like the tiny breeze from a butterfly's wings or the gentle dusting of a summer cottage after a long winter absence, and he found himself thinking again of outcomes and consequences instead of simply reacting to the world as it came. His trust in believing rose from the ashes. Perhaps in time he would return to the world in which others existed.

And yet something out here, atop the high, cold and exposed peaks of the Rockies told him young love wouldn't last and that it was better to expect loss than to be caught off guard again. He considered all this, thoughts and ideas that he would never share, as he sat and spit for twenty minutes watching the dawn break and the day begin.

To the south, rays of sunshine broke free from the mounting screen of white and grey, revealing the rocky, forested mountains, fresh and new for the first time and quelling Edgar's musing. He stood and stretched his legs with the moan of a grown man. His muscles ached from four nights' sleep on rough, uneven ground. Gingerly, he started his climb again through the ankle high snow. It wasn't long before he found the familiar batholith of granite for which he had been searching.

The old timers had named this place Windy Ridge and it rarely failed to live up to the name. There were few places on earth as brutally exposed to the elements. It was a paradox of the earth and a metaphor for life in the northern Rockies, a high outcropping of the roughest, most inhospitable terrain imaginable set amidst heavenly views of the continental divide's most astonishing landscapes. The spine of the ridge was so steep a person could look out at endless expanses of timbered mountains and the wide yellow plains that surrounded them, miles in the distance, and yet miss a bull feeding sixty yards away. It was an anomaly in itself, steeped not only in elevation but in Drummond history. This ridge had served as his father's sanctuary, and that heritage served as the majesty of its appeal for his younger son.

The fact was that Edgar had never slain a bull, and it was fact that had often brought him shame, particularly now, knowing his father never lived to see him accomplish the highest honor possible in a Drummond's eyes. His father had once told his sons that it was his dream to watch them both take bulls, together, from a single herd on a cold, clear mountain morning. But such a feat is not easy. It takes time and luck. And the Drummond family would prove to have little of either.

Edgar did shoot a muley buck both years he hunted at camp with his father, and he would never forget the pride in his old man's eyes as his son field dressed the animal and labored to get it back to camp and hung. But by the same cruel twist of fate that seemed to taunt his very existence that greatest glory had eluded him and now his father was gone. He had seen a bull taken once though; been present with his father on a successful harvest. His father had shot that bull down off the point of this very ridge. He was nine years old at the time, too young yet to carry a rifle, but the details of that hunt were etched into the very bedrock of his memory. He often dreamt of that hunt and he could taste and smell it even now. The instantaneous chaos of emotions turning thought upside down was something he would never forget, nor feel again. After hearing the roar from his father's rifle and witnessing the impact of bullet meeting beast, in the dull drone of the echo and the silence and surrender of life that followed, something frightening was lost by the boy, forgotten, never to be regained.

Edgar had told the story of this hunt to others in the presence of his father. It was his story, the only story he ever told, the story of his warrior father, a source of pride and a bonding moment that bridged two generations of one blood. It was a story of their family's greatness and he took pleasure in being the only remaining relic of the feat – aside from the antlers which lay piled and mostly unseen in a cluttered heap in the shed behind the house, along with a couple dozen other antiquities that couldn't be eaten.

But Windy Ridge was sacred to him for another reason as well. It was the last place he had shared time alone with his Uncle Marvin; his father's brother and possibly the little brother Edgar would have become had death and disappointment not had such epic affect on him. They had come here together on a morning hunt two years prior. It was Edgar's first legal season and the camp had dwindled to just the four; Tom, his two sons, and his brother Marvin, who had no children. Young Edgar had spent the majority of camp hunting with his father, watching, listening and learning. But for that one hunt, Marvin had offered to take him so his father could have some time alone, and Edgar had been overjoyed when his father agreed.

The snow being deep that year, they had set off from camp long before daylight on foot with his uncle breaking trail. It had taken a long time to reach the ridge, and when they did he remembered it being the most merciless environment he had ever

109

experienced. Snow drifted and swirled to the will of the gale's fury, and their path ranged from barren dirt in some spots to wading through four foot drifts in others. With the wind chill it had to have been thirty below and even through countless layers the cold made Edgar's head ache, and he could barely open his eyes against the blinding grit of the polished grains of ice.

Uncle Marvin was nothing like his brother. He was a goof-off, always telling jokes and talking about girls and drinking whiskey while their father remained ever stoic, stern and serious. As a boy, Edgar had often wished he was Marvin's son, particularly when his father showed the full fury of his temper. But Edgar realized as he grew up that Uncle Marvin's lighthearted spirit didn't mean he lacked his family's characteristic ferocity. Despite appearances, Marvin remained thoroughly independent, stubborn and short-tempered.

He was a younger brother, like Edgar. And like Edgar, he didn't seem to put much stock in material possessions – Tom attributed this to his lack of responsibility and the fact that the things he broke or lost were never his own. Marvin was a grinner and Edgar had always figured his uncle had found the secret to a joyous and carefree life. He carried candy in his pockets and used to sneak treats to the boys before dinner despite their mother's repeated requests. When she found out, she would scold him, but he always ended up playing sheepish and inevitably got a grin out of her. It seemed he was that way with everybody except their father. Nobody could stay mad at Marvin. He might have been a free loader and a carouser, but that was always excused as Marvin being Marvin. Edgar had once dreamed of being just like his uncle.

Of course, hunting with Marvin was different too. Whereas the slightest rustling of pant legs was unacceptable with Edgar's father and talking was forbidden, Marvin kept a running dialogue the whole time. He was constantly stopping to light cigarettes and asked Edgar about his hobbies, his girlfriends, whether or not he had ever made it to second base – whether or not he knew what second base entailed – about his dreams and aspirations. He pretty much talked about everything except hunting. Edgar enjoyed their talks, although he said little.

That last morning they had hunted together, they had crept down along Windy Ridge for about a half hour before Uncle

Marvin decided he had had enough with the cold and the wind. So, they ducked back into the trees and headed straight for the parks at the bottom of the bowl without even waiting for the morning to get light enough to glass back toward Six Point or Camp Ridge. This lack of discipline would have been completely unacceptable to Edgar's father. He told his uncle as much, to which Marvin had replied, 'Yeah. Well your pops, he don't believe in short cuts.' When he had said this, he was leaning against a tree smoking a cigarette, and although Edgar still wasn't really sure what he meant by it, the moment would have lasting impact. It was the first image he remembered of his uncle, and it completely changed the way he saw his father. Uncle Marvin had shaken his head as he spoke the words and there had been a strain in his eyes that Edgar had never noticed before. It was the family strain, and although the look was one of irritation, even at thirteen, Edgar recognized the admiration. It was the first time Edgar would ever think of his father as anyone but his dad.

It was also one of the last times he would ever see his Uncle Marvin. He died in an ice-fishing accident that same winter. The circumstances surrounding the accident were strange. Drummond men died in car wrecks and industrial accidents, at poker tables and even in bed with other men's brides on a few occasions. But they never died in the wilderness. Nature was supposed to be their sanctuary, the one place where they were at an advantage. Besides that, neither Shannon nor Edgar could remember Uncle Marvin ever ice-fishing.

All these memories came to Edgar as he moved along the ridge checking the parks and open timber all around as shadows climbed the surrounding mountains. Visiting such places had that effect, like cherished old movies rich in legacy, both pleasing and painful. He felt those memories touch him the night before, but it had been his first hunt alone and he had been rushed by the anticipation. That's why he decided to come back to let the past settle on its own terms. Plus everything was different at dawn. He had invited his brother to join him, told him again of his hunch, but again, Shannon had declined. For reasons he never shared, Shannon would not go near Windy Ridge.

The haze was gone now as a breeze rose from the gulches. The sky to the north cleared to reveal portions of color: winter blue mostly, cold and pure, but to the southwest three layers of building strata told a different tale. The low billows of white had formed a flat grey lid miles long. Edgar knew this day would bring snow.

Through the murk of the diminishing haze he scanned the surrounding ridges carefully through his binoculars. He had never seen an elk from across the gulch but always looked out of habit. The flat benches and big subalpine firs made ideal transition country. Besides, the dedication to diligence had been drilled into his head by his father: 'Always be sure to give them big firs a once over,' he had said time and again. 'You won't always see elk there, but if you always *check*, sooner or later you'll spot a bull moving through there to bed down on one of those benches.' His father was full of hunting advice, and almost no other kind. And despite giving his best effort at times, Edgar rarely forgot any of it.

When he had convinced himself there was nothing out there, Edgar strolled blatantly to the tree-line on the edge of the ridge forgoing any efforts at stealth. It was almost eight and the elk should still be on the move. Fingered openings ran down between the patchy tufts of white-bark pine and snowberry bushes that sprouted out as the terrain turned less desolate, providing long lanes of sight over the decaying deadfall and denser vegetation that grew in the ravine below. But on the northwestern face of the ridge the morning lagged far behind the spine and not a squirrel chirped, nor a bird sang. He wandered downhill through the snow-covered trees always keeping the open ridgeline above within sight. The snow was still fresh and light which made for quiet movement but also slick footing and he was unable to move too quickly along the side hill without falling. He saw no sign of elk; little sign of anything aside from snow and trees and the tall, hollowed stems of last summer's bear grass. The only tracks were his own from the day before, mostly erased by the previous night's dump.

Another hour passed but the sun never managed another showing and the timber remained dim. He had nearly reached the bottom parks when he noticed traffic coming off the crest to his left and crossing his path perpendicularly. There was a low saddle here, near the end of the ridge and the elk crossed here often. He knew the tracks were fresh, for they were clean and free of snow. There were three sets; one that looked big. His heart rate rose.

He removed the sling of the gun from his shoulder and held the carbine in both hands like an advancing soldier in an old war film. Whereas moments earlier he had been thinking of everything but elk, he now fully expected to find a trophy bull staring back at him any second. The excitement was dizzying. He sneaked along, his mind at once focused and conscious of the slightest disturbance; each step was followed by a cautious inspection of his surroundings. This went on for maybe twenty minutes before he grew distracted and his preoccupied negligence returned. His pace hastened noticeably, dropping the prudent care for stealth. The weight of the rifle became noticeable once more. The morning had reached full stride, and it felt like midday though he guessed it couldn't be later than ten o'clock. The forgotten fog seemed like days ago. Following the tracks, Edgar was free from choosing a path. He walked confidently, mindful of scanning for movement. He had failed to notice when the forest around him awoke with noise. The tracks led him down away from the ridgeline and into the bowl then weaved from one side of it to the other. The tracks chose the open timber for him. The terrain altered in elevation, but the rises weren't steep enough to disrupt his awareness with the acute sense of hunger or thirst. The cold, pungent air felt fresh in his lungs. The travel was easy.

Finally he stumbled upon three frozen ovals and his heart raced anew: elk beds. The stench of their piss was irrefutable. He checked the snow within the indentions in an attempt to judge the age of the beds. Bits of hair lingered in the compacted ice formed where the animals' warm bulk had molded the snow. The droppings around the beds weren't steaming but weren't frozen or crusty either. Edgar guessed the elk had come off the ridge around first light, meandered down here and bedded sometime that morning. They couldn't be an hour ahead of him. He scooped handfuls of yellow snow from the largest indentation and scrubbed it into his jacket and pants. Then, he rubbed his boots, bottoms and sides, in the feces and piss as he had seen his elders do to mask the sweat of his feet. His focus was entirely present and optimistic again as he debated his next move. He felt like he knew what he was doing and a growing sense of pride.

In his vigilant inspection of the area it took him a moment to realize he had overlooked a very obvious fact. The discovery of

113

the beds had caused such a commotion he had given little consideration to the reasons for the elks' departure. It was late morning. Why would the elk leave their beds now? As the tracks went from a methodical, meandering path before bedding to three distinctive lines after, one apparent difference became clear: the presence of dirt clots and pine needles in the departing hoof prints.

These elk were running.

He had paid no attention to the wind which had risen up the ridge in the early morning. Now, he noticed it was swirling. One moment it crossed his path and the next it touched slightly at his back, in the direction he had been traveling. They must have smelled him. Blood pulsed against his temples as a loud buzzing filled his ears. He cursed himself for his stupidity. These elk were long gone. But maybe not. The words of his father taunted him from somewhere within. 'If they hear you, they might wait to see movement. If they see movement they might freeze long enough to get a shot. But if they smell you, the gigs up.'

The words echoed through the rustling breeze as Edgar jogged hopelessly along behind the tracks. The thin, cold air burned his lungs. He ran for a long time; his heavy packs weighed his feet and made his efforts at haste through the snow and timber appear awkward and sad. He ran against his frustration, falling to his knees repeatedly and gasping for air as he finally reached desperation. 'A guy's better off to chase speeding trains than jumped elk through closed timber.' Finally, he collapsed in a shameful sputtering tantrum. He was suddenly cold; worn out; desperately thirsty; hungry and disappointed. All these realizations hit him at once. He rolled onto his back and stared up through the snow-covered limbs of the conifers, watching the storm clouds roll in and solidify. He had no idea where he lay, but he didn't care. He was done caring. In that moment hate consumed him.

He hated hunting. He hated the lore and the memories and the advice; the expectations of legacy. He hated elk. He hated curses. He hated his mother for abandoning him and his father for leaving him in such silence. He hated everything and anything until he had nothing left, and all the walls he had built and fortified came crashing down. Right there in the cold snow, in the middle of nowhere, the hardest boy alive cried and cried, until he cried himself to sleep.

Chapter 14

Oliver Carino dropped the pencil and sat clenching his fist against the arthritis, damning his deteriorating health and every punch he had ever thrown. He sat at a table in the back room of the gym. The cramped quarters served as the office along with a half dozen other functions. Like the entire church, the room was dark and damp and smelled like sweat and mildew. A space heater glowed hot in one corner below the first aid cabinet.

Oliver was filling out the physical and release forms for a fighter he had been training the past few weeks. The guy suffered from a chemical imbalance and was borderline schizophrenic. He had been living down at the shelter and could barely read or write. Training had gotten him off the booze, and if he stayed focused it might help him get his life on track. He was in his early forties, couldn't spar much, and would probably never win a fight, but he had a lot of good years left in him if he could learn to stand himself. Oliver felt for the guy. It was the kind of situation that still gave him a sense of purpose.

If only his damn hands would work. They were twisted and worthless anymore. He was too young to have such hands. But he labored through the pain, scrawling out his barely legible script, cursing himself under his breath for his handicaps. When he finished, he was worn out and bothered. He stood, still proud but no longer straight, and hobbled slowly out to the gym where he hoped the sounds of fine tuned bodies in acts of strenuous effort would ease his tension.

He was right. The sour smell of sweat went from faint to overwhelming as he exited the office and the rhythmic grunts and exhales of exertion that met him in the hall brought relief. He leaned against the doorframe and took it all in, trying desperately to ignore the cramping in his wrists and knuckles. The small gym had two rings, eight mats, a few weights and bags and not much else. The gray concrete walls and ceiling were caked in a brown sludge from years of sweat and grease and gave the place an authenticity of toughness. A few tough individuals had trained here over the years. Their posters hung on the walls, fading alongside the memory of their deeds. Most of the nostalgic memorabilia featured boxers. But only the old timers still boxed. The new guys all practiced mixed martial arts. And there were fewer of them who stuck with it every season. Lots of fresh faces turned out in the winter, but as the weather grew warmer and the workouts tougher, they came less and eventually not at all.

Tonight, there were eight people: two old Irish hands sparring as they had done nearly every Tuesday night since Oliver had moved to town, and four young men training with Sil and his nephew, Roy. Sil had two on the mats grappling. Roy was running the other two through a strength and conditioning circuit. It was quiet for winter. The average night this time of year ran about a dozen guys plus the three trainers. Thursday and Friday, there would be more, say fifteen or twenty. Twenty-five was rare and pushed capacity. Guys end up waiting in line or stand around jawing, wasting everybody's time.

All these kids did was talk. And not just the youngsters. Oliver couldn't believe how grown men carried on anymore. They gossiped like school girls and nothing was kept hidden or sacred. A lot had changed over the years.

Silvio Mancini had opened the gym in the late seventies after marrying one of the Yuhas girls. They met in Las Vegas but never made it there, so the Brooklyn born Mancini agreed to give his wife's hometown a try. He never thought he would make it five years, and yet, four kids and six grandchildren later, they were still here. One of the only 'true' Italians in town, initially, most people who didn't know him assumed he was a Native. It was an error that got a lot of redneck noses busted those first few years. Sil had been an accomplished pugilist, carrying a 22-8 professional record with eighteen knockouts. The book on him said he had poor footwork, but his right could kill a man with or without gloves. Luckily, it never did, and eventually the fighting stopped, partially on account of Sil's temper subsiding with age and partially due to the fact that a few busted heads tends to spread a message quickly. It probably didn't hurt that the third generation New York Italian ended up training a few of the toughest Natives in the area too, and one of them, former gold glove, Victor Running Water, became his beloved disciple and close friend.

Running Water ended up disappearing after he accumulated a hefty debt with local bookie and crime lord Zeke Kale.

Subsequently, Sil never took much offense to being called an Indian. Although by that time, his reputation was well known, and the mistake was rarely made.

On a May afternoon in 1998, random chance had brought Oliver Carino and Silvio Mancini together. Oliver was passing through town en route to Seattle where he had two fighters on a card promoting the fledgling sport of 'ultimate fighting'. He stopped, alone (since his wife passed in 1992, he nearly always traveled alone unless a fighter needed a ride), at a local Italian spot for lunch. His skin color drew a few quizzical looks from the locals, but one man approached him cordially and asked if he wouldn't mind a little company. That man was Sil, the owner of the restaurant, and a man that knew a thing or two about feeling unwelcome in a foreign land. When Sil discovered Oliver was a trainer, he insisted he order for the weary traveler. And while Oliver ate three delicious courses, the two men got to talking. Sil had never heard of the art of jiu-jitsu and was immediately fascinated by Oliver's tales of the still rather underground sport. The meal was on the house, and the two men exchanged contact information. Over the course of the next few years, they became close friends, and when the mixed martial arts revolution erupted, Sil begged Oliver to come out west and help him train.

Oliver, who had learned and practiced jiu-jitsu during a stint in Brazil after his last tour in Vietnam, was living in Detroit at the time and growing tired of the city's hardships. He decided a change of scenery might do him some good. In his sixty years, Oliver had been mostly a gypsy voyager anyway. There was no place he really called home. He had only come to Detroit in the late eighties after his wife had discovered she had breast cancer and because the Josephine Ford Cancer Center located there was a leader in breast cancer treatment. Even the best doctors wouldn't be enough, however, and the cancer had eventually claimed her life.

Born in Rio to a Brazilian mother and a marine father based there, he was an only child, and the family moved stateside when he was two years old. For the next ten years, they bounced around from Atlanta to Alaska and everywhere in between, until his parents divorced, after his father started a new family in the Philippines. Oliver's mother was a citizen by that point, and they

117

spent the next several years slumming through working class cities of the Midwest in a state of betrayed limbo. Oliver fought, stole and was arrested on several occasions. He lashed out at the world that had wronged him and refused to speak of his father. His mother was a sturdy woman though and always provided for her son. She did her best to guide him and that love left its impact. But for many years, that affection remained unseen, buried deep below his confusion and pain. Although she always talked of returning to Brazil, she would never get closer than Florida.

They moved to Miami when Oliver was sixteen, where they found some sense of belonging in the Latin community despite being unable to escape the poverty they had long since learned to accept. Oliver continued to fight and began to run with gangs. But his mother's prayers never fell upon a deaf ear, and somehow, someway, he always returned home alive.

Three years later, he was drafted. He served three tours in Vietnam, and the vicious impartiality of war changed him. Through its brutality, he found God and appreciation for all his mother had done for him. He learned to trust and depend on others, and he let go of the resentment he had been harboring most of his life. On a sunny fall afternoon in San Francisco, while home on leave, he met his father and forgave him face to face. The meeting was brief and a little awkward, but Oliver walked away with a sense of closure and never thought much about the man again. In 1974, his mother passed away. She died of a brain tumor; as would be the case with his wife later, she was much too young to die.

Oliver was devastated. Unable to deal with his grief, he decided to travel to Rio to find his mother's family and search for peace. He found only the latter, in a local girl, Alicia, who reminded him of his mother in her reserved manner, fierce loyalty and uncanny honesty. She became his sunshine, purpose and eternal joy. They married. But they were unable to have children. The complications only intensified Oliver's growing faith. He took up jiu-jitsu and fell in love with the slum children that came to practice the art on the sun-drenched beaches of Rio. He saw the opportunity and optimism the sport gave to people who had nothing else outside of soccer. Then one morning, while attending mass, God touched him somehow, reminding him of the places he had grown up and the troubled youth of his own country. He

118

decided it was his calling to bring jiu-jitsu home and make amends with his past. His wife understood. She said she had always known, since the day they first met, that something would call him away. He was a man searching, she said, and was not done moving, but she said that someday, somewhere, he would find his peace.

They moved back to the States where Oliver began his quest to teach inner city youth the rewards of jiu-jitsu. They started in Texas, where Oliver worked to collapse some of Houston's fiercest gangs. Then, they wound up in LA before opportunity drew Oliver back to Chicago and the Great Lakes region where he had first learned to steal, fight and survive on the streets. He discovered he missed the seasons, and Alicia found steady work with the school districts. The couple bought a house, and Oliver opened his own gym. The gypsy voice in his soul fell dormant, and his eyes stopped drifting to the horizon during conversations. All was perfect until Alicia's immune system began to fail. Suddenly, she was constantly falling ill and unable to perform activities for any length of time. Oliver insisted she see a doctor. A checkup led to tests and more doctors and the diagnosis of a tumor in her right breast. Oliver spared no expense to find the best help available. After much effort, he was able to get her into the Ford Center. But the cancer spread quickly. Alicia grew weak, thin and aged years in a matter of weeks. By the time, Oliver found a place to rent in Detroit, doctors told him his wife had less than a year to live.

Six months in the hospital, and their perfect life was gone. Both the house and the gym back in Chicago were both lost as the bills piled up. Oliver paid no attention. He couldn't work anyway. He spent every waking hour at his wife's bedside, watching her bright, young face whither and age as the cancer stole her away. He remembered his mother and prayed constantly for guidance.

Alicia's death nearly cost Oliver his faith. He fell and he fell hard, spending his days staring at the cracked, yellow walls of his cramped tenement while cockroaches searched the floor for crumbs from what little he ate. At night he walked the dark streets of Detroit aimlessly amidst the sirens and the horns, the bums and the hustlers and the whores. But after a couple months on the bottle, he fought back, refusing to surrender. He knew this wasn't what his mother or his wife would have wanted. They both

119

expected him to stick to his promises. So he returned to the church and eventually to the gym, all for the sake of the two women he had and lost.

Now he was here, in Montana; sixty years old, with a body far older than his years. He had reached the reflective stage in life, and he wondered often about the mark he would leave behind. There was no fear of death, for the people he loved most awaited him; of this, he had no doubts. But it was natural for a man in his position, with no children and no significant other, to want to see just one final impact through to the end, leave one lasting impression on someone who would remember him as he was now and not as he still imagined himself in his youth.

Tired and reflective, he leaned against the doorway gazing at nothing and thinking of not a single thing in particular, simply striving for clarity, when a man entered the gym quietly through the heavy double doors at the side entrance. The man wore a tattered jacket and dirty work jeans. At first, his arrival went unnoticed, even by Oliver, who was the only one in the gym not consumed by activity. His eye caught the newcomer's movement, but it wasn't enough to break his meditative reflection. It wasn't until the man stopped along the adjacent wall near the lockers and began taking in the gym as only one unfamiliar with their surroundings would do that Oliver broke his stare and gave the man full consideration. Even after a once over, the old man had shuffled half the distance between them before realizing he recognized the face; then he couldn't put a place to it.

Amidst the effort of his methodic saunter, Oliver scoured his faulted memory to fit the face to a name or recollection.

"How we doing this evening, son?" the words came out naturally, without effort or thought. He introduced himself, and was reaching for the young man's hand when recognition struck him and his heart nearly skipped, sending him into a convulsive fit of coughing. The stranger didn't ask him if he were alright. He said nothing. He had seen the change in the old man's eyes when recognition struck and knew the reason behind Oliver's fit.

It was him alright.

"Excuse me," Oliver said, slightly embarrassed. His pulse throbbed blood through aged arteries, and the excitement of it all made his head spin with overexertion. He felt dizzy. He needed to sit down and take his pills. "What brings you in tonight, son?"

The question was a nervous diversion, as the old man tried to steady himself. But the young man wasn't watching Oliver, he was still scanning his surroundings, and he made no effort to answer the question. He knew that Oliver knew who he was and why he had come. There was no need for theatrics or formalities.

As his memory came back to him, Oliver realized while he hadn't recognized the mysterious assailant from the night weeks earlier. The dead flame was absent or had subsided. The kid was sober, and there was a purpose behind his eyes. Something had changed in his life recently, and Oliver had enough experience with such transformations to know that the young man before him stood clinging to some newfound hope or chance purpose he held little faith in.

"Do you want to train, son?" Oliver asked gracefully, easing back a step and giving the untamed spirit before him space. He waited patiently; the sounds of continued activity around him added texture to his prayers. No one else in the gym noticed the old man's cautious efforts to corral the stallion before him nor understood the importance of that moment in Oliver's eyes, for it was of the most difficult type of battles, one without the simplicity and brutality of force. This was a struggle of care and experience; one wrong move, and all would be lost.

"Yeah," he answered.

Oliver did not smile or sigh though he was overjoyed. He asked if the boy had ever boxed or wrestled before as he had done a hundred times before.

"I wrestled." The hollow-faced lad offered.

"Ok, then, that's good, son." Oliver replied. The rest of his recruitment interview abandoned him, and the two stood facing each other just as they had done on the street that cold, violent night. "Welcome to Sil's Gym, son." He said. Palms up and open he spread his arms to the room around him. "When would you like to start?"

"Right now. Tonight."

This is typically the point where Oliver would go over the gym rules, fees and general prospectus. But Oliver saw no point or room for wasting time.

"Good. Good. Ok then…Do you have workout gear or do you need some?"

The young man pulled a pair of gym shorts from his jacket pocket.

"Good. There is an office in the back where you can change if you'd like to follow me, and there's a couple lockers right here against the wall. I'll just need a minute, and we can get right to work." His feet felt light and his body alive as he moved giddily toward the back room. Hope and optimism had that effect on him.

Chapter 15

Checking the list for the third time, Jill remained distressed. On the list were the names of Shannon's key donors and supporters that were to be invited to an early September campaign brunch and golf scramble. The event was large scale, an exclusive and explicit who's-who gathering meant to sway the influential power players still riding the fence and sure to be one of the crucial countdown events leading into the election. The scheduling of the event had been a last minute decision by the party's candidate for governor and left Shannon's team in a panic. With the election less than six months away, Shannon's small campaign staff was completely overwhelmed with other responsibilities, and Jill had agreed to help anywhere she could lend a hand. She finished the invitations for all the names that were given to her, including a few independents she had added herself, but she couldn't shake the feeling she had left out someone important. She was sick with worry and wished her husband would answer his phone.

Although she had volunteered willingly, the growing strain of her ever hectic schedule coupled with her father's persistent pressure to do more left her in a state of constant anxiety and unhappiness. To make matters worse, she rarely had a moment alone with her husband, and when she did the discussion always focused on the election; him, his career, his problems, his life. Her life and their relationship had become second issue and she felt she had no one to talk to. She couldn't remember the last time her dreams had been the topic of a conversation or anyone asked her how she was feeling. Plus, Shannon had spent little quality time with the girls over the past year, and Jill worried about the pattern of priority she could see taking root. At first, she had assured herself that it was only a temporary issue and would resolve itself after the election. But after eighteen months of living through the madness of a never ending campaign schedule, she watched her husband grow steadily more distant and worried that those occasional reassuring words that 'he was sorry' and that 'it was almost over' had become nothing more than a hollow statement. Lately she was having more and more trouble believing those words, and worse, looking into his eyes as he spoke them, she didn't know if he believed them either.

It had been months since they had been intimate and that too was worrisome to Jill. Shannon had always been controlled and a bit rigid, but lately he had grown almost robotic in his detachment. The fire in his eyes had grown cold. He never told her she looked beautiful anymore, and the only passion Jill saw from him were rare but furious outbursts when the stress boiled over and the couple had a screaming match. Jill was not accustomed to such fights. She had never heard her parents raise their voices to each other in anger and in the early years of her own relationship, the couple rarely had a lasting argument; the first time she heard her husband use profanity was during a rare night of drinking after his brother returned home from overseas. Shannon had always had a bit of a temper, but he was more prone to cool jabs of cynicism and dramatic sighs. He could control it then, and they talked things out. Now, Jill had grown to almost relish the quarrels as they had become her only opportunity to vent her own frustrations and see her husband through all the smoke and mirrors. Her biggest problem was that she was beginning to lose faith in her husband's genuineness, and it terrified her to think she actually knew nothing for certain about the man with whom she had fallen in love. These insecurities left her feeling more isolated and alone.

She set her pen down on the table covered in stray papers and envelopes and released a long exhale. She looked around her at the beautiful home her husband had provided her, the art and furniture of her dreams laid out just as she had always imagined it growing up. Portraits of a perfect family hung along the hallway just visible in the afternoon shadows. The great painting of a regal bull above the mantle, head back, mouth gaping amidst a primal scream toward a potential foe lurking in a nearby stand of aspens in the depiction's background. The scream was silent of course, aside from a subtle steam that could be seen exiting the elk's snout, and the challenger was not quite visible from where Jill stood, but the painting, titled Fall Fury, had always been her favorite of their western art collection. Jill had never become an elk hunter, even after countless seasons spent sharing a bed with one of the most obsessed.

In honesty, Shannon had never really tried to turn her. He had taken her out many times, particularly in the early fall, during the rut, where she had seen elk in their cautious migrations from open field to dark timber and back in conjunction with the rising and setting sun. She felt the spine tingling chill of their shrill challenging bugles as they pierced the crisp autumn air. But she had rarely been out on rifle season excursions, when the days grew short and the cold and snow blanketed the mountains of western Montana, and she had never once been to the legendary Drummond camp despite voicing a persistent desire to visit those first few seasons. For whatever reason, Shannon kept the camp's location guarded from his wife and daughters and eventually Jill accepted this fact. She never once suspected him of using hunting as an excuse to mess around, for it was the one place her husband returned from unable to hide his emotions, the one time he became transparent. Like clockwork, each fall he fell into a quiet, distracted daze; half excited, half afraid. He spent days, sometimes weeks, at a time out in the high, rugged wilds among the ghosts of his ancestors like a modern day pioneer. And depending on his luck, he would return either coated in frustration, sorrow and disappointment or bathed in joyous glory, as immediately evident as the soot, blood, dirt, sweat and smoke that clung to his clothes and skin.

Jill stared at the painting. She realized she had always loved the piece in part because this was how she envisioned her husband: the mighty stag vanquishing all challengers. Yet lately, her feelings were changing. And looking at the painting now, she saw it in a new light. Perhaps her husband wasn't the mighty bull but rather the silent challenger sneaking in to steal a few cows from the vocal and distracted champion. She shook her head at the notion. Now she was thinking of her marriage as it compared with the breeding habits of four-legged animals? She needed rest. She hadn't slept well in weeks. She lay awake nights and listen to her husband's peaceful breathing and wonder enviously how he kept everything to himself; everything below the surface.

She walked to the window and looked out to the quiet streets of their picturesque neighborhood. It was an early summer afternoon and one of those rare, almost perfect Montana days. It was the kind of day she cherished more than anything as a young girl; the daylight hours so long; the nights growing milder each week. She remembered her family's long weekends at the lake, where she met her 'summer' friends and played from dawn until dark along the dock or on the steep, dry hillsides covered in mighty ponderosa. She thought of all the great memories she had shared with her husband and her two darling girls. They were growing up so fast. Soon they would be teenagers and they would want cell phones and independence. Was she wrong to want more now? Was she being selfish? She knew that her father would say yes, but her mother, whom she had hinted to several times about her growing concerns, seemed to say life was too short to be unhappy. Although Jill never went as far as to admit she was unhappy for fear of sounding selfish. Or perhaps it was a fear of facing the reality of a less than perfect marriage. It created quite the conundrum and only furthered Jill's suspicions about the frail fabric of all her relationships.

But who else could she talk to? She certainly couldn't discuss her problems with the other wives the Drummonds mingled with. They were mostly snobbish types, many with two or three divorces under their belts already. Most had become acquaintances more for networking benefits rather than the kind of natural bonds that built true and meaningful friendships. Jill did not like to share similarities with those women. Some of them probably experienced similar loneliness and questions of doubt, but Jill knew they were far too vain to admit anything beyond the superficial stereotyped dilemmas they had grown to cherish: the need for a maid, entertainment versus charity schedule conflicts, the ignorance of the 'lower class', jokes about their lack of a sex-life and how all was fine so long as they had enough red wine. Jill feared that to confide in such strangers would probably cure

125

nothing and likely only stir up damaging gossip. Besides, she had never felt close enough to any friend, except Shannon, to truly open up. She too carried a bit of stoicism after all.

So she would have to confront him. But she had tried that before, and the result always left her feeling like nothing had been resolved or with a sense of guilt for creating more strain. This time would have to be different. She had to get everything out, hold nothing back. It was the only way. And if nothing changed than tough decisions would have to be made. The dread of it all made her stomach turn and she grew sick. She rushed to the sink. What was going on? Not even to her mid thirties and she had everything a mother and wife could ever ask for, and yet the fear that it was all just a hollow shell, payment for the concessions of her character, grew day by day. Jill had been raised by a man who hid his emotions well. She had no issues with stoicism. But this was different. Shannon was becoming not so much stoic as enigmatic, and now that Jill had begun to doubt the true intention of his righteousness, she had no way of ignoring her nagging mistrust. It grew constantly.

She ran the faucet to clean the sink and wiped her mouth with a paper towel. Outside, a young mother still dressed for spring frost pushed a stroller along the sidewalk. The child too was bundled, his or her face invisible from Jill's distance. The scene brought Jill memories of her first child, the constant bliss that accompanied the achievement of a lifelong dream and the assurance and optimism of young love. She thought that would be it; that the confidence she felt at the time would infuse with the beat of her heart and wash over her for the remainder of her life on earth. Reflecting now, she couldn't recall when her concerns for self had returned to her; after Melanie's first year perhaps. But then it had been nothing, a miniscule pinprick of desire that felt selfish in comparison to her husband's valiant, selfless mission to provide, protect and make the world a better place. The seed had grown slowly over time though and eventually its voice became impossible to ignore.

Those days too had come and gone, and Jill stood in an immaculate kitchen trapped in the silence between granite countertops, stainless steel appliances and marble tile. But she wouldn't cry. She was a Drummond now, and she refused to cry.

126

She gathered herself and moved back to the table and looked at her invitations, trying desperately to release her personal toils if only for the time being. She was struggling when she heard Melanie's voice,

"Mommy, there's no cartoons on and I'm bored." Her R's sounded more like W's as she stood on the carpet just beyond the kitchen still dressed in her pajamas, her blond hair a ratted mess, dragging her blanket behind her. She was adorable as always and her words shook her mother from her haze. The urgency of the golf event had negatively impacted her daughter's schedule as well.

"Okay," Jill answered, forcing a smile, "What do you say we get you dressed then and walk over to the park?"

"Otay." Melanie responded, not quite excited.

"Do you need help getting dressed?"

"No mommy," Melanie squirmed. "I'm a big guwrl."

Jill laughed which pleased her little clown.

"Okay, well how about you run up to your room, and I'll follow you just in case?"

"Otay." Melanie set off eagerly.

"Pants and a sweatshirt honey…" Jill called after her. She shook her head, smiling. It always amazed her how little it took to remind her that her problems weren't life and death. Things could be far worse. This, of course, only left her feeling selfish again.

She straightened up the table and was searching for her purse when the house phone rang. It took her a moment to find it.

"Hello," she said with practiced sweetness.

"Jill?" She immediately recognized the voice of Steve Zowiky.

"Yes." She answered as she once again began the search for her purse. "Is this Steve?"

"Yeah, doll." The voice responded warmly. "How the heck you doing today?"

Jill managed a forced laugh as she tried to sound as chipper as possible, "Well, I am *doing* I suppose. Shannon put me in charge of organizing our invitations to this stupid golf scramble that Quinn's people threw on us last minute, and I'm stressing out a little about the list we've compiled."

"Wow, and I thought I was having fun today." Zowiky chuckled. "Well, as long as I'm invited we're good. Team Drummond will win the whole deal."

"Of course you will Steve." Jill conceded, an actual smile stealing her face. "I'd expect nothing less."

"That a girl. So hey, you got any clue as to where the solemn steed's at right now?"

"Not a clue." Jill admitted as frustration returned to her voice. "I left him a message at the office this morning and I've been trying his cell all day. Nobody seems to know where he is, and I really need to talk to him about these invitations soon."

"Huh. That seems a little odd. Yeah, I need to grab his ear about something time sensitive too. I figured maybe he slipped out of the office for a little afternoon delight."

"Fat chance." Jill snorted. Immediately she realized it wasn't the type of low brow response she typically gave and grew self-conscious. "No, he hasn't been home. But if he shows up or I get a hold of him, I'll be sure to have him call you after I'm through with him."

"Everything alright with you, doll?" Steve inquired. Apparently, he too had sensed something odd about Jill's responses. She flushed with embarrassment.

"Of course," she said. But she couldn't seal it. "You know how it is with Shannon. He can just be…difficult to talk to sometimes." Again she wished she hadn't said so much.

"Yeah, well he is a busy guy and has a lot of irons in the fire. You know how he feels about you."

"Sometimes." She squeaked. She was suddenly on the verge of tears.

"Well, I know how he feels." Steve tried. But for once there wasn't much assurance in his voice. "Look, Jill, if you ever need anybody to talk to or anything…" The statement stopped there; left in limbo. Jill's head raced. This was Steve Zowiky she was confiding in. What was she thinking?

"Uh, thanks a lot Steve. I do appreciate that. But really, everything is fine. It's just been a stressful morning. That's all."

"Okay. Right. Of course." He murmured. "But the offers still on the table. I mean if you ever do need it."

The sound of Melanie's voice carried from far away. She was in her room calling for her mother. Jill suddenly realized she had been walking in circles around the kitchen and still hadn't found the purse she originally set out to find.

"Thanks again Steve. I have to run now. I'll let Shannon know you called. Thanks. Bye bye." She didn't even wait to hear Steve's farewell. She hung up the phone and set it on the table. Then her fingers rose to her temples. Her brain was a blur of activity. Was she losing her mind?

Melanie called out for her again, and she pulled herself together and headed that direction. She found her daughter with pants on backwards hanging out of a flannel shirt with a scarf draped around her. She laughed.

"What are you doing child?" She asked with humorous authority. She knew her daughter was hamming it up. She had it in her.

"I dunno." Melanie giggled.

"You are one crazy girl." Her mother conceded as she began to piece her youngest back together. She couldn't believe it, but as she helped her daughter and they shared in playful laughter, Jill actually couldn't shake her thoughts free of Steve Zowiky, her husband's longtime, moronic best friend.

Chapter 16

The crisp, clean cruiser remained stopped at the stop sign a long time. There was no traffic coming or going in either direction. The only other vehicle around was a twenty-some-year-old Dodge pickup that had pulled to a stop behind Deputy Gale, and the driver didn't seem to be in enough of a hurry to provoke the officer in any way.

So they both sat and waited; nearly a full minute passed before Gale touched the gas gently and turned the wheel to the right. As the shiny Crown Vic pulled onto the blacktop and headed north, the Dodge rumbled off in the opposite direction, trailing shorts spurts of black exhaust and leaving the frontage road otherwise abandoned. To his left, across a barbwire fence and

129

some two hundred yards of dry weeds, the highway ran parallel to Gale's position. It too was empty. On his right, endless hayfields stretched out for acres and acres and ran off toward the mountains. It was July and only the tiniest spots of snow remained drifted in the shadows of the highest rocky bowls, well above the tree-line. The peaks themselves were bare. The alfalfa was flowering and ready to be cut. In one field, a swather was making its rounds. In another, antelope stood still as decoys.

Gale had lost sight of the grey Buick he had been tailing some miles back. But it didn't matter. He knew where it was headed now. He drove another four miles and then merged onto the highway heading toward the canyon. He debated calling Grisham but decided against it. There was no point. The old man would provide no guidance and no aid. For some reason, he refused to take a definitive stance where the kid was concerned.

Grisham had confronted Edgar once about his fledgling brothel, demanded a cut and that was it. Gale didn't know if the old man had grown too attached to the kid or preferred to allow the joint to remain open as leverage against the kid's brother, as that Drummond's prestige and power grew. Either way, Grisham wouldn't discuss it. The old man had grown less open to debate in the past few months, especially with the whole Drummond situation. Gale couldn't understand it. The older brother had some political clout sure, and he had served as useful in the past. But it wasn't like any civil servant wiped their ass in this town without the old man's approval anyway, and Shannon Drummond was proving to be proud and obstinate prick. It seemed only a matter of time before his arrogance would cause problems. And Gale didn't like problems. He wanted things to stay the same. To him, it seemed easier for the old man to just run a less insolent pigeon against Shannon in the primary. Not that Grisham could simply decide an election. But his support could definitely give a viable candidate a huge windfall.

And Gale didn't even want to get started on the younger brother. That crazy bastard was a ticking time bomb waiting to explode in everyone's faces as far as he was concerned. Yet still, Grisham refused to make a move.

130

Gale had decided the old man was losing his edge. He was too indecisive; wasn't as sharp or ruthless. He no longer invoked the same fear in people.

To make matters worse, the old man's crew was absolutely terrified of this Edgar kid for some reason. They refused to cross him. Sure, they all said they would off him if the order was given. But Gale knew they would do it in a cowardly way, and that's how people get caught and investigations dig deep and names get named. Most of Grisham's morons admitted they would prefer to leave the kid alone. They feared his vengeance more than Grisham's wrath. Their loyalty was teetering. Grisham would never admit it. But Gale knew the old man wouldn't be in charge forever. He had anticipated a change in leadership for some time. Again, this made him nervous. To make matters worse, Grisham seemed to be grooming the kid as his possible successor. Gale was no idiot. He could see the events unfolding. But he had plans of his own. And he would be damned before he let some emotional alcoholic run a hundred year old crime syndicate into the ground. He just had to stay a step ahead of the competition, bide his time and wait for the right opportunity to present itself.

That's why he had decided to follow the kid to his hideout; even if he had yet to decide what he would do once he got there; maybe rough the kid up a little; teach him some manners; show him who was in charge; how things were going to be in the future.

Climbing up out of the valley's wide open, irrigated fields, he passed Cattle Flats and the last of the nice two story ranch homes. From there the hills grew undulated and taller and the signs of civilization grew sparse. The earth dried and grass thinned to yellow tufts amidst desert pavement and graying sage. Then the red rock appeared on either side of the highway and the cows vanished. The river rolled down from the mountains and ran along beside him and soon the sage gave way to sparse ponderosa and jack pine. Up ahead the road twisted behind a steep rock face and disappeared. From there, he would be out of cell service for eight miles while the guardrails ran through the heart of the Rocky Mountains. Just before the corner a massive, worn billboard showed a newborn child and read, 'Life….a beautiful choice.'

The canyon was a different place entirely; as steeped in lore of questionable character as it was in sheer vertical feet. Long ago, the route had served as an old Indian trail between hunting grounds along the Rocky Mountain Front. After the discovery of gold, small war parties of braves had holed up here and refused to be moved to reservations – proud warriors resisting to accept defeat. In the 1860's, the territorial legislature approved funding for a wagon road to be built through the canyon in order to connect the rich mines of Butte and Helena with the river barges to the north. With the sheer rock face on one side and the river on the other, the mule trains that carried the valuable cargo were left vulnerable to robbery and native attacks. In response, private groups of vigilante militia built posts throughout the canyon and provided protection for hire. After the railroad and later the highway were built, these services were no longer required, and all but one of such posts vanished. Still the short span of river remained a popular haunt for criminals, fanatics, conspiracy theorists and other antisocial types. The people of the canyon were always outsiders, and they adapted with the times; first as bandits and marauders, then as bootleggers, drug smugglers and, more recently, in the booming businesses of prostitution and high stakes illegal gambling.

It was a tough place, a place that not even Zeke with all his ruthlessness had ever held full control. Grisham, learning from Zeke's mistakes, mostly stayed out of canyon affairs. The law too liked to forget the place existed. It was on the edge of the county's jurisdiction and almost no tax revenue or votes came from the area. So the sheriff's department tended to let the citizens police themselves, taking exception only when innocent or influential people were involved or the canyon's business spilled out into the valley floor where it could no longer be ignored.

Despite its reputation, day and night were different worlds in the canyon. Gale remembered taking fishing trips with his father as a boy and wondering how such awful stories could possibly be true about a place so beautiful. That was part of the compromise. Hunters, hikers and fisherman were given free range of the recreation opportunities provided during the daylight hours. The ugly side didn't show its face until well after the sun set, and darkness consumed the deep, mystic chasm carved down through the sedimentary shale and limestone of an ancient sea bed.

It was early evening when Gale's cruiser rolled into the damp shadows of the steep rock walls; almost seven. The sun glared off the potholed road and far wall of the canyon, but already the river was shrouded in darkness; even in summer, the night came earlier here. But in the twilight now, the rock glimmered in blinding brilliant violets and reds. The rock jutted out in uneven terraces hundred of feet high, the clear straight lines of its layered sediment evident like a timeline of the earth's age. Here and there the lines vanished where metamorphic pressures changed the rock slowly over thousands of years or where a slide erased the legacy in one violent instant. A few miles further and a green sign indicated an exit; Coyote Creek; population three hundred and forty-eight. Gale crossed a cattle guard and then a short bridge over the river. On the far side of the water, there was a bar, a tackle shop, a ramshackle gas station and a few run down cabins that constituted a motel. Up and down the road, log houses and aluminum trailers dotted the widening gorge with the same resilient grit as the scraggly brush and pine clinging to the abrupt rock walls above.

There were tourists in clean SUV's and Jeeps with out of state plates outside the motel and each of the businesses. It was peak season, and the town's population had quadrupled. But it was still fairly quiet, as foot traffic wasn't all that common. The appearance of the cruiser entering town didn't draw much attention from the visitors, still in their button up fly-fishing shirts, tan hats and neck wraps, but it immediately drew attention from the locals. Two men, hardly older than teens, dressed in oil stained coveralls stood beneath an open garage door at the service station and watched Gale creep by with frowns on their peach-fuzzed faces. A much older man, fat and gray-haired with an unkempt ponytail and sunglasses sat on a motorcycle outside the bar, smoking a cigarette and watching Gale through invisible eyes with the same stern intensity, unfazed by the evident uneasiness his still presence caused the tourists drinking at a picnic table nearby. By the time Gale passed the bar, two more inbred looking types had exited the establishment and joined the surveillance. They had their heads cocked back high with an instigative assurance rarely shown to law enforcement inside the city limits. They stared long and hard and one of them slapped a cigarette from a pack of smokes and hung it from his lip without taking his eyes off the cruiser.

133

Gale was not a timid man, and he met every look without hesitation, welcoming the challenge with a self-righteous smirk. He was a big, strong man, and he had seen countless men of this kind over the years: mostly inefficient but scrappy, they tended to draw their courage from an early afternoon bottle habit and the practice of a few drunken brawls. These were the sort of men that pulled knives in a fight and could be dangerous if cornered but with proper preparation and handling were mostly harmless. They all seemed to have a few priors and despised authority, but not many of them would take on a man of Gale's size one on one; let alone do anything more than verbally provoke a peace officer. Gale had learned from his experience with scum, a lot of guys weren't afraid of going to jail, but most people would do anything to stay out of prison. Gale didn't waste any time. He just kept on accelerating.

A half mile outside of town, a sign indicated a private drive; Muskrat Road; No Trespassing. The road, if it could be called that, wasn't much more than two tire ruts. But Gale turned off, guiding the low vehicle expertly over massive potholes and exposed boulders. The drive led uphill, first through a narrow meadow between towering cliffs and then climbing the southern cliff along a series of tight switchbacks through steep timber. Atop the cliff, the road opened upon a dilapidated ranch spread across a flat butte in the brilliant light of the dipping sun. The effect was not unlike exiting a dark tunnel into the light of day, and the intensity of the summer sun felt exaggerated.

The butte was bordered by the cliff on three sides and the timbered hillside on the other. Rotten and leaning posts strung with loose barbwire ran around the edges to keep three or four mules on a thistle plagued, nearly grassless five acres of pasture. The sun fell behind the cruiser as the driveway turned left through an open gate and became graded gravel. Both the metal gate and the wooden posts supporting it had been recently renovated. Up ahead, a massive chestnut tree grew in the yard of the main residence, which was surrounded on two sides by small sheds, chicken coops and a pig pen. Beyond the house, a hedge of cherry trees partially hid a large barn. Only the gables were visible. Allegedly, this barn was the location of Drummond's whorehouse and casino.

134

There was split rail and barbwire fencing everywhere, much of it in the process of repair. The house itself was white, although much of the exterior was being overtaken by a green hue that appeared to be a moss or lichen. It was a decent enough home, or had been in recent decades: two stories aboveground, boxy with a covered porch in the front and large, second story deck in the back overlooking the timbered hillside and road below. It sure didn't look like the location of an exclusive high-stakes casino.

As Gale made his way down the long drive, he couldn't shake the feeling that it was more than just the half-starved mules watching him. He inched his right hand to the stock of the short barreled shotgun he kept beneath the dash and freed it from its scabbard. He hardly expected an ambush, but it never hurt to be prepared for the worst. He had the radio off and, besides that, back up would never make it here in time. He rolled down both front windows to listen. It was very quiet. All he heard was the sound of the tires moving over the gravel and the occasional squeak of his struts. He was almost to the house when he noticed a towheaded teen with no shirt on watching him from the corner of the building. He slowed to a stop, but the boy disappeared.

"What the fuck?" Gale said to himself aloud. Scenes from "Deliverance" flashed through his mind.

There were two vehicles parked in front of the house: a white Ford Bronco and a rust and primer colored Ford pickup; no sign of the Buick. The boy seemed to be the only one around. Gale sat stopped for a moment and debated his next move, gingerly checking and rechecking his mirrors and scanning through the windshield for a sentinel of any kind. Everything seemed too quiet, too easy. Finally, he decided sitting there parked in the open wasn't helping anything and continued on toward the barn. He was halfway to the rear pasture, just passing the cherry trees when a skid steer appeared in his path and he was forced to slam on his brakes. He quickly pulled the shotgun and exited his vehicle aiming the weapon through the crack between the windshield and the door and shouting simultaneously,

"I better see some fucking hands right now, or I will blow your fucking head off!"

The tractor stopped and Gale could see the teen raising his hands, frozen in fear.

"Get the hell out of there." He shouted without lowering the barrel. "What the hell are you doing?" The boy climbed out. He was panting like a dog but said nothing. "You better tell me what you're up to boy, and I better believe you or your life is about to be cut real short."

"I was just going to move some hay to feed the mules," the boy stammered.

"The fuck you were, kid." Gale recognized him now as being fourteen or fifteen years old, skin and bones and showing the effects of a lifetime of poor hygiene habits. The deputy guessed he hadn't had a bath in well over a week. "I saw you see me back at the house. You knew where I was headed. Now, you tell me, are you buying time for them boys hiding out in that barn?"

The boy didn't answer, so Gale pumped a shell into the chamber for effect. "You better speak quick boy." He spoke calmly now, so the boy would know he meant business. "Don't you let this uniform fool yah. If I pull this trigger and erase your face, everyone in this world will believe whatever cockeyed story I tell them about why you forced me to do it, you little shit. Nobody gives a rat's ass about the death of some poor kid up in the canyon. In fact, I'll probably get a God damn medal for it… Now start talking!"

The boy registered the words and swallowed hard.

"I don't know nothing." He said, trying his best to remain stoic.

"You stupid bastard kid."

Gale took two steps and slapped the him hard across the face with the back of his big right hand. "Get this fucking thing out of the way." The boy debated and Gale sent him to the deck using the shotgun's barrel. When the boy got up the hesitation was gone. His face was bleeding from somewhere, and he climbed quickly into the skid steer and jerked the tractor out of the way. As Gale climbed back in the car, he left the loaded shotgun beside him on the seat and shouted, "Now you get your ass out of here boy. Because if I see you again, I swear to God you'll be locked up in juvi by week's end. I swear to God."

Quite shaken and full of adrenaline, Gale shifted the cruiser into drive, kicking up gravel and dust, as he sped across the open pasture to the barn where he found the old Buick parked amongst a half dozen Harleys. The sight didn't exactly excite him, but he had come too far to simply turn around and drive off, and besides he was pissed off now. So he left the shotgun on the seat and climbed out of the car and adjusted his collar. His nerves were shot from the run in with the boy and he tried to hide it with a stretch and a look around, figuring for certain that his approach hadn't gone unnoticed. But he didn't see anyone and this fact only heightened the tension. The last thing he needed was for a group of petty outlaws to feel caught off guard and cornered and panic. There was nowhere to run up here. That left a shootout as the only option, and Gale didn't exactly like his odds.

As he looked around he couldn't figure why an ex-marine would choose a criminal location without adequate exit corridors? It was a dead end, and it didn't make sense to the deputy. He walked as calmly as possible toward the barn, but endless questions continued to arise with every step and swam through his head alongside the growing notion that he had made a very grave mistake coming out here on his own.

Maybe Drummond had game trails that wound down the face of the cliff? Maybe he and his posse had already run off?

But it seemed more likely he was just a sloppy drunk and hadn't put in proper planning. The kid had been tuned up the few times Gale had ever met him, mostly in Grisham's bar, and the deputy had read the kid's introverted brooding as cocky self-assurance. That's part of the reason why Gale had decided he couldn't leave the future of his supplementary income in the hands of the little Irish prick; he couldn't exactly live the life he lived on a deputy sheriff's salary.

The main structure of the barn looked to be thirty years old but still sturdy. The front entrance was a heavy sliding panel door that had been recently updated. At the corner of the building, there was a steel door that had also been added. Gale stood before the door and gave one more look around. Crickets chirped incessantly in the sparse grass and spotted knapweed that covered the uncultivated pasture. The evening was cooling, but it was still hot and a warm breeze touched the sweat on his neck. He saw no point in knocking. He tried the handle. The door was unlocked, and he opened it and entered the barn to find it surprisingly well lit.

Long rows of fluorescent bulbs ran below the beams twenty five feet overhead. The interior was simple: a spacious open drive bay with eight or ten horse stalls all finished into rather luxurious private rooms. In the rear was another small room walled with exposed-sheetrock and possessing the barn's only window, a three by three single pane facing back toward the open bay. A shade had been drawn down over the glass, but fluorescent light trickled through. There was no steel reinforcement in the entire structure. The floor was brushed concrete, and the air was cool and quiet. Gale could smell the mustiness of the old barn wood. In the middle of the bay eight men sat or leaned around one of a dozen or so empty tables. They watched the newcomer enter in silence showing little surprise or shock. Gale's heart thumped hard in his chest and without much pause for thought, he drew confidence from their apparent lack of preparation. His wide chest broadened as he strolled, smiling toward the occupied table,

"Well I'll be damned," he whistled. "Now what would all you low life scum being doing way out here in the middle of nowhere?"

A hasty scan of the table turned up no weapons, no papers, nothing at all really; just a few packs of cigarettes and a can of Copenhagen. He recognized Drummond and his driver, Quinn O'Leary, amongst the mostly older faces of leather clad bikers. "You boys ranching out here?"

Nobody answered his inquiry.
"Cuz you sure don't look like ranchers."

The men remained motionless where they stood or leaned. One man chewed at a toothpick.
"What's wrong boys? Didn't think the law would ever find your little whorehouse?" Gale was close now, and he could see the details of each face. None of them looked around for support or fidgeted in any way. None of them looked afraid. They all kept theirs eyes on him, and nobody spoke. There was a presence of discipline Gale had never seen in such men; a military discipline. The silence made the deputy uneasy. "Look, we can do this the easy way or we can do it the hard way…"

No response. Gale sighed.
"Looks like you guys want the hard way…"

The deputy's weariness grew. Seconds ticked.

138

"What are you a bunch of fucking mutes?" His frustration soared and got the better of him. "Somebody better say something right fucking quick."

"What business brings you way out here this evening, sheriff?" It was Drummond who finally spoke. His voice was steady but low, less powerful and distinctive than Gale had expected. It was nothing like Grisham's confident, rhythmic speech. It was rather plain; not the voice expected of a leader of men.

"Well, well, well, if it isn't Edgar Drummond," Gale smiled, cooling slightly, "I'm glad you asked.
"You see, as a peace officer for the *county*, your little business out here is inside my jurisdiction. And that means it is *my responsibility* to insure the public that everything is on the up and up, and that nothing illegal is taking place out here on this charming little property." As he spoke, he slid a palm along the side of his scalp, smoothing his hair back and then wiping the perspiration from the back of his head and neck. "Unfortunately, I can't do my job if I'm being kept in the dark on what it is that's going on out here. You see some members of the community may not support what it is you boys are doing out here, and they in turn may ask my fellow deputies and I to come out here and pay you a little visit, and that would mean putting a stop to the whole shebang…Now, that would also probably mean most of you lowlifes would be sent back to the clink. Not to mention it would cost you all a decent chunk of change, I'm sure."

Now, I'm a fan of capitalism and I don't want to be stopping anyone from making a little money."
"I mean really…nobody wants no trouble. But, the only way I can prevent trouble from ever happening is if you boys cut me in. Nothing drastic. I understand the overhead of running a small business. I understand it's all about margins. So, let's say, ten percent?"

For the first time there were some sideways glances toward Drummond from around the table. Gale smiled and waited. He had spoken long and mistook his long-windedness for significance.

"Sheriff, I'm very sorry to have had you drive all the way up here for that purpose." Drummond said calmly, his eyes locked on the man to whom he spoke. "I think you've been misled. There

139

is no money to be made here." Gale saw the steadiness in the kid's eyes and could see he was clear-headed and unmistakably sober. "This is simply a club of sorts, a place to relax for outdoor enthusiasts. Any gambling done here is small time and strictly for entertainment purposes. And the bedrooms we've added…those are just our bunks." There was no smile, no fear, no conceit, no tell of any kind in the kid's face. He spoke the words simply, and Gale realized right then that they had known he was coming. But Gale wasn't overly concerned either. He hadn't expected this sort of extortion to be an easy task, particularly when he stood alone. After all, a man that couldn't be broken or controlled by Grisham was not a submissive individual. The sheriff had known from the start his goal might take serious work. He maintained his poise best he could, laughing when he wanted to explode,

"Oh, so you guys just come out here for an entertaining nickel ante game of poker on the weekends, huh?" But then his brow narrowed. Despite all he knew and had accepted, Gale wasn't accustomed to people standing up to him either. "So you wouldn't mind if I came out here late one Friday or Saturday night with a dozen deputies to crash the party?"

"Just bring a warrant." Drummond snapped, a forked vein bulging from his forehead.

"Alright you little shit," Gale shouted, slapping a hand on the table as he lost what remained of his cool. In an instant, everyone stood and tensed except Drummond, and the sheriff quickly remembered where he was and that he was alone here. He lowered his voice, but his anger remained obvious, "I was offering you a great opportunity to stay out of jail. A chance to keep making money for a very small fee. But we'll see how cool and calm you are when the SWAT team rolls in and I burn this piece of shit to the ground."

"We'll see you then, sheriff. Thanks for stopping by." No one else had uttered so much as a peep still, and Gale could see he was dealing with a well organized group and not the bunch of drunken slackers as he had originally expected.

"Yeah," he sneered. "We will see you then."

He moved his ice cold stare down the line from one face to the next. Then he backed toward the door without turning. "As for the rest of you faggots, I'd be careful about hanging around here.

You've been warned. And you better remember you ain't got many ways to run from here."

"You should probably remember that too, sheriff." Drummond replied with a straight face. Gale stopped frozen near the open doorway. His body tingled with rage.

"Are you threatening me?" he asked faking a smile best he could. "Are you really that stupid?"

"Not at all," Drummond replied. "Just pointing out a detail you apparently already noticed."

Gale had heard so much about this kid being such a hothead; he couldn't believe he remained so calm.

"I did notice it. Maybe you should've been a little more careful choosing your location."

"Sheriff Gale," Drummond stood as he addressed him, and for the first time in his career Gale felt threatened in his uniform. "I want you to understand that I bought this property for a reason...And you can take that how you want to take it." He smiled politely before adding, "I'm sure I'll see you around."

Gale exited the barn without another word, climbed in his car and whipped it around in a cloud of dry, July dust. Nobody followed him outside and there was no sign of the boy. The sun was just setting and the crimson glare made it impossible to see anything as he guided the cruiser directly toward the massive ball of fire. In his frustrated state, he wanted more than anything to come back here with a load of officers and beat every one of these bastards to a pulp, even if he couldn't get a single charge to stick. He would cave Drummond's head in with his boots and make him cry out like a helpless child. Who the hell did this kid think he was?

But the further he drove the clearer his mind grew, and as he rolled out of the canyon and into the first starlight of the valley, with all the lights of town below him, he realized he would have to bide his time. This was no time to start a war. The time would come, and he would know when it arrived. He had to use all his resources and be smart. He still had Grisham to worry about. If he couldn't control this Drummond, he would have to work on the other.

141

Chapter 17

Edgar awoke to find himself leaned against a big fir, coated in a fresh layer of white powder. He was cold and stiff, but the barrenness of the world held his immediate attention. All around him existed nothing but pristine and endless white, contrasted against the distant gray hues of boundless storm clouds. There were colors but no light to them, no signs of life except the grey trunks of the trees and their few uncovered needles, green here and blue in the distance.

And yet the void was so empty the snow seemed bright against the inescapable gloom beyond. An aura-like glow emitted from all directions and placed great strain on the hidden tops of Edgar's eyes, beyond the lids, deep in the socket and back to his brain where the pulse annoyed and distracted, making it impossible to concentrate his thoughts. The light was flat once more but not from mist or fog. He blinked continuously, already annoyed and trying to distinguish reality from dream. Somewhere far off, a wind could be heard building, then approaching and finally whistling violently overhead. From his seated position, Edgar felt hardly a gust as the gale swayed the tree tops high above. In its passing, he heard whispers. Big light flakes fell upon his face, like a drizzle hung motionless in the air.

Edgar zipped his jacket and breathed warm breath into the collar where it radiated upon his chin. Several minutes passed before he stood. His skin was cold. His butt was wet. His bones were stiff and dull from his cold slumber. He ignored the urges of hunger and thirst. He ignored the whispers in the wind. He ignored the silence of the slow falling snow. He craved only his brother's companionship and shelter from the lifeless white that was everywhere and everything. Exaggerated flakes fell in steady, vertical silence, white upon white upon gray. Looking up into the flurry, distance and time were undistinguishable. Edgar wore no watch and recalled little comprehension of place. For a moment the stillness felt novel and filled him with a sense of tranquility and he thought surely he must have died and this world was exactly what a realist might expect of the afterlife, neither heaven nor hell, simply cold and quiet, white and empty.

A medley of emotions danced in the pit of his empty stomach, but he was unable to distinguish any one from another. He had to shake himself from his trance-like daze to consider how long he had slept. He figured it couldn't have been more than an hour. He remembered the elk he had jumped and the tantrum that had followed. He felt embarrassed by his actions. He felt restless and alone. The quiet, stoic boy, who had always faired well on his own, suddenly could not cope in this place, with this life. He listened. There was no sound beyond the few simple wants in his head and the whistling of the wind. The sparrows and squirrels were gone. Not a crow cawed. Not a raven beat its black wings. Thinking back on the morning, Edgar tried to summon back his rage, but he fell short.

There was no sense of panic. He hadn't traveled that far. Besides, the Drummonds knew these woods well and a true woodsman was never lost. He scanned the terrain. The snow had covered the distinct dimension of the surface, leaving the earth flat. He knew he was in the broad basin west of the ridge and south of the rocky peak. The snow had accumulated significantly and his tracks to this place remained only as the remnants of craters, scarcely identifiable, the only signs of life in a world reborn since he had left it.

He retraced his steps without thought or question, his mind distracted by the desperate grasping to complete some idea he was unable to formulate. Upon passing, he stopped to inspect the elk beds a second time. But the new snow had erased the evidence, and the scene was only the remnants of a mess like the imprints left after children wrestled, and his brain felt too stale to revive past grievances. So he continued backtracking, his eyes glued to the ground and his weary mind distracted by idle thought. Only his steady, labored breathing kept his thoughts company, and he tried to concentrate more on the prior.

His legs fatigued quickly. The muscles burned as lactic acid levels rose in the absence of water. Yet he pushed on. It wasn't long before mild dehydration brought on slight hallucinations. The rising emotional discomfort blocked his reasoning. He thought little of his fate as he hastened his stride.

It was cold. But the temperature was deceiving because of the moisture and lack of light. He could see his breath, but walking

143

radiated heat from his core, and the surrounding peaks provided shelter from the vicious bite of the wind. The tip of his nose felt the numbing sting of cold, but if he could keep his boots and gloves dry, he decided, frostbite shouldn't be an issue. To the boy, the weather seemed only an annoyance and was the least of his concerns.

Meanwhile the snow continued to fall, quietly accumulating with the patient stealth of cancer. He paid little attention, for in his mind he didn't have far to travel. His life's journey had been forged through the steadfastness of his determination, the dealing with hardships as they arose. Planning had never been his forte. He didn't fret over details, as did his brother. He simply made decisions and willed his way to accomplishment. He never failed against human opponents for he never faltered once his mind was made up. Such stubborn determination could not be duplicated by any man alive. Every step he had ever taken had brought him closer to his destination, but he had never stopped to consider where that destination might be. So he trudged along through snow, compelled by disposition to outlast some nonexistent adversary, defying doubt and fear as if born in a world where such things had never existed, a world where there was only the will and the way and the outcome. The world through which he trudged was fine with such terms and accepted him without hardship or special treatment, and thus he moved with some appearance of harmony even as his boots occasionally sank nearly knee-deep through the hardened crust.

He didn't know how long or how far he had gone when he formulated his first clear notion. The concept wasn't loneliness or resentment exactly, but rather a throbbing indifference – a disease that didn't violently choke reason like anger but rather suffocated it gradually without symptom. He didn't stop to consider that he had been gone since before dawn or that his brother had expected him back at camp around noon. In the indented maze of the bowl he forgot about the epic expanses of the wilderness in which he traveled. He forgot about elk and family, the past and the future and everything else that existed beyond the sight of his eyes and the falling snow. Nothing mattered but lifting one foot and then the other. He had no fear of perishing for life did not matter enough for him to consider it. His greatest concern, his only concern, was his brother, whom he did not want to disappoint.

Suddenly these thoughts, along with the rising guilt that accompanied them, warped into an overwhelming impatience. He must get back quickly. He must not worry or disappoint his brother.

This nagging vision, in turn, further hurried his pace and distracted his judgment, wasting precious resources in the process. His thighs struggled to operate in this harsh environment. Lactic acid built up. He had no source of energy. His mouth grew dry. He began to feed on handfuls of snow from the surrounding shrubs and deadfall, but his thirst was unquenchable, and the false sense of food only made his hunger pangs worse.

A few hundred yards from the bottom of the low draw he decided to abandon his meandering tracks and cut left up the steep ridge to save time. The decision was made in haste with no consideration of consequences. In his distracted, weary mind, he figured the detour would save him twenty minutes or more. But he wasn't thinking clearly. He was rushing, falling frequently, and his hands grew wet inside his gloves.

It was a foolish decision; the type that cost men their lives. But he knew the lower park formed somewhere along the drainage ahead, just not exactly where. The sense of familiarity was exaggerated by his mood and condition. He failed to realize his route would be perpendicular to the ridge from which he came and that he would be heading west rather than northeast toward the apex where the ridges came together.

As he marched on, his head began to ache and his reactions dulled. He didn't realize he was slipping into the early stages of exhaustion and possibly hypothermia. He hadn't had a drink in hours. He knew only that he was strong and determined; the earth would submit to his will. Thoughts of giving up had yet to arise. Still, he knew that in this place and under these circumstances death was always on the table. But this was the fate of all men that braved the wild, and he saw no reason why he should be given special favor from the laws that governed all life on earth.

As he hiked and heaved and coughed, a single desire consumed him. All he wanted was to reach the tent, sit by the stove and ease his brother's burden. He had to save Shannon somehow from something, though he didn't know what. He simply knew there was a potential for greatness in his brother that was unique amongst men. He had always seen it in his brother, and he expected even as a young boy that his father had seen it as well. If his mother had ever seen it, she had lost it, as she had lost all ability to see people as individuals and grown to expect that great change could only come from some divine source and not from those that walked upon the earth.

He rushed off course breaking trail in the fog of his trancelike revelations, stepping to the rhythm of his pounding heart and wheezy breathing through the clean surreal of untouched wilderness. He climbed straight. Up the hill he went. Sweat swelled along the line of his wool cap even as his fingers grew numb inside his gloves. The ridge grew steeper with every vertical foot. The snowy path grew slick and more difficult to navigate. He slipped and fell and swore. At some point he took the cap off, and steam and stored body heat poured from his head. He was making wrong decisions; too many wrong decisions. But he had lost too much. He could lose no more.

Reaching the flat of a plateau, he stopped to catch his breath and looked around in search of something he recognized. The rifle slung on his back felt burdensome and uncomfortable. He fell to his ass in the snow and panted for oxygen. He sat for a long time until his butt grew numb again and the wind chilled his sweat-laced skin. Then he stood and leaned against a tree, shivering. Nothing looked familiar and living creatures no longer seemed to exist. It was only the endless timbered mountains and the snow and his loneliness. When his toes began to ache he tried to start again, but the butte was flat and he was unable to choose a direction. He didn't notice that his shivering had grown worse.

Eventually he reached a knoll of rock leading down steeply toward a deep ravine and had to turn. He had strayed too far. He didn't recognize his surroundings and didn't know where to go. He felt lonely and angry but refused to be afraid. To panic would help nothing. And so he fought against it, fighting for his brother's sake, but the endorphins of panic along with stanch, hereditary pride blocked his common sense and compounded the mistakes he had made. Finally, the familiarity of anger consumed him; the way of his upbringing. He assured himself he was atop the bluff along the

Main Ridge near the head of Windy Ridge. But he didn't know if left was north or south, for there was no sun and no sky and no signs of the familiar landmark of Black Bear Mountain or the high rocky point of Windy Ridge.

And so he made his second crucial mistake. It wasn't the decision of a rational mind. He needed to stop and admit he was lost; search for a landmark; backtrack; start a fire; get warm. He needed to proactively behave in a manner geared toward survival. But he didn't recognize that his rationality was waning and he had forgotten his hunger and thirst, so he ignored his father's teachings. He was young and had been given so little time to learn. It was only through sheer hubris and a stubborn ignorance that he was able to start marching forth again, deciding that if not for the storm he would see the familiar peak of Black Bear Mountain to his left.

But he was no longer able to ignore the cold. The timber was less limbed here, and the terrain exposed. The wind howled and the snow drifted. There was no horizon to speak of; no means to gauge progress. His pace slowed to a crawl. Soon he was overcome by exhaustion and his head began to spin. A voice told him to go back, but still he forged ahead, blinded by the circumstances of a life carved from obstinacy. He could see only his brother and Shannon's words of encouragement and belief from his childhood returned to him, providing fuel from an empty tank. He hiked through the drifts, one step at a time, while the untamed wind tore through his man-made layers until his bones ached from cold and fatigue. His face frosted and he tucked it inside his jacket. And still, everywhere he looked there was only more snow, more distance, more unwelcoming naught. The trees, the landscape, the air – everything belonged to the callous white and cold of winter's indifference.

Then the ridge fell off ahead again, and the last of his confidence crumbled. He knew this had to be impossible, that he couldn't be where he thought he was, but he wouldn't surrender yet even as panic found fear in its dormant shell deep within his heart. He changed course yet again. The sky's luminescence had darkened but remained unchanged to the point that he gave no thought to time as the route between day and night. There had been no past and existed no future. There was only this and it felt hopeless and eternal. He saw no sign of a sinking sun. As far as he

147

knew, it was still early afternoon. But time was ticking. To his right, barely visible through shaded timber and swirling snow, the tiniest crack of cold blue shown through the storm; the afternoon was growing late and the hidden sun's radiation diminishing. The darkness grew not in the clouds but beyond them and the wind took on a deeper, more taunting growl. With darkness, the temperature might quickly drop another ten or even twenty degrees.

He took shelter in a stand of snarled juniper among sturdy whitebark pines. The wind died down, obstructed by the tightly knit branches of this natural fortification, yet he could hear its howl now and again in the distance, waiting; patient; searching for a victim. The snowfall had eased as well, collecting in his new sanctuary with that detached persistence reserved for processes of nature; billions of tiny, insignificant particles falling continuously with unnoticeable change. He found the endless silence of such precipitation deafening.

Edgar's skin ached from the wind's brutality, but he was a hard and determined boy, not easily broken. His hands were numb and he balled them into fists inside his gloves. His feet felt like frozen anvils. Yet he pushed forward. In the thick brush he stopped more, stumbled more. Each time, his resolution faded further. Deadfall snagged on adjacent trees and stretched out vast distances, erasing any game trails. He took longer breaks and traveled shorter between stops. Was it too late to turn back? Would the wind have erased his tracks across the open hillside?

Finally, somewhere in the ever tightening maze of blow-down the last of his iron will abandoned him. His inner voice was no longer his own. As the words of his father finally found him, he surrendered fully to the grasp of panic.

'A stubborn man may last a long time in extreme cold, but to the winter his plight is of no consequence. The winter does not pardon those unwise enough to pit themselves against it in a battle of wills. Jesus may have forgiven, but nature knows no such pity.'

Pushing his way through an endless jungle of impasses, he fell into hysterics. He tried to run but only compounded his struggles. Cold and wet and pain met his every mistake. He swore. He screamed. But as his father had promised, the mountains gave no pardon – not even to echo his cries. Fear fed off his frustration, distinguishing what was left of his resolve in a hurry. He grew frightened. He shook and his jaw chattered. He became the boy that he actually was, fifteen years old, an orphan, hard and alone in a world governed by physical laws rather than divine intervention. His internal dialogue became a wall of distant narrators, whispering doom through sinister, plotting voices. His shin struck a hidden stump. His feet slipped on the rotten, snow covered logs he climbed over. Then a low branch stole his hat. Another dumped snow down the collar of his jacket. The moisture crept down the flesh of his back, furthering his bewildered state. Rage mixed with the fear and hopelessness. He fought and struggled without direction like a caged animal, like a madman. Just when he decided to turn back, the timber opened, and in that fragile instant of relief he felt a twinkle of hope.

He saw gray light ahead. He was exhausted and weak. A family of magpies cawed playful laughter. The sound of life was immediately sweet music to his ears. How could he possibly move backwards, away from his destination? He could not face that thick maze again. He looked for the sun, but still it could not be found. But he convinced himself the trail was near. And yet still the voice taunted him. A feared four letter word had crept into his conscience and taken root. It became the only word that existed. He was lost. There was no escape. There was no turning back.

Through the wind he staggered on. He was tired and his body begged him to lie down and sleep. The gloom and fatigue spread with each passing minute. Desperately, he fought to remain conscious, standing, sought signs of human existence, confident his brother would be searching for him by now. Every indention in the fresh snow received a thorough examination, even rodent tracks. But there was so much terrain to search. Why had he ever turned off his tracks?

His brother would find him.

But the contemplation of death found him first; it wasn't dying that scared the boy, rather the dreadful question of who might mourn his passing, who would remember his existence. What would it do to his brother? It was a heavy burden for such a young boy, even one as tough as Edgar. Finally, he could fight no more. He dropped his rifle and collapsed to his knees in the powder where he began to sob.

149

The tears came slowly and sparsely, sniffles that were fought against and almost inaudible, rather than the sorrowful wails from his earlier tantrum.

But somewhere deep down he knew Shannon would never fail him.

He wiped the tears away and refused to be consumed. He couldn't leave his brother alone in this world. He couldn't quit.

He struggled back to his feet and cried out for help.

None came.

Shannon would never abandon him.

Nothing but silent, snow-covered conifers listened in every direction. Nothing but white without distance or shape could be seen. He couldn't handle the isolation or fear any longer. He began to scream and continued as dry, frothy saliva crept from his mouth and froze on his chin. Snot, spit and tears soaked his face. He screamed until he grew hoarse. He screamed until he thought he would vomit. But this time he found no peaceful slumber to save him from his reality.

Shannon had never let him down.

Then he had nothing left. The darkness fell long as his eyes closed. He began to fade off, to let go and drift toward that final, quiet sleep, the great unknown.

But Drummond's never die easy, and on the verge of a life abandoned, some evolutionary function kicked on and a baser instinct took him over. His eyes struggled open; fluttering against the burn. In broken revelations he searched for reasons to live and found Holly in the untapped recesses of his deepest subconscious. Her smiling face spoke no words, but in its caring concern, he heard a call to rise. Only later would he realize that, although it was his girlfriend's gentle image staring down on him, it was his brother's solemn voice demanding him to endure – not his mother's or his father's voice, not the voice of the girl he loved, but Shannon's.

'Just survive, and I will save you, brother.'

And then these thoughts left him. The subconscious voice that controls guilt and shame; the same voice that had mocked him in his struggles, gave him one final scolding for his incompetence then abandoned him forever.

150

He rolled slowly to a seated position and searched the snow with bare, shivering hands of purple flesh until he found his rifle. He scooped it up best he could and examined it in deliberation. The cold metal stuck to his numb skin. The snow had stopped falling at some point and the white around him had gathered the indigo tint of twilight. The darkness came quickly. Feeling had melted away, but he knew that he needed heat and help soon if he wanted to keep all his fingers and toes. He saw the lifeless weapon he held in his quivering arms. It was a line of humility he thought he would die before he would cross. But that had been his stubborn pride. Now he wanted only to live, and he knew that at least two people out there wanted the same. He drew strength from this knowledge, and the voice within spoke in primitive, singular terms paying no attention to the waiting death that hovered over him. All the thoughts and emotions that had heeded him in his quest for shelter faded to black and the instinctive voice within guided him with short concise directions. It spoke and he acted, plain and simple.

He struggled to his feet, leaned against a spruce, braced the butt of the rifle against his shoulder and fired a shot into the fading gray. The violent discharge awakened something within him – an honest creature, desperate not even for love or approval but purely to survive. A few seconds later he fired a second shot into the abyss above and the earth shuttered. As he fell back to his knees in the deep snow, the silence returned and he noticed his gloves lying beside him. He hadn't remembered taking them off. He shook the snow from them and put them on and pulled his hat down low. He blew on his hands and rubbed them together for warmth.

And it was in that moment that he realized how little life meant in the grand scheme of things, but also, he realized beyond everything that affected his life, this is who he was and would always be. There was neither pity nor pride in his recognition. There was no feeling at all and little reflection beyond recognition of a cold, hard fact. He would die; whether it was today or tomorrow or fifty years from now. His time would come and the world wouldn't miss a beat.

He took an inventory of his pockets. There he found a half book of matches, a wad of toilet paper and several candy wrappers. It was a start, but he needed fuel to burn and limped around in progressively larger circles until he found a pitchy, old grey stump jutting out of the snow. The upper three quarters of the log was sheltered by buck-brush and the canopy above, leaving it void of snow and bone dry. Edgar checked the matchbook and knew he would only have a couple tries. The evening was growing colder by the minute and if he fell asleep again without a fire he would not wake up. But the wind was dying and the stump should burn if he could get a flame hot enough to get it started. He took his time patiently digging the log free using his boots to clear a perimeter. Somewhere far off, he swore he heard a coyote howl.

Shannon would come.

After he had cleared and dried the area, he broke open the stump using gravity and the small hatchet he carried in his fanny pack to expose the dry, pitchy wood from the rot as his father had taught him. His hands ached with excruciating pain as he worked but the hurt and use helped regain feeling in them. Once he had carved out a good sized hole, he gathered dry needles from the undergrowth of a dead pine nearby and lined the cavity. Next he added the paper, wadding it loosely to increase its surface area and exposure to oxygen. Then he fanned branches around the stump to form a wind block. After aligning everything just right, he removed his gloves, drew his hands inside the chest of his jacket and did his best to thaw them out by blowing down through the collar as he rubbed them together. They continued to shake, purple, cracked and bleeding, but through patience he was able to steady them enough for use. Hunkering down near the crevasse, he pulled his jacket up over his head and worked within it to provide additional protection from the wind. He pulled the matchbook from his pocket and angled it inches from the fuel.

He lit his first match and as its tiny flame began to burn was able to ignite the paper. As the flame slowly rose to life, its color changed and Edgar gambled, placing the remaining matches along with the book into the hole below the flame. He cupped his hands around the tiny flame and watched and waited. The evening had grown silent, and the darkness was falling as the shadows all around stretched and broadened.

His brother would save him.

He watched the flame flicker and dance and the paper blacken and vanish. It was a slow process. He didn't pray. He

152

didn't think about the parents that were gone, his girlfriend or his luck. He didn't think about the life he had lived, mistakes he had made or the future at risk. His mind was blank beyond that flame and the knowledge that his brother would find him and the desire to stay alive until he did.

Slowly, the needles began to pop and burn and then the flame spread to the pitch inside the log, but as the paper burned out, the fire shrunk to the tiniest glow. Edgar's life depended on the fate of that last orange flare. He blew gently into the gap. The pitch smoked. He could feel the warmth and knew the initial fire had dried the gray wood around it. Carefully, he exhaled again and again, blowing lightly.

Then the smolder took with a sudden fury. And within minutes the stump was engulfed in a crackling fire that would grow to an inferno. The flames fed off the pitch and the cold surrounding air and gave off a thick black smoke that rose in a straight column through the darkening sky. The pops and cracks were celebratory sounds of warmth's approach. Soon, there was heat.

Edgar sat down upon the patch of ground he had cleared and stuck his hands inches from the insatiable flames as they began to grow and jump and dance and turn from orange to yellow-blue. Anything was better than white. And as the fire spread to the rest of the stump, the white around the log hissed and retreated, rescinding it's domination in protest, melting away to expose the dead grass and black soil below.

As the warmth spread to Edgar's body, he knew he had to gather more fuel or his stump would burn out. It was hard to leave the warmth of the small fire, but he struggled to his feet and searched nearby for anything dry enough to burn. After ten minutes he had gathered a few small armfuls of branches and dragged over another large stump that had been protected from the snow. He piled his fuel beside the flame and fed it quickly. Then he sat before his fire and watched it and accidently smiled. His father would be proud. His brother would be proud.

The night was dark now, and the moon and the stars were hidden behind the overcast and the smoke from his fire seemed to supply the black that surrounded him. He found his rifle and again he fired two shots, but the clouds were unfazed and the darkness

153

never budged and the silence quickly returned. Still, the shots felt less desperate and hope had returned. He sat again before the warmth of the fire, and soon he began to hum and then to sing. He knew few songs and the songs he sang were mostly old church songs or choruses, and he carried on as loud as he could muster in defiance of the world's indifference, but soon his voice grew hoarse and he had fed the last of his fuel upon the bonfire he had built and still the wilderness remained unchanged beyond the bright glow from the dancing flames. He began to grow very tired again, and he struggled in his fight to remain awake. He noticed his boots were melting and backed away only slightly, yet not too far for he knew the fire would shrink soon and he craved the heat. Just as he faded off, he stared into the high leaping flames one last time, registering all the colors and movements of his murmuring savior. And then he closed his eyes. And he wasn't sure if he opened them again or if he was dreaming, but from somewhere he heard gunshots; distant rifle fire echoing across the lonesome darkness.

Chapter 18

"That's it son! Strike and move! Stay low!"

The sounds of dull thudding kept cadence to Oliver's instructions which he mixed delicately with criticism and praise as Edgar bounced from one foot to the other, striking the bag with violent speed and power before ducking back into his guarded dance. He wore tight borrowed trunks and his pale, scarred flesh glistened with perspiration. The kid was skin and bones except a few flat plates of muscle clumped around his chest and stomach and a few sinewy fibers running up either arm that knotted at the bicep and shoulder. Oliver wasn't all that surprised at how little meat there was to the kid's makeup. He had seen the type before; scavengers, survivors without a wasted ounce on them. Like a wolverine, they were most dangerous when cornered. The hardships of a tough life flowed through Edgar's bloodstream and magnified his every strike. His body was riddled with scars, burns and bullet-holes; his flesh etched with faded ink; marine code, ammunition and Old Glory; two massive antlers climbed his back from just above his hips to his shoulder blades and between them the phrase, 'Only the baddest bull breeds' screamed out in Old English script.

"Now shoot!" Oliver shouted as he dabbed sweat from his own brow. "Come on you gotta be faster, son! Down to that knee and explode UP!"

The kid was lightening, and although he didn't have the lungs and had numerous flaws in his technique, there was no doubt he would be a champion. If he lasted. His type of raw talent was rare and it wasn't the opponent or the training that the questions of potential hung upon. It wasn't the fight in the ring that mattered, but the fracture from within. And the kid was a model example.

After those first few weeks of gung-ho discipline, the kid's demons had returned. He started missing practices. No phone calls or warnings. His schedule was random to begin with. Sometimes he stayed away a week or more, which meant Oliver had to be ready and available at all times. Some nights the kid wouldn't show up until eleven thirty when the gym closed at eleven. Oliver tried to discipline the kid, but his words just seemed to bounce off the surface. There was never an excuse, no reason or explanation given at all. Edgar would train on his schedule or no schedule. So Oliver stayed later and later, sleeping in the back room most nights if he slept at all, waiting for that knock at the door. He grew obsessive. His health continued to deteriorate, and he felt his desire as a race against the clock.

Sil began to worry. He warned his friend of the implications of such erratic behavior at Oliver's age and in his condition. He was constantly reminding the old man to take his medications and forcing him to eat. Some nights he begged him to go home, take a few days off and rest. There would be more time to train. Sil saw the raw talent the kid possessed, but he couldn't understand why Oliver allowed him to walk all over him. There were other fighters who needed help too. Fighters more deserving of the old man's patience and knowledge. Sil couldn't stand the way the kid broke the gym's unwritten rules and came and went as he pleased. He saw a lack of discipline and saw the slim chances of Edgar reaching his potential for what they were. A few times the

155

kid showed up so plowed he could barely stand, and Sil threatened to ban him once and for all, but Oliver wouldn't allow it.

The kid was creating a rift between the old friends. But Oliver insisted all was well. He insisted the kid could be saved. He saw the way he trained with passionate fury when he was present. Even when he reeked of booze and it seeped out of him until his flesh took on a green tint he followed Oliver's directions and showed continuous improvement. And when he was sober and focused, it was like nothing the old man had ever witnessed. But what really mattered to Oliver was that so long as the kid remained in the gym the dead flame couldn't spread or cause harm. It couldn't engulf his soul or claim more victims. He felt that they were extinguishing it a little at a time. Because of that, no price could be too steep. Try as he might, Oliver couldn't shake the memories of that first violent night, and he held in his heart that those events had been a message from above.

The only victims under Oliver's watch were the kid's sparring opponents, of whom there were few remaining. It didn't take long before no one wanted to step on that mat in front of him. He was too physical, too detached. And when others lost their temper and tried to cheap shot him, find some advantage or chink in his armor, there was no sign of pain. Only swift and evenhanded retaliation. No man, fighter or not, liked to risk serious injury without hope of victory, especially in training. So most openly refused to spar with him. Others found excuses. Eventually, only a few men, all much bigger than the kid, would train with him, and he outwrestled them all.

Tonight, these men were not around, so Oliver had him walk through takedowns and submissions with a skeptical partner and then pushed him through bag work and cardio to keep his heart rate up. The kid still had the smoker's cough and sounded as if he were hacking up a lung half the time. Oliver ran him through a few thirty minute circuits until the kid started vomiting and couldn't stop. But Oliver felt no pity for a young man so old and stood by shaking his head, continuing to push little by little, reminding the kid he had only himself to blame for his lack of endurance and trying to find his breaking point.

"Alright," Oliver finally conceded, disappointed that the kid couldn't seem to get past that cardiovascular tipping point. He never showed signs of fatigue against an opponent, but solo cardio and weight training failed to keep him motivated. It made evaluating his true endurance, and thus his capabilities, almost impossible. Oliver figured that eventually tougher opponents would solve the problem, but he worried about how the kid might fair against professionals that were able to take advantage of this weakness. "Let's get you in the ice bath for twenty."

Oliver used the ice bath or massage table after practice as a means to talk to the kid, try and get inside and open him up. At the very least he could keep him around a little longer, tire him out and keep him off the streets, away from the booze and the temptations that came with the dark of night.

Usually he would talk, and the kid would grunt a few responses. But he did seem to listen, and Oliver remained optimistic, believing that all men can be reached and that sooner or later he might break through. He started each night's dialogue by sharing the stories of his own life, trying to relate to his young apprentice, stopping only occasionally to ask the kid a question or make some point that might get him to offer anything in return. Tonight the kid was clear-eyed, and he decided to try and do some digging right off the bat. He grabbed a chair and after Edgar had climbed into the stainless steel tub the two sat quietly in the dimly lit room a few minutes, as the kid caught his breath and the old man collected his thoughts.

"Well your first fight's next Saturday," Oliver braved finally, breaking that void of companionship the kid so easily seemed to induce.

The door was closed and the gym beyond it nearly empty. The room was dimly lit and quiet aside from the old man's wheezing and the occasional splashing of water made by the kid's movement. "You gonna show up right?"

"Yeah, I'll be there." The kid laughed. It was a good start. The kid's eyelids were almost closed, and he looked calm and tired, almost peaceful. "I'm sorry I missed practice the other day." He went on. "My schedule gets pretty hectic sometimes." Those two sentences comprised as many words as the kid often spoke over the course of an entire workout. Oliver was filled with hope.

"Not sure which day was the other one," the old man joked, "but I understand people are busy. A man's got to work, and his

157

hobbies can't come before his well-being or that of his family."
The kid didn't answer, and the old man wondered if he had hit a
nerve. "Do you have any family around here, son?" He had done
some research on the kid's family and already knew from asking
around that the kid had grown up here, that he had lost his father as
a teen and that he had a brother running for attorney general.

"Yeah," the kid offered flatly. "I got an older brother and
an aunt."

"Oh yeah? I suppose it was your older brother's thumpings
that hardened you up as a kid, huh?"

"Nah," the kid replied. "He was good to me. I'd say the last
time we ever fought I was eleven or twelve."

"Probably cuz he knew you could whoop him." Oliver
offered.

"No." The kid answered with his usual certainty. "He was
tough... Different kind of tough."

"Were you close?"

"Yeah. We were close. He basically raised me, taught me a
lot about this world."

"But you're not close no-more?"

The kid shrugged. "My brother, he's got a family of his
own, and a great career... busy schedule. I'm sure you've heard
the ads on the radio?"

"Oh, yeah," Oliver played dumb, "I guess I never put it
together before. Your brother, he's a big shot politico, right?"

"Yeah," the kid said. "Something like that."

"You must be proud of him?"

"Very."

"How many years between the two of yah?"

"Almost six."

"And what about your parents?"

"They're gone." A tension rose in the kid and his eyes were
open now as he shifted restlessly beneath the cold water. Oliver
knew this opportunity was a fragile one, and he decided to ease off
a bit. They both sat quietly for a moment.

"So you served in the Corp, correct?"

"Yes."

"And you saw combat in the Middle East?"

"Some."

"I was an Army grunt myself." The old man pulled back his sleeve to reveal the faded markings inked there. "Drafted. I served three tours in the hellholes of Vietnam and Cambodia under Westmoreland. Lord Almighty. Got to see the world so to speak. It wasn't pretty what I seen over there, but I did a lot of growing up in the service.

"Who'd you serve under?"

The kid stared ahead and his head almost nodded. "Can't really say."

Oliver was caught off guard and more than a little surprised.

"Oh... Hmm." He fell quiet a moment. "Special Ops?"

"Yes."

"DEVGRU?"

"Something like that." The kid answered as he picked at a scab on his right arm. He was somewhere else, remembering a forgotten part of himself, and the old man couldn't help thinking he hadn't been there in a long time or gone there willingly.

"Well everyone appreciates all you've done to serve and protect this country's freedom, son." Oliver said softly. It was the only thing he could think to say. "I know it can be tough, carrying the burden around with you. I've been there. Have you ever talked to anyone about it?"

"I'm talking to you right now."

"But I mean really hashed it out. There are people out there that can help...professionals." The old man pried before fading off.

The kid said nothing.

To ease the mood Oliver backed off again, told a few of the lighter stories from his time spent overseas; token anecdotes of gambling, Vietnamese women, drinking, trying pot, and the mind-warping humidity. He offered laughter at the opportune times, but it felt forced and the kid remained a statue. He was somewhere else entirely. Twenty minutes passed without a response, and Oliver knew his chance was slipping away. He changed directions a second time.

"You still dating that same gal?" The old man tried, desperate to pull the kid back. He felt guilty for the downward spiral in the kid's mood and worried about the consequences of their conversation.

159

"Yeah. We're moving in together."

"That's good." It was a spark of hope. There was something there.

"Maybe."

"What do you mean, maybe? Are you nervous, son?"

"A bit."

"That's natural. It means you're human. I'm sure things will work out." The subject seemed to bring the kid back to the present and Oliver knew he had to be careful not to lose him again. "Will it be your first time living with a woman?"

"Yeah." A glimmer of pride and hope showed through in the single word.

"Ooh hoo," the old man chuckled. "That's good. That's real good. You'll be fine. Just be yourself, son. Try your best. Choose your battles. That's all you can do. I still remember when my wife and I shacked up for the first time...Mmm hmm, to be young again." He bent at the waist and his bones ached as if to validate his words. "Do you plan to marry this gal?"

"No." The word was hard and certain. It caught Oliver off guard.

"Not the marrying type? There ain't nothing wrong with that. Of course, there ain't nothing like the love of a good woman either. A good woman can cleanse a man of all the sins he wears on his hands. A good woman's love can change him forever."

"Yeah." The kid agreed.

"Yes sir. You seen the changes yourself, I bet? You know how it is."

"Well, I sleep in a bed a lot more now. That's for sure."

The old man laughed and that got the kid laughing too. Oliver felt like they were making progress.

"Son, you are a wild one. Didn't your momma never bring you in out of the barn, boy?"

The kid's smile faded at the mere mention of his mother.

Oliver quickly made note of this and subconsciously chided his choice of words. The kid didn't look too far gone though, so he decided to press his luck.
"What happened with your parents, son, if you don't mind me asking?" There was a pause and all at once the air in the room felt heavier. Oliver felt a desperate tug to backtrack. But the words

160

were already spoken. Then the kid surprised the old man again when he answered,

"Our mom left when I was a kid. Our dad passed away when I was fourteen." There was a pause as Oliver waited for more. When it was clear the kid was finished, the old man was forced to fill the silence.

"That's a shame, Edgar." It was the first time he had called the kid by his name. He didn't mean to it had just felt natural. "That must have been tough on you boys?"

No answer.

"At least you had each other." The old man offered gentle as possible.

He wondered suddenly, as he had done before, how two individuals faced with the same situation could turn out so seemingly different. Doing the math in his head, he realized the older brother would have been around twenty at the time their father died, nearly done with the raising age, which probably explained part of it. But their mother's leaving must have affected them differently as well.

The silence went on another minute before Oliver started in on the details of the fight. The kid remained on the verge of insecure vulnerability. Clearly, he didn't let just anyone in and it was apparent from his demeanor and body language that he was unsure of the trust he was showing the old man. Oliver was unsure of how to proceed. He wanted to hug the kid, tell him it was alright to hurt and congratulate him on the progress he had made in the past half hour. But he knew better. He needed to debrief and deescalate the tension. But he didn't do that. Instead, he took another gamble.

"You know your parents loved you, don't you son? They might not have made all the right decisions, but none of that was your fault, and they'd both be proud as hell of you if they was alive today…"

The words were too boilerplate, library book psychology. Oliver should've known better than to offer such a generic statement to a kid that bought zero bullshit.

In a flash the kid was out of the tub and upon him, stark naked and dripping wet. He grabbed his cotton sweatshirt tight in his right hand and held his nose inches from the old man's face.

161

His heavy breath blew hot against the old man's skin. Staring eye to eye, Oliver saw tears welling along the surface of the kid's retina.

"Listen," He huffed through clenched teeth, desperately trying to hold himself together. "I know you're a good man, and I know you're trying to help me with all this father figure shit and relating to me as a soldier. But don't you ever pretend that you know who I am, who my parents were, or where the fuck I came from, you hear me? Because if you do, I'm done with all this rehabilitation bullshit and I'll leave you shitting dentures." Through the rage and harsh words, there was a calm presence. It wasn't a threat, simply a reaction. The kid was scared and vulnerable and pissed off. This was how he translated his emotions. He hadn't had a conversation about himself in so long that very old and deep wounds had been reopened. His lifelong defenses were simply reacting to protect him.

"Alright now, son." Oliver said softly without moving a muscle. At that moment he didn't care if the kid pulverized him. He knew if he hit him he would probably kill him with one punch anyway. He didn't give one thought to his own well being. His only concern was for the kid. "You just calm down now. I'm sorry for overstepping my bounds. We're just talking here. I'm just trying to get to know you a little bit, and by the looks of it talking things out a little more might do you some good."

The kid twitched, and his arm cocked at the elbow as he loaded that, scarred and knobby fist at Oliver's eye level. "The rage that lives in you won't do you no good, son. I've been there. You don't have to believe me if you don't want. But believe me when I say this hate and anger won't bring you nothing but more hardship. If we don't get to the bottom of what fuels it, we're just wasting our time. You need to let go." The kid tightened his grip on the shirt and the old man shook with the force of it, but he didn't flinch. He knew the kid wasn't going to hurt him. If he were he would have. The worst of the emotion had passed.

"Enough." Edgar said.

There was more to say, yet he swallowed the words.

Oliver could see that the kid understood everything the old man said. But he was hesitant to reveal anything more, for he knew not what type of explosive, destructive action might come with

162

uncovering such fiercely concealed pain so quickly after so long. He knew all that harbored hurt was at the surface now and that such torment needed to go, and he wanted desperately to get it out, but such a process would take time. He didn't know how to take the next step. He had never been taught to share or process through dialogue.

Yet a threshold had been crossed. A bond was being forged. And in the boy's wild eyes, all of this was told. In that moment of uncertainty, fear and hope, Oliver recognized hope. A hope that if the flame didn't consume him too soon, they would get there, and this soul could be saved.

Suddenly Oliver realized he hadn't been living for a long time. It wasn't only this kid that he so desperately sought to aid. He too had been going through the motions for far too long, burdened by the loss of his mother and his wife, abandoning the world of the living and awaiting his own end. He now recognized that his recent frustrations with the kids he had been training stemmed from his own guilt, and the two weren't all that different in that way. Sometimes it takes a close encounter with danger to show people a truer reflection of the life they lived, and Oliver saw more than he bargained for catching his reflection in those cold, hard eyes.

Droplets of water dripped from the kid's skin and hair and soaked through the old man's jogging pants. The tiniest sensation of cold registered against the flesh of his thighs, and in it he remembered life and regained an appreciation for such feeling. The seconds passed like hours as the intense stare down lingered a moment longer. Then the kid turned grabbed his clothes from the bench nearby, pulled his pants on without toweling off and left the room in haste.

After he had gone, Oliver was left in the silence of a dreamlike fog. He became very conscious of the effort of his own breathing, inhaling and exhaling, until the world around him completely vanished. He sat there like that, wheezing, and reflected a long while, and, although at that moment he couldn't recall the past two minutes if his life depended on it, the tiniest details of the altercation were etched into the very bedrock of his soul. It would be a day or two before he could replay the scene in his memory, but he knew immediately that what little time he had

remaining in this life would be intricately woven into the fate of
the wild boy who had just spared it.

Chapter 19

The sterile, white room on the fourth floor of the county
hospital reminded Shannon of so many awful memories, and he sat
in the stiff, plastic chair beside the window and shifted his gaze to
the world outside whenever the effects of the tiny room became
too much for him to tolerate. His mother's sister lay in the bed
three feet from him. A woman he now realized he hardly knew.
And yet, outside of his brother, she was the last remaining member
of his family, laying sick and still amidst the clutter and clamor of
modern medical machinery, just as his father had done years
before, on the same floor, of the same hospital.

A dedicated smoker for nearly half a century, Aunt Dotty
was reaching the end of a long, unwinnable fight against lung
cancer; although right now, she was watching Wheel of Fortune.
Shannon hadn't known the game show still aired.

It was a Tuesday. Work had brought him to the vicinity,
and stress and a sense of obligation had brought him the rest of the
way. He hated hospitals, but he needed a break from his own life
for a while. This was his third visit to Aunt Dotty's room. He had
found the previous trip strangely therapeutic and figured why not
try to recapture that sentiment. The first visit he had come alone,
on an evening similar to this, and spent more time in the car
fighting himself to enter the building than he had spent at his
aunt's side. That visit had been tough. His guilt had weighed heavy
upon his shoulders. But then, keeping his promise to his brother, he
and Jill had brought the kids one day after school, and that trip had
gone quite differently.

Aunt Dotty had seen Melanie only once, as a newborn, and
she was so touched by the visit that she began to cry. When the
child asked her elderly aunt if she was crying because she was
sick, Dotty laughed through the tears and a coughing fit and
explained that she was in fact crying for joy, an odd behavior
Melanie would understand when she grew older. It was a heart

164

warming moment all around made especially memorable when Melanie understandingly held her Aunt's hand and assured her that 'mommy cried for joy too – whenever daddy bought her a shiny necklace or flowers, which wasn't very often.'

Shannon smiled at the memory, but there wasn't much else to smile about on this visit. Dotty wasn't doing well. Her eyes had sunk back away from the light of the world, and her skin had become the color of iodine. Even limited communication wore her out quickly, and the nurse had told Shannon she was sleeping nearly eighteen hours a day.

Shannon had taken the news with a straight face. After all, he hadn't exactly remained close with this woman over the years. But now, sitting beside the familiar face that had always reminded him hauntingly of his mother, he noted how vastly it had changed from his childhood memories, and a hollow sorrow engulfed him as he wished he had included this lonely, independent woman in more of his life's experiences or at least those of his daughters. In all those years of limited contact, she had never complained once. If Shannon called, she had answered. If he needed anything, she helped anyway she could. And yet as the years rolled by and life grew ever busier and more complicated, he had left her forgotten, punishing her in a way for the sister that had abandoned him. It had even occurred to him at times that this was his reasoning on some subconscious level. But he had grown so skilled at compartmentalizing guilt that he never had much trouble pushing these thoughts from his mind.

Now, with everything else going on in his life, he realized the assessment had probably been pretty close to the truth.

He had actually tried to contact his mother after his first visit. It was the first time he had reached out to her in over twenty years. He called the last known number he had for her, but it had been disconnected. He investigated a little on the internet, but his efforts were half-hearted. In truth, he was glad he hadn't found her. He wasn't ready to open that door and probably never would be.

Besides, Dotty only mentioned her sister in stories of those earliest years of his childhood, and he knew the two hadn't been in close contact for many years. She too, it seemed, had been scarred by the abandonment of her sister and sole blood relative. Perhaps the Drummond curse wasn't reserved for Drummonds.

Dotty's only visitors were Edgar, Shannon and a handful of close friends from her past; the nurse said there were three or four of them, though Shannon had never crossed paths with any one. Sitting there awaiting death's arrival, he couldn't help but wonder who and how many would visit him when his end came near. As he stared out the window, he contemplated a moment on that most distant future.

It was late September now, and the days were growing shorter. The nights were growing colder, and the colors had already begun to change. Two weeks had passed since the neighbor's tomato plants had fallen victim to the first frost, and the snow flurries couldn't be far behind. Many years there was snowfall throughout September though more recently Central Montana had enjoyed several consecutive Indian Summers.

It sure didn't feel like winter this evening. The temperature had fallen just shy of eighty that afternoon, and although it would dip down around freezing after dark the summer still felt eternal, if only in the valley. Shannon knew all too well that the high mountain peaks on the horizon would be no picnic this evening or tomorrow morning, before dawn, after twelve hours without radiant heat.

Shannon was ready for winter. It had been a hot, grueling summer, and the cold and darkness had a way of slowing life down. He had little time for the lake or other summer leisure he had once enjoyed, and if he had to play one more round of golf or attend another boring baseball game to get a vote he thought he might snap. Mostly, he was just ready for the viciousness of campaigning to be over. The primary had been more exhausting than he had ever imagined. It felt as if it had been a wasted year of waiting and wondering, and he eagerly looked forward to regaining a sense of routine in his life. He longed to get away from the people and the incessant noise. But he knew this would be his toughest fall yet. With six weeks until the election, a recent poll had him mere percentage points behind Berkman and he seemed to be gaining momentum every day. It seemed independents were buying into Shannon's platform of Montana as a family.

Just getting out for an evening drive was going to be difficult, and it broke his heart to think there might not be a Drummond camp for the first time in thirty-eight years. Although

166

he had been alone for the majority of the past decade, and the camp had hardly been a social experience for far longer than that, it was still a crushing blow to his family's proudest and perhaps final tradition.

Still, it was bound to end eventually. He had no son, and it didn't appear Edgar would be having any children. His daughters would grow up, marry, and the Drummond name would vanish into the oblivion. If their husbands didn't hunt, decades of knowledge on the high country would be forfeited. The deeds of the Drummond clan, their history, would be forgotten. The world would go on. Such change was inevitable; but that didn't make it any less a shame in Shannon's eyes.

Still, nothing was certain yet. Perhaps Jill and he would rekindle old romances and have another child, a son. Perhaps this would be the year his brother returned to the wilderness of his youth and escaped from whatever wild, untamed frontier had since replaced it in his soul. Perhaps, perhaps, perhaps. Those pages remained unwritten.

Far in the distance, high above all else, Black Bear Mountain stood dark and powerful even amongst giants, beckoning and daring. Shannon set his sights upon its timbered, toothy peak in the late afternoon sunshine and wondered when he would again reach the peace and safety of his hallowed refuge. The picturesque magnificence of those sharp arêtes, carved by long extinct glaciers, had grown to bother him in recent years, not out there amidst the presence of those rugged mountains, but from the distance of the valley, here in town looking out toward that fall and winter home abandoned. It was a feeling that plagued him; a realization that those mountains didn't care one way or another if he or anyone else for that matter came to explore and experience what that hallowed wilderness provided. Such habitat was indifferent to companionship, and beyond the desire for water, sunlight and oxygen, without need. The wilderness cared not who spoke what of its greatness and beauty, learned from its vast silence, wrote of its topography, or documented its history. Such was the attitude of all things eternal; confident and indifferent.

Shannon had picked up archery hunting the fall prior, both to extend his season and to give him more opportunities and excuses to get out away from the constraints of a life that he felt continually funneling him toward an existence without choice. But he was a terrible shot, unconfident beyond twenty yards, and he hadn't even drawn his bow yet this summer as his schedule grew ever busier. He clung to the notion that, win or lose the election, it would all be over the week before Thanksgiving and he would be able to disappear for those last few days of the season for some well deserved time off. The snow was usually deep by then in the high hills and he looked forward to that horizon with great hope for escape. But who knew what was to come?

Dotty coughed, and he turned back from the window and returned to the here and now.

"Is there anything I can get you, Auntie?" he asked, doing his best to mask his discomfort and the incessant wanderings of his mind.

"No, hun. I'm doing just fine." The elderly woman replied. "Now why don't you run along, I know how busy you are, dear." Without turning her head she reached for his hand but was unable to find it.

"Nothing more important than this on the schedule, Auntie." He said and took her hand and held it. Her hand was cold and the flesh loose and furrowed.

"You're such a sweet boy, Shannon. I've been so blessed to have two such darling nephews. And my grand nieces. Oh how beautiful those girls are." This she said without a hint of insincerity. Here she was, never married, without children, succumbing to a slow, painful death and yet she held no qualms or resentment toward the world she was leaving. Only pride for the family that had had so little time for her. Her courage and contentment amazed him. There was much he could learn from her attitude. "I hope you know your visits mean the world to me."

"Thanks, Auntie." Shannon said. He looked into her eyes, clouded from cataracts, and as she closed them a moment his emotions began to show through. "I only wish you'd had more time with the girls...I guess I just lost sight of...stuff...priorities...with work and everything...the time just flies by..."

"Oh don't you go feeling sorry for this old lady, hun." She stopped him, trying to squeeze his hand. She turned her head and smiled at him. "I've lived my life, and I couldn't be more proud of you boys. I just hope the two of you find peace with each other and with the Lord before it's too late. I'd hate to see you end up like Lizzie and I. Life is too short to dwell on silly sibling grudges." Her smile vanished, and Shannon could see she was somewhere else for a moment. "Take it from me, dear."

Shannon didn't know how to reply, and so he just held her hand and watched her while Pat Sajak responded to a wave of applause in the background. It was Aunt Dotty that spoke again,

"Your mother and father would be so proud of you, Shannon." Tears welled in Shannon's eyes.

A moment later, Edgar entered the room. He was dressed in a white polo and clean jeans. He wore no hat and his hair was cropped clean and close to his head. Shannon almost didn't recognize him as he stopped just inside the doorway of the dim room, and stood smiling against the contrast of the brightly lit hallway.

"Well, hello darling." Aunt Dotty greeted him when she noticed his presence. Shannon turned away so he could wipe his eyes, and then stood, nervous, but also glad to have his brother find him here.

"Hello, Auntie." Edgar replied, his smile growing more evident as he beamed in the direction of the bed. Then to Shannon, he added, "Brother," with a nod of his head.

"Good to see you, Edgar." Shannon moved toward his brother who remained still and the two shook hands. Upon closer inspection, Shannon realized it wasn't just the clean clothes that he didn't recognize; there was a new look to his brother – vibrant and cheery. His skin had pigment to it, and he looked healthy. It caught Shannon off guard, but he quickly grew fond of the new Edgar as he returned to his seat and allowed Dotty to direct the course of conversation.

Sure enough, Edgar spoke more and clearly, without the slur of bourbon, and even his tone seemed more chipper than Shannon had heard it sound in years. The elder Drummond had heard rumors of his brother training to fight and listened with great interest while his aunt asked Edgar how the boxing matches faired.

"Good," he answered. "But it's not boxing. It's less structured. I'm allowed to wrestle too."

169

"Oh," Dotty moaned. "That's right. You told me. I am an old woman, dear. I forget things."

"It's nothing, Auntie."

"You were always such a talented wrestler."

"Thanks, Auntie."

"And what of this pretty girlfriend of yours? Any news?" She asked. Her speech was slowing noticeably. Edgar blushed, still smiling.

"We're living together," Then turning a winking eye toward his brother, "against my niece's wishes." The brothers shared a laugh at this, and although Dotty missed the humor it pleased her greatly.

"Oh that's wonderful darling... And you said you're living in the old Parish?"

"No. Krystle had an apartment there, but we're living at my place for now."

"Oh good." Dotty said, but her look showed some disappointment and the words were coming together very slowly now. "I always hoped one of you boys would settle around Lewis Street. Your father's people have so much history there."

The conversation dawdled from there. Soon, Aunt Dotty was fading in and out. Edgar and Shannon made light comments to fill in the gaps and every now and again the old woman murmured, "My boys, my dear sweet boys." Then a nurse entered the room, and the brothers said their goodbyes. In the hallway they lingered as Shannon searched for words to express all that weighed upon his mind.

"So you're fighting?" He asked for a lack of a better place to start.

Edgar shrugged. It was one thing for him to talk about himself to his dying aunt and another to be the focus of a conversation with his brother.

"I'm training." He said; his smile gone now but the light still there beneath his skin. "I've only fought once."

"And?"

"I won."

Shannon felt an apology swell his throat, but he didn't know what he was sorry for or how to express years of words unsaid.

"Good…Congratulations…And congratulations on moving in with Krystle. We'll have to have the two of you over for dinner as soon as this election's over."

There was a lull in the conversation as Edgar took the compliment with a shy smile and Shannon ran out of filler. They were left standing amidst decades of sentiments unsaid while the hospital continued to buzz with activity around them. Edgar stood patiently, at ease in his brother's company in the absence of words. He cherished these seldom moments of genuine bliss when their blood bonded them without effort and hope lingered. His renewed sense of pride was reflected through his appearance and extended by the magnitude of the meeting. There was a glow of optimism in him. He was proud of his brother for being there; proud of their family for enduring.

Shannon didn't share his hopeful outlook. His brother's cool demeanor and slick threads only reminded him of this mysterious whorehouse or casino and his arrangement with Grisham. He was high strung and exhausted, and he couldn't see the moment with any clarity. All he recognized was the added pressure of being a Drummond again. And combined with the stress of the election and his problems with Jill, it was too much. The silence constricted him. His palms began to itch.

"So, what's this I hear about you running some sort of an escort service or casino or something up in the canyon?"

In his brother's face, Shannon watched their moment evaporate and he couldn't help but feel the slightest sense of satisfaction, followed by immediate guilt.

"I don't know." Edgar said evenly and there was still time to save the progress made, but Shannon had moved in one direction and his momentum built quickly.

"Edgar," he said looking around before leaning forward to keep from being overheard. As he did so, he lost the casual comfort he had found in Dotty's company. He forgot why he was here and the apology he had planned to articulate. He was just the guarded individual trying to distance himself from the curse once more. "I know you can take care of yourself, and I know you are only doing what you can to get back on your feet.

"But I am so close to something very important," then almost as an after thought he added, "and I don't want to see you get burned."

171

"I appreciate your concern, brother." Edgar responded without changing tone. "Everything is fine." He tried to find a smile but only half his face complied.

The apology Shannon had originally set out to give swirled itself into his frustration at his brother's composure. Without taking a moment to calm himself, Shannon pressed on,

"Look Edgar, I know you think I wronged you in some terrible way when we were younger, but I was doing my best with the very difficult situation that I was given. I can't spend my entire life making amends for it. So I'm sorry, alright? It wasn't easy for me either. You weren't the only one who had to deal with those losses, remember? You weren't the only one that hurt. I was doing the best I could."

It was coming out all wrong, and he could neither control nor stop his words. He would wonder later where such barbs had even been forged. How had he not know such feelings dwelled within him?

"At some point, a man has to take responsibility for his own actions and stop blaming the world for every hardship thrown his way. I can't wear the burden of this family forever."

He was no longer guarding his volume or careful of being overheard by the people moving up and down the hall. Edgar waited, wooden, until he was certain his brother was finished.

"I hold nothing against you, brother." He said. "I couldn't be more proud of you, and I'm sorry if I've caused you any stress or any pain." The calm detachment of his words soaked Shannon in regret and embarrassment.

This wasn't how it was supposed to go. Shannon was supposed to be the calm, collected older brother. He was supposed to be the civilized exception in a family of back-wood rednecks. All he had wanted to do was to apologize for the past and open a road to change for the future. But a single pinprick of insecurity had collapsed his entire effort and exposed all his buried pain in a competitive urge. He realized in that moment that he was not the agent of justice he envisioned himself to be; he had not escaped his family's fate, only altered his own perception of it.

He felt like a complete and total fraud. And yet, still, his denial fought against him; too much work had gone into keeping the flaws he viewed as weakness concealed for too long. Those habits had been ingrained in him since youth, and as his brother stood stoic and strong, his instincts demanded he do the same.

He had made a mess of it all, and an opportunity was slipping away. He tried desperately to seize it, fighting to control his ego even as his wounds lay open and vulnerable. But the underlying need to 'win' remained deeply entrenched in his personality and couldn't be simply turned off.

"I'm sorry." The words came out and all he had to do was repeat them once more and leave the seed to grow. The roots would grow strong below the surface, and in time, the healing would blossom. Yet, it wouldn't happen. "I've had a long day, and I'm just really stressed out right now."

Leave it, Shannon, he thought to himself. Stop right there. "There's no reason to take it out on you."

Enough had been said. An amends of sorts was made. Progress.

But why shouldn't Edgar apologize too? How could he just stand there and say nothing – show no sign of receipt? Not even a thanks? Shannon despised that cool composure that hid everything. It was his father he faced all over again.

Edgar stood still and emotionless.

And then Shannon cracked.

"I just wish you would grow up, Edgar, and see that the irresponsibility of your actions affects more than just you." And it was done.

He forfeited that tender opportunity and gave no effort to gain it back. He didn't know why. It was beyond him, and he absolved himself from fault by concluding as much. It was beyond his control. But that didn't help him from feeling terrible shame as he watched the glow dull and then vanish in his brother's face.

Why couldn't his little brother defend himself this one time? If he was really so tough, why did he never once stand up for himself?

"Alright, brother." Edgar rasped at almost a whispered. "I'll see you around."

And as he walked away, slowly, down that long hallway, all the sights and sounds and smells of Shannon's surroundings returned to him as if he had been shaken from a trance. He stood against a wall and wondered why it should prove impossible to

173

make amends for any of it. Then he wondered how long it had taken Edgar to find that glow and whether or not he would ever regain it.

He felt like a tiny, insignificant and petty man.

Chapter 20

"You know I ask myself sometimes, if you were always such a cold, emotionless son of a bitch," Jill told her husband.

She spoke the words with blame and hurt though her rage was winding down.

"I wonder how I could've simply ignored those qualities in you before.

"But I know that's just me being selfish. The man I fell in love with had love in his heart and compassion for mankind."

Her face remained flush and tear-soaked, but she was through yelling. It did no good, and she was tired of wasting energy.

"You talk about your father, how he was impossible to understand. But you have become him, Shannon, and you only think you are so different." Her face soured, as if the words were so obvious. "That single-minded, uncontrollable yearning? The self-destructive detachment? You have it too." Then, her face showed pity, "Only you call it ambition. And it's burned you from the inside out."

She closed the suitcase she had packed hurriedly, without thought and marched out of the bedroom leaving Shannon alone in his final remaining sanctuary; the room they had shaped and shared together; the one place he could always escape what haunted him and safely let his guard down.

He listened to the soft tap of her shoes as her footsteps met the red oak in the hall. The sound vanished as she reached the stairs, but he continued to listen with held breath until the silence ended with the door to the garage swinging open. Every sound, even the silence, was amplified by Shannon's inability to speak, his inability to move, the inability of his usual charisma and bullshit to mask the problem without fixing anything. It was his

174

inability to change, and he realized his wife was right; he had become his father.

Despite all his efforts to distance himself from the Drummond curse, the hands of fate had found him.

But had he really tried so hard to escape his father's legacy?

He looked around him at the picture frames that told the story of their lives, the massive oak dresser Jill had fallen so in love with upon first sight, even the azure color, textured upon the walls. His wife had chosen it for its calming effects.

He had taken such a drastically different route, and yet here he was, with his children downstairs, unable to stop the only woman he ever loved from leaving his life.

He heard the mechanical groan of the garage door rising. Then a car door slammed in the driveway and he listened to the tiny squeak of footsteps approaching through the snow. Jill reentered the house with determination and went straight to work on packing a second load. Shannon had no idea what she packed, nor did he care. She deserved anything and everything for all that she had put up with.

He moved to the railing, where his feet stopped, and he stood and stared helplessly at the front door left ajar. As Jill made her second trip out into the cold December darkness, Shannon's guilt enveloped him and he crept inadvertently down the stairs to the entrance hallway, where he felt the cold winter air blow in like late evening insecurity. It was nearing the dinner hour, yet the night had already blanketed the earth entirely and the streetlights reflected off the carpet of snow providing a slight pink shine to an otherwise vacant world. The temperature was in the teens. The air was thin. The skies clear. Shannon remained in his work clothes, minus the jacket; his tie hung loosely from his collar. He wore no shoes, for he had been in the process of changing when the seemingly familiar disagreement had turned ugly in an instant. The sting of the entering draft pulled him closer to the door where he stood and tried to reflect on the events leading up to this moment.

Shannon had entered the house fifteen minutes prior. The smell of tacos had registered in his weary mind as he made his way to the kitchen where his wife shuffled about opening cupboards and rattling silverware like any other evening. He hadn't kissed her

– tried to remember suddenly the last time he had, as he replayed the scene in his head. It had been too long since he had shown such routine and casual affection, and he couldn't think of when or why such chivalry had abandoned him.

His wife had greeted him with a generic question about his day or work; something along those lines. He hadn't answered. He hadn't even heard her words. Instead, he had retaliated with some snide question of his own: did they really need every light in the house on. It occurred to him now what a silly accusation it had been, being greeted with a bright, welcoming, warm and cozy house and the rising aroma of seasoned beef and perfume. It wasn't as if the money were an issue. It hadn't been for some time. Besides, he didn't need any of it. He would be just as content living in the little house out on Weekender Lane that he had been raised in, that they rented out now but never updated. All the rest was for her and the reflection of success. It occurred to him suddenly how unimportant most things really were to him.

There might have been more, but he had glazed over the details from routine or distraction – whatever reason. He had turned and headed up the stairs to change. Then what?

He was still reviewing these earlier events as his wife stormed past him yet again without so much as a glance. She had an overstuffed bag of the girls' things in her arms and Shannon realized there would be no convincing her to stay. There was a part of him that wished to grab her, match her passion with a firm kiss, at least force her to talk to him, hear his tired excuses one last time. He knew if he spoke them honestly enough, she would hear them differently. She would see that he still existed below the hardening shell. But he had spoken so many insincere apologies and held back true emotion for so long that he no longer possessed the ability to differentiate. He didn't know any longer which he was him and which was an idea he had created, and it wasn't a switch he could turn on and off.

As he stood trying to find some thread of courage, a tiny movement caught his attention, and he noticed his daughters' blonde heads peering out from behind the edge of the mahogany trimmed archway to the living room. There was a flashback to his childhood – his own parents fighting. Strange, it had always been the screaming that had frightened him, but eventually those

176

arguments had grown routine and such emotion had been lost. That eventual lack of response was the blame he had placed upon his father. And now, another generation of Drummond children experienced an unchanging destiny.

And yet, even this night, the missed opportunities had been countless.

She had followed him up to the bedroom. The events of his day had remained heavy on his mind, and he had tried apparently unsuccessfully to pretend he was paying attention to whatever reasons she had come to address him. At some point, she had asked if he were listening, and he had answered that of course he was, without looking up from the emails he thumbed through on his Blackberry. He wasn't ignoring her, only trying to regroup and unwind before being engaged. At least that's what he honestly thought. It was a familiar moment, one he assumed all marriages experienced to a certain extent. In fact, there was little uniqueness even as the mood turned sharply toward anger and voices were raised. He told her she was acting irrationally, pointed out that she was being selfish and childish, but her father's words failed him this time. She wouldn't be appeased. So Shannon had tried to deescalate the feud by taking blame, apologizing, explaining that it had been a long day and he simply needed a few minutes to get settled. But she wasn't buying that either. She told him his generic excuses wouldn't work any longer. She told him that beyond his excuses, apologies and promises, they had nothing left to call a relationship. She told him that their marriage had become an idea held together by joyful memories of the past and doubtful promises of the future. They had no present and hadn't for some time.

Even then, he hadn't fully realized that this argument was any different than others. He knew he loved his wife, and assumed, as always, that she knew it too. They were simply experiencing a very trying and busy new phase in their lives, and he figured she had evolved in her tactic from experience – a quality he saw as admirable.

He tried to explain for the hundredth time that he only worked so hard for her and their family. But she countered with the reminder that he had promised her things would change after the election, and she wouldn't even let him speak assurances that things were slowing down. She cut him off time and again. And when he promised he would have ample quality time for her and the kids very soon, she called him a liar and began to cry.

That's when things had grown ugly. After matching her emotions for a minute or two, Shannon had gathered himself and refused to shout any longer. And it was only after she regained her composure without letting down and began to pack a suitcase that Shannon realized there would be no compromises, that this time was different.

Now, she was telling the girls to put their jackets on and making a third trip to the car. Shannon stood on the cold concrete of the front steps, just out of the driveway's bright spotlight unable to speak. Or was he only unwilling. And in that cold, desperate moment he saw his father's son come full circle, as the cold soothed his bones in the silence.

There were differences of course, as his father would have never worried about what the prying eyes of the neighborhood might witness from such a scene. But it was the same stubborn pride crippling them in the end.

"Darling, be reasonable." He pleaded, quietly, trying to appeal to his wife's unyielding loyalty; her passion for logic. It was effort after all. But it went unanswered. Jill situated the children and moved back to the driver's door, slamming it one last time behind her. Beyond the snow covered lawns, the black streets lay empty as far as the eye could see in either direction, and the silence consumed the world. He fought his pride but wouldn't shout and was swallowed by the same silence that had stolen his mother.

Years of conscious crafting wouldn't allow him to make a scene. So he stood helplessly in the cold shadows, steam bellowing from his lungs, skin goose-bumped, heart pounding. He listened to the caravan's engine as it labored the loaded vehicle back into the cloud of its own exhaust. Then the shifting of cold gears took his family away from him, and the vehicle disappeared down the block.

He remained there, stuck, unable to reason until the motion light clicked off, and a shiver from the pitiless cold forced him back into the house.

Then he shuffled aimlessly through the empty rooms, heat slowly returning to his bloodstream. His mind had become a puddle of confusion, and the energy of his thoughts was lost in his

178

thinking about them, where they came from and what such rationale meant. At one point, he picked up the phone before realizing he had no one to call. He thought of calling Steve Zowiky but couldn't imagine what two grown men talked about in such an hour of need.

He was a Drummond, like his brother and his father before them, and as that admission soaked in, the thought of it haunted him and somehow soothed him, for in that acknowledgment so long denied rested the simple reality that he was who he was and all the running and hiding was unnecessary. He was the Attorney General of the state of Montana. But even if he went on to become governor or the President, he would still be the same insecure kid that lost his parents at a young age and never slowed down long enough to consider the ramifications such trauma might have on his perception of reality. He had thought by changing everything around him on the outside he could escape the ominous sense that some tragic coping would always lay ahead, just around the next corner. But that feeling never went away, for he never resolved what it was inside that weighed him with that burden in the first place.

He poured himself a glass of wine and sat down on the leather sofa in the front room. The light from the adjacent kitchen provided only dim perception of the small, comfortable room he had rarely stopped in.

He remembered only one other time he had sat on this couch, and that had been on an evening his brother had been over for dinner and, for whatever reason, Edgar had stopped here, sat down and simply stared out the big front windows for a long while. It had only been a few weeks after Edgar's return home, and they had just finished a pleasant dinner in the formal dining room. Shannon couldn't recall what meal had been served, or any of the conversations, but he remembered clearly and quite fondly that the tension that had long stood between them had dissipated on that evening, and when he had found his brother in this room, neither had said a word. Shannon had simply sat down beside Edgar in silent camaraderie, and the two had shared a few special minutes in each other's presence.

It occurred to Shannon now that he hadn't spoken to his brother since before the election, since that evening at the hospital.

He had intended to apologize for that incident, but time and again, failed to pick up the phone. He had visited Aunt Dotty weeks later, hoping to run into his brother, but she said she hadn't heard from him since.

That next visit had come on the heels of his election upset, and it had turned into a distracting PR event – even in victory, the local hero finds time for his family.

As if anything could be less true, he thought.

In the month that followed, there had been parties and celebrations, endless congratulations and hoopla, but still his brother stayed away and he was unable to reach out. He needed Edgar to make that first move. He wanted so desperately to hear his brother congratulate him that it embarrassed him.

Eventually he grew petty over the slight and convinced himself it was of no consequence.

In light of this evening's events, Shannon realized how blind he had become to the world around him. He also realized, sitting on that couch thinking back on the moment he had shared here with his brother, the tension between the two hadn't lingered so long because his brother had failed to forgive him for what he had done all those years ago but rather from the fact that he had never accepted that forgiveness. He had never forgiven himself. He had never really tried. Instead, he had simply tried to earn some higher absolution by achieving a level of success that would somehow prove he had never been wrong in the first place. Along the way, he had allowed his ambition to slowly but surely eat up his other characteristics in an effort to burn the evidence.

He set the empty wine glass down and tried to shake free of this type of thinking. He was simply overcompensating. He felt guilty about the fight he was having with Jill and as a result was taking on additional blame. It was only natural to do this in the wake of such a guilt stirring event.

Only that wasn't what was happening and he knew it.

It was quite the opposite actually. A pattern of behavior was showing through, one he had noticed before on countless occasions, and now he was trying to ignore it.

The emotion.

Drown the emotion.

It worked when his mother left, had gotten him through his uncle's death and then his father's; and it had helped him forget the pain and disbelief he had seen in his kid brother's eyes when he had done the most unforgivable act of his life. The night he sacrificed his brother's undying trust and admiration.

Of course, he was sorry for what he had done. He knew this. Edgar knew it too. But he had never forgiven himself. And he no longer knew if there was any way he ever would. Every time he saw his brother, he would see that guilt.

He stared out the window a long time that night, searching for change and trying to ignore the dim reflection he couldn't help but catch in the cold, clean glass.

Chapter 21

Wrapped in a blanket at his brother's insistence, Edgar sat upright on the edge of the cot and watched Shannon pace anxiously back and forth.

The elder Drummond wore the same solemn look he had worn since finding his brother.

Shannon had been pacing for nearly an hour, stopping, now and again, only long enough to check on Edgar, see if he was doing alright and if he was sure he wouldn't go home. Edgar was tired of the questions and refused to answer. Such concern only furthered his embarrassment. At first, Shannon had offered no choice in leaving, calling Edgar's stubborn refusal, bullheaded idiocy and ignorance over and again. He told his little brother that it wasn't courageous to ignore frostbite or hypothermia.

The fight hadn't lasted long though. Edgar hardly argued. But he wasn't about to budge either. He told Shannon if he wanted to go home, he was welcome to do so alone. It was an empty threat, but the message was noble. Mostly, he was just tired and needed rest and warmth. Yet when they arrived back and camp, he refused to lie down until his brother did. He was shaken up and still a bit frightened, but otherwise he felt only drained and numb. The tips of his fingers and toes remained void of sensation. But he didn't need a doctor, he needed his brother. He had him and all would be fine now. His primary sensation was an overwhelming sense of relief at being here, now, with his brother and no longer out there, alone.

The mistakes he made had been his own. This he knew. But he would not compound them. He would be damned before he disgraced his father's memory and the legacy of his family by abandoning the first hunting camp since the death of a patriarch without the brothers getting blood on their hands because he had gotten mixed up out in the family's backyard for a few hours.

Not that heading home would be easy even if the boys wanted to leave. With all the new snow and the way the wind had blown that afternoon, the trail would be impossible to navigate in the dark. Shannon hadn't told his brother, but he had tried the bike in his search for Edgar and found it to be a futile struggle. It would be even more difficult for Edgar to manage such a difficult trek in his exhausted condition. Shannon figured they were pretty much stuck, at least until sunrise. This knowledge was part of the reason Shannon hadn't persisted in forcing Edgar to go home immediately. An emergency exit would likely require a long hike, at least to the truck, and if the wind had drifted the roads down lower, that too may well be stuck without a few days of rising temperatures. It was a dilemma that left Shannon uneasy and uncertain. But at least his relief in finding his brother safe was providing him with some optimism.

When Shannon found his brother, Edgar had been slumped in the snow beside a dwindling fire on the short ridge west of the one they called Windy. Shannon knew exactly how it had happened without having to ask. He figured Edgar had been coming back east across the bottom of the bowl and turned north too soon, climbing the short ridge and mistaking it for the one he had come down that morning. From there it was only a matter of following the ridge up as it ran northwest toward the perpendicular main ridge and Black Bear Mountain on the far side. Eventually, he would have hit the main trail that ran east and west across the next ridge and back toward camp. But somewhere toward the end of his journey, where the ridges flattened out forming a high, flat butte, he had abandoned course and continued due west, away from camp. A solitary knoll had been carved here in the bowl's forming as the original Medicine Mountains' glacier had slid

182

southeast and a creek had run down from the high plain left in its absence. It was an anomaly in the landscape that could fool even an experienced woodsman into thinking he was climbing the steep face of the trail ridge running east and west between camp and the dark peak. The decision left the younger Drummond just south of where that short ridge branched away from the other. In fact, the location of the fire ended up being just under a half-mile from the trail leading back to camp.

It actually may have been a fortunate break, for if Edgar had missed the trail hidden beneath the deep snow, he may well have fallen off the far side and ended up down on the high plains between Haystack and Big Bear. That would mean moving away from camp and the area in which Shannon had narrowed his search. As it was, the flat butte that ran wide between the three glacial carved rises was perfect for pinpointing the sound of Edgar's distress shots and had led Shannon to his brother quite quickly.

Sick with a grief that had grown exponentially since sunset, Shannon had rushed over to revive his brother, only to have him open his eyes upon proximity. The pale boy had then stunned his brother further by standing quickly on his own competence, grabbing his rifle and slinging it over one shoulder. Only then did the brothers embrace, sharing a hug that was full of emotion, firm and lasting, and timed by the boys labored breathing. Words weren't necessary or readily available. That hug had said it all. Following it, the younger Drummond had then assessed the fire with a short, blank stare as if to give the entire tribulation one last moment's consideration, to face what he had experienced and what he had learned; then said rather evenly, "Let's go."

Shannon had brought food and water, and his brother attacked both savagely as Shannon quickly tended to the fire. He spoke to his brother, but Edgar had little to say. It was evident he had cried, and Shannon couldn't imagine the depths of agony such release must have required. In the beam of his flashlight, he inspected his brother against the other's will and found him relatively unscathed albeit frightened and pink with cold and still shivering. His eyes were lusterless, as black and impenetrable as the night that surrounded them and his face wore an exhausted, hollow look. But Shannon examined him thoroughly and found no

183

signs of pneumonia or obvious threats of either hypothermia or serious frostbite, and Edgar shared with him nothing that might confirm his concern nor alleviate it. Whatever thoughts or feelings the young boy had experienced or was having now would be his own and go unshared. Shannon had tried hugging his brother a second time, but his brother hardly hugged back and the feeling of him trembling under his touch shook him with terror and so he stopped abruptly and stood back and watched him uncomfortably.

He had then tried chewing Edgar's ass, venting his concern as his father had always done in a wave of rhetorical questions and harsh statements about preparation and using one's head. Edgar seemed to enjoy the sound of his brother's words, the cadence and volume. But still he said nothing and Shannon quickly composed himself, and with nothing left to say or do they began the long trek toward camp.

It was the darkest night ever known, yet rather than backtrack Shannon cut a sharp path northeast, back onto the open flat and into the thick mess of deadfall Edgar had twice circled through. They traveled through the new snow behind the beam of a single flashlight, and it lit the way white underfoot and cast a blue glow out the distance of a thrown stone. Occasionally Shannon had to stop and judge their direction using his compass and when he did he couldn't help but shine the light back in his brother's direct, and the younger Drummond would stare back into the bright white light without squinting and as his eyes dilated the color returned to them, though they remained haunted and discouraging through the mist of his breath.

During that journey, Shannon felt for Edgar like he had never felt for another before and he saw glimpses of his younger brother from his memories over the years, and in them Edgar was very young and smiling, still so full of hope and faith, and Shannon secretly made a concession with God and the stars above for past grievances. He tried not to imagine what might have been had his brother not been returned to him safely, but those thoughts too slipped in and he was glad at times that his own face was hidden from the light. He didn't know what he would do. He had lost a mother and a father already, and it was unfair, and the strain of this latest incident left him on the brink of a complete and total renouncement of his faith in the world in which they had been

184

born. On the third of such looks Edgar seemed to sense the neurosis swirling in his brother's mind and he assured him he was fine and that was the last he spoke of it; not once did he acknowledge a word about being lost or scared.

When they reached Edgar's bike, blanketed in unmolested snow like some anomaly of nature only recently accepted, they fought it down the ridge, riding double and walking it much of the time, as far as Shannon had made it hours earlier and then Shannon had followed his brother back to camp, pausing each time the poor, worn out boy dumped the bike in the slick snow. It was after midnight when they arrived back at camp, but the sky had cleared overhead and the stars shown down brightly upon the tent like a fairytale ending.

Arriving at their destination had immediate impact on Edgar's spirit. He dismounted the bike, entered the tent and lit the lantern as if returning from any other evening hunt. His calm demeanor helped in easing his brother's fears, and Shannon took a seat on the bent metal folding chair and ran his fingers through his hair sighing.

It was then that Edgar gave the short account of that morning's hunt, jumping the elk and losing their tracks. He spoke maybe five sentences and a long pause followed. Then Shannon rose from his seat and knelt before the stove and lit the fire that he had prepared that afternoon. When he finally asked whether or not he thought there had been a bull with the elk he had jumped, it erased the reoccurring image of his baby brother, his last remaining love, his family, cold, lost and alone, at the mercy of the mountains. Edgar had answered yes, simply and confidently. The trauma diluted, no further attempt was mustered on either's part to rekindle thoughts of a worse case scenario and only much later did Shannon remind his brother of the protocol of being lost: stay calm, think, don't panic, back track if possible and if not follow a creek bed to a river or road, start a fire earlier, stay warm and dry, read the sun or stars for direction, and always remember that nothing in the wilderness will harm you except your own ignorance.

Otherwise, they said little and listened to the fire crackle in the potbellied stove.

185

That night Shannon cooked soup from a ham bone, can of beans and leftover scraps from previous meals. He submerged himself in the preparation, but still the weight of this new scope of responsibilities consumed his every thought. He had become a father when his died but had never considered the true burden of his fate until now. Vulnerability had just never applied to Edgar. He had to be fed and clothed and directed to school and such, but there had never been any real concern for his well being. Such thoughts would have seemed out of place, a waste of time before this day. But now that had changed. It was as if the trauma of this event had created a rift between them even as it drew them closer together, and it left them ultimately feeling somehow more alone even in each other's company. In an instant the vastness of that divide between them had become obvious and yet what effect this new perception would have on their relationship and their lives remained to be seen.

It was early morning now, the darkest hours of the night, and the tent was quiet. In the haze of wood smoke and grill grease, they had eaten as a distraction, without enjoyment despite Edgar's insatiable appetite; then sat beneath the meager light of a single lantern looking anywhere but at each other. Then Shannon had began to pace. The hissing of propane appliances and occasional crackling from the stove broke long stretches of silence as an older brother marked his path back and forth across the tent's dirt floor, struggling to cope with the guilt and stress of an avoided disaster, and a boy too young for such sentiment coped with the shame and embarrassment of having brought these burdens upon his last remaining hero.

Finally Shannon's mind tired and he stopped, and he cut the propane to the lantern. But neither of them slept well in those still hours before dawn.

Edgar awoke countless times in cold sweat from fitful dreams. Each time, the darkness felt foreign, and he expected to find himself alone. He would wait in silence until his eyes adjusted to the dark and find solace in his brother's motionless silhouette and steady breathing. His brother's still profile provided him a sense of peaceful reassurance along with the warmth radiating off the stove. Then exhaustion would overtake him once again. He never remembered the details of those dreams. And he knew nothing of the terrible cries he called out from his sleep or that Shannon lay wide awake beside him, haunted by his brother's struggles, hardly closing his eyes for fear of the visions that awaited him; visions of a curse that couldn't be real, for he did not believe in such nonsense. And yet, he couldn't convince himself of this fact for what felt like the thousandth time in his life.

The moans and muffled sobs chilled him to his bones; the first audible anguish he had heard from his brother in years. Those dreadful sounds brought new horror to the hollow face his flashlight had framed out there on that cold, desolate knob capturing all the torment and pain the family suppressed and suffered, suffocating the hope and optimism he fought so valiantly to maintain. He couldn't understand how despite willfully avoiding each and every pitfall of his family's past, the same fate seemed to find him at every turn. A dangerous resentment was breeding within his soul. With each howl, his jaw clenched tighter and the battle waged forth.

Dawn was breaking when Shannon rose and stepped into his slippers and left the tent for the john, and in spite of his exhaustion and the feeble shape of his psyche, Edgar rose silently behind him as if the previous twenty-four hours had never happened; as Drummond's had always done. There was enough light in the tent for Edgar to find the lantern and he lit it and poured himself a bowl of cereal and sat bathed in the propane glow and ate, half awake and void of thought. The relative humidity had plummeted while they slept and a Chinook raced off the leeward side of Black Bear. The snow was already heavy and water trickled from the trees with the rhythm of a dozen metronomes set at various tempos. The warm, dry air greeted Shannon's sap and smoke caked skin like a visit from an old friend. They were at least an hour and a half late in rising, and the soft lavender of dawn spread quickly around the horizon like a halo as Shannon sat upon the throne and listened and watched and waited for the new day to arrive. His joints ached with fatigue, but the ulcer in his stomach had subsided and a relieved drowsiness washed over him as the spinning of the earth returned form and color to the great mountains. He sat a long time, grateful to be free of the tent, its darkness and the stale air of fear and doubt and guilt. He gave thanks for the sentiments of blue skies and the Chinook which he

187

hoped would decongest the trails, allowing for the option of escape even if it wasn't really an option they were free to choose.

Every few minutes another gust rushed down from the peaks high above, and each one took a little of the early winter with it. Such a wind could change the world quickly. It would have impact on the elks' movement and the boys' attitudes.

But how?

Shannon couldn't concentrate.

He had come here to hunt and to find peace. But troubles plagued him. He had to remember that everything was fine, that this was his sanctuary, the place where troubles could wait. He breathed deeply and considered his father's wisdom, eventually settling upon a relevant nugget he had heard numerous times. 'A man has three seasons to dwell on the problems that invade his life, but in the fall, elk deserve his undivided attention.'

Shannon wondered if his father would say such things if he had faced such struggles. But when he considered the question deeply he remembered all those stories of destitution and suffering that the old timers used to tell without flinching, and he realized those stories had once been trials too and only became easily told anecdotes long after the fact, and he knew that the Drummond's before him had had it just as hard if not worse.

His ancestors had known nothing but poverty and struggle, toiling endless hours in dark holes beneath the earth by candlelight in search of a vein that never paid off and a hope that never lasted; lost limbs, lost fortunes, lost lives. And yet they had forged on. They sowed their seeds. They accepted their existence. Their scars left them stronger, more in tune to the sweet and sorrowful song beneath it all. There was no doubt they were men of a tougher generation; they had to be. The prayers they prayed asked for little more than bread to eat, health to work and the welfare of their family. When war broke out, they didn't wait to be drafted, they volunteered enthusiastically, ready to defend an idea of liberty that had never benefitted them in a personal way. They were men of a different time and era, quiet men, stout and hard. They were men of Edgar's mold.

Shannon wondered now if he would make those men proud.

As the dawn continued and the first rays of the sun bathed the world around him in all its glory, the warmth soothed Shannon's wounds. Birds cawed and sang and somewhere a squirrel gave its first daring challenge of the day. The world seemed to be taunting the earth with the message that no storm could destroy their determination to live and in that courage his mind let go of the darkness: the damp, smoky air and the pleading wail of his brother. Hope was born anew.

A gray-jay hopped around in the canopy above him, cocking its head inquisitively with an erratic, jerky motion.

Edgar had gotten a little mixed up in the woods, but he had been found without harm.

The bird hopped down the branches, ever closer, until it perched just seven feet high a single tree away. There it stopped and watched Shannon with the same impetuous head cocking. Where it came from or what its existence entailed when no man watched were among the mysteries of a great unknown. Shannon remained still and steady, and the bird seemed to wonder if he were part of the landscape.

It was a learning opportunity. Things may have been far worse. He had started a fire and showed his resolve.

Shannon found a few random peanuts left amongst the lint in his pocket and he tossed them at the base of the small pine. The bird spooked at his motion, fluttering his wings rising to a higher branch a few trees back.

Really, the whole situation was a fortunate one. Plus, he had tracked elk to their beds and shown blunt disappointment at having jumped them despite all that had happened. He would make a fine hunter. All would end well.

The bird glided down to the ground beside the peanuts, considered Shannon carefully a moment longer then scooped a single nut and quickly rose again to the closest branch. Just as it concluded all was safe and prepared to dive again, Shannon stood, finished his business and started back in the direction of the tent, sending the bird scurrying off.

Edgar stood waiting beside the bikes in the small meadow beside the tent, overdressed and oblivious to the change in the weather. He watched his brother's approach with the same curious interest as the little bird had shown. Shannon stopped a few feet

189

before him and glanced skyward in a moment of consideration. Then he looked at his brother, and he saw not the burden of his fate, but the tender boy, his own flesh and blood whom he cherished.

In spite of the rising temperature, Edgar kept his chin tucked behind the collar of his jacket, hiding his disposition. As the gaze lingered, Shannon could see that he wanted to turn away but didn't. The elder Drummond smiled, and the result was instant relief in the boy's face. Soon, they both stood smiling at each other in the rising light and warmth of the morning, neither of them daring to move or speak for fear of ruining this moment of peace and release.

Finally, Shannon spoke, "We got a late start this morning." Now it was Edgar's turn to look up and gaze around. He nodded slowly, taking note of his surroundings for the first time, yet said nothing. Shannon knew he would give no response, but he paused regardless. "I don't know how much the elk will move with this snow-eater blowing in. They might bed down." Again Edgar agreed with a single head nod. "Yesterday was a little traumatic for us both." His brother turned away from the fact, and Shannon went on quickly, "What say we spend a day in camp, rest up and recover…we'll get after them bastards this evening when the snow melts and they return to the parks to feed?"

Edgar didn't know if there was a right answer, but he didn't dare give the wrong one, so he stood wooden giving nothing away. Shannon often detested his brother's ability to do this, but this morning it reminded him of those Drummond men of past, their father and their heritage. In the dawn's warm rays it brought them closer together. So he gave his brother a playful shove and he laughed; it felt good to laugh. Then they both laughed. They laughed until Shannon's eyes welled up with emotion he wouldn't allow to breach the walls he had refortified.

"Alright then," he concluded, looking away at nothing. Edgar looked away again too, giving his brother the moment. Shannon wiped at his eye quickly and turned back, satisfied. "Let's get this tent mucked out. I'll make you a proper breakfast. Then I'm going to read a little and go back to bed a while…I didn't sleep too well last night."

Edgar sprung into motion, unzipping his jacket as he moved toward the tent. Noticeably lighter, he went as if a weight had been lifted from him shoulders; the escaping guilt almost visible as the aura about him regained its glow. Quickly, he double-bagged the trash and hauled it across the flat expanse of the campsite some eighty yards, where a tree had been notched for climbing. The trash was hung from the tree more than ten feet high to discourage bears from entering the camp. The second bag helped not only to mask the scent but also added a subsequent line of defense against chipmunks and birds until the garbage could be hauled away or buried. They had never seen raccoons at this elevation.

Next, he organized the wood pile, restacking the logs closer to the stove to replace that which had been burned. Then there was kindling to split, so he choked up high on the wedge and began dividing a dry, dead log continuously smaller. The warm, moist air formed sweat upon his skin.

While Edgar worked, Shannon watched. He couldn't help it. His brother was fifteen years old. It had been too long since he had stopped and watched him grow, too long since he had considered him as more than an unfair burden of responsibility. He rolled back the flaps of the tent, securing the corners to let in maximum sunshine and warmth. The stale air of the night before exited in even exchange and Shannon brought the coolers in to the shade. He closed the valve to the lantern and opened the valve on the large propane bottle connected to the cook stove and struck a match above the burner. The blue flame rose to life and he adjusted the knobs while his brother washed pans in a plastic basin behind him.

Edgar worked in the half-light of the tent's open entrance, and the exaggerated depth from the shadows showed him in full glory. Shannon photographed the image in the permanent base of his memory. He knew then, as he pulled partially thawed elk sausage from paper wrapping and dropped it, sizzling, to the hot surface of the pan, this would always be his family's place, regardless of fate or curses or change. He knew that his father watched over them here and that they would kill a bull before the week was through. He knew these things without consideration just as he knew the future would hold struggles and accomplishments,

191

both hope and heartache, joy and pain, and eventually acceptance and peace. These cycles repeated themselves just like the seasons, regardless of man's efforts and society's change. He knew the old timers were right about these things, just as he knew that he would never understand his brother, whom he loved.

Chapter 22

The opponent waited in the ring as Oliver led the kid across the concrete floor toward the center of the pavilion. Raucous heavy metal with a driving, thunderous bass blared from countless, unseen overhead speakers. Strobe lights flashed across the dark, half-filled Civic Center grandstands. Despite a decent crowd, the floor below the high ceiling remained cool and the air far less musty than the cramped church gym on a fight night. The music had been generically picked for the amateur bout, but the old man knew the kid didn't care. He didn't hear it. He had already been deeply entrenched in his coma of focus ten minutes before they left the locker room. Wherever he went when he went away, he was there now, and the journey back would likely take hours. Like a gladiator forged from the salt of the earth purely for combat, or an archangel cast down for the reckoning, the kid had a way of becoming inhuman and indifferent.

Oliver had witnessed the transformation enough times now to where it no longer completely terrified him. He knew the kid was in there somewhere, compartmentalizing the pain, and he remained confident that each time he stepped in that ring some of the fuel that fed that dark flame was burned. He honestly believed the violence within the kid had to be unleashed in order for him to find salvation from his demons. Priests and shrinks weren't a realistic possibility for some men. Some men's issues were too deeply ingrained. They couldn't talk their problems out. Some men were born warriors.

Still, every time the kid vanished inside himself, Oliver's blood ran cold. He didn't know how many more battles his old heart had left in it. Each fight became a gauntlet for both men. And

Oliver felt his own fate firmly intertwined with that of the kid's now until the end, as if the kid's heart beat blood for both bodies.

Tonight would be Edgar's fourth fight but first real test.

His opponent, a 6-2 amateur from Cheyenne, Wyoming, was a tall, sandy-haired Dane hoping a decisive victory over the 3-0 newcomer would help speed along his quest to turn pro.

It couldn't hurt.

Without any official scouting, Edgar was already creating quite a buzz in the small, rather tight-knit world of regional mixed martial arts. The few locals and hardcore fans that had witnessed him fight in the dingy church gym trumpeted tales of his tools across the pages of internet chat-rooms. Word spread quickly – the Attorney General's Marine brother could fight; not that this was news to any avid wrestling fan from Cork County who remembered the kid's high school exploits.

The kid hadn't faced anyone special, but there was something there that seemed extraordinary. All three of his victories had come by way of early submission. Each copied a patent formula. He shot early and hard, took his opponents down with violent power and choked them out mercilessly. Everything transpired with the sense of predation, as if his opponents were prey rather than competition. None had made it beyond the first round; their feeble efforts to fight back or protect themselves – all futile in slowing the wrath of the wiry young man with the bullet-hole scars who moved like an impending doom.

Maybe it was his uncanny grappling instincts, that natural strength in his hands and fingers. Or perhaps it was the fierce detachment in those hollow eyes that simply beat opponents before the bell even rang.

Whatever it was, it left those who witnessed it with a lasting queasiness and discomfort, as if the carefully constructed illusion of mans' culture and society's safety crumbled at the sight of his brutally butchering opponents with such blunt force and ease. Everyone seemed to agree that he was hard to watch. Yet with each fight, the crowds grew, for the theater of violence was impossible to turn away from.

Tonight's fight would stand to separate the facts from the rumors. His opponent was more experienced, and he would have an idea of the kid's game plan. The lanky Dane would be the kid's first opponent with more than five fights under his belt, and the first with a preferred style of fighting. He was a quick, heavy-handed puncher with four or five knockouts, a history of boxing success and a proven jaw. He had three inches on the kid and even at the weigh-in outsized him by nearly eight pounds.

In the ring, that gap probably doubled. The big bastard was fit and his physique showed it. He wouldn't be intimidated or walk straight into an easy submission. If the kid was to be anything, tonight would be a proven first step.

Oliver knew the striker's strategy would be to take advantage of the kid's aggressiveness, try to land a heavy right-hook or combination before Edgar could tie him up. He would wait until the kid came inside to shoot, and counter his forward momentum with the length of his reach. If he connected, it could be over quickly. If he missed, he would sprawl and hope to keep the fight upright. He didn't stand a chance against the kid if the fight transitioned to the mats.

It was cut and dried. That simple.

They had trained accordingly with a focus on boxing and defending against a striker. Oliver knew that if the kid managed to counter a few punches, an opportunity to shoot would present itself sooner or later. But the kid had to be patient, and he had to be smart, guard his chin. He hadn't shown the same proficiency as a pugilist as he did as a grappler, and the old man chided him in training when he continued to fall back on his chaotic, street fighting instincts. He told the kid that his undisciplined style wouldn't save him forever and promised him that if that if he lost his temper and tried to punch it out with this guy, all the toughness in the world wouldn't save him from a knockout blow.

He hoped the kid had listened.

The lights came up as they entered the ring and the arena stirred with anticipation. Oliver removed the towel from the kid's head and watched his eyes immediately dilate, locking upon his prey as it hopped around shadow boxing across the ring. It was a feral, hungry look, the most primal expression the old man had seen in all his years around hardened men of conflict. Of course, he had seen that look at least a half-dozen times since that first night outside his home, but there was no growing comfortable with it. The look was like that of a mountain lion starved and prodded, then unleashed upon a preschool. Oliver stood before that icy glare and repeated the game plan over and over as he slapped the kid's shoulders. The kid didn't move or flow like other fighters. He was as cold and motionless as a corpse despite all the distractions and anticipation.

"Alright, kid," The old man grumbled loudly to be heard. "Remember, hands up, side to side. Don't let yourself get predictable. In and out, up and down. When you see he's off balance, that's when ya shoot with everything you got."

Then the announcer's voice came over the P.A., drowning out the old man's instructions and the half-tuned Butte Civic Center crowd roared to life with whistles and unhinged shouting.

Two professional bouts headlined the card, but the crowd was louder and rowdier than Oliver had expected. He guessed the attendance to be around fifteen hundred; almost thirteen hundred more than the cramped confines of Sal's gym allowed. They had come to see blood, to see one man humble and embarrass another, and they stomped their feet in rhythm as the fighters were introduced.

The kid was introduced as undefeated local, Edgar 'Irish Eyes' Drummond, and the crowd erupted with approval. Oliver looked around him at the heavily Irish-Anglo crowd standing in ovation and couldn't believe it.

The rumors had definitely spread along the Interstate.

The kid showed the crowd nothing in return for their praise. He was a statue, and yet he wasn't tense beneath Oliver's touch. He was loose, almost calm.

The referee called the fighters to the center of the ring where he gave his final instructions. They touched gloves and returned momentarily to their corners. The bright white light above beat down upon the ring. The music stopped, and the hum of the crowd lulled to intermittent murmurs. All eyes were focused now on the ten by ten square of canvas.

The bell rang.

As the fighters returned to the center of the ring they moved quickly in a counter clockwise direction, hands up, ready to box. Edgar wore green shorts with white trim and moved like bottled nitroglycerin. The taller Dane, in all black trunks, obliged

195

to meet him, throwing a straight left jab as the gap closed between them.

Before the Dane could fully extend his reach, Edgar took a stutter step onto his left foot, touching for only a fleeting moment before delivering a lightening rod left hook against his opponent's inactive right hand, driving both into his cheek. As the force of the blow rocked the Dane's head, the Cheyenne native brought his left-hand back to protect himself, and as he did so received a right and another left that were only partially deflected by the one-inch padded gloves the combatants wore.

Taking a step back, away from the onslaught, the Dane tried to create space with a pair of blind, defensive jabs. But the haphazard attempts came up empty, and as he loaded his weight for a hook, he was left exposed. The kid landed a straight right jab in the center of the Dane's face that noticeably stunned the taller fighter, and the uppercut that followed a split second later, straightened him to his full height. His eyes rolled back in his head and his body fell limp and long to the canvass. The instant his back touched ground, Edgar was upon him, but the ref moved quickly and probably saved the big man's life.

Six seconds.

Fight over.

The crowd lost their minds, not realizing the graphic events just witnessed would stay with them for the coming hours and days, affecting the comfort of their psyche and their sense of safety. For now, that hadn't registered, and the thousand plus witnesses stood and cheered until they grew hoarse and lost their voices. Shrill whistles and screams drowned out the bell and announcements that followed. And after a full minute had elapsed in the wake of the six seconds of fury, the tall Dane in the black trunks remained horizontal with a doctor now standing above him shining a tiny penlight in his unknowing eyes.

But the crowd could care less about this man's well-being. They had the security of not knowing him. This is what they had come for – to watch a crime that sickened them in the streets outside of bars become a sport with two trained and willing contestants under the watchful eye of an impartial referee and emergency medical technicians standing by.

The chant of Drummond began; deep and low, unrecognizable at first.

Drummond. Drummond. Drummond.

The fans chanted slow, deliberate, the decibels growing. The single word of esteemed worship echoed off the high ceiling of the Civic Center and eventually brought Edgar back to the land of the living. He heard the chant and examined the crowd for the first time. The lights had come up, and the scene became a ceremony of homage. They were pleased with him. And this pleased him. He enjoyed hearing his name chanted in praise and approval.

His hands rose slowly over his head, and the chant turned to shrill cheers that only grew more deafening as the crowd erupted all anew. He took them in with a slow three hundred and sixty degree turn beneath the hot lights and found his place of belonging. But it was foreign and overwhelming, and after a short moment in the spotlight, he slunk back to his corner and the safety of the old man's familiarity.

The indifference was gone now from his face, replaced by a very innocent human look that fell somewhere between joy and sorrow. The old man wasn't sure if the kid were about to smile or cry.

"Just had to prove me wrong didn't ya?" Oliver said, only partially hiding the frustration in his voice. "Had to do it your way huh?"

But the kid said nothing, showed nothing. It was impossible to know if he even heard the old man over the deafening roar. Music was playing, but it was indistinguishable from the overall noise.

Oliver embraced his champion in a celebratory hug. The kid didn't hug back, but he didn't pull away either and the old man didn't care. He was used to the boy's guarded mannerisms and felt he benefitted from the sentiment just the same. He used it as a diffusing mechanism, something to remind the kid that he had done nothing wrong, that this was a safe place to exercise his hurt and work out his pain. He was reminding the kid that people cared about him. The boy's tight muscular torso quivered beneath his grasp, and the old man whispered approval and praise in his ear.

The Dane was standing now, with the help of his trainer and a medical assistant, but still appeared unsure of his identity. The referee called Edgar to the center of the ring where his arm was raised victoriously.

"And your winner, by knockout, six seconds into the first round... give it up ladies and gentleman for Montana native son....EDGAR...IRISH EYES...DRUM-MOND....DRUM...MOND!"

Again the crowd erupted, holding nothing back despite the card only being half decided. This time Edgar was ready for it. He reveled in the glory of his accomplishment, recollecting his days as a high school wrestling star still so full of promise. He played it cool, but the ovation would stay with him for days. He would lie down that night and be unable to turn it off. He was known now, and his quiet privacy, the normalcy he had been striding toward would be shaken. But he had found a place of belonging and a skill that brought enjoyment to others without forcing him to be someone or something he was not. It was such a glorious moment, such a chance redemption. It bred hope in his soul, and gave his life that needed purpose and meaning. It saved him, and the old man watched it happen and whispered a silent prayer of thanks for the existence of such a possibility.

Chapter 23

Shannon navigated the busted up 1978 Ford three-quarter-ton slowly through the untouched powder that covered the winding, washed-out rocky road. Edgar sat on the bench seat beside him, staring out the passenger window as the snow fall accumulated on the silence around them. In four low, the old pickup grinded along with steady resolve, its steel studded tires packing the soft surface down and leaving behind the tracks of exploration with a barely discernible crunch. Beneath the grunt of the engine's labored whirling and all the squeaks and groans of tested struts and cold metal, low fuzz produced by the radio's cracked speakers was just audible. It was a country station, one of three AM stations that came in this deep in the mountains. Like a time machine it played the same sad Waylon and Willie songs the boys had listened too while making the same trip fifteen years earlier. Shannon hummed along to the songs as the steering wheel bounced left to right and back again.

The rig's best days were behind it, and Shannon doubted the old Ford would survive too many more trips. But he had said that last year, and he had said it the year before. When it came to saying goodbye to a trusty partner, the thoughts and words were one thing and the doing was a whole other.

The pickup had belonged to their father. Shannon had half-heartedly tried to sell it that first year after Tom's death, when the boys could hardly afford milk for their cereal, but no matter what the offer, he always found it not enough. So he had kept it. It became his truck, and he had handed his Buick down to Edgar.

His brother totaled that Skylark inside of sixth months. But Shannon drove the clunky old Ford for years, clinging to the courage of its determined resolve until Melanie was born and, with two young children, his wife convinced him he needed a vehicle more suitable to kids. Something with room for car seats.

"Besides, citizens don't want to see their elected officials slumming around town in beat up old pickups." She had said, pleading to his vanity in the face of loyal resistance. It was a statement he still wasn't sure rang true.

But his wife was the boss, and so he had bought the Explorer off a neighbor when he noticed it for sale. He didn't even bother trying to sell the truck this time though. He just parked it behind the garage and insured it every hunting season.

It had been a reliable rig for a lot of years, climbing up those rutted out, drifted in old logging roads, hauling bikes, four wheelers, cords of wood and elk carcasses. All a guy had to do was turn the hubs in and give it hell. More than a few times it had earned its keep and the benefit of the doubt in situations where getting stuck meant a solo hike of several miles through less than ideal conditions.

That truck had hauled his grandfather's horses and the boys' motorcycles and outlasted them. By the time Shannon and Jill had been married those old bikes were more problems than they were worth. One or the other was always broken down, leaking oil or impossible to start, plus with the growing popularity

199

of four-wheelers and snowmobiles, more and more hunters were intruding into the Drummond's favorite areas. What had once required a few days for horses was now possible in an afternoon. Not even the deep snow of late season kept them off the trails, and Shannon found himself forced to rise earlier and earlier to stay ahead of the competition. So finally, he had sold the bikes while his brother was overseas and bought a used ATV. The decision had instant impact. With chains on the Ford and the four-wheeler, Shannon was exploring more terrain in a day than the old timers used to hunt in a week. Nothing was out of reach.

But man's growing advantage came at a price. As distances grew increasingly less difficult to travel, hunters were willing to hunt further and further from their backyards. This meant more unfamiliar plate numbers and more pressure on wildlife already feeling the squeeze of civilization's advancing intrusion. Horses had required land and hay, dedication and money to care for them year round. But anybody could park a four-wheeler in their garage, gas it up and change the oil. Suddenly everyone had the means to access the dark timber and remote peaks of the Rockies.

But even as technology was equalizing the means of travel, accessibility was slicing the pie into smaller and smaller bites. The days of sprawling ranchland touched only by cattle were disappearing even in Montana. It seemed small-scale, family ranching was a dying game of too much hard work for too little return. More and more sons and daughters of ranchers were going to college to become bankers, lawyers and politicians. When the ranchers grew old, their life's work, their family's legacy, the success of generations measured in acres of sweat and blood and prayer was sold to a developer or an out-of-state investor with little interest in growing alfalfa or raising steers. These properties were either subdivided or they were outfitted. If they were subdivided, that meant more people further from town. It also meant less winter grazing land, which in turn meant less elk.

If they were outfitted, that meant no trespassing signs hung from fence posts where sign in boxes had once stood. Outfitting typically involved larger properties of prime big game country, and it was a system dominated by the rich, mostly out-of-staters. The hardships of the hunt were replaced by a life of comfort, ease and $10,000 guaranteed success hunts.

Shannon remembered Grandpa Earl telling him stories as a child about the Indians warning his own grandfather that the pioneers' system of permanent settlement and fencing of the land richest in resources, and their obsession with owning the beauty of the earth, would eventually deplete the country of all it had to offer. But in an area as vast and open and rugged as Montana such threats always seemed preposterous. Tom had said as much as an eager and able young man, writing off the stories of his ancestors as the words of tired, bitter old men. But Shannon knew his mind had changed as his years had piled on, and now his eldest son's sentiment too was beginning to change, though he had no sons to pass the ways of the wilderness down to.

As Shannon hummed and thought and reminisced on such unstoppable forces, his brother sat beside him in silence, watching the snow fall and looking neither before nor beyond the moment. Shannon glanced over at his still and sturdy figure now and again, and each time he did it pleased him a little more. He was happy to have his brother beside him, and the pride of being a Drummond had returned to him after such a long absence. Had it taken his wife's leaving to open his eyes? Or had it been Aunt Dotty's death? Was the change in him only temporary or the start of a new chapter in his life?

By the time they reached the trailhead, the morning was well underway. Shannon parked the truck and the brothers stepped out of the heated cab and into the cold, unforgiving world of a mile high winter. The snow was already eight inches deep and a twenty mile per hour wind blew it across the face of the ridge until it fell in all directions. It was fifteen degrees colder here than it had been at five am when Shannon pulled up to his brother's apartment, which put the temperature in the low teens before factoring in the wind chill, and the air was thin and crisp and stung the lungs.

Shannon threw on his jacket, hat and a pair of gloves while his brother went straight to work unhooking the ratchet straps that anchored the four-wheeler in the bed of the pickup. By the time Shannon was ready to help, the machine was free and the ramp leaned on the edge of the tailgate. His brother stood behind the truck in a grease-stained navy sweater and dark green wool pants, struggling to light a cigarette amidst the swirling gale. The sweater had holes all over and the pants had melted orange in places from drying too close to a stove or fire. He wore no gloves and his grimy orange beanie rested above his ears, the point of it swaying south with the wind.

A shiver shot through Shannon's spine, and he couldn't be sure if it was the morning's frigid temperatures or the sight of his brother standing there so unfazed by the full fury of winter's wrath. He was a sight to see; nothing about him out of place here; even after years of absence from the wilderness of his youth, he arrived back and simply belonged as a native species born to the wild and well adapted to such an environment. As he got his cigarette lit, a smile climbed one scruffy cheek and he cupped his squinted eyes in his brother's direction.

"Well," Edgar asked in a gruff voice barely audible through the wailing wind. It was a voice that sounded more and more like his father's all the time. "You gonna unload the bitch, or we going to wait and see if this wind flies us to camp?"

Shannon laughed.

"Put a coat on, you moron." Shannon joshed, feeling as happy as he had felt in ages. He still didn't feel like an older brother yet, didn't know if he ever would again, but he felt like a brother and that was enough. He was in his favorite place with the only man that could ever understand where he came from and why he was the way he was.

But he didn't let the moment linger, for he knew that no good could come from it. He climbed into the bed of the truck, fired up the Suzuki, choked it and backed it down the ramp. Then he left it running while the brothers loaded gear high on either end. By the time they strapped the last bungee down and started out the trail, there was hardly room to squeeze them both on and the gear was already covered in a fresh coat of white. Shannon had to crane his neck around the tent and stove to navigate. Even so, it would take a second trip to get all the supplies and food out to camp, and possibly a third trip for their hunting equipment and clothes depending on the talent of their engineering.

It didn't bother the men though. They were already moving to the less hectic, more natural rhythm of the mountains. It was the rhythm in their blood. Besides, they both remembered the days of packing camp in on the bikes and nothing could be that bad.

As they crept along the trail beneath the monotony of snow-covered pines and firs, the memories of that first camp after their father's death came rushing back to Shannon as if it had just happened the previous weekend.

It had been slow going that season. Edgar had dumped his bike a half dozen times on the way out the trail, banging up equipment and spilling a cooler of food everywhere. Shannon had done his best to take it easy on his brother, but he realized now that Edgar had never truly experienced adolescence or much of childhood for that matter. He had come down hard on him a few times and made the next three trips solo while Edgar waited patiently at camp alone. Luckily, there had been no snow yet that fall, and Shannon had been able to finish the job with enough of the afternoon left to set up the tent and stove before darkness fell. Thinking back on those days, he couldn't believe all that they had accomplished on those Kawasaki 250s. But at the time he had hardly considered any of it; they were just two boys desperate for answers that would never come to light.

He remembered that camp more than any other; every moment, every decision and the few words they had spoken across the wounds left exposed and bleeding in their hearts. He couldn't forget if he tried. And although they never spoke of it, he knew Edgar remembered it as well. It was the beginning of the second phase in their lives; the fall from innocence; though they had hardly experienced more than a taste of that before the salt and blood had grown familiar upon their tongues. Shannon had long forsaken that trip as the start of the downfall of their relationship, but as the echoes and smells played back in his mind, he realized it had only been a gut check, and it was his response to the mounting pressure and his refusal to face reality head on that had truly severed the inherent bond between brothers. After all, Cain had slain Abel; Shannon had merely kissed a girl.

Two miles in, half-way up the knob of the third ridge, the four-wheeler high centered and the men were forced to dig it out and chain it up. It took them twenty minutes to do so, and by the time they started again, another inch of snow had fallen. The depth of it now covered the tires to the center of the rims and the trail was only visible as the width of a particular distance between trees. But it was soft and without form as the wind had yet to have enough time to compact it. The metal of the chains' loose links jingled against one another and slapped hard off the fender as the tires chewed their way through the unstable substrate. Even with the chains on, several spots required repeated runs to bust through, and by the time they reached the campsite the gear on the machine's rear rack was caked in two inches of frozen crud.

The storm clouds were low and dark and gray. The snow continued to fall and the wind continued to blow. The meadow where the Drummond men had made their elk camp for three generations was an untouched field of white surrounded by ageless pine, the boughs of which shook and whistled and whined in the wind. The snow was knee deep over the hidden flat where the boys would assemble their shelter. Still, the thought of turning back or bagging the trip never crossed their minds.

It took the men half an hour to dig a spot out for the dimensions of the tent and another hour to get it up and tied off. When they had finished and the ridgepole was tied off and the tent was stable, they stopped and shared a moment of tired satisfaction, huffing and panting in the cold thin air as they stepped back and contemplated the fruit of their labor. This would be their home for the next five days and nights, and the bleaker and harsher the world around them grew, the cozier that tent looked. With ice hanging from the stubble of their faces, they shared a smile and a few heavy sighs, then went to back to work with a sense of pride and growing satisfaction. After the stove was in place and the stovepipe straight, Shannon headed back out the trail to grab another load while Edgar went to work falling a couple standing-deads with the chainsaw. It was a harsh and dangerous environment; winter; deep in the highest, most remote mountains of the continent. But the Drummond brothers operated without doubt or fear, more comfortable in this setting than that of the civilized world they had left behind. It was a Saturday, but the date hardly mattered. For the next few days all that mattered were dawn, dusk, fresh tracks and well placed shots. They had until Thanksgiving before the responsibilities of Shannon's job would drag them back to town. It had been one year since he had won the election, and this would be his first true vacation. Yet he had agreed to help dish out Holiday meals at a food bank – though secretly only to see his estranged wife who coordinated the event –

and thus couldn't take the full week off. Edgar too had promised Krystle he would be home to carve the turkey, their second together.

But between now and then, only hunting and companionship mattered. Five days of quiet solace. Five nights of solitude and solidarity. Ten hunts if they managed one this evening. But tonight's hunt was the farthest thing from Edgar's mind as he busied himself sawing fallen trees into ten foot logs and dragging each back to the camp where he blocked them to saw again. Despite the cold and snow, a sweat broke on as his brow as he worked and smoked, and by the time Shannon returned with the wedge and the rest of their gear, his younger brother had thirty stout logs cut in two and a half foot intervals ready to be split for the stove.

After they had moved everything into the tent and set up, Shannon spelled his brother on the firewood and Edgar sat on a log to rest. The snow had slowed but never stopped, and the old canvass tent was already coated in white. The wind too had died down, and the ridge grew quiet. Only the consistent crack of the axe falling upon its target echoed down into the gulches where it was deadened and lost. Edgar lit a fire in the stove and started stacking the split wood beside it in the corner of the tent. As smoke rose through the stovepipe and collided silently with the falling snow, the sky around them continued to darken without ever having shown light.

Shannon noticed the subtle changes as he set the ax down to catch his breath. His back ached and his body was fatigued and stiff from the day's expenditures. He decided they had enough wood split for the time being. He broke trail to the spring and filled water jugs from the twenty year old pipe, then returned to camp and took a seat outside the tent on a log and stretched his hands open and closed. His body had adjusted to the temperatures, and he had actually removed clothing layers as he had labored through a half a cord of firewood.

To rest felt good. As he watched the smoke dance from the stove pipe into the cold atmosphere, he realized this was the first time all day he had stopped. He glanced at his watch: two and half hours until dark. It had been a long day. It wouldn't be easy to get a hunt in.

His brother appeared, pushing aside the flaps of the tent, and Shannon noticed the bottle of Jim Beam clenched in his left fist. The sight of the bottle gave him a momentary discomfort, and he looked his brother square in the eye. But Edgar didn't seem to notice. He sat down on the splitting block across from his brother and unscrewed the cap from the bottle and took a long pull. Shannon could smell the bourbon over the snow, sweat and smoke. After his swig, Edgar wiped his mouth and offered the bottle without taking his eyes off the tent.

"No thanks." Shannon replied with the wave of his hand. Only then did Edgar turn to face him for the first time.

"Shut up and have a snort." He insisted. "You've earned it."

Too tempted by the second invitation, Shannon obliged him, taking the bottle and tilting it to his lips for a short pull. The warm liquid burned like fire in his throat. He coughed.

"There you go." Edgar laughed a deep, hoarse laugh, taking the bottle back. "You know, my old lady has me playing the sobriety card more and more frequent lately," He said, pausing for an ironic swig. "While I admit it keeps a guy out of trouble, still can't figure why sober folks think they've figured out something so damn special." He coughed and spat and wiped his mouth with the back of his sleeve. "Like dying of boredom is so much more honorable than a lifetime spent treading water." Shannon wasn't sure what his brother meant. He didn't want to know. But he took his turn again on the bottle all the same.

They passed it back and forth like that for a couple minutes in silence before Edgar set it, uncapped in the snow beside him and searched his pockets for a cigarette.

"It's been a long time," Shannon broke the silence, "since we've been out here together."

The bourbon coated his empty stomach in a layer of warm discomfort, dulling the focus of his eyes and lowering the voice of his internal dialogue. His brother nodded in agreement, and they both stared at nothing as the smoke from Edgar's cigarette rolled off the glowing end, stinging Shannon's nose and eyes. They sat that way for a long moment as waves of time lapped upon the shores of their perception. So many hunts they had taken out here. So many memories; so many experiences.

As the bourbon sank lower and lower in the bottle, their tongues loosened and they began to speak more openly.

"You know I'm sorry right?" Shannon asked, pulling the statement from nowhere.

"Yep." Edgar answered simply and yet with a degree of certainty and finality. And this time, Shannon left it at that.

"You know," he went on. "I've really gone and fucked my life up."

He didn't know what response he had hoped for in return, certainly not pity, not from Edgar, not now or ever. But still he felt the need to share the statement. And his brother simply listened as he finished his smoke, tossed it and took another short swig from the Beam.

"I used to hate Dad for letting Mom leave. I blamed him. I mean I blamed her too, but I could forgive her because I never needed her for much as the years went by. She became this ghost, this idea I guess, and the less I thought about her, the more pious and without fault she got in my head, I suppose... But Dad was still around and he was unchanging and stubborn even as everything else changed around him. I guess that always pissed me off, like he wasn't trying, or he refused to explain anything he did or why he did it. I needed explanations. I needed someone to talk to."

He faded off a moment and glanced over at his brother who had began to build a fire between them with the scraps hacked from the split logs. Edgar didn't seem to be listening, but when Shannon stopped he stopped what he was doing and looked up. And in his eyes Shannon saw something that convinced him to continue, "My marriage...I mean my family...Jill and the girls...they are all that ever really mattered, and yet I never could give them the one thing they ever asked for."

He reached for the bottle as the tears welled in his eyes. "The same way I could never give it to you...And I wonder sometimes if this is my fate? Our family's curse? Or if I simply tried so hard to understand our dad that...I don't know..." A single tear broke free from his eye and collected grime as it rolled down his cheek.

"I tried so hard not to make the same mistakes with my own wife, my own kids."

He stopped there, leaving his thought hanging, refusing to go on unless his brother agreed to at least the premise of the conversation.

Edgar seemed to sense this and after a moment of pause found words.

"Do rabbits exist only to feed predators?" It was a strange statement and so far off topic that Shannon suddenly thought his brother must be quite drunk.

"I mean, were rabbits put here merely to feed other animals?" Shannon realized his brother was trying to make an analogy. But he wasn't accustomed to metaphorical speech, particularly from his brother, and he was unsure of what Edgar was trying to express. He listened intently all the same through the fog of the bourbon and the continuous silence of the now passing storm, just happy to be sharing something honest for once. Edgar went on, "And for that matter, why do so many animals hunt the rabbit and depend on it as prey, while nothing preys upon the wolf or the bear except man?

"Did God decide these relationships or did they come to exist on their own and God simply refused to alter them?" He stirred the fire which was beginning to crackle and expel heat and held a log above the growing flames without adding it.

"You could spend a lifetime pondering such questions, and all you'd get back would be more questions that arise with each answer. Why are we here? Are we forsaken?

Life is difficult enough just living it. It's best to leave that other shit to the philosophers and priests, the men of books…That's why I love it out here… Because none of that shit matters out here.

"What you see out here is what you get. Don't bring that shit out here."

Edgar dropped the log on the fire and watched the flames lick and grow around it. Shannon let the words sink in. The words were a glimpse inside his brother's mind, a mind he had always found so guarded; one that he had never understood. It made sense that his response to Shannon's most honest confession ever shared would be veiled in metaphor and open to interpretation.

Shannon was taking longer pulls from the bottle now and feeling drunk.

208

"You know," he murmured, "I've tried so hard to escape our upbringing and avoid the risks and pitfalls I saw as responsible for damning those I'd loved growing up. And yet here I am, all alone, having failed my own marriage and children, hunting the same mountains that haunted our father and his father."

"You're not alone, brother." Edgar corrected him.

They sat in silence again no better or worse off. The wind had died down and the shadows of the trees grew long as the sky began to show itself to the north already palely lit by the rising moon. And then the call of geese could be heard approaching. They sounded far off at first but then appeared overhead minutes later as dark arrowheads chasing the storm across the twilit sky. Shannon watched them with jealous wonder. But it was Edgar who spoke,

"Cowards." He spat. Then he lit a cigarette and turned away.

And when the lively migration had passed and the honking faded off and the sky fell dark and only a few stars showed themselves, the fire died down without anyone offering to feed it, and hunger and cold forced the men into the shelter of the tent.

Chapter 24

The persistent caw of a raven awoke Shannon from his nap, and he rose lazily from his cot to find a chipmunk searching the dirt floor for scraps.

One flap of the entrance had been tied open, and the tent was well lit by the sun, warm and welcoming. There was still heat radiating off the stove and a neat stack of split wood replenished beside it. Smell was the first sense Shannon was aware of, mixed scents of the pine drying, and the smoke-drenched canvass walls and the sour reek of wet boots and socks and body odor. Given enough time at camp, the sweat and the smoke became second nature; the nose grew dull to such familiarity in search of new stimuli. But those smells were always there and especially evident upon awaking, stiff and sticky, coated in dirt, soot, sap and layers of salt from the sweat of long hikes in altering temperatures; there as a reminder of the length of one's stay; the lengths to which a man would go in pursuit of his maddening desire to fill his tag and stock his freezer. Only Shannon was not a man. Not yet. He was still a boy, young in years. But that fact did nothing to change his situation or lighten the weight of his responsibilities or desires.

He stretched and gave a yawn, causing the chipmunk to dart off. He felt both rested and relieved and yet he knew if he didn't get up now he could easily fall back to sleep in the cozy calm of the tent. His brother lay sound asleep below him on his tarp, fully dressed, still and breathing peacefully. He looked young and vulnerable and ordinary, like any other sleeping boy. He looked like a sleeping boy should look, and Shannon watched him for a few short moments and he smiled. The previous night's predicament felt long ago and embellished, all but forgotten; the impacts unknown and far away.

He checked his watch. It was a quarter after one. He climbed to his feet and began to move about without a clear purpose, intentionally causing a stir. He had slept heavy, and he awoke slowly, sore and more aware of his body's condition and his mind's fatigue than he had been that morning. He sniffed his pits and winced and then dripped dish soap in a pan of water and set it on the stove to warm. Then he poured himself a cup of water and sat down and drank. He refilled his cup three times and still his thirst felt unquenched. He stretched his neck and rubbed his eyes trying to shake off the cobwebs of exhaustion. Finally, he forced himself back on his feet and found a rag ripped from an old t-shirt and dipped it in the lukewarm liquid and cleaned his face and neck and pits and behind his ears. Then he washed his hands thoroughly and put the same shirt back on. There was fried chicken in the cooler, and he pulled out a breast and sat back down on the rusted folding chair and ate it and gulped down half a Mountain Dew. After his snack, he pulled on a sweatshirt and stepped into his slippers and ventured outside to piss and assess the day.

The wind had tapered off and the afternoon was calm and beautiful with a deep distant blue in the sky beyond the canopy of the secluded glade. Sparse wisps of high, white cirrus ran across the epic arc as reminders of distance and time. The chinook had done its work and gone, and yet the ridge was still warming under the glare of an enormous sun. It was a gorgeous break from the previous day's gray and the world was abuzz with the sounds of life and the bustling activity of winter preparations. Anticipation seemed to sing in the crisp mountain air. Shannon shaded an eye with his hand and took in the sweep of his surroundings with greater attention to detail. There was little snow left on the trees. But the ancient pines and firs and spruce that mingled indifferently in that high, steep country seemed apathetic to the momentary relief. Shannon knew better than to think the warming trend would be anything long term. The sun wouldn't climb any higher, and he expected with the clear skies and a vacating pressure system the radiant heat would rise up the mountain that evening and cooler air would rush in to replace the void. He expected a much colder night.

He turned his gaze south where the highest trees were set ablaze in orange brilliance. The sun lit the earthy tones of the wet landscape, creating a spring-like feel. Yet the shrubs were bare and the shadows were already climbing the timber on the north face of the adjacent ridge. In a few hours the sun would fall quickly toward the western peaks off in the distance beyond First Ridge.

Shannon wondered for a moment how many others, like them, were out there in all that terrain, scouring the timber with their obsessions and silent solitude. The mere thought of these imaginary men succeeding out there stirred his soul and focused his mind. As the raven beat his wings forcefully and circled the campsite high above, Shannon sat down on a stump and turned his focus to that evening's hunt.

It wasn't long before he heard Edgar rise behind the canvas wall that stood between them, followed by the crackling of the plastic chicken container Shannon had left out on the card table. The hinge of the cooler squealed then the lid fell shut and a moment later his brother joined him in the sunshine, half-dressed and dirty, chomping on a drumstick. He had the can of pop his brother had opened in his left hand and gnawed at the chicken bone in his right. When he finished he tossed the bone absently into the brush. A spot of grease glistened on his cheek. Something in the air seemed to surprise him and he considered his surroundings for a moment before draining his drink and crushing the can and tossing it the direction of the fire pit where it fell short, silent in the snow.

211

"We should get going soon." He said, and Shannon nodded in agreement.

Edgar stood a moment longer then disappeared back behind the wall. Shannon turned his thoughts to the elk his brother had jumped the previous day and contemplated where they might have gone. It was crazy given how many elk there were in these mountains to worry about one small group or another, but it couldn't be helped. Those elk were more than just a hypothetical, more than the ghosts he had been chasing. Then again, if they were jumped they could be anywhere by now. It was hard to guess at the behaviors of spooked elk, like guessing at the actions of desperate men. And there would be little hope of tracking them in the melting snow. Besides that he didn't want to go to Windy Ridge. He wasn't ready to face those memories. That left pretty much everywhere else. A blessing and a curse. The country was simply too vast for two boys to hunt alone, and yet the mere thought of sharing it made his blood boil.

He had to concentrate.

Where would a bull elk be at dark?

With nothing to go on, it was a guessing game, as much luck as skill. And he longed for a hunch or gut feeling but found none. His mind couldn't seem to fall in sync with the pulse of his surroundings. But he was growing closer.

They had tried down low and seen nothing. With the recent snow more truck hunters would be out in the valleys pressuring any herd that remained bunched and brave lingering between the foothills and hayfields. Those elk often filtered up through Pickett's Gulch and spilled onto the parks along Camp Ridge and Six Point. But he couldn't visualize them there and his mind wandered on unconvinced.

He wanted to stay high. Despite his lack of success he liked the sign he was finding north of the main ridge. Big lone bulls seemed to like it up there, and he liked the odds of running into one by poking around Haystack Hill long enough. It was so wide open and with two guys they could better cover the expanse of the whole park. There was still a lot of snow in the timber, no reason a bull wouldn't take the chance to come out and feed where the wind had cleared the long grass.

How to hunt it though? Should he show Edgar his honey hole or send him out the trail along Prospector Ridge?

Mid-thought, Edgar came out behind him in his patched, dirty orange coat ready to go. He had his snow cap on and his heavy gloves though the temperature remained in the forties. His chin was tucked into the collar of his jacket and he looked impatient, awaiting his brother's instruction. His presence forced Shannon from his indecision. The elder Drummond swore aloud and shook his head in last second deliberation, before finally climbing to his feet, anxious and rushed. Haystack Hill it was. He would have to choose their hunt once they got there.

He went in the tent to grab his gear while Edgar waited outside. The afternoon light glowed bright on the canvass, and he found those mingled scents of the smoke and grease and wet wool somehow less unpleasant. In fact, now fully awake, the clutter and the smells and the other quiet signs of camp life gave the twelve by fifteen feet of shelter a sense of belonging that had long been absent. He gave his temporary home away from home a final once over and checked his pack to ensure he had his flashlight and other essentials. Then he grabbed his rifle and checked the chamber, clicked the safety and slung it across his back. He closed the flue and filled his water bottle and exited the tent, zipping the flaps closed behind him.

"You on safety?" he asked his brother.

"I don't have one in the chamber." Edgar answered.

"Better take a second to check just in case."

Edgar did so, opening the bolt on the Savage and insuring that the chamber was indeed empty. He showed his brother to satisfy him. Shannon winked, and Edgar smiled.

"Where should we go?" Shannon asked though his mind was already made up. Edgar cinched his brow below the curve of his beanie as he gave the question consideration. Before he could answer, Shannon bailed him out, "What do you think about Haystack Hill?"

"You were there night before last." Edgar remembered. "Did you see any sign?"

"Not much." Shannon admitted. He was proud of his brother's inquiry. "But I haven't seen much sign anywhere and that

213

doesn't mean a bull won't come wandering out on that big park tonight."

Edgar agreed with a nod. "Think we can get out there on the bikes?"

"Should be able to. At least as far as Prospector Ridge. That chinook gobbled a lot of snow this morning.
"If you see any drifts remember to squeeze through the timber just off the trail."

Okay," His brother said. "Meet at the trailhead atop Prospector Ridge?"

"Okay." Shannon replied.

The younger Drummond climbed on his bike and kick started it to life. The roar of the two-stroke shattered hours of tranquility and yet added to the growing sense of stability. Things seemed to be returning to normal. As if there was such a thing. Shannon expected his brother to let him lead but wasn't surprised when instead Edgar tore off across the meadow, kicking up mud and slush and vanishing into the trees.

The ride brought him further bliss as he emptied his mind of everything but the trail, the terrain and the image of a bull raising its horns in the waning twilight upon Haystack Hill. The images of glory swelled his heart, and he rode with familiar bravado, proud to be a Drummond once more. He raced over tree roots and climbed hills through the slushy snow, sliding his rear tire back and forth.

The ground had hardly thawed and the travel wasn't too bad, and he guided the machine with grace and skill bouncing along the rutted out trail at high speeds as easy as a child might skip down a sidewalk. He wore no helmet, nor did his brother, neither ever had. It wasn't a skill issue – Shannon probably dumped his bike now more than he ever did as a kid. He rode it so much harder. No, it was ignorant habit, competitive masculine valor, like most poor decisions they made. Even Shannon, the cerebral Drummond, wasn't immune to the treacherous clutches of the family's bravado. It was in his DNA – the freedom, the independence, the love of all things untamed – part of his identity. As he tore across a familiar stretch of loose rock without a second's hesitation, his thoughts turned to his younger brother again, the courage of a fifteen year old boy to press on after the trauma the previous night's experience. Shannon knew Edgar would hunt alone again without hesitation and the pride in his belly radiated outward. His brother was a hunter and a Montanan of the purest kind, and those labels would define him as they had defined their father and his father before him. That is all he was given and it was what he had left. He clung to it dearly.

As he pulled up alongside Edgar's waiting bike, the craving for conquest rose in him suddenly and without warning as it had only a few times before. He felt no shame in that desire. In fact, it brought him more pride, more lust, and he shivered with excitement. Enough time in the mountains had a way of shedding the bulk of one's emotional needs, but this meant the more primitive emotions were left sharpened and exposed. His brother may have been more clearly shaped in the hardened caste of Drummond men, but it was this relentless yearning that was their lasting legacy.

Tonight would be the night. Tonight, he would kill.

He knew this in a way that couldn't be possible. He knew it in his bones. It was the hunch he had been waiting for and it hit him hard. They would be in the right place at the right time. He would be in the right place at the right time.

As he climbed off his bike, he could barely contain himself. The intuitive, reckless urging he had long chided his family for consumed him, erasing all the harbored guilt, doubt and insecurity. He couldn't understand any of it, and at the moment he didn't care. He noticed his brother watching him and thought his look felt more particular than usual. Maybe Edgar could see the change in him, or maybe he felt it too. Maybe it was something in the air or the weather that triggered a chemical change in them.

He cocked a cartridge in the chamber and re-clicked the safety, prompting his brother to do the same. He spoke a few final words of encouragement and then the conversation stopped and they were off. Boots swishing in the soft snow.

It was still early, a lot of daylight left.

It was probably too early.

No, it was never too early.

Shannon marched swiftly along the trail, slowing only now and again to consider a detail or particular that seemed worth another look. He backtracked slightly away from the bikes, circling

215

around the ridge, crisscrossing his earlier hunt. His tracks from two days prior were barely detectable where their paths crossed and new tracks of squirrel and grouse and hare checkered the slumping snow. There were deep craters where snow had fallen from trees and deer sign and a paw track that Shannon guessed to be feline, probably a lynx or bobcat. The pressure system that followed the storm seemed to have everything on the move and they walked away from the sun, noses to the wind, as the daystar moved across the southern sky, two boys in search of understanding and the meaning of something pure in the form of a reclusive, extraordinary stag somewhere on the steep, rugged spine of the world's final continent. Its last frontier.

Their path took them through mostly mature lodgepole, almost limbless to fifteen feet or more with sparse canopies. A few patches of spruce grew high along the ridgeline, and all about, the vine-like stems of an unfamiliar berry bush that seemed to flourish in the moderately tight timber here coiled above the snow showing its remaining leaves in the yellows and reds of fall. By staying on the top bench within sight of the ridge and the peak beyond it, they remained in the direct light of the late afternoon as the shadows climbed the steep, V-shaped gulches below. In the distance, the vast, flat valleys stretched out toward massive unfamiliar ranges that sat upon the curve of the earth dark and blue in the cold tint beyond the sun's passing reach. The crimson rays crept slowly away toward the south, yet the pivot fields would remain bathed and beautiful until the orbs topmost bow dipped below the highest western crag of Black Bear Peak.

Shannon had walked passed his blazed trail to the lower, hidden bench, but he kept its orientation in his mind and worked his way down slowly to where the noisy woods' rose gave least resistance into the drainage. When he knew they were close, he stopped and debated the next move. In his mind, he still saw a trophy bull, feeding across the hillside park at Haystack. Edgar waited beside, him his carbine held waist-high before him in both hands. Buck brush and bear grass grew rampant on either side of the dry draw they straddled.

Shannon could see that last night's episode had changed the boy, awoke something in his awareness of the mountains and of hunting and of manhood. There was a new attentiveness and maturity about

216

him. But Shannon knew they should stay together. It was too soon for him to be alone again. He didn't know this hunt well enough. But the bear grass got so noisy down below that it would be hard to stay quiet. He checked his watch. It wasn't even three. They would be waiting a long time on the park if they kept along the ridge.

"Do you know how to get to the park from here?" Shannon whispered, slightly ashamed and avoiding eye contact.

Edgar nodded, pointing up the hill and in the direction they had been moving. Shannon raised a naked hand to his chin and fell back into silent consideration. His deliberation lasted nearly a minute.

"Alright," he said finally, no longer quiet enough to be considered a whisper. "I'm going to drop down into the timber here and work my way around below the park." He pointed in a general direction south of their position. "You stay along this bench. It's better hunting then up along the ridge.
"When you get to the park, stay tucked back in the trees but find a good spot where you got a lean and can see the majority of it. I'll plan to sit below you on the far end.
"If you see me there, or it starts getting dark, slowly work your way up through the edge of the timber so you can check that upper meadow. There is good feed on it, and sometimes they come out right at dark."

Edgar gazed into the timber, envisioning it all. He nodded slowly.
"Dad showed you that upper meadow before right?"

Edgar nodded again.
"Do you think you can get there?"

Again, he nodded.
"Okay. You just stay right along the edge of the timber moving up that hill." Shannon repeated. "You can't miss it. It's only about a mile. A lot of times they'll feed out on the far left where it bottlenecks or hang back and feed right in the timber off the park. Be ready, use your binoculars, and move slow. There is no rush."

Edgar nodded.
"Okay." Shannon looked at his brother directly trying to think of anything he had left out. Edgar was looking away, and it gave him the opportunity to extend the length of his inspection. He debated his decision a moment longer.

217

"Alright buddy," he said and he smiled but his brother's face remained wooden. He wondered what his brother was thinking in that moment but realized he would never know because he would never ask and Edgar would never tell.

"Good luck."

Neither of them moved at first. All that went unsaid hung heavy in the thin mountain air. The temperature was dropping as quickly as the sun but their breath remained unseen. Finally, Edgar slung his gun and started off deliberately up the hill through the brush. Shannon watched him go and felt goose-bumps form on his arms. Something was going to happen. He could feel it, and he knew now it wasn't just the sentiment of the previous night's scare. He was going to shoot an elk tonight.

Almost giddy again, he moved down quickly through the thick, noisy brush in search of the hidden bench below. Any guilt dissipated quickly and anticipation hastened his step. He hadn't walked fifteen minutes when he came out amongst the open firs. Another quarter of an hour and he found exactly what he had been wishing for: a big lone track came up out of the gulch below, hit the bench and headed east toward Haystack. At the sight of the track, he froze and looked all around until he was satisfied the big bastard wasn't out there looking back at him, and then he knelt to better examine the track. It was a big track: wide, deep and deliberate. It had to be a big, lone bull. His heart pulsed harder, and his brain kicked into full alert. He could see the old monarch easing along, watching, smelling, listening; hungry and taking care to choose an open path with plenty of room for its massive antlers.

He brought his rifle to his hip, the barrel directed out in front of his feet, and slowed his pace to a systematic stalk. His hands were steady, his movements smooth and silent. He was a confident predator – a natural killer.

This bull was right out in those firs in front of him. It was just how it had been for his father the afternoon he first discovered the bench. Shannon would bet his dirt bike this bull was heading for the park too. He couldn't be more than an hour behind it. Either he would kill it in the timber or his brother would shoot it coming out on the park.

He hastened his speed slightly.

218

The track meandered left to right and back again, sticking to the open timber. The shadows had climbed to the lower edge of the bench. Whenever the track edged toward the hill, Shannon stayed low and tried his best to gain ground without getting caught. The ground was dry in places where tufts of mountain grasses, still vibrant green and waxy had soaked up the melting snow. The walking was quiet and easy. The track veered down off the bench rather sharply, surprising Shannon, and he stopped and checked his watch again. It was only four. Still a few hours until dark. It occurred to him that this bull may have traveled along this bench in the morning and bedded down somewhere amidst the snarled pine and nasty brush below. Impossible to know for sure. But he didn't believe it. This was a big bull, and it was coming up out of the bottom of the gulch heading for the park at Haystack Hill. He just knew it in his gut.

He decided to sit down for a minute and have a snack, give his brother a little time to get to the park and get set up. He had a granola bar in his pocket, and he pulled it out and ate it and then unzipped his pack slowly and removed his water bottle and drank while considering his next move. It was hard to sit still. His adrenaline pumped.

At a quarter after four, he couldn't sit any longer and started after the track again. He didn't follow it down off the bench though. He stayed high in the big timber, keeping an eye on the steep slope to his right. But when the track went further down, he had to do the same to keep an eye on it. As soon as he got off the bench, he was in the shade of the peaks behind him. The slight breeze shifted and blew down into the gulch. Shannon knew there was a spring down there and a couple wallows. He had seen them before. But he wasn't that familiar with his current surroundings, and he knew it got thick before the bottom. Eventually, he found himself doing exactly what he hadn't wanted to do: following the track down through a draw into the thick lodgepole, noisy brush and windfall. He lost track of the bench and meadows above it leading out to the park. He was hunting desperately and he was letting the elk set the terms.

As a branch snapped, he stopped again. It was nearing dark, and the bull would likely be on the move. If it didn't sense a threat, it would feed toward the park. He should climb straight back up and wait. The breeze was almost unnoticeable down here, but he knew it was swirling and that this elk would use it to its advantage. An unnoticeable breeze to humans could be enough wind to bust an elk at over two hundred yards. The problem was that he knew he would have to cross out in front of the track to get on the far side of the park. If the bull crossed his track that fresh, it would bust him for sure. The gig would be up. The second guessing and self-doubt was driving him crazy. It wasn't like him.

He decided to stay on the track and just ease along.

The sun had passed over the ridge behind him, and the gulch grew dim and mysterious and quiet. He was moving at a crawl now, choosing the path of least resistance carefully and stopping constantly to look and listen. The silence made his ears ring, and he thought he heard noises that probably weren't there. No squirrels or birds seemed to reside down here in the earliest shade of the day and the deeper he dropped the crunchier the snow grew.

His optimism was sinking fast. But then his luck paid off, and the track began to climb, still moving steadily away from him, away from the sun. The entire time he had been on the track, the elk had never bedded, shit or pissed, and Shannon was no closer to guessing how old the track was than he had been an hour earlier. But now he smelt it. Dank and strong. A bull elk. Distinctive. The stink left over from a long, hot rut.

He knew he was close before he even saw the pile of droppings still steaming with the sprinkled about piss unique to the male of the species. He checked his scope to be sure he had it dialed down for the dense timber. He had about a hundred yards of visibility in places, as little as forty in others. The subtle breeze continued to shift back and forth, and it was growing darker in the timber. He knew the moment was close at hand. He also knew from experience that the difference between returning to camp having been elbow deep in elk blood and heading to bed frustrated beyond console could be a fraction of a second. An inopportune twig snapping or aiming just a half inch high or low.

He crept further up the hill scanning second by second for the tiniest movement, a glimpse of that off-white looking slightly out of place. He knew his brother was somewhere out there just

220

above him. If Edgar was set up across the park he would have every advantage. The odds were set in his favor.

But Shannon couldn't resist. He crossed the subtle bench and continued right into the bear grass and buck brush pressuring the track carefully. The last of the small meadows was just a few hundred yards further between the upper bench and the open park. If only he could ambush that bull before it fed out in the open. This was his last conscious thought before he caught a flash of elk hide in the timber.

It was just a flash. A microcosm out of place. But even through the tiger stripes of dying light and dark shadow it registered in his brain, causing a chemical reaction, the release of a wave of neurotransmitters that were quickly snatched up by the receptors of adjacent dendrites across the synaptic clefts. As he raised his rifle he estimated the shot at sixty yards, but that was only a guess made in a fraction of a second. He saw the white tips of horns, tall and wide, as a head turned away from him and he saw the dark eye as he locked the stock's butt against his shoulder. It took less than a second for his muscle memory to sync his eye to the scope but then another second or two to find hide again. Four seconds total from the instant he saw the critter to the moment he framed it in his crosshairs. But the bull had seen him first and taken two or three steps in that time span. There were trees and shadows everywhere. All Shannon saw was ass as he gently squeezed the trigger.

Even in the heat of such a moment, Shannon didn't jerk. He had learned early on that Drummond's never jerked.

As the eruption of man's technological advantage tore through the wilderness, the ungulate reached top speed. A commotion of panic rose. The rifle tracked its movement from right to left as it fled west away from the park and the source of the thunderous explosion and north up the ridge toward the security of the dense timber. Shannon saw only flashes of the majestic beast as he smoothly rotated the bolt toward his shoulder and cocked in another shell without taking the scope from his eye. Boom. Another report rung out at over twenty-seven hundred feet per second and still the prey crashed through the timber without the slightest deliberation of a path. This wasn't the silent bounding of a

221

deer, but rather a chaotic and noisy exit through any and all obstacles. Limbs snapped and hooves thundered.

Boom. Another shot; three in all; smooth, quick and rhythmic but without avail. Then the rifle fell silent as Shannon raced in pursuit of the fleeing bull. He could hear the heavy body crashing through the timber over the pounding of his pulse. But the muffled clap of hoof beats was already growing distant. He ran hard with everything he had jumping logs and ducking branches powered by the adrenaline pumping his legs. But he was no physical match for the powerful strides of four churning limbs, reverse jointed for efficiency and speed. The bull was born to run, and it crested the ridge before Shannon could reach the open and crashed down through the dark timber and into the gulch beyond.

Shannon followed the dirt clad tracks far longer than was probably practical, mostly out of duty and anger, disbelief at having an opportunity like this slip through his fingers. His pace slowed, but he continued to run, lungs burning, panting, refusing to face his failure even as it stabbed him below his ribs and pounded against his eardrums.

Finally, he stopped, fell against a tree and heaved for oxygen. The snow was much deeper on this side of the ridge, and the darkness set a violet hue all around.

"Fuck," he swore aloud, spitting the thin saliva and mucus from his dry, chapped lips. The word tore through the tense silence that followed the discharge of every firearm.

It had been a nice bull. Of that he was certain. He wasn't sure how big, but he knew it had not been small. Maybe he had hit it. It was possible. He wasn't that far away even for thick timber. He hadn't seen any blood in his pursuit, but that didn't always prove anything. He searched out the track, found it and followed it a little further, investigating with his flashlight. The trail was white and brown without a hint of red.

Who was he kidding?

He didn't hit anything. He had screwed up. He had rushed through noisy bear grass and woods' rose following a track he knew was headed directly for his brother. The bull had heard him, smelled him. It had seen him coming. His mind searched for excuses as he hiked back up the ridge. There was no guarantee that bull was going to come out on the park. Certainly not before legal shooting light was over. It might not have come out until after Edgar had moved on to check the upper meadow.

Shit.

It was his brother's bull. He had selfishly sent his brother off to the park to protect his honey hole and then stole an elk right out from under him; stolen it from his family. Even if he had shot it in the timber, it wasn't the right way to hunt it. Edgar would have heard the shots loud and clear. He was probably headed in Shannon's direction. Shannon worked at the details he would share in the retelling of the hunt. There was difficulty in deciding how honest to be. There always was.

He reached the crest of the ridge and realized the sun was only now beginning to set. There was still thirty-five minutes of shooting light left on the parks. The timber had deceived him. He hung his head and headed east to meet his brother.

Chapter 25

It was just after eight on the first Sunday evening in September and the wide, deserted street was bathed in the crimson glare of another beautiful, late summer sunset. The near horizontal rays collided with the dry-grass foothills that lined the gulch to the east and west. It was the transition time bars and taverns experienced in the evenings that time of year, just prior to the commencement of the NFL season, when even the dawdlers of the after work crowd had gone home, but before the true night owls could afford to be out. Playoff baseball hadn't started. Not that anyone went to bars to watch playoff baseball anymore.

The twilight lingered long and the wind eased. The hatch was probably just starting on the rivers. It was the first weekend of bow season and hunters were already rationing their vacation time and sick leave, forfeiting their spare summer social hours in a compromise with fed-up wives.

That left Shannon all alone crossing the vacant boulevard. But it didn't stop his nervous glances all around. The occasional breeze blew down from the mountains and across the valley, unable to muster enough momentum to be a bother, and yet with enough bite to serve as an early reminder of winter's rapid approach. There were thick, fun clouds overhead to catch the light in various shades of purple and gold, and the moon was out early to administer these colors' slow meander across the sky.

Shannon had parked the Explorer in a rear lot above his old office three blocks away and taken an odd roundabout loop to approach his destination from the opposite direction. It was an action he had performed without prior planning; a subconscious attempt to be diligent and careful, although if anyone *were* monitoring his activities, his path alone would appear quite condemning and prove awkward to explain.

The evening was cool, yet certainly not cold. The temperature had dropped eight degrees since five o'clock but now held steady in the mid fifties. The leaves of the young maples that lined the sidewalks were only just starting to lose the dark boldness of their green. They grew from black iron hoops that had protected them as young saplings, and although they hardly needed the safeguard any longer, Shannon's daughters would be his age by the time those trees reached full maturity and shaded the street with stout branches overhead. By then, their roots would begin to buckle the concrete slabs of the sidewalk, and the city would stifle their growth, hacking their branches and exerting control as if the trees had chosen that ground and it had been only through the act of man's mercy that such chance had been deemed tolerable.

The Attorney General was dressed casually this evening in blue jeans and a maroon Montana Law sweatshirt. He wore a faded navy baseball cap tucked down fairly low on his head, another decision that could probably create the exact kind of suspicion he hoped to avoid. As he reached the far sidewalk he stopped beneath the awning at the bar's entrance, hesitant as he always was being so unnatural in this demographic of the world. Except for a short stint following law school, Shannon had never spent much time in bars. He never found much use for them. In the framework of his psyche, such establishments had always conjured images of his family's failings and hardships, places where a man's problems were compounded and his secrets exploited, even as he was lulled into a false state of comfort and camaraderie by the sweet nectars of sin.

224

Yet as he had climbed the social ladder, he was amazed to discover it wasn't the habit itself that condemned men to their outcomes and judgment but rather the specific location of their indulgence, the company kept there, and the effect alcohol had on their disposition. This realization had boggled his mind. He decided he lacked whatever specific skill set was required in differentiating those who gained from participation in the art of social inebriation from those who would be labeled more harshly as drunkards, and thus he had abandoned the political strategy of cocktail hour before his career ever really got underway, and as far as he could tell the decision had never really impaired him.

As he stood indecisively outside the heavy oak door, he tried to assess the bar's inhabitants through the small rectangular windows on either side of it, but the room was dim and the glass too opaque from smoke and grime to gauge any particulars. This left him little choice in the matter as he saw it, so he mustered his resolve and grabbed the brass handle ready to accept his fate. He found the grip sticky to the touch and almost gagged. This dampened his confidence, but he managed to maintain his resolve and opened the door and entered the establishment wearing an air of superior disdain that was now impossible to disguise. Not that he tried very hard to hide it. He saw no need to. There were only a handful of patrons in the joint, and the majority of them didn't even look up from their drinks, busy as they were projecting an image of abject misery that any artist worth his or her sand would revel to capture.

The bartender, leaned on the near end of the rail reading the newspaper, gave Shannon a quick nod of recognition then went back to what he was doing.

All at once, the sour, pungent odor of the room gave Shannon a slight head rush, and he found himself wondering why anyone would pay money to hang out at such a vile and depressing establishment. He drew a cocktail napkin from a stack upon the bar, wiped his hands and tried to avoid eye contact as he made his way toward Grisham's office.

Toward the back he passed the usual crowd of Grisham's goons, perpetually stuck as they seemed to be at the card tables, smoking and drinking regardless of the time of day as if the parameters of the outside world were irrelevant. They watched him through the tainted eyes of men who had seen the veil of idealism pierced by abusive fathers, crooked civil servants, deviant priests or teachers that had simply given up on them, and had exchanged the optimistic lies of their dreams for the more realistic materialism of cash in hand. In their haggard, half-drunken smiles, Shannon thought he felt their delight in seeing yet another supposedly unsoiled, high-ranking man of the system come to beg for a handout from the puppet-master pulling all the strings behind the curtain.

"Is Mr. Grisham in?" Shannon asked trying to hide the rising taste of shame on his tongue, pretending the visit were an unplanned, random occurrence, as if he had simply been in the neighborhood and decided to stop in on an old acquaintance.

But nobody bought his bullshit, and the only answer he received came in the form of a few indifferent head nods and the jerk of a thumb in the direction of the hallway. These men saw through his ploy. They just didn't care enough to call him out. Besides, no one could do anything to change the system. Everyone who wanted something was in the same boat. The rules exempted no one. The only difference was that those who benefitted from the arrangement were obligated to play along; while those who didn't bitched and moaned to help themselves sleep at night. That's how things had always been here and how they would likely always remain.

Still, Shannon felt the heat rise to his cheeks as he swallowed his pride and continued down the clean, well-lit, tile hallway to the closed office door, where he stopped and took a deep breath before knocking.

"Yes?" the door responded with a grace inconsistent to everything else around it.

"It's Shannon." He said low but firm, glancing back down the hallway and into the murk one last time as if speaking his name aloud here was to commit a grave crime in itself. But no one was there to watch his fall. No one cared. And for a moment he couldn't decide which was worse, the continued habits of transgression his own life followed or the fact that no one else seemed remotely interested enough in the grand scheme of things to put a stop to such behavior from their elected officials. He heard the sound of a chair squeak beyond the door followed by the slow rhythm of oxfords clicking against the tiles. A final admonishment flittered through his thoughts: character was defined as what one did when no one was looking.

It was so true. The first time Conrad had told him this quote, long ago, Shannon had felt a numbing cold momentarily paralyze him, for he knew not only the profound truth in the statement but just how accurately such an assessment summarized his own insecurities. At the time, he had been unable to distort or rationalize the ugliness of his character on only a couple occasions, yet since then he had done everything in his power to hide the malicious nature of it. Everything except make amends to change it. And worse, he had since used that quote on numerous occasions in the company of the young and idealistic believers in transparent democracy.

As the door opened, and Grisham stood before him, crisply dressed in cream slacks, white collar and black jacket, smiling as sly and subtle as the devil himself, Shannon sincerely wished, if only for a minute, that his true character could be exposed to the shock and disgust of all and the whole massive system of interconnected deceptions crumble before one more innocent person could be hurt by the greed and ambition that had so often tarnished the truly successful at their core.

But there was no such miracle, and Grisham invited Shannon into the room with the charm, grace and ruthless cunning unique to those possessing a competitive ambition far greater than any guilt or shame could ever overcome. And although Shannon had always held firmly to his disdain for Grisham, before this moment, he had secretly respected such unsympathetic single-minded determination and taken smug satisfaction in his failure to age. After all, Conrad was Shannon's idol, but he had always seen Conrad's nature and virtue as being unobtainable. Grisham on the other hand was just as intelligent, refined and successful and yet far more powerful; less susceptible to the oscillations of societal drift. For while the burdens of the world's plights piled upon his father-in-law's broad, righteous shoulders, curving his spine toward mortality's grave and rendering him more and more helpless to outcomes in the world around him, Grisham remained a fixture, in charge and in control, never changing, immortal in the scope and impact of his actions.

Or so Shannon had long thought.

But now, for the first time, he noticed the signs of stress in the old man's composition and tried to recall how long it had been since his last visit. It couldn't have been more than three months. But had his hair been so thin then? His eyes so deeply sunken? His skin so loose and pale? His stature so meek and frail?

Shannon thought not. This man, who had long served as the model of consistency in his eyes, refusing the hand fate dealt him time and again, even as the passage of each brutal winter dealt heavy blows to everyone and everything around him, had suddenly aged a lifetime in a few short months. Grisham still carried himself with the same class and confidence, yet some factor of the power and intimidation that had always stood front and center was missing, and in its absence Shannon saw his own lonely, wretched reflection. And it terrified him.

"Please sit." The old man instructed as he did so himself. Shannon obliged. And when they were both seated, Grisham opened the dialogue, "How are you my boy?"

"I'm well." Shannon said bluntly. Though he used such frivolous filler in his own meetings, he was fully aware of its purpose and it irritated him now that he sat in the position of inferiority.

"And those pretty girls of yours?" Grisham continued, watching Shannon's face closely for any sign of a tell. Shannon had never spoken a word of his separation to the old man, but he was well aware that Grisham knew his life in great detail, as he knew everything, as his kind of scum had a hand in all things, everywhere and always.

"You wanted to meet," Shannon cut the bullshit. "What about?"

Grisham laughed, or tried to, but as he did so he had to suppress a coughing fit with his handkerchief, and Shannon stole the upper hand for a moment.

"Always straight to the point," Grisham said, collecting himself quickly. "Like your brother in that regard and your father for that matter. No time for chitchat with a Drummond. Just work, work, work."

Shannon maintained his poker face and waited.

"We have a problem," Grisham said, breaking eye contact in an unusual lapse of authority. As he glanced momentarily away, toward his desk, Shannon was allowed rare opportunity to examine him more closely. He was a rather small old man when viewed beyond the veil of his reputation and the hypnotic control of those carnivorous eyes and the soothsaying voice, and Shannon wondered suddenly how this man had possibly come to hold so much power without resistance for so long. But the thought was a fleeting one, for as Grisham's gaze met Shannon's once more, the quick pierce of fear returned, and Shannon remembered it was in that look and the total absence of compassion, that the promise of death to all who opposed him was vowed. All at once the old man vanished and only those piercing yellow eyes of clarity in purpose and swift action without mercy remained.

Shannon shuddered to think he had buckled under the harsh gaze of those eyes so many times. But he also felt a rising pride in his father, who Grisham openly admitted had never been swayed by either himself or the allegedly more brutal Zeke before him.

"The problem is your brother, Shannon." The statement was unsurprising. It was a fact Shannon was dealing with more and more. Plus, Edgar was a trump card Grisham had been threatened for some time now, whenever Shannon refused his favors.

Still, it was odd coming so directly, without first asking for anything in return, especially from this man, who had coddled Edgar and excused his reckless behavior for so long.

It made no sense to move directly to the threat without asking for anything first. It wasn't Grisham's way, and Shannon felt a new uneasiness set in as he waited to hear more.

"As you know, your brother has been running a business of some repute in the canyon for some time now. Whores, high stakes poker, some minor gun running." Shannon was well aware as Sheriff Gale and Grisham had been leveraging exposure of the business for two years now. "I've always let it slide because quite frankly it was always small potatoes. It never cut into my business much, as I've never been too interested in the hillbillies of the canyon, and it never seemed to distract your brother from his responsibilities here – on the contrary, having something of his own actually seemed to motivate him and keep him focused, and at least occasionally, sober."

"Plus it's served as pretty useful blackmail more than a few times." Shannon interjected, trying to maintain a reasonable sense of honest transparency in regards to the narrative. Grisham paused, raising his eyebrows in surprise at Shannon's sudden courage. Shannon, too, was caught off guard by his own blatancy, and he warned himself internally to be more careful.

"Regardless," Grisham winced with evident annoyance. He straightened himself out before going on, "the problem is your brother's little operation has grown significantly larger, and I'm afraid he's grown a bit too big for his britches."

"And what would you like me to do about this?" Shannon asked, immediately ignoring his own warning. "You don't really think I would have made all those deals with you to keep this under wraps if you thought I had any sway over my brother's activities did you?"

"If you interrupt me again, I'll cut your tongue out, set it on this desk and let you stare at it while I finish." Grisham replied quickly, with cool force that was a little too calm for comfort. A vein bulged in the old man's forehead, and Shannon swallowed hard.

"As I was saying," Grisham continued. He lowered his voice, but he was clearly ruffled and dropped the nice guy act. "Your brother is becoming a liability and a dangerous one at that. And, he has to go, Shannon."

"What?" Shannon asked incredulously.

"Your brother needs to be killed, Shannon," The clarification was spoken more bluntly. "And I'm asking you to do this for us."

Grisham took a small sip from the coffee mug on his desk while the brevity of his words set in to the man across from him. Then he returned the cup to its coaster. The weight of the silence seemed to linger endlessly.

"Normally I would do this myself, but as you know, your brother is a bit of a hard boy to pattern. He has no habits, no schedule, no wants or needs. It might get a little messy, and that could lead to a long drawn out ordeal, negative publicity…possibly open warfare…innocent people could be hurt."

Another dramatic pause.

"I don't think that's what anyone wants.

"Do you want that, Shannon?"

But Shannon couldn't speak. He felt dizzy and fought the sickness climbing from his stomach toward his throat.

This had to be a joke.

He wanted to get up and walk out on this madness but found himself unable to move. His ears began to ring, and he felt faint.

"I didn't think so." Grisham pierced his lips and nodded in acceptance. "The second option would be to bust his place in the canyon, make a high profile arrest...or more likely kill the bastard and make it appear that he resisted. But this too causes me some unease.

"I don't exactly see your brother going peacefully, and his little club up there is pretty well fortified.

"A shootout looks bad even when it is police sanctioned and that'll surely bring federal agents sniffing around... Besides if he was killed in a shootout with police that would look pretty bad for the Attorney General and even worse for his chances at making a run for the Governor's Office in a few years." Grisham leaned forward and the crow's feet around his eyes tightened as his chair squeaked. "That is the ultimate goal, isn't it Mr. Drummond?"

The old man was saying everything but the truth. The naked, obvious truth: that he had evidently grown afraid of Edgar.

Shannon suddenly realized he had no idea what his brother had become. He had become so caught up in his own life and his problems with Jill that he didn't realize his brother had become some kind of rival linchpin in the local criminal community. How had he ever let it come this far?

He had to clear his mind and listen intently, knowing the deal was about to be offered.

"Option three would be that you take care of this problem. He is after all, your problem too."

"You can't possibly be serious?" Shannon cried.

The old man brought his palms together, tapping his pointer fingers momentarily before his lips. Then he went on.

"Now, I know such an idea might seem particularly inhumane, but I'm certain that if you give it some somber thought, you will see the advantages of this unusual predicament.

"First and foremost, he trusts you. You can get close to him, closer than anyone else anyway. You can insure that the job will be done quickly and without great suffering on your brother's part – a promise that I can't make with the other options…"

"Are you really asking me to kill my own brother?" Shannon interrupted, unable to stop himself. Even as he spoke the words, it sounded insane.

"Not exactly," Grisham grimaced slightly in the face of the inquiry's bluntness. "Your brother, Shannon…he's already dead. "I'm giving you an opportunity to show him mercy. Consider it a form of euthanasia. Didn't you once support such legislation?"

"This is madness." Shannon blurted, pushing back his chair and rising quickly to his feet. But his legs were wobbly and his entire body quivered. "I refuse to even discuss this any further. I can't believe you would even discuss it. And if you try to murder my brother I'll…"

"You'll what?" Grisham dared him. "Huh? What will you do?"

"I'll warn him! That's what I'll do! And then, and then… I'll go to the feds and I'll tell them everything I know! I'll take us all down!"

The door swung open and two of the larger men from the poker table were in the room. They grabbed Shannon by either arm. Shannon struggled, but he couldn't free himself. "Let go of me!" He shouted.

Meanwhile, Grisham rose calmly and smoothed his hair, regaining his composure. One of the goons kicked the door closed behind them.

"You will do no such thing, Shannon," Grisham said, his voice returning to its conversational tone. "Do you really think I'd leave such a decision in your hands if I didn't know better? "When your brother first came back, and he showed up here, drunk, broke, beaten… near death. He told me that you had nothing to do with each other, that your relationship had been severed years ago.

"Now, I never did get him to divulge what grave travesty had broken your brotherly bond. Even in his darkest hours he wouldn't cave on that. But it must have been something terrible. For I've never seen darkness quite like that which lies deep within that boy's tortured soul…and I've seen some tortured souls in my day, Shannon." As Grisham spoke he clicked his way slowly around the desk until he stood directly in front of Shannon with nothing between them but the grip of the two burly goons.

"Whatever happened between you two… it killed your brother, Shannon. He's not the quiet kid you remember. He is a murderer, Shannon. He's carried out acts so brutal, even I have to look away… So don't you all of a sudden start playing all high and mighty on me." He straightened his back and flexed his neck.

"It's a difficult task, Shannon. I know it is. A heavy burden. But we all must make our sacrifices." He put his hand along Shannon's cheek, and Shannon looked away but only for a moment. "If you pull this off, I'll make sure everything you ever dreamed of is yours. Money, vacations, power."

"Fuck you," Shannon spit. "You might as well kill me right here, right now, you piece of shit. I'll never hurt my brother."

"Oh yes you will." Grisham sneered.

"You know we're a lot alike, Shannon, you and I. You might not like to hear that, but someday you will see and you will understand that sacrifices are required for those who will rise up and lead in this world.

"I used to think your brother took after your Uncle Marvin and that you had somehow escaped the family curse all together.

"You didn't drink or fight or gamble. You seemed to lack that illogical, obsessive quality of your people. But if there is one thing I've learned about you two these last few years, it's that Edgar was built in the stubborn image of Tom Drummond, and you Shannon, you are the reincarnation of your Uncle Marvin." Then his face suddenly grew very stern again, and his labored breathing wheezed as he gritted his teeth. "Let me make this a little more clear to you, Shannon. You're not going to warn your brother and you're sure as hell not going to throw your entire life away by turning yourself in. You're going to take care of this problem for me, for us, and you're going to do it before the close of the year."

"And if I don't?" Shannon grit his teeth defiantly.

"If you don't, I'm going to kill your brother anyway." He smiled. "I'm going to torture him for hours and leave nothing to recognize… And afterwards, I'm going to kill you, and your pretty wife Jill, and then I'm going to wipe your seed from this earth."

"You son of a bitch! I'll kill you with my bare hands!"
Shannon tried to attack with everything he had but couldn't escape,
and Grisham laughed and the gold of his crowns glimmered under
the fluorescent bulbs. It was a hideous laugh, pure evil. Then he
punched Shannon hard in the stomach. The blow knocked the wind
out of him but did nothing to dull his hate.

"I wish it wasn't this way, boy. I like your brother. I like
him a lot. But like I said, he chose his fate. Now you must choose
yours."

He punched him again, hard in the midsection, and the
strength he carried surprised Shannon greatly despite the situation
he was in. He stopped struggling and hung limply in the two men's
arms and pulled his head up until his eyes met Grisham's. Still, he
said nothing.

Finally, Grisham turned from him and walked slowly
around the desk back to his chair.

"You know, I'll be gone someday, Shannon.
"Someone will have to replace me." He wrung his hands in
unsatisfied contemplation. "I had hoped that man would be your
brother. But now, I know I picked the wrong man." And then he
smiled that devil smile. "But perhaps I only picked the wrong
Drummond?"

Chapter 26

It was a couple hours before dawn, the morning prior to
Thanksgiving, and Shannon hadn't slept. His brother had risen a
few minutes earlier and he listened while Edgar stoked the stove in
the dark. With his eyes still closed, he heard the loose hinge on the
iron handle squeak as the stove door opened followed by the
forceful loading of split pine logs and the crackle of the hot coals
slowly spreading fire to new fuel. He turned on his side, let his
eyes half open and watched his younger brother, all grown up, as
he sat in the dull glow of the stove.

He knew he couldn't do what he had come here to do. He
had known all along. And yet he had put those thoughts off time
and again and said nothing. But now, after several days of silence

and nights without sleep, he felt like someone other than himself, like a powerless observer watching his life unfold. He watched his brother add a branch of red needles to the growing fire and the surge and crackle that followed. He continued to watch silently as Edgar placed the percolator on the flat top of the otherwise cylindrical stove. He watched him stretch and spit and scratch at the crotch of his baggy old long-johns before taking a seat in front of the growing fire and gazing into its flame. Then the words just spilled forth.

"You know this will be our last trip out here."

Edgar turned slightly on the stump on which he sat to listen to words that had already been spoken. Then he turned back toward the now crackling fire and coughed.

"Why do you say that?" he asked.

"Because you have to leave after this." Shannon answered quickly, his hidden eyes misting with emotion. "You have to go away from here, and you can never come back."

Edgar didn't turn this time. In fact, he showed no surprise at all. He just stared into the dancing orange glow and rubbed at his whiskered chin.

"I don't think I'll do that brother." He answered, simply; as usual, his voice giving nothing away.

He tilted his head back slightly as he spoke, stretching his thick neck tight, and his words vaporized as steam. Then Shannon watched his silhouetted profile become a clear face momentarily as he leaned forward again, stirred the burning logs with a branch, and then closed the stove door, his image fading away. A rising wind howled against the canvass walls as the tent fell dark.

"You have to Edgar." Shannon spoke across the cold void. His eyes adjusted quickly to the dark, and he could see the tent now in growing detail. He swallowed hard but never hesitated, "They'll kill you."

It was a harsh, terrible statement and the words came out so blunt and bold, just as they had felt rattling around in his mind for the past several weeks. And then as if to make sure he had spoken and not just thought the statement, he said it a second time with more direct certainty, "They're going to kill you, Edgar."

Edgar didn't even offer an argument. Nor did he ask of whom his brother spoke.

235

He just sat there still as a statue, and the darkness fell quiet and calm beyond the fire sucking fuel from the pitchy wood and another ruffle of the canvas walls. And in that moment's silence, Shannon was certain once more of how real all of it was; for the first time since that night in Grisham's office, there was no ignoring reality. He wished his brother would ask him how and what he knew, coerce the story from him. But he didn't.

The percolator came to a boil, and Edgar stood and removed it from the stove. He set it on the table and lit the lantern that hung from the ridge pole. The new lantern burned propane, and it hummed low and steady as the pale light and the noise seemed to end any chance of Edgar easing Shannon's burden. Edgar poured himself a coffee and sipped it, and Shannon rose from his cot and joined his brother near the stove as heat returned to the tent and his body adjusted to the chilly conditions outside his sleeping bag. Their breathing became less visible with the passing minutes, and they sat in their long underwear, turtle necks and wool sweaters eating cereal from paper bowls and drinking coffee from tin cups the same as they always had. Shannon thought about the past and how nothing really changes. He thought about his girls, how much he loved them, and he thought about the state of his relationship, if he would ever win his wife back, if their relationship could be salvaged. Then he wondered as he had done constantly in the past few weeks, how his life had ever come to such turmoil.

After they ate, Edgar pulled his wool pants and jacket and gloves from the rope above the stove where he had hung them the night before and dressed without bothering to check if anything was dry. Shannon stepped into his slippers and unzipped the tent flaps to take a piss.

There was no moon and the world was black, cold and desolate, but fairly calm. Only occasionally did the wind build up from a lower relief, far away, and charge across the ridge, and when it did you could hear it in the trees approaching from a great distance, rising up, gathering strength and then rushing off in the direction of the approaching sun. Like the dark, the wind was cold and had a bite to it. But Shannon had grown acclimated over the past week and he stood against it hardly flinching in his long underwear and sweater.

Only the snow interested him. It had snowed since their arrival, not hard, but consistently, and even their tracks to the spring and the john from the night before were decently filled. Shannon shined his headlamp all around and guessed another two or three inches had accumulated overnight. Not much, but when there was already two feet on the ground, every bit might mean the difference between making it back to the truck on the four-wheeler or hiking out.

The snow had stopped for now, and the skies were clear. The stars shone by the thousands, bright, yet tiny against the black expanse of the universe. As Shannon pissed, he watched the hot urine burrow into the blue surface, down and down as steam rose. Still, he never saw the earth. The snow was that deep. He didn't know how one man would get this camp out. But he could worry about that later. Packing out camp should be the least of his concerns. He had enough to worry about this morning. He knew his life was about to change forever. This was no time for considering the hardships he would face down the road. This morning would be the most difficult of his life. His responsibility was inconceivable, and he tried to think of anything else, yet it was impossible.

He knew what must be done. He had put this obligation off too long. He knew Edgar wouldn't hold it against him. After all, it was Edgar's own doing.

He took a deep breath of the cold, thin mountain air and watched the smoke he exhaled slowly. Then he returned to the tent, drank another cup of coffee down to the dregs and dressed, trying to clear all thought.

"It must have snowed again all night," he told his brother.

"Not much." Edgar countered, scratching at his greasy scalp and yawning.

"If the wind blew any harder last night than it's blowing now, we won't make it out the trail very far."

"Then we'll just have to fight our way out as far as that Jap sumbitch can make it and hunt from there. It's not like there's a bad hunt out here."

Chewing and clawing and rocking side to side and back and forth, the four-wheeler made it further than Shannon ever expected. A few times, they were stopped but able to reverse out of the drift, back up and hit it again with more speed and break through. Then just before the rise at Windy Ridge, he buried the machine in a long, drifted open saddle and high-centered it to an instant stop. The wheels spun and spit snow for a moment, but it would go no further. From here, they would hunt by foot and travel wouldn't be easy. It was still twenty minutes before legal shooting light. Edgar pulled his leg around his brother and hopped off first, sinking knee deep on his first step and nearly losing his balance.

"Looks like we'll be hunting Windy Ridge this morning." He said, removing the slung rifle from his back. He held the weapon before him, inspecting the frosted barrel in the lights of the four-wheeler. He batted the frost from the gun then gently fingered the snow from the lenses of his scope.

Shannon refused to believe this cruel twist of fate. He throttled the gas a couple more times, and the engine wailed as the chained tires spun helplessly, but the machine failed to budge.

"Shit." He whispered. He climbed off the machine slowly and stood in the deep snow examining the situation and considering what it meant. Then he turned to his brother. It was still ten to seven, and Edgar was already loading snuff in his lip. He stood watching his brother, waiting. A little brother to the end.

"Well, no point in us both hiking up there." Shannon said, taking a short look around. First light drew near, but the horizon remained dark yet. "You take the ridge, and I'll parallel you just down off it on the Pickett's Gulch side."

Edgar spit.

"Snow will be deep." He pointed out.

"I know, but if I jump something I want it to stay on the park, so you'll have a better chance of getting a shot."

Edgar spat again but said nothing. Shannon knew his brother disagreed with the plan but wouldn't argue.
"Alright, then," Shannon sighed. Then shaping his mouth into a small circle he blew smoke and watched it. Only then did he remember the cold cruelty of his responsibility. Of course, it would happen on Windy Ridge.
"Better give me a ten minute head start then just in case they wind you and run my way."

Edgar nodded and Shannon started off to the south drudging slowly through the deep snow. The going was tough, almost ridiculous. Every other step his packs sunk through the baseless powder knee deep or further. He couldn't remember ever being out here when there had been more snow. He needed snowshoes. Every twenty feet was a journey and as he worked his way down through the head of the gulch and started up the far side, he found himself wondering how or why an elk would stay up here fighting this bullshit to survive even a single day when there were all those lush hayfields a few miles below.

Despite the bitter cold, his labors made him sweat and before long he had his hat off and his jacket open. About three quarters of the way to the park, he stopped to catch his breath and turned his headlamp off. He waited for his eyes to readjust to the darkness of the timber. Above him, to his left he could make out the rocky spine of the ridge where it met the graying skyline and ran east toward the farthest mountains. The rising sun was just beginning to bathe those high, distant peaks in the pale predawn grey, and he knew the ridgeline above would wear a thin band of gold in another ten minutes. He hastened his pace, eager to get out in front of his brother where Edgar wouldn't see him through the glare of the rising sun.

A new day was arriving on the endless expanses of conifers that rolled up and down and up again in all directions. The constant struggle to survive would make a shift change soon, but the forest around him remained silent as only the ridgeline details became obvious where the black trees met the creaming skyline. The pines around him wouldn't receive light for another fifteen minutes or more. The individual trees were just tall, conforming shadows of resemblance. The only difference between any two was height and as Shannon looked around if he didn't know any better, he would think the world's flora were uniquely coniferous and ran off toward eternity in all direction, concealing no life, nor summer, nor ocean beach amidst the winter's gloom.

But he did know better, and a few minutes later as he struggled and slid along the dark side-hill of the gulch just above the thick mess, and the gray lifted toward the pale color of dawn, not yet blue or yellow or even violet on the horizon perpendicular to his course, he caught the first signs of movement on the naked spine above. Edgar's orange not quite glowing yet still distinguishable from the pale snow appeared from nowhere and mimicked his own movements down toward the change in the sky. He knew that his brother couldn't possibly see him. He estimated the distance at about six hundred yards, although it must be closer, as he knew breaking and fading light had a way of skewing distances. He kept slightly ahead of his brother scanning the open fingers above him while staying hidden from above.

As the crag broadened and the park along the rocky spine fanned out and the timberline fell, he stayed low. His brother disappeared from view for a few minutes and then reappeared where he had stopped beside the single, old, hollowed-out fir, long dead but rooted deep in the rocky surface of the exposed ridgeline's highest point of relief, unwilling to yield or fall to the most brutal elements of nature's arsenal.

From that distance, Shannon couldn't tell if Edgar was searching the benches across the opposite gulch or scanning the near timber for his brother's position. Edgar's orange was fully distinguishable now, and when he vanished behind the girth of the tree Shannon knew him to be there only because there was nowhere else to hide. The landscape lay otherwise motionless, cold and lonely along the top of the world.

Shannon climbed to where he could see the spine of the ridge before removing his orange jacket and hat and tucking himself into the shadows along the bottom edge of the park, where he sat and waited for daylight to reach his position as the sun's radiation crept down the hillside. It was cold without a jacket, but he had a second beanie, a camouflage one, in his pack and he put it on and sat on his jacket, rubbing his gloved hands along the length of his arms to create warmth.

He wondered what his brother's eyes saw from his elevated three hundred and sixty degree perch. His own view was limited, but he could see the wind kicking the snow off the exposed grass and rock in the blinding light above and he knew he would see his brother soon enough, haloed in light as he moved down the ridgeline against that wind.

Shannon's nose grew numb as he struggled to catch his breath and he cursed to himself and fidgeted uncontrollably as the first hints of blue lit above the soft blond of the horizon.

What was he doing here? What was he about to do? Was this even possible?

240

The stars were gone, and the first rays of light stretched out over the jagged ramparts to his right as the land's details became apparent. He thought of his father and how angry and disappointed he had been in that man the last time they had watched the dawn rise upon this very ridge.

That had been so long ago, and his outlook so different then. At the time, his father's words had been so ignorant and foreign, and as the years went by that forfeiture had grown cowardly and unforgivable. But now the crime seemed petty and almost frivolous in the hindsight of a life lived and the wake of his own mistakes and misdeeds. He tried to focus the blame where it had always lain, but nothing was as it had once seemed and such blame was no longer easy. His efforts were useless. His own wife, the only woman he had ever loved, was gone now and he recognized and could appreciate the same powerless inability to win back not just a mother or a wife, but a complicated and unique individual. He couldn't blame his wife for leaving, and he couldn't blame his father either. As consumed as he was with the same stubborn pride that prevented him from even making the first step toward change, he knew what his father had done was nothing compared with what he himself had done; what he was *about* to do.

Back then, his father had spoken those words so easily it seemed, as he continued to scan the snow covered mountains from approximately the same spot that Edgar now stood; that gnarly fir dead even then, or dying. And Shannon remembered how he had begged him not to let her go, looking up from teary eyes at his hero, a man capable of anything.

'I can't make her stay.' His father had said simply of the boys' mother, his wife. Just like that. And it was that statement that had always seemed such a plain and inconsiderate lie. Tom Drummond hadn't even looked his young son in the eyes, and perhaps that is why the emotion, the struggle, had gone unnoticed for so long. In Shannon's young mind it had all been so simple. He could have fixed it. Whatever it was. It could be fixed. He had pleaded as much with his father crying desperately, but his father had been indifferent. Or so it had seemed. He had told Shannon that someday he would understand. But Shannon didn't understand. He couldn't.

241

It was only now in the rising brilliance of a huge and unobstructed dawn with his baby brother making his way down the spine of the steep ridge toward his death that Shannon admitted he had never tried to understand. He had never tried to accept that some things really were beyond a man's control; that a man was only a man, and he could only control his own decisions. And as he admitted this, his whole life came rushing at him from a whole new angle. And he thought of his girls and Grisham's vicious threat, and how a man cannot shape the world to his desires but only his actions in accordance to his character.

He knew that he had only his own cowardice to blame for this dilemma and that even if his father had tried to keep his mother from leaving he would have likely failed. And as his brother stopped and raised his rifle toward the sun and away from Shannon's position, he raised his own rifle in Edgar's direction. He found the orange of his brother's jacket in the crosshairs of his scope, but his eyes were blurry with tears and he had to blink and wipe at them. He knew in that moment, everything his father had stood for and why his kind was so unique. As he found his brother again in the scope, Edgar was looking away. He cursed himself and the world he had sworn to change. He cursed the day his insecurities had led him to the act of heartless cruelty and selfishness that had sent his brother down the path he had traveled; frightened, angry and all alone. He cursed the fogged glass of his scope that prevented him from seeing his target clearly. And he cursed the God he had never admitted believing in and yet never fully shaken the doubts of, for never giving either of the brothers, or any Drummond for that matter, a fighting chance.

The blast tore across the heavens and the echoes answered back from all directions. It was a single pure and deafening roar that seemed to Shannon as if it would never end. But then it did end, and it ended swiftly, although his mind no longer registered this fourth dimension. He sat there with his finger still on the trigger as the echo changed from a single fading ring to muffled sobbing to a rising clatter of approaching thunder, and he knew that he had done the unthinkable, the unforgiveable, and now God himself was racing to earth to strike him down for this final travesty he had committed.

242

But then as his sobs were drowned out and he was able to get his scope to stop quivering up and down, he made out his brother's blurry face just above the crosshairs, staring back at him, alive and awaiting the fate that had yet to be handed him. His expression was blank, without fear or even curiosity, and he only looked at Shannon for a moment or two though it felt like forever before he turned his look back to the spine of the ridge where movement caught Shannon's attention.

They came toward him four abreast over the spine of the ridge, their desperate stampeding muffled to a tiny fraction of their effort as they hit the deep, windblown snow. Their movement slowed such that Shannon could see the breath steam from their snouts and the panic in the coal black of their eyes as they closed in on the timber ahead. There was fear there, but the noble critters would give away none of it. They were alive and as long as they remained so they would fight for every beat of their heart. There were at least thirty of them, maybe more. It was hard to tell, and Shannon picked out one of three or four small bulls quickly and raised his rifle yet again and shot the beast in the chest without hesitation as it struggled toward him a hundred yards yet from the safety of the timber. As the rifle pin discharged the shell from its casing the ringing in Shannon's ears canceled out the growing clatter of the approaching herd and the sorrow in his heart. The bullet struck the majestic bull and knocked him back, stealing his legs from under him as he fell into the snow his horns thrashing and legs struggling to regain solid ground.

The stampeding elk instantly swung about again and mayhem ensued as some turned left down the open ridge toward the sun, others turned back the way they came and a few young calves simply stopped too tired or confused to do anything more.

Unhindered by the events unfolding beneath it, the sun continued its climb behind Shannon and to his right, and as the yellow rays lit the ridgeline in full radiance, the individual crystals of the snow sparkled perfect all around except where the blood stained the powder around the struggling bull. In the time it took Shannon to discharge the spent casing and jack another shell into the chamber, the bull climbed to its feet in defiance of death, desperate to live, to survive. But as Shannon put its head in his crosshairs it lay back down and heaved, awaiting its end. The details of the animal were haloed in light as it turned its head toward him, and as he exhaled slowly and prepared to end the noble bull's pain, he caught a flash of his brother as he had seen him in what already felt like a distant memory.

He lowered the rifle a moment and looked again. The last of the herd was vanishing now in one direction or another, but the mortally wounded bull made no further effort to stand. It was dying and it seemed to watch Shannon with its final breaths, stoic and still beautiful even in the violent struggle of imminent death.

He looked up the hill again to where his brother stood watching. Edgar hadn't moved, but the glare made him almost impossible to make out without the aid of the scope. The bull turned its head away from Shannon. It lay about halfway between him and his brother. He estimated the distance at a hundred and twenty-five yards; about the same distance from the timber and the spine of the ridge. The area was roughly a circle, and the bull lay in the middle of it.

He considered all of this only a moment longer. Then he raised his rifle and swiftly shot the bull in the head. It kicked twice and fell instantly dead.

Shannon lowered his rifle again and hid his face as he cried. What had just happened seemed impossible to him, and yet it had just happened. He couldn't understand any of it, and he made no effort to move. When he finally pulled himself together he expected to find his brother coming toward him. But his brother was nowhere to be seen. The dead bull lay alone upon the trampled park, its hide and horns sticking up out of the deep snow.

Maybe his brother hadn't seen him, he thought. The glare from the sun would have been directly in his eyes; plus he wore no orange. But he had to see him. They were so close, and he was staring right at him when he saw his face, set against the dark timber with his gun raised. Maybe Edgar thought he was raising his scope to watch him shoot? Or because he had heard him shoot? Or because the first of the elk were already cresting the ridge?

Finally, he could sit still no longer. He was cold and numb and forced back to present. He pulled his jacket back on and climbed the hill, making only a slight inspection of his kill before hiking past his bull to the crest of the ridge where he found his brother just over the other side in the northern shadow gutting a five point bull slightly larger than the one he had shot. Feeling slightly faint, Shannon walked over and stood a few feet behind his brother, but his brother never looked up from his work and after a few minutes of silent observation, he felt cold and ashamed and afraid and made his way slowly back over the ridge to the warm sunlight of the southern facing side and began field dressing his own kill. His confused and strange thoughts ceased to exist as he delved into his work and the warmth returned to his body as he plunged his uncovered arms elbow deep into the animal's warm blood.

After he had removed all the entrails and the windpipe, he went down the hill and found a large branch and busted it off and used it to brace the ribcage open. Then he threw a little snow in the cavity, wiped his knife on his pants and used the snow to clean his hands and arms best he could. He didn't bother with skinning the critter because he planned to return with the chainsaw and cut the carcass in half for dragging. As he finished his work and freed his mind once more, the dread of what he had so nearly done returned to him. He was stuck in the process of deciding how to face his brother and respond to the accusations he would make when he noticed his brother coming down the ridge toward him.

The crosswind was picking up and hit him with a blast of arctic chill as it raced down the ridge. He squeezed his hands as they shivered and tightened against the cold and glanced back toward the sun which didn't seem to be rising so much as skimming along the distant peaks. He reached for his gloves and jacket as his brother arrived beside him.

Edgar tossed the blood-stained saw he carried into the snow beside his gloves and then searched his pockets and drew a pack of smokes. Shannon watched him pull a cigarette from the box with dark streaks of blood still running down his bare arms and his hands soaked in crimson. Edgar didn't seem to notice even as he raised the cigarette to his dry, cracked lips and lit it. The bits of meat and flesh stuck to his fingernails an inch or two from his mouth. He smoked in silence for a moment, standing over his older brother gazing out at the surrounding horizon of distant mountains while Shannon watched him closely. Then he grabbed the bull by a horn and examined it without looking back at his brother.

"Nice little bull." He said.

"Thanks," Shannon replied, examining the animal closely for the first time.

"Did you ruin much meat?" Edgar asked, pulling at the brisket for a closer look.

"Huh?" Shannon asked startled.

"I asked if you ruined much meat?"

"Oh, I don't think so," Shannon sighed, though he hadn't really inspected that closely. "Maybe this front quarter a little, but the bullet hit that shoulder hard." He faded off and looked away again as the chill overtook him. The wind kicked snow up off the surface and into his eyes. "What about you?"

"Nah," Edgar grunted. His cigarette had gone out, and he cupped his bare hands to relight it. "Shot that sumbitch right in the head."

They sat for a moment in silence like that, Edgar smoking and Shannon holding the saw. It was cold, very cold.

"Did you get your ivories?"

"Shit. No, I almost forgot." Shannon went to work digging the bull's canines from the gum. When he had finished he held the short, rounded tusks in his hand and examined them. Edgar knelt beside him, pulling his own set of ivories from his pocket and holding them near for comparison.

"Well, I guess we better cut this bitch in half, huh? We got a long day ahead of us."

Shannon considered his brother's words, but his heart wasn't in it.

"I wish you'd go, Edgar." He said on the verge of tears again. "I mean even if you didn't leave Montana, at least leave town?" His brother smoked and spat.

"This is my home..."

"But they are going to KILL you!" Shannon shrieked. "I don't think you fully understand what we are dealing with here."

"We?" Edgar asked, making eye contact.

Shannon sighed. Then he sat for a moment trying to decide where to start. "Grisham has his hands in everything...You couldn't possibly understand the complexity of the situation."

"I understand better than you might think, brother." Edgar cut in. "I fully understand now." They looked at each other for a

246

while, and each saw something that seemed to explain something else.

"But I still don't think I'll leave, brother. Those problems are my problems, and I already tried to run from my problems once. It didn't help any. Those kinds of problems don't go away until you face em head on." Edgar looked around him. Then he flung his cigarette. "You got to love it up here." He said. "It's Drummond country. No one can change that, ever." He looked at Shannon. "No one can take anything from us that we don't give. Don't you forget that."

He nodded his head in agreement with his own statement and paused a long time just standing there in the cold wind staring, before adding, "Everything is going to be ok, big brother." It was a familiar promise. A meaningless promise that was never true. But he spoke it, and for some damn reason it helped. "This is my deal, and I'll never let nothing happen to you or your girls." Then they were quiet again.

"Jill had an affair with Steve Zowiky." Shannon said. He didn't know why he said it especially then and there. But for once he couldn't hold it, his burden, alone any longer. He had to talk to someone and it seemed like as good a time as any to talk to his brother. He was broken and fully exposed, he might as well get things off his chest. "I don't know. Maybe they're still sleeping together.

"I don't know."

Edgar listened to the words and took them in. Then he put his hand on his brother's shoulder and Shannon cried.

"We're gonna be ok, brother." Edgar repeated the words. "As long as there are elk in these mountains, there will be Drummonds here to hunt em."

Chapter 27

The first pulse of the small battery-powered alarm clock shocked young Shannon swiftly from his coma, and he bolted upright. The slow, rhythmic beep was an immediate annoyance that shaped his mood as he searched the darkness blindly for his flashlight. Finally, in a fit of aggravation, he gave up on the flashlight and grabbed frantically in the direction of the sound. A ruckus ensued as he knocked over the rusted and warped old TV tray beside his cot where the alarm had rested and everything he had piled on it dropped to the earth. The clock kept right on beeping, and by the time he got it and was able to make it stop, he was beyond irritated and on the verge of a blowout.

He had been angry for four days. Ever since he missed the bull in the timber near Haystack Hill. Angry and disheartened. Angry and hungry. Angry and tired. Worn out. The scene played out in his mind like a bad song on repeat morning, noon and night, and each time it grew harder to swallow as if that one chance summarized the despair of an entire life's effort, the pointless struggle against imminent failure.

As the quiet returned, he sighed and laid his head back down to give his eyes a moment to adjust to the darkness and make some attempt at salvaging his morning. In the absence of the alarm it was nearly silent, aside from the occasional rustling of slight morning gusts. But he could still hear the pulsing beep in his ears taunting him in his failures until the echo faded to a high pitched ringing and his thoughts turned again to the grave futility he had come to escape. Could fate truly be predestined? Could an entire bloodline simply be damned by God? Did curses really exist? And if so why this family? It had all seemed so improbable before, and yet he had lost every battle he had waged against such hopeless thought, eventually always fading back into abject despair.

And now he was alone. Alone like every Drummond before him. Alone even in his brother's company, perhaps more so than he had ever felt in solitude. Before there had always been a boundary between privacy and lonesomeness in his own subconscious, but he no longer recognized where that stood and his failure compounded a growing bitterness toward the world.

A building gust howled against the canvass walls, drawing one side in then the far side out as the frigid air slipped in under the sagging tent walls and threatened to bring the whole structure down on top of the two boys. The whir of the fabric tightening was followed by the snap of the canvass testing the stakes that held it in place, and it pulled Shannon temporarily away from his infectious insecurities as he set about in search of his flashlight once more. For a moment he couldn't help but consider what other boys his age would be doing; sleeping no doubt; after a long night of boozing or studying or whatever else twenty-one year old boys did on Friday nights.

But such fate would never be his, and he knew such thoughts were only time wasted. This was his place, and his life would be unique. The world would act and he would respond. That is how it had always been. There could be no effect without a cause. This was a law of the physical universe and he had come to accept it as one of the few certainties of life. That and eventual disappointment, a let down or hangover from even the highest of highs.

It wasn't until he had located his old hand-me-down torch and began to move about that he became fully aware of his state of being. His eyes were swollen with sleep and his sinuses plugged up. He was sore, and his body and mind fatigued. The brothers hadn't return to camp until well after dark the night prior and although the dawn was arriving a few minutes later each day, Shannon continued to set the alarm clock earlier. It was two hours before legal shooting light now. Saturday morning. And Shannon was out of time. He had to be back to work on Monday or he might lose his job. This fact clouded the clarity of his usually rational mind. He had dreamt of being fired and missing the bull, the two events simultaneously intertwined, and in each replay the bull grew larger and more remarkable and the outcome of losing his job left him more destitute and without options. Both scenarios played out in the same repeating nightmare of inescapable failure. Now he was awake and still experiencing such dread. He felt helpless, no longer in control of his life and the course it was taking, like a massive object rolling down a mountain and starting to gain speed.

This gripping pessimism only drove him harder. Last night had been his first full night's sleep in days. He was barely eating. His exhaustion finally trumped the credibility of his imagination.

He lit the lantern, and as the kerosene growled he called his brother's name in a hoarse voice that sounded alien from building phlegm and lack of use. It was very cold, and the sight of his breath in the soft light of the lantern only increased the chattering of his teeth. He dressed quickly, layer after layer and pulling his beanie down low. His knees and back ached, and his hands were already numb and hard to work with. They were like blocks of ice as he used them to stoke the stove, wiping at a dripping nose constantly with the back of his sleeve.

They were out of milk, so he sat, shivering, before the new fire and ate cereal dry from the box and drank as much water as he could stomach. Both coolers were nearly empty, but they wouldn't starve. They still had plenty of cubed game steaks, hash browns, and a half loaf of bread. But they were out of eggs, sausage and lunchmeat. The granola bars were about gone too along with the chips and candy bars, licorice and peanuts. There was only so much mustard and butter could do to make a meal.

Shannon boiled water and drank two cups of thick, gritty coffee, savoring the warmth without enjoyment while he sniffed at his runny nose. As he sat, Edgar rose and dressed and ate. Edgar preferred pop, but the few cans left had frozen and exploded, so he tried the coffee. It was awful stuff and he couldn't manage more than a few sips. He ended up standing like a zombie close to the stove shivering slightly with both hands wrapped around the cup.

The tent was just starting to warm as they gathered their gear in discouraged silence beneath the pale light of the lantern. The shadows ran long in the far corners of the tent and the gloom hung thick as fog. Speech had grown so scarce over the past few days that the rare word or question almost echoed. They could read each other's thoughts, but those too had grown sparse and neurotic to the point the brothers went to great effort to ignore each other's body language. Their psyches could no longer handle the reflection of their own doubt. They had forgotten the enjoyment that had once brought them to this place, just as they had forgotten the joys of hope, and yet they wouldn't even consider quitting, nor would they succumb to the apparent madness of the entire predicament.

250

They were consumed solely by the loss that addicted them and the obsession with of a harvest they were convinced could somehow save them.

Even young Edgar had tossed aside the last of his frivolous pretending. His daydreaming and fooling about had nearly ceased since he had been lost and found. He stayed mostly focused now, singular in thought and desperate to get home to Holly's voice, her touch.

The younger Drummond knew they had to slay a bull or risk further tarnishing a family legacy that could support no further damage. In the past four days they had hunted the hell out of every spot known to their ancestors. Before daylight until well after dark, with obsessive determination, Shannon had led them up steep hillsides, across rocky gulches, drainages and draws through thick stands of new growth to hidden wallows and springs and across more parks and plains and meadows, snow, sleet and wind than many humans ever experienced in a lifetime. He led them to tall feed and water, places where elk had to go. He led the way like a man possessed, like his father in the midst of those hardest years when everyone he loved was dying or dead or done living and his marriage had teetered on the brink and then collapsed. And like Tom Drummond, somewhere along the way the elder son had accepted the somewhat irrational understanding that elk hunting and life were directly related and if only one truly mattered it must be the prior.

Those first two days after the Chinook were mild. Then another bitter storm had blown in arctic air that sat heavy on the mountains, and it had only grown colder since. There was no thermometer around, but Shannon was certain the temperature hadn't topped zero in the past seventy-two hours. The snowfall had been mild too. The wind and the cold seemed too brutal for snow. Three inches had fallen ahead of the front, followed by occasional skiffs and constant cloud movement: white and wispy, high and low, thick and unstable, foggy then smoky, growing grey but rolling over the mountains and on toward the east too quickly to gather. At times it felt like it was snowing as the wind kicked up frozen grit off the ground and the trees, and swirled it around until the grains were coarse and cut the flesh like tiny diamonds.

When it was calm, it was gorgeous, so silent and cold with the sun's flat rays almost visible like frozen cords connecting the star to the random hunk of mass where life had come to flourish. The air seemed to freeze in those moments and tiny crystals sparkled everywhere. But then the sun would move on as if tired of such a vacuum of activity and the wind would return worse than before. Gusts of up to forty miles an hour, unrelenting, made the cold unbearable on the open parks and exposed ridges. It blew most of the afternoon and all night whistling across the wilderness, silencing the living world aside from the branches of the trees that swayed and snapped in violent symphony. No amount of extra layering seemed capable of protecting the boys from its bite. Throughout the long, restless nights the tent walls rattled and bowed and once the stove pipe was blown over and the tent filled with black smoke until Shannon could get it back in place. Yet so far their shelter had remained standing like the trees that braved the lifetime of a century in that extreme climate of constant change.

Despite the weather, and the boys defiance of it, and their expansion of terrain explored, the lack of elk remained a constant. Sign was almost non existent. Shannon had never seen so little sign amidst such an extended stay in camp. They searched high and they searched low, but they hadn't caught sight of so much as a cow or calf since the tragic missed opportunity below Haystack.

Except rabbit tracks, the occasional spooked grouse rising and a lone raven calling out its passage in the pale afternoon light there was little sign of life in those mountains. And with every mile the boys' outlook grew more dire.

The previous day had left them utterly thwarted. After spending the morning scouring a series of parks just above the hayfields where they could glass for miles across the rolling hills and plains of the mountain-valley border, they had stopped back at camp just long enough to pack a couple sandwiches and more water and set out again before noon to hike from camp out the ridge they called Blue Grouse, down into the bottom of the drainage of Hollow Creek, and back up the steep, short and until then nameless ridge that flattened out onto the plateau above camp. These were desperate hunts. Hunts that even Shannon hardly knew. But desperate times called for desperate measures, and they were finding luck nowhere else.

252

Just before sunset, as they meandered, half-starved and half-lost, across the broad flat atop the most western ridge that ran off the Main Ridge searching for an observation knob where Shannon thought Black Bear and possibly Windy Ridge would be visible, Edgar had finally asked his brother where they were. Shannon had done his best to describe the location using vague references to unseen landmarks.

"But what is the name of this place?" Edgar asked, for surely every ridge and gulch and park had to have been previously explored and named.

"Well, dad always called the gulch between us and Windy Ridge, Asshole Gulch, because people used to hike up from the road years ago and leave a lot of asshole tracks," Shannon explained. "But I don't think this little ridge really had a name since no one ever hunted up here much."

"But the gulch couldn't be called Asshole Gulch on a map?" Edgar asked, his confusion contorting the look on his wind-burned face.

"No," Shannon answered. "None of the names we use are official names found on a map, except Black Bear Mountain…And the creeks, I guess. Most of those are all real names." He paused for a moment of reflection. "Haystack Hill might actually be called that too… I'm not positive.

"But the ridges and the draws and the parks and gulches and the springs and the wallows, granddaddy and the boys at camp, they just made those up over the years."

It was clear from the boy's face that Edgar enjoyed this news.

They continued on, climbing whenever possible, for another twenty minutes before the boys stumbled back across their own tracks and Shannon cursed.

"Where the hell are we?"

Being a ways from camp, with darkness approaching rapidly, Shannon decided to simply backtrack rather than explore the ridge any further. It was a decision he would have likely made regardless, but Edgar's recent episode definitely made the decision easier. They had gone another ten minutes when Edgar broke the silence again.

"Lost Brothers Ridge." He exclaimed, just as the timber was starting to purple. The remark led Shannon to turn and face his brother with a look of curiosity.

"That's where we are. We'll call this ridge Lost Brothers Ridge."

"We aren't lost," Shannon said with the wounds of his brother's crisis still too fresh on his weary mind to see any humor in the suggestion. Not to mention the word alone held little honor in his views. He looked away from his brother, up and all around them. It was then that a second meaning in the name drifted to mind. He looked back to his brother who was now beaming ear to ear. For the first time all day Shannon smiled. He didn't know why, but he couldn't help it.

"We aren't lost." He said again.

"No, we ain't lost." Edgar agreed, still grinning. "How could we ever be lost in our own backyard?

"I just meant we don't know where we are."

"But by simply naming this place." Edgar went on. "We find ourselves! We find ourselves just off the trail somewhere atop Lost Brothers Ridge."

Shannon laughed.

"Alright." He conceded. "Lost Brothers Ridge it is then."

And for a fleeting moment all was right once more and the act of hunting became what it is and what it should be; what it would always be. And the absurdity of considering it only in regards to the success or failure of a harvest came to light and all perspectives changed. Edgar was pleased, and his pleasure pleased Shannon.

But for such an outlook to last requires much contemplation and contentment, and as the darkness and temperatures fell and the silence prolonged, the object of their desire regained its mythical worth and that new, brighter perspective faded.

It was full dark before the boys found the trail by the glow of the flashlight and another hour before they made it back to camp. The stove had long since grown cold and the tent was as cold, dark and unwelcoming a place as the wilderness surrounding it. Edgar had lit the lantern long enough to fill the stove and get the fire burning hot. Then they had eaten chewy, undercooked elk loin steaks without any sides or sauces, or words and turned the lantern out again and listened to the wind mock their failure until their exhaustion won out.

Now it was Saturday morning, the second-to-last morning they had, and as they left the shelter of their tent, Edgar was certain Shannon would take them to Windy Ridge. It simply couldn't be avoided any longer.

But Shannon had other plans. He had decided to take the bikes to the end of the old logging road that wound up and around Black Bear Mountain to the rugged peak's northern side. It was an area he knew little about. He had never hunted it. Few had. So far, inaccessible and steep that even their father thought packing an elk out of it would be more trouble than it was worth. Yet Shannon remembered his grandfather telling tales about bulls that would hunker down in the dark timber of that tallest mountain where man rarely ventured and defy logic where the snow never blew off.

"You're avoiding Windy Ridge." Edgar pointed out after Shannon had shared his plan.

"Avoiding it?" Shannon stammered. "Why would I be avoiding it?"

"Don't know." Edgar shrugged. "But that don't mean you ain't."

"Stop using the term ain't. We are not hillbillies."

Edgar watched his brother closely but said no more.

He was right. Shannon was still afraid to face Windy Ridge, afraid to meet his father's ghost at Tom Drummond's favorite place on earth: the first and last place an eldest son remembered his father telling him that he loved him, the only place he ever talked of God and the non-physical, and the place where a harsh reality had been realized and a surrender spoken that could never be taken back or forgiven. Shannon had spent endless sleepless nights trying to forget that morning and those words. He could never accept that his father, his hero, had given up on a commitment that a young boy knew should be life-long or that he had spoken the words so easily. These were all memories that had impacted him instantly and forever and that he wore like a shirt or second skin, memories that would eternally remain synonymous with that barren and exposed batholith.

"Bring everything you might need," Shannon told his brother gently. "We'll be gone all day."

255

Edgar grabbed the last of the juice boxes and dug through the coolers for snacks but found nothing else of interest. Shannon adjusted the flue and turned off the lantern. The kerosene was low. The morning was still full dark as the boys exited the shelter of the tent, but a crescent moon provided enough light to give the snow's packed surface a wet, shiny gloss and the boys' eyes adjusted quickly to the contrasting shades of blue around them. Shannon gassed up the bikes while Edgar held the flashlight, and the smell of spilt gas lingered as Shannon set the container holding the last half gallon alongside a tree and they started out the trail single file.

It was a long and soothing ride through dark timber and open meadows. The beam of the headlight and the roar of the two-stroke announced their existence with a boisterous supremacy. The sting of the wind numbed Shannon's cheeks and nose, slowed his thoughts, soothed his soul, as he felt the subtle swelling of pride that came from rising before the sun to pursue a dedication older than civilization itself, particularly now that the quest had stopped being for enjoyment's sake. Edgar had his face covered with a neck warmer but the constant friction of the cold air against him found chinks in his armor and squinted his eyes until he saw only a fraction of what lay before him – the spinning rear tire of the Shannon's bike, he kept in the center beam of his headlight. The cold kept him awake and alert. He too he felt the renewal of dedication in the unbreakable bond with his brother and it reminded him why they came out here and why things still made sense here, where words weren't wasted on promises that couldn't be kept.

They rode for nearly an hour, but there remained no hint of dawn when they reached the deep and drifted snow covering the high flat plain at the base of Black Bear Mountain. In the dark, it was impossible to navigate the drifted snow. And the bikes struggled. The brittle sage stood out like purple knots on the rolling white surface. They fought valiantly for several hundred yards, Shannon breaking trail where he knew a trail remained somewhere underneath, and Edgar desperately following, but eventually their progress ceased and the bikes were abandoned, hot and layered thick with dirt and snow like ancient relics revealed at the end of some fantasy ice age.

The boys too were covered in snow kicked up from the tires, and Shannon swatted frozen chunks from the back of his brother's jacket and cap. They were both numb from the ride and Shannon could feel his brother quivering. He saw no benefit in words though and said nothing. They set into motion quickly toward the timbered base of the mighty mountain with the wind so loud that they could hardly hear the crunch of their boots. The moon was hidden behind the mountain now, but slight, misting clouds reflected its light on either side of the peak with the mountain itself black and ominous and unwelcoming. In defiance, Shannon watched the iconic rise in the earth's crust and his contempt for all things holy and spiritual and set in stone grew with each stinging breath.

His father had once told him as the pair stared out at the mountain that the way the ground itself climbed skyward toward the unknown with such might and daunting will proved early on in the earth's creation that it would be a world forged by toughness and determination. He said that the Bible had gotten it wrong; that the meek could never inherit this world.

As Shannon marched toward the dark, timbered tower he had his own symbolic thoughts in mind and set forth to prove that the mountain's height and stature represented nothing but the same hands of constant, violent change that had indifferently watched centuries of death and war and hate like the hoarding barbarian leaders charging the gates of Rome, not to pillage it and enslave its people so much as to prove to themselves in the face of their own deaths that no place or people were held sacred over any others in some deity's twisted game. The world was a place where wills collided and the champions would be those unwilling to yield or fall short regardless of the obstacles.

Edgar lagged behind his brother, laboring through the hardened drifts, tripping over sage and occasional sinkholes in the snow nagged by a responsibility to brother, blood and to the family legacy. He had to hustle to keep up, and he was panting hard against his efforts. His bones ached. But there would be no complaints this day. Still he craved dawn and the radiant heat it would bring as the cold consumed his every thought and his nose, fingers and toes hurt from the minor frostbite he had suffered only a few days prior.

Shannon felt no such discomfort. He was cold but the past week had done much to acclimatize his body to the harshest of environments and the past few years had made him indifferent to anything nature threw at him. He was older and he needed this far more than his little brother. He wouldn't quit, and he would be damned before he would be denied. His brother had him as a guardian and a beautiful girlfriend as a compassionate companion. Shannon had neither. He would have the glory of the kill for nothing else would suffice and he would accept no less. In this state of psychosis, he forgot his brother was with him and only registered Edgar's existence when they reached the shelter of the timber and he heard the footsteps stomping far behind him. He paused to consider his location.

A blood-red ripple grew on the circumference of the horizon, but the mountain remained dark and impenetrable. He had to use his flashlight to guide the way. He held his rifle in one hand, his eyes, ears, and nose scanning constantly for change. He moved quickly and fell in sync with his new surroundings. Edgar, lacking the advantage of the flashlight, struggled to keep pace, yet refused to fall far behind. And while the first violet hues spread across the sky, Edgar strove to close the growing gap between him and his brother. But the growing light only amplified Shannon's lunatic pace.

Then, as the darkness lifted, the elder Drummond abandoned his winding path and veered straight up the mountain pushing through thick stands of four foot pine and any other obstacle that stood in his way and Edgar fell further behind. He lost sight of his leader but had to stop to catch his breath. He was pushing his lungs and body to their limits.

The sky above the trees was clear and the light spread quickly, steadily. He expected the temperature was rising already. He pushed on, eventually finding his brother five hundred yards up the mountain, squatting behind a huge fir on the edge of a small clearing. At the sight of him, Edgar slowed, remembering for the first time they were hunting. With eyes peering he crept along toward his brother's position. But when he was within fifty yards of his brother's side, Shannon stood and began to climb again.

Edgar saw no tracks in the clearing, and although he had only recently taken the time to look, he knew by his brother's demeanor there hadn't been a single track on the entire climb. He followed his brother up the mountain, red-faced and panting despite the extreme cold. Shannon found a creek bed and followed it for several minutes before growing discouraged and turning off, side-hilling the mountain to the southwest, moving away from the rising sun. Edgar followed his brother's tracks, the rifle growing burdensome, whether slung or held in his hands.

They traveled in this direction for a half hour or so, both stumbling and sliding through the timber until Edgar caught Shannon again at the face of a rocky cliff, and they were forced to climb again. It was tough going for even a nimble climber, and Edgar slung his rifle and clung to the sparse needled saplings for support as mini avalanches cascaded off the steep slope. He could see the horizon of the summit above them. It wasn't far, and yet Shannon still moved at a pace of desperation. He only stopped when he fell hard on his left hip. Edgar whispered up toward him, asking if he was alright. He answered yes, examining his rifle which he had protected against his outside hip during the fall. These were the first words either boy had spoken since they left the tent.

As they reached the top of the bluff, they stopped again. There was nowhere left to go. The sun rose over the peak above them, and the day arrived in a miraculous instant. Suddenly, everything was bathed in the bright, warm beams of gold. Small birds appeared from nowhere and filled the morning with their songs.

The brothers stood and looked out at the world from its own penthouse. Still huffing for air, Edgar was blown away by the view and overwhelmed by the majesty of it all. The cold and distance and the vastness of it was all spectacular. He had never in his life been at a height where he could see so much. But Shannon never lost focus for even a moment. He glassed the area intently for ten minutes as the morning sun climbed over the mountains and revealed three hundred and sixty degrees of terrain, growing in both clarity and detail. In his searching he saw three mule deer feeding across the plain far below. But no elk.

He cursed aloud as he lowered the binoculars.

Below them a golden eagle sat perched on the snag of a hollow dead with few limbs half-rooted in the base of the rocky cliffs. The bird was hunting same as he, and shifted its head back and forth across the high plain at the base of the mountain. Shannon spat and wondered why any critter capable of flight would ever choose this over whatever unknown paradise lay far away.

Chapter 28

Oliver sat at the counter drinking coffee as the morning rush came and went around him. For breakfast he ate wheat toast, dry, and grapefruit which he had never learned to like. Mostly he had ordered the citrus fruit because it seemed so strange that he could in Montana in the middle of a cold, bleak winter.

He came to this little cafe once or twice a week, had been for years. The place served cheap, decent grub and a great cup of coffee. There was a routine. He was friendly with the waitresses, and they with him, and he had gotten to know many of the regulars and enjoyed making small talk. Generally he came to relax. But lately that hadn't been so easy. Everyone wanted to talk about the kid. And the subject usually made him uncomfortable. This morning, in particular, he hoped to avoid it.

Despite his love for the boy and the pride he felt in watching him grow, the old man never stopped worry about him. And in the past few days that concern had grown considerably.

The kid hadn't trained in weeks and the old man hadn't seen or heard from him in all that time. Even for the enigmatic young brooder this was unusual, especially with such a monumental fight nearing; especially with how far they had come.

The past few nights, Oliver had experienced a recurring dream of futile despair, death at his doorstop, and he couldn't shake the feeling that something terrible was coming down the line. He could feel it in his bones and despite his best efforts to deny it, write it off as unwarranted anxiety brought on by the boy's unexplained absence, he knew in his heart it was something real and perhaps inescapable. He had done everything he could to reach out to the kid, but even Krystle couldn't say where he was and the grave concern in her weary voice was undeniable when they spoke, and anything but reassuring.

With each passing hour his obsessive distress had grown more severe, until he could think of nothing else. The night prior he had awoke countless times in cold sweat, and he had come here early this morning, for a lack of a better place to go, in search of a moment's solace, distraction from the anguish that plagued him, thinking that perhaps he could use the conversations around him to deter his dread. So he drank his coffee and tried to think of other things, anything, as he shied away from others' eyes and did his best to keep to himself. But he was an old man, and his mind was singular and focused, and there were no other thoughts to be found amidst the lives being lived all around him.

It was an early December weekday, like any other. The cafe was already decorated for Christmas. The snow had fallen for two straight weeks, and it was cold, and the cold tore through the cozy café every time the jingle bells rattled above the glass door. No one could remember a winter so full of snow and cold so early, and everyone spoke of it tirelessly. It was a cold that whispered of sinister fates and depressed people, worried them or drove them slightly mad. It was eight o'clock in the a.m. when the bells jingled and the sheriff marched inside the café. Oliver had seen him before, tall, thick and unnaturally handsome; a man who stood out even if his uniform didn't scream for attention. It wasn't just the badge but the way he wore it, like a polished challenge or a dress uniform reserved for award ceremonies. His name was Gale and he usually came in closer to ten with another deputy, and they sat in a booth that seemed to be reserved for them near the door where the sun shone upon them through the big windows, and they spoke loudly and laughed in the bright light and made their presence felt while they drank their coffee and looked with smug superiority at the faces surrounding them. Oliver had made the mistake of making eye contact with that face before. The look he had met on that occasion was one that seemed to expect a thank you and perhaps a bit of fret despite a lack of recognition.

This morning the sheriff was early and he was by himself. He didn't sit in the booth though it was empty. Instead, he made his way deliberately toward the counter where Oliver sat alone. The old man watched his approach in the reflection of the mirror that ran the full stretch of the wall before him. And though he had never spoken to this man before, he knew immediately why he came, and a shiver ran down his arched spine.

He knew that the pretty faced man bearing the righteousness of a badge that approached him came not for the sake of justice but with a darker, unlawful purpose. He could see the arrogance and the ignorance. And he knew that there would be no going back. He knew that this man thought of Edgar Drummond as a nuisance and nothing more. And it would be that mistake, that miscalculation that would unleash hell on earth and lead to death and sorrow.

He didn't know how he knew any of this for it only occurred to him right then as the man in the tan pants and brown jacket came toward him. Perhaps it was his age and years of experience with violence and inevitable suffering that was the burden of those that seemed born to bear crosses or maybe it was something deeper and more metaphysical in nature. Whatever it was he didn't doubt his instincts for a moment, and he saw no point in avoiding what he knew to be inevitable. He set his coffee cup down and turned to the man just as he arrived beside him and set down on a stool leaving one adjacent between them.

The snow had paused in its assault sometime in the night. But a few inches had been added to the three feet already received on the valley floor in the past weeks. Behind the sheriff and through the window the pale light of clearing skies reflected the breaking dawn off the new snow. The white covered everything clean and fresh aside from the windshields and metal of garage kept vehicles which redirected the horizontal rays in all directions. The light would be blinding in a matter of hours and then darkness would start its long arrival once more.

Gale's huge form, made bulkier by his jacket and presumably several layers below it, looked odd piled high and narrow on the bolted, chrome stool. He removed the Montana Peak from his head and revealed his blonde locks still wet from a shower and shining with product, brushed back along the sides of his sturdy skull and flattened from the hat except where the ends curled in the back. His skin was pale from the cold except in the cheeks where a rosy tint shone through. He wore black gloves on his large, steady hands. For a moment the old man considered how

262

this man might fare in the ring, but the thought was interrupted as the sheriff addressed him,

"How she going this morning?"

"Can't complain." Oliver answered with a shrug of his shoulders. His insides quivered and his head grew light.
"Mighty cold out there again, but the coffee's hot and it's feeling fine and cozy in here. I can't seem to brave leaving just yet."

Gale gave a slight chuckle and had a subtle look around him. He seemed to be considering the patrons in the establishment for the first time. The waitress was down the counter a ways, and the nearest tables were beyond earshot of casual volume without making efforts to eavesdrop. After a moment, he seemed satisfied with whatever it was he had paused to consider.

"Yeah, she's wintering out there. At least the sun's looking like it might show itself today."

"Yes, sir." Oliver turned to the windows along the wall. "Sometimes I think the clear days are the coldest this time of year though. Seems like as soon as that old sun comes out, it's already fixing to set.
"I had fourteen at the house this morning, and I'm not mighty sure it's rose any since."

"Nope," Gale agreed, turning to follow the old man's gaze. "Not much. Supposed to stay cold for a while too." The waitress made her way over and greeted the deputy by name, and he smiled at her and asked her how she had been and after she had given a generic answer, he ordered a coffee with cream and sugar and adjusted himself in his chair while she went to fetch his drink. When she delivered it, he thanked her with the same practiced smile. After a sip he addressed the old man through the mirror.

"I'm not sure if we've ever been properly introduced," he said, his voice smooth and sweet and friendly. "I'm Sheriff Brad Gale."

"Fine to meet you, sheriff. My name is Oliver. Oliver Carino." They shook hands and Oliver had to hide a wince as Gale squeezed his arthritic fingers with a vice like grip.

"Oh yeah," Gale's face pickled as he tried to pretend he had just made the connection, "You train fighters down at Sil's gym right? You train Edgar Drummond, is that right?"

"I do." Oliver admitted. "I do. I train several young men."

"But the Drummond kid, he's the champ right? Unbeatable ain't he?" Gale narrowed his eyes now and scrutinized the old man as he awaited a reply.

"Son, if there is one thing I've learned in all my years, it is that no man is ever unbeatable at anything.

"But that kid, Edgar, he is something special."

"That's what I've heard."

"He's won nine bouts now and not one opponent has even challenged him."

"Is that right?" The sheriff frowned.

"Yes, sir. He's set to fight a professional fight in Vegas after the first of the year, and this fellow he's fighting is also undefeated. Stronger than the kid and faster too. So we'll have to wait and see before we anoint anyone as unbeatable. This fella could present a challenge."

"He could? But you don't think he will?"

"Well, sheriff, to tell you the truth, I don't think anything can stop Edgar Drummond, but himself. Like I said, he is something pretty special. It will be interesting to see how the events unfold.

"That is if the events unfold."

"What do you mean by that?"

"Well, I haven't seen the boy in weeks. No one has. Hell, I was about to ask if you all had him locked up."

"No," Gale replied, the disappointment in his face evident. "I have to admit to you though, we are looking for him."

"I had a feeling you might say that. Do you mind me asking what for?"

"I just need to ask him a few questions. That's all."

"I see." There was a pause as Gale tried to decide how to proceed.

"Let me ask you something."

"Go right ahead, sheriff."

"Is there much money to be made in this fighting that he does? I mean is there as much money in it as say professional boxing?"

"No, sir. Not yet at least. It hasn't caught on quite like boxing has. But there are purses, and for certain professionals it can be a rather profitable career. This fight would be Edgar's third fight as a pro. And if he won it, I think he would be able to afford to train and to fight full time. But I wouldn't say it would make him rich."

"What about betting though?"

"Of that, sir, I couldn't tell you. Never been a gambling man myself."

"Do you think Drummond's favored?"

"Probably not. Like I said this other cat has more exposure and he's fast and strong. Edgar's pretty unorthodox in everything he does. Plus, he's in terrible shape, for a fighter at least. He smokes cigarettes like a chimney, and he hates to run.
"Frankly, I think every time he wins it's an upset of sorts…Boy the people of Montana sure are getting behind him though. They really see something in him they admire."

"Interesting."

"Yes sir."

"Why do you think that is?"

"Well, sir, if I had to guess, I'd say it's that they see he's real. In a world of boot deep bull-crap, pardon my language, he is what he is. I suppose that's refreshing sometimes… Plus he was a Marine. People love veterans."

The sheriff didn't have anything to say to this, but Oliver couldn't help noticing his agitation seemed to be rising. He detected something more than criminal at hand. He sensed a personal vendetta of sorts.

"So when do you expect to see him again?"

"Hard to say, sheriff. Like I said, the kid is on his own schedule."

Gale looked away and chewed at his lip in deliberation. Then he turned back to the old man but said nothing. There was something on his mind though, and it must have festered as he sat and finished his coffee, for after he drained his cup he climbed quickly to his feet and reached for his wallet and removed a card.

"Well, next time you see him, I want you to give me a call you hear?"

"Will do, sir."

"But don't let him know we spoke, you understand?

"Excuse me, sir?"

"I said when he comes in for training or calls or whatever, I need you to go in the back and call me but don't alarm him in anyway."

"Well, I'm awful sorry, sheriff, but that doesn't set quite right with me. Has he done something wrong?"

"Well, you said if he wins this fight, he'll be able to afford to train fulltime, but if he's made no money up until now, how does he afford to train and travel and feed himself? You ever ask yourself those questions?"

"Well, I don't charge him to train, there is a small charge for the gym, but Sil sponsors the kid, so that is waved too."

"But how does he eat or pay his bills?"

"I'm not sure there, sir. I believe he works at a pub downtown."

"No. I don't *believe* he does." Gale answered quickly. He remained standing and his agitation was no longer masked. He stood over the old man frowning down on him. "He quit that job some months back. I don't believe he's been employed since."

"Well I'm sure he still has his military compensation."

"Yeah, maybe. Like I said, I just want to talk to him. That's all."

"Well, it sounds awful important. But I'd just feel more comfortable if I relayed the message to him rather than called you behind his back like that."

Oliver's hand began to twitch and his mug rattled against the counter. He released it as Gale took notice. The old man felt his toes grow cold and he struggled to find his breath. He coughed. Gale asked if he was alright.

"Yes. Thank you."

Gale asked the waitress to bring water. Then he turned back to the old man and waited.

"Listen old timer, if you know where he is, you best tell me. The truth is Edgar 'Irish Eyes' Drummond is currently under investigation in connection with several criminal activities in the area, and I'm just trying to do my job. If he is innocent, then I can help him. And if you stand in the way of my investigation, you will find yourself in a great deal of trouble, Mr. Carino."

"Well, sir, I do understand that and I didn't mean to stand in the way of any police work. I will cooperate in any way I can, sheriff. Like I said, I have not seen him in weeks and that's the honest-to-God truth…I'm sorry for prying. Just trying to look out for the boy that's all."

"That's fine." The sheriff nodded. It was clear that he now believed him, and he believed the fear he had instilled in the old man would work when the boy came out of hiding. "I'm trying to do the same."

He dropped a few bills and a coin on the counter then slapped it to catch the waitress's attention. He stood still while she picked it up and smiled and winked when she thanked him. Then he addressed the old man through the mirror,
"Does seem a little strange though, don't you think? A man with no vocation can't seem to keep a steady training schedule despite that fact that his next bout may earn him a great deal of money."

"Yes, sir, but I don't spend much time wondering about what a man does with his free time. Keeping my own life together is tough enough as is, you see?"

"Come on Mr. Carino, who are we kidding? You really think I buy that you've never wondered about your prize fighter's private life, especially when he has a huge fight coming up and all of a sudden he's gone AWOL." Gale made a puzzled look like he smelled something fishy. Then he turned to face the old man again. "I know that *you* know what this kid's capable of. We can pretend that he's a trained fighter, but we both know he's a military grade weapon of destruction, and we both know that he is a drunk. And when he's drunk, which he usually is, he's as dangerous as hell on wheels." He searched the old man's face for a reaction. "But regardless, it's of little concern. I'll find what I need, and I'll make the arrest."

"You speak as if the man is already guilty." Even in the face of intimidation the old man couldn't help but reveal his loyalty.

"You train fighters, Mr. Carino, and I do police work. I'm pretty good at judging a man's character."

As Gale spoke he stood erect a moment and set his hat upon his head and cocked it at an angle in the mirror and tucked the strap beneath his chin and gave Oliver a condescending look. "Sounds like you might take a little more interest in choosing your

267

clients." Then he leaned back in close and his face hardened into a grimace.

"And whether you choose to protect this scumbag or not, you tell your boy I'm not afraid of his lonely boy act one bit." He said this in a low growl. Then he stood straight again and gave the room one more unconcerned look around. "Now you have yourself a nice afternoon, Mr. Carino." He pulled his gloves on with the same confident deliberation he showed in every movement. "It was nice meeting you, and I'm sure I'll be seeing you around." And he turned and walked out into the cold white world.

Chapter 29

Krystle lay dozing on the couch in front of the television when Butch startled her. Something had caused the dog to rise from his spot beneath her, and as he rushed toward the door the tags on his collar jingled. The muscular mutt stood at the door and a growl grew deep in his throat, but he did not bark. Krystle turned, leaned over the back of the couch and rubbed at her tired eyes, frightened, yet hopeful to hear Edgar's key at any moment.

Butch was a young blue-heeler/pit-bull cross, as loyal as he was lethal. Edgar had brought the dog home a few months earlier, right around the time everything began to change. He said the dog was a gift, a temporary substitute for the child the couple had yet to conceive. But as the summer had faded to fall Edgar had grown increasingly more anxious all the time and she often caught him watching the dog as if waiting for some warning of the unknown. She had never seen fear in him, and the appearance of it now felt so out of place she was afraid to inquire as to the source. Then one night he had told her not to answer her phone any longer if she didn't recognize the number and to stop answering the door unless someone was expected. He told her this and in the next statement assured her no one would ever harm her. This he promised. It was not a promise Krystle ever wanted the circumstances of her life to dictate. But this was only the beginning.

Soon after, Edgar told her that if the dog ever went berserk, she should grab her jacket and move to the back bathroom and be

268

ready to escape through the window. He said she should call him immediately and gave her an address where she would go if such a situation should arise. He had her memorize the address so that no trace of the location would be left in the apartment. He said such things calmly and then promised again that she was safe and in no danger of any kind. He spoke the strange paranoid contradictions side by side, one then the other and as always without explanation.

And still she had stayed. As crazy as it sounded, these were the kind of compromises she had accepted when she had agreed to take one final chance, a leap of faith with the man she couldn't stop loving. In exchange, he had promised her several things and so far he had been true to his word. First, he married her in an impromptu, businesslike ceremony at the courthouse. Second, he never drank at home or kept liquor in the apartment. He still stayed out some nights and refused to call or say where he had been or what he had done. But he swore to her that he was faithful to their vows, that there were no other women now or ever, and she believed him as he had never lied to her. She knew she was enabling him, but it was a codependent relationship from the start. Besides, she was a stubborn woman. She had grown used to this new arrangement, this new life, and if she was honest with herself she would admit that she was happy for the most part, or at least content, which was happier than she had been since early childhood.

Then around the time he brought Butch home, something changed. From that day on, he stayed away more nights and sometimes days at a time and even his usual solemn stoicism grew more distant and wary. There had always been a certain detached hollowness about him, like he knew something about death that no one else knew and that he wasn't allowed to share, but now something about his weary guardedness told her that it was no longer just he who stood on the brink of something dangerous. She began to notice the vehicles parked outside, his "friends" who were always around, in the shadows. She knew they were there guarding her.

Now, it had been over a week since she had last seen him. Eight days since Thanksgiving and hours, days and lonely nights since she had discovered she was with child. With Edgar gone, she had been forced to deal in helpless solitude with the entire

269

smorgasbord of emotions that accompanied a pregnancy. She had told no one else, and the stress of the news along with the growing fear for her husband, herself, and now her child was causing her health to deteriorate rapidly. She knew something was wrong, could feel that something horrible was coming. But she didn't know what, and the uncertainty only made the lonesome dread worse. She began having terrible headaches and stomach aches and flu-like symptoms. She wasn't getting enough to eat, wasn't getting the nutrients she needed. She needed to see her husband, share this news, be held and comforted to alleviate the burden she bore. She needed to hear him tell her that everything would be alright once again, even if it wasn't true.

She knew Edgar would be excited regardless of circumstance. They both wanted children. Since their reunion, even before their marriage, she had tracked her cycles and he had obliged her in every way a man could. But she worried that she was reaching an age when such a dream was no longer realistic. For months on end, they tried and tried without luck. Then on Thanksgiving Day their situation, his life of secrecy and silence had caught up with them and exposed dangers unfit and unfair for a child to be born into and moved her emotional stance from something she felt guilty about suspecting to something obvious and unacceptable and terrifying. And now, discovering she was pregnant had changed her mind all over again.

Early that fateful Thanksgiving afternoon, Edgar had returned from a week of hunting with his brother still covered in blood, yet refusing to say anything more about the trip than it had been a good hunt and that both brothers had been successful in slaying bulls. He told no specifics of the hunt itself. He was anxious and distant and sorrowful. As dinner approached she had to shake him from a series of absent dazes and force him to shower and dress. When he returned from the bedroom unshaven, with bits of blood still stained to his hands and packed beneath his fingernails, his hair was wet but still greasy and unwashed and the stench of campfire and death still clung to his skin. He was like a zombie, and she was furious and demanded he tell her what had happened. He gave no answer; neither reason nor excuse. And the hurt that reflected off him like a force field prevented her from mounting substantial argument or ultimatum. She begged him to tell her what was wrong, yet he just sat there in the kitchen staring at her and at the floor and out the window and at nothing at all.

She was a strong woman made stronger from their time together. There was too much to prepare for their special holiday together to waste her time worrying. She pulled herself together, assuring herself he was only worn out, exhausted and distracted, knowing he would never let anything happen to her, to them. She assigned him a few last minute chores to help with dinner, which he performed. But he did them mindlessly, and she ended up redoing most herself. Perhaps strangest of all was the way he told her how much he loved her time and again; randomly; perhaps a dozen times over the course of the afternoon; ten more than he had spoken on their wedding day; more than he had spoken in all their time together.

Krystle's mother and her latest boyfriend, a real beauty named Gene, had joined them for the holiday feast she had labored and stressed over for days. When Gene's jalopy pulled up, Butch had barked and Edgar had drawn a loaded pistol from some concealed place on his person and pushed her into the pantry closet and leaned against the door frame of the kitchen with the loaded weapon pointed at the door where the dog crouched barking and growling.

When the doorbell rang it had taken all the strength she had to calm him and maintain any semblance of composure herself. Edgar gave no apology for his reaction and didn't chew a single bite at dinner. He simply sat and stared at her across the table with a plateful of food set in front of him. It was the most difficult hour she had ever experienced in all her life.

If her mother or Gene noticed the silence or tension that hung between the newlyweds, they made no mention of it. They had arrived drunk and loud and continued right on through several bottles of wine. It was probably only through their incoherent ramblings that the friction could be lubricated in Krystle's mind, and the absurdity of the entire situation helped to create a dreamlike malaise that likely prevented the night from ending in catastrophe.

The couple had left around nine thirty, just as their buzzes began to mount a turn toward ugly and Edgar began clearing the table. Krystle had given her mother what she half expected to be their final hug, wiped the tears from her eyes, closed the door and followed him into the cramped kitchen to confront him. Enough food to feed a hungry family of four remained upon the table atop her grandmother's silver and fine china and a brand new white tablecloth checkered with turkeys and little pilgrims.

He apologized in the face of her festering rage but continued his refusal of explanation. When she pushed and hit him, the act was lacking in sincerity, and he stood his ground and accepted the blows without reaction. The contact marked the first physical dispute since their latest reunion and she swore to him that he had blown his final shot and that he would never see her again, and he said only that he didn't blame her and agreed that it was probably for the best. Then in the vacuum that followed, he told her again that he loved her and there were tears in his eyes and she huffed and panted and cried as he tried to apologize yet again without authenticity. The silence beyond the emotional display only heightened the suspense and Butch stood tensely by and watched the melodrama unfold with seemingly great interest.

Edgar was stifled by the weight of the situation and his efforts to calm his wife came out broken and indecisive as when children apologize without understanding what they have done wrong. Otherwise he had remained familiarly wooden, unable to hold her or tell her that everything would be alright. While it was evident he was somewhere else, he seemed desperately trying to get back to her and the world in which they were able to coexist. His concern for her was obvious. She knew this, as she knew him, as she had never known another before, and after the violence had been sapped from her person she fell to the kitchen floor, exhausted, and lay there amidst the mess and chaos sobbing. At that point, Edgar had recovered quickly and moved closer and stood beside her. He kneeled quietly and set his hand upon her shoulder. And later, she had looked up into his hardened young face and seen his iron resolve returned, and she remembered feeling relieved and safe at last. He told her that he was done doing what he had been doing. He said that she had cooked a fine meal, and he thanked her and assured her that she would be an excellent mother someday soon. She realized only later, that it was almost like he had known; as men like him, men who lived entirely in the present, had always known.

It was after four a.m. when he had finally joined her in the bedroom. She awoke as he climbed under the cold sheet beside her. His body was warm and hard and still carried the aroma of smoke and something wild. He laid a hand upon her shoulder and her body involuntarily tucked into his and his strong arms had embraced her and his legs touched the length of hers as if electricity jumped between them. They lay in this way for what felt like hours. She had never felt such safety or belonging. Then they made love that she initiated with pecking kisses of sleepy confusion that had grown fierce and angry in reaction to his scratchy beard and the aroma of his wild stench and her frustration with the inability to rid herself of such a man.

First, she rode him, in complete control, gyrating with the sheet tucked around her waist, scraping her nails against the tight, dry flesh of his chest and shoulders, feeling every bulge and scar of his hard, sinewy frame. When he tried to increase the tempo, she raised herself slightly away, discouraging and avoiding his attempts until he gave in, relaxed and let her regain control. Finally, when she had nothing left and collapsed heaving in sweat and exhaustion, he pinned her beneath him with his palms wrapped around her tiny shoulders, firm and yet tender, and drove her to several climaxes with deep, rhythmic pulsing that increased with speed and power as her moans climbed to vulgar screams and profanity. She clawed at his back and pulled his hair desperate for some reaction from him. She cried. But he made no sound other than the low grunt of his labored breathing. The sex continued on this way until dawn broke and pale light rose through the closed blinds, and in dimness she tried to make out the details of his face which she had not examined closely in so long. But the shadows hid him, like his silence, and so she watched his heavily scarred and inked flesh flex and work beneath the shine of the thin coat of perspiration that covered it and sharpened it against the dark.

She awoke the next afternoon around one feeling hung over from exertion and aching from a satisfied soreness in a way she hadn't felt in years. Edgar was nowhere to be seen, which disappointed her but failed to surprise her. She called out for him but only Butch appeared. The dog climbed upon the bed and lay smiling at her as if slyly hinting at the secret they shared. She had gone to the bathroom and to the kitchen for a bowl of cereal but otherwise remained in bed all day. Beyond the room, the evidence of the previous night's failures at normalcy remained untouched as they had left it. And she ignored it best she could. But as the day wore on, her lazy satisfaction sank toward a depressed loneliness. And yet Edgar never returned. She found herself fighting the despair that she might never see him again.

The following evening Sheriff Brad Gale had approached her on the sidewalk outside the bar as she arrived to work in the cold wind of an early December afternoon. He told her that he was looking for Edgar, and her heart had sunk. But her concern had not been for his safety. Instead she had desperately clung to the hope that whatever reason the inquiry was in regards to it must have happened before Thanksgiving, for it was so important that her husband keep his promise. Gale made it apparent that he was unaware the couple had married. Krystle gave nothing away. She lit a cigarette and tapped her toe impatiently smoking as the mixture of the cold and the longing and the curiosity and the disappointment turned her sadness to anger. She grew quickly irritated with the bastard's secrecy and told him as much. She called him an asshole with a badge and told him that even if she knew where Edgar or anyone else was she would never tell a cop. The conversation had quickly grown hostile, and she had tried to excuse herself, saying she would be late to work. But Gale had grabbed her wrist as she turned, and she had to contain herself as her fear and anger warranted a reaction. In the exchange that followed, he called her a slut and a whore that should remember her place and know damn well that her boyfriend was as good as dead. She told him to fuck himself and shook her wrist free and stormed into the bar where she went straight to the bathroom and shook in terror.

She didn't cry, not until later when she could take the mounting fear and anxiety no longer. Throughout the night she found herself unable to catch her breath or hear voices of patrons and coworkers. She forgot drinks and entire orders. But she made it through the shift. The bartender walked her to her car. Someone on those deserted streets was watching her. She could feel it. She was certain she wouldn't make it home. But she made it without incident.

274

The moment she locked the door behind her, she broke down.

She cried all that night and the next day.

Then the morning sickness started. A few days later, she had taken a pregnancy test. It was positive, and she had taken another which was also positive. From that moment on she had shown no signs of her fear or loneliness outside the apartment. She had lost count of the days of her vigilance.

Butch moaned and whined at the base of the door and finally the key slid into the lock and the lock turned and the door opened gently. Edgar slid through the dark crack and into the dim room. He wore a black hooded sweatshirt beneath a camouflage down jacket and wool pants and snow boots and a black stocking cap. His face looked thin and pale beneath an unkempt reddish-brown beard. He patted the ecstatic dog on the head and told it to heel and only when it had did he turn to Krystle who had risen to her feet and stood with the couch between them in sweatpants and one of his stained Carhart sweatshirts. She held her breath.

In that silence anything could have been expected and nothing that followed could be called surprising or out of place, but somehow Krystle kept her emotions in check. She rushed to him and they embraced, and she could tell by his reaction that hers surprised him. He held her at a distance and examined her, and she knew that he knew something had happened, that something in her had changed. After a moment, he squeezed her back as she squeezed him, and he kissed her upon the forehead and the mouth with his dry, cracked lips. Only then, did she finally break and begin to cry. His hug tightened further.

"Where have you been? And what the hell is going on?" she wailed against his chest quietly. It wasn't a demand or accusation but a plea. The relief of her release overwhelmed her.

"It's alright," he whispered. His voice was as dry and chapped as his skin, and she knew he hadn't spoken aloud in some time. "It's alright."

"No, Edgar," she pulled back and looked him in the eyes with desperate honesty. Her face was twisted and red from crying and creased where it had pressed against his jacket. "It is not alright. You have been gone for *too long*. This is not fair. This isn't what we agreed to. You told me you were through doing whatever you were doing and I accepted that and trusted you without asking questions. But now the police are looking for you... cops are telling me that you are dead man... Someone is watching me, following me, watching the house...We are in danger Edgar, I can feel it." She blurted her words rapidly, unable to control herself any longer. "What did you do?" She demanded. But before he could answer she continued on, "We have to get out of here! We can't stay here! Oh what have you done?"

"Shhh," he hushed her gently and waited for her to calm herself, but she couldn't. The cork had been pulled. "It's alright," He whispered again, pulling her head back to his chest and petting her hair gently with his rough hands. She sobbed against him and felt her body go limp.

"I'm pregnant, Edgar."

His hands moved to her shoulders and he moved her back slightly, examining her all anew as she looked up into his face. His was a face of concern and yet excitement and there was a gentle kindness in his eyes, a glowing of pride. "I'm pregnant." She said again. She didn't know where the words came from or if she had even spoke them aloud. She began to cry again.

"Are you sure?" He asked cautiously.

She nodded her head, and through her tear drenched eyes she saw him smile a crooked half smile through his scruffy beard. He pulled her to him tight and he swung her gently from side to side. Then he began to laugh and the laugh grew from a chuckle to near hysterics. She watched the change in him, and amidst such dread it was a beautiful thing, and she wondered for a fleeting moment how amazing a man he could have been if only he hadn't been born himself. But then she realized that such brilliant and fragile beauty could never exist without the contrasting sorrow or desperation that gave it such splendor. And in that moment she remembered why she loved him and no one else, and she was almost happy though she still couldn't stop her tears.

"What are we going to do, baby?" She asked, almost smiling now herself. It took him a few moments to gain composure.

"I need you to get out of town for a few days."

She couldn't believe his words and as those words sank in, she crumbled worse than before.

276

"No," she said. "I won't leave! I won't let you leave me ever again!" She shrieked and as her tone rose shrill he had to hush her again. "No, Edgar, I'm staying with you. I'm going wherever you go." She cried. "You can't leave me not now, not ever again. We have a child now!"

"It is only for a few days." He said gently. "I got you a room at Fairmont Hot Springs. It's under the name Mrs. Reynolds. Becky Reynolds." She began to argue, but he wouldn't allow it. "Don't worry about ID or anything. The room is paid for and they won't give you any hassle. Now listen to me. This is very important. I need you to pack quickly, get in your car and I need you to drive there tonight. The roads are clear, but I need you to be strong and drive slow and safe. I need you to stay at the hotel for three nights and not leave the hotel for any reason. Do you hear me, Krystle? You can soak in the pools and do whatever you want at the hotel, but you do not leave that hotel under any conditions without hearing from me first. Do you understand?"

No," she shook and quivered from head to toe. "No, I don't understand. I don't understand any of this. I won't go. This isn't fair. You told me you would change. You promised me things would be different. Why is this happening to us?" There was an understanding in his face that was so compassionate, she thought he might cry. He rubbed her shoulders and kissed her cheeks.

"I know it's unfair, baby. And I wish I could go back in time and change everything. But what is important to me is that you're safe, that our baby is safe. That my family is safe. So I need you to do this for me. It is the last demand I will ever make of you. "Now, if I haven't contacted you three nights from tonight, I need you to call my brother. He will know what to do. He will take care of you…of both of you."

"But," she was on the verge of another tantrum, but he hushed her and held her.

"No buts."

Then he kissed her lips gently and the kisses grew deeper and more passionate. "We're going to have a child." He exclaimed. "I'm going to be a father." And they smiled and they hugged and touched and kissed some more.

Then, despite his initial resistance, she led him to the bedroom where she undressed him. She had so many questions to

277

ask. There was so much left to be explained. Those issues were let go. She knew it must be done. Events had been set in motion. So despite a nagging fear that these would be their final moments together, she ignored those fears and found strength from somewhere unknown and untapped and she made love to him. Not like the last time. This time they left the lights on and they were both gentle and moved slow and touched each other with the slightest caress and shared long and wet and passionate kisses and equally long, powerful glances. There were tears on her part and gentle care and understanding on his. When they had finished, she was tired and without clue or care for the when or the where. She had lost all contact of time and the world outside, the world beyond the two of them, for that was her world and all that mattered.

But he immediately rose and began to dress, and she was forced to remember once more that that other world was just a dream and that perfection didn't exist and nothing ever lasted, not joy, nor sorrow nor pain or nothing else. Everything human was fleeting.

She watched him from the bed as he pulled his jeans on and then his socks and his boots. As always, he moved with swift determination. She was calm and exhausted and lost in a trance. He told her to get moving, but she lay naked and unable. She didn't notice Butch rise or hear his tags jingle on his collar as he headed toward the door. She didn't notice Edgar noticing either. And the next thing she knew he grabbed her with a speed and strength that wasn't human and he shoved her beneath the bed, jamming her elbow hard against the frame and causing her arm to go numb. Afterwards, she didn't know if she had screamed or cussed or made any sound at all. All she remembered was the pain in her arm followed by the sound of glass shattering and a concussive shutter that shook the house at its foundation.

The explosion left her ears ringing and her vision dark and wobbly. It was followed by a flash of light. Then she must have entered a state of shock as visions of summer and childhood swept over her and everything slowed way down. She remembered thinking she had dozed off with the television on full volume.

But it wasn't the television. That had been destroyed in the blast that tore the living room apart. It was three masked men in black suits that entered the apartment following the explosion. They carried semiautomatic weapons and fired in heavy repetition without aim. The small caliber shells sprayed in all directions tearing through the sheetrock of the tiny room in a scene that would almost seem comical if it weren't so real.

Edgar counted the rounds from habit, but it was no use. All three weapons were firing simultaneously and without pause. When he heard the first click of an empty clip he slid out from his position and shot two shots from the .44 that had stayed within reach even during the climax of their lovemaking. He shot from his back and rolled out of the slide behind the far corner of the door with the angle of the hallway between him and the gunmen. The assailant closing in on the bedroom fell with an agonizing scream, compounding the chaos of the warzone. His partners dove for cover in a room left void of such structure, sending a panicked volley of return fire in the direction of the bedroom.

Then there was silence and Edgar waited and followed their movements by the sound of their boots against the hardwood. When the man in front reached the hall he fired a few rounds down the hallway at floor level, terrified of meeting the same fate as the original leader. From their tactic, Edgar immediately deduced they had no other explosives left and were now growing concerned about ammo. Between shots he charged from the bedroom in a low squat, weaving back and forth as he returned fire. In the mayhem that followed he was nicked in the earlobe as the assailants lost their remaining nerve and turned and fled covering their retreat with several errant sprays in all direction. Edgar shot the trailing man in the back of the head as he retreated through the doorway, slumping him dead in his tracks half in and half out of the destroyed apartment. A final few rounds rung out and thudded upon the bricks outside the building.

Edgar immediately returned to check on Krystle. The bed remained as it had been left from their lovemaking and aside from a few errant scraps of shrapnel from the blast and bullet holes along the far wall beyond the doorway the room wasn't in terrible shape. His wife lay where he had left her, shaking in terror beneath the bed. He pulled her out and checked on her. But her shellshock left her inert and she didn't speak. He cupped his hands over her ears and spoke his instructions as he would to a fellow soldier rather than the pregnant wife that she was.

"I need you to get dressed and hide in the back pantry." He pulled a small caliber revolver from the dresser and placed it in her shaking hands. "If you hear anyone enter that doesn't announce themselves as being police, shoot them." All of this took approximately a minute. The screeching smoke alarm ticked away the seconds.

Then Edgar did the unthinkable.

He left Krystle behind and pursued the remaining gunman out into the cold winter night with no shirt on, running with the pistol swinging up and down, unhidden in his left hand. He looked like a videogame mercenary, blood dripping from his ear onto his tattooed shoulders, chest and back; his skin blue from the cold and ink.

He chased the vehicle for a full block, but it had long since sped off down a side street. He was left screaming in the dark deserted streets for the cowards to face him, screaming for Grisham and Gale in vulgar, nonsensical statements, spewing saliva and pounding the pistol wielding fist against his chest while the veins bulged in his arms and throat.

In the distance police sirens filled the night, closing in quickly. He turned and ran back to the apartment, where the front wall was practically leveled and bits of flame smoldered on the walls and devastated furniture parts. A few neighbors were on their porches now, unable to resist the dangers of their curiosity. Edgar had to step over the fresh corpse of the second gunmen to enter the apartment.

"Krystle." He called out. "Krystle."

Butch lay against the wall near the broken down door, half severed and yelping. Edgar knelt beside the dog and gave it a single gentle pet along its head and down its back.

"Good boy, Butch." He said softly, and then stood and fired a bullet into the dog's head.

In the reverberating silence following the shot, the wounded assailant cried out for assistance. Edgar walked over to the man who had removed his mask. He recognized him as one of Grisham's goons, a man named Chad with a wife and two young children. He was around thirty years old. Edgar stood over the man and the man turned to look up at him and he reached up trying to plea for mercy. Edgar looked into his desperate eyes and fired two shots into the would-be assassin's chest. He found Krystle a moment later, still naked and quivering on the bedroom floor, the pistol clutched in both hands.

"Krystle," he whispered. But she didn't respond. "Come on, baby." He said heaving her limp naked body over his shoulder. "We have to go."

Chapter 30

Shannon pulled the Explorer into the garage and shut the garage door and entered the house through the laundry room. He turned on the hallway light and the glow ran off toward the kitchen and the staircase, highlighting the eerie quiet that had become his home. He had yet to grow accustomed to it and didn't suspect he ever would. But tonight, it hardly mattered. It had been a long day, perhaps the longest of his life, fielding phone calls with television cameras and microphones everywhere he turned. He was exhausted. And the silence was a welcome change. He set his bag down beside the banister at the base of the stairs and hung his jacket on a hook in the front entrance hallway, flipping light switches as he moved.

He had done his best to do damage control. But when a homemade bomb levels your brother's apartment, the rumors of his criminal habits begin to circulate rather quickly. Add multiple witnesses describing that brother as a shirtless, tattooed psychopath, running down a snow covered street in the frigid cold firing a pistol and screaming profanity laced challenges at a fleeing car filled with machine gun wielding mercenaries, and it becomes a bit harder for a major political figure to spin, than, say, a family member arrested for an assault or DUI. Mostly, Shannon pled unaware of any cause behind such events and had done his best to profess his brother's innocence until proven guilty. He used every opportunity to remind the country of his brother's heroic military career and tried to paint Edgar as the possible victim of circumstance. That might have been easier had his brother or least his new wife stuck around to meet police and paramedics after the incident. Instead, what remained of the hundred year old building stood taped off as a crime scene, and a million questions and fears hung on the held breath of the town's sixty thousand or so residents.

Federal investigators and national media were arriving to town in droves. The tiny airport had never been so busy. Every political and social ally Shannon had added to his inner circle on his swift rise to the top had vanished in a smoke screen of unanswered emails and secretaries' regrets in telling him they would have to return his call – when all three parties knew this to be untrue. He was sure to be impeached, convicted and watch what was left of his life wash down the drain. That was, of course, assuming Grisham didn't stick to his word and have Shannon killed, which at that moment seemed both the most likely and perhaps favorable outcome of the biggest news story to come out of Montana since the capture of the Unabomber.

His own life hardly mattered any more. It was only the life of his estranged wife and their two little girls that he held any value for personally. That is why he had agreed to speak with the FBI agents first thing the following morning. He wanted to ensure his family's safety. And at this moment he was worried sick about them.

Shannon had tried hinting as much to Conrad in a phone call he was certain had been eavesdropped on by investigators or Grisham's men or possibly both. Obviously, Conrad wasn't pleased to hear that the safety of his girls might be at stake, though he did seem receptive to the warning. The old general had little else to say to his former protégé. He could care less whether the cause of this incident was of Shannon's doing or beyond his control. Shannon didn't blame him. Regardless of the circumstances leading up to this, he should have prevented it before death or the threat of death was ever involved. He wondered what, if anything, Conrad knew about Grisham's power, the real power beyond the surface. But it was hardly the time to ask and there was sure to be more questions than answers.

The only certainty was that this was his fault. It was all his fault. If not for the blind concessions he had made time and again, for years now, he or a fellow idealist may have been able to assail some of Grisham's growing power, certainly avoided this: two dead and two loved ones missing. He had known about so much for so long, and yet he had done nothing but use the information he was privy to for his own selfish gain. In his own mind, he and he alone had brought these horrific events upon the very people he vowed to serve and to protect. He prayed the heightened state of affairs would keep Grisham lying low for a while. But he knew enough about psychology and primitive instinct to know a predator is most dangerous when cornered or frightened.

If only he hadn't been so selfish, so greedy. If only he hadn't been so ambitious. If he hadn't carried the nagging guilt of his family's demise, he may have found a way to bring Grisham down, expose Gale for the growing threat that he was or at the very least reached Edgar before this steadily mounting crisis had reached such a violent detonation.

Poor Edgar. He was such a good boy. And that was how Shannon imagined him all day in his subconscious. Each time Edgar's name touched his ears, Shannon saw only his kid brother, as he had been at fifteen, after their father's death, just as he had appeared for years in thousands of guilt ridden dreams. And Shannon knew why. His guilt had nagged him every day since that kiss; that almost innocent mistake. But it wasn't an innocent mistake. Not when a boy so young has faced such hardship and has only an older brother and nothing else left in this world. In that case, Shannon's momentary lapse in judgment was to become Judas.

To think that perhaps a tiny peck and fleeting embrace of console and understanding in a moment of imprudent disregard for the repercussions of such an act, on a drunken, youthful night, so very long ago, in the wake of such unbearable loss, such unexplainable emotion, could possibly lead to such far-reaching and substantially devastating outcomes. For the rift that had risen between his brother and himself, the rift that eventually became this deep, wide and impassable chasm, now so clearly seemed to begin with that moment, when an older brother betrayed a younger in the most unforgivable of ways at the most unthinkable time.

And finally, Shannon was prepared to accept the blame for everything. This time, he wouldn't secretly pass the fault to anyone else deep down inside. Not his mother nor his father nor his brother. Even if only to himself. This was on him, and for once he couldn't spin it in his favor.

He clicked the switch in the kitchen and the jolt of the fluorescent tubes stuttered a sterile light on the clean surfaces of the room. The sameness of everything disappointed him some. He had half expected to find an assassin here waiting for him – an easy way out. He leaned on the counter and sighed, unsure of what to do next for the first time in a long while. Suddenly it occurred to him that if he hadn't always been so certain and determined in his decisions and reactions this whole terrible episode could have been prevented a hundred times over. But such thoughts of autonomy in the course of one's life had been losing traction with him for some time now, and he suspected that a simple solution was likely never possible. The Drummond curse had never felt so real.

He dialed Jill's cell for what may have been the hundredth time. It rang and rang again, until the voicemail picked up. He had left a dozen messages already expressing his urgency to speak with her. There was nothing left to be said to a stupid machine. So he hung up and set the phone down and ran his fingers through his scalp, desperate for a course of action to come to him.

When providence failed to provide a solution, he pulled a glass down from the cupboard and filled it with ice and opened the cabinet above the fridge where he stored a small assortment of liquors that were rarely touched in the absence of company. The days of joyous gatherings in this home were gone, not likely to return, and he had found himself more and more of late having a drink or two in silent reflection and remorse in the lonesome emptiness of the big house. He grabbed the Scotch, the Macallan, aged eighteen years, but then changed his mind and decided bourbon was a better choice for the situation. He poured a little Beam over the ice and let it set to work on the frosty cubes before adding a little more and then a tiny bit more still. He took a sip from the drink and held it in his hand and stared into the shadows of the dining room. What would he have done if a gunman had been waiting here for him? Would he have taken his fate like a man or fallen to his knees and cried and begged to be spared? Would he have fought to survive?

Eventually, he drank the drink down to a third of its original volume and added fresh ice and more bourbon. Then he walked about the house flipping on lights until he reached the living room where a seven foot fir tree stood fully decorated in the corner visible from the entryway. It was a beautiful tree particularly in the dark; full and shapely; one of the finest he had ever harvested, it was in actuality the top of a much taller tree cut down then poached for its upper symmetry. But even with its colorful lights all aglow, reflecting the shine of dozens of ornaments and four stockings hung on the mantel beyond, it was only another morsel of deception in the sham that his life had come to represent – or possibly always been. For this was no happy home. Even if he piled gifts beneath that tree and the smells of its sap and a cured ham filled the lower floor of this big beautiful home, it would be an artificial joy and even his girls, so young still and full of innocence, would only succumb to the charade for so long.

He thought about these things and all the illusions his life was built upon and wondered when and where it had all begun. At what moment had he contracted with himself to accept such deficiencies? He thought that perhaps he had simply been born without something that was fundamentally necessary to genuine human connection, but then he realized this too was an excuse freshly formulated by his loyal subconscious, and as he walked slowly across the unswept hardwood, drink in hand, he stopped in the entryway and hit the switch and light poured down from the vaulted ceiling and subdued the newly added Christmas glow. It took him only an instant to detect the presence of a dark, bearded figure sitting in the armchair opposite the tree and another moment to recognize this man as not a would-be assassin but his own flesh and blood. But when he had grasped this realization, it took several seconds longer to reach a reaction.

"Edgar?" he asked the haggard figure in the black hoodie and black beanie and torn camo jacket. The figure looked up, and his eyes adjusted to the light.

"Hello brother."

A million new thoughts buzzed through Shannon's consciousness, but he was tired and calm from the bourbon and he breathed instead of spoke, and took his brother in.

"Are you alright?" He asked.

"Could be better."

Shannon moved slowly closer to his brother. He was about to sit down in the loveseat facing him when his brother nodded toward the drink. "You got anymore of that sauce?"

"Of course." Shannon said without a hint of laughter. The room had been radically rearranged with the addition of the tree, and the décor's placement was foreign to him and he had to look around a moment to find a place to set his glass. "I'll be right back." He said.

He returned a moment later with a second glass filled with ice in one hand and the bottle of bourbon strangled by its neck in the other. He handed Edgar the glass and offered to pour from the bottle. His brother took the glass and dumped the ice into his hand losing a few cubes that spilled into his lap. Yet rather than fuss with the spilled ice, he put the handful in his pocket and raised the now empty glass toward Shannon. Shannon filled it half-way and set the bottle on the hardwood beside the chair. He picked up his own glass and moved to the loveseat, watching his brother the entire time. Edgar drained the drink in two gulps. He pulled a cube of ice from his pocket and chewed it while he filled the glass full, took a sip and then brushed the spilt cubes to the floor and set the drink in his lap.

"I'm sorry." He said, raising his eyes to meet the gaze of his elder brother. The eyes were void of all life.

Shannon ran his free hand through his scalp and his own eyes welled with moisture as he sighed.

"Yeah," he said looking up toward the ceiling as if hoping to rise there and escape this whole mess. "Me too."

They sat that way for a moment and each took a drink and Shannon tried to imagine again how it had possibly come to this.

"This is all my fault." He conceded. "When Dad died I just couldn't fill…"

"Stop." Edgar cut him off. Shannon looked back and their eyes locked. "Enough with the blame and the guilt and the reasons why… None of that matters anymore." He said.

"You told me to leave. You gave me that opportunity and I didn't take it, and I placed you and our family in harm's way."

"Why didn't you leave?" Shannon couldn't help but ask.

"Where would I go?" Edgar replied.

Shannon had no answer.

"I'm a grown man, brother. I know you can't see it sometimes. But I'm grown. And along the way I made choices and those choices were my own and they had nothing to do with you or with Dad or with Mom or with any of the shit that's happened between us." He looked at his brother as he spoke and it was a serious look, but his eyes were clear and dry. It was evident this was something he had thought long on. "This thing should've never come to this, and if I'd have known…if I'd have known this would happen, maybe I could have stopped it. Maybe not. Hell, I don't know, and it don't matter. What matters is that you told me to go, you gave that chance, fair warning, and I refused, and now we're here… But I'm going to fix it. I'm going to end it."

"No. No one else has to get hurt." Shannon demanded. "No one else has to die…This is as much my fault as it is yours." He spoke honestly. "And it's time I will take responsibility too. I'm talking to the FBI tomorrow morning, and I'm coming clean about everything. We'll set this right."

"You think that's going to solve anything?" Edgar sat forward and his brother thought he might laugh. "You think this situation can be solved with talk or with law?"

"Yes." Shannon answered, nodding vigorously. "That is how the world works, Edgar. That is how a democracy operates."

"That ain't how this works, brother. That ain't how this has ever worked. There are two dead men in a car parked down the block. Those men were sent to make sure you *didn't* talk, and you can trust me when I say there will be more before the law ever lifts a finger to change anything in this town. Nobody cares about us, brother. They just don't want that danger to feel so real, so close. They don't want it to set foot in their own safe little world. See no one has a problem with death or pain or the horrible evil that we all know exists. They just don't want to see it. They don't want to think about how they would face it. They want it kept behind locked doors. They want it restricted to far away places."

"Jesus Christ, Edgar." Shannon felt sick and his drink trembled in his hand. "So what do you suggest, we go around killing people? Start a war that will get innocent people killed? My girls killed? Get Jill or Krystle killed?"

Edgar turned and looked out the window into the dark evening and his brother watched what he could see of his reflection from across the room.

"I promise this will all be over soon, brother."

"Edgar, I'm talking to federal agents in the morning. They can help you. They will protect you. They will protect Krystle."

"They aren't going to protect nothing, Shannon." He spoke the words gently, almost at a whisper, as if he wished the words weren't true. "That's a fantasy and you know it as well as I do. We protect our own. That's how it's always been."

"If that's what you believe then I'm asking you to let *me* protect *you*. Just this one time. Please!
"You leave tonight. I'll watch out for Krystle and I'll see that Grisham gets what he deserves. I'll make sure Gale is charged too."

"Krystle's pregnant."

Shannon didn't know what to say.
"She's pregnant, brother." He had emptied his glass again and now he was filling it as he spoke. "I'm going to be a father." He shook his head and a shadow climbed the right side of his face and Shannon could see his smile, a crooked, sheepish half-smile. But as his words trailed off, the smile left his face and his gaze fell back to the floor and Shannon watched the options melt away.

"So we'll deal with that too, Edgar." He said softly. "What's important is that no one else suffers for our mistakes."

"They won't." The younger Drummond answered with sudden resolve. "I need a day, maybe two. Give me forty-eight hours and this'll all be over."

"It's not that easy, Edgar. There are bigger players in this thing than you think. Go away tonight and I'll barter a deal. I swear it... You're a military hero for God's sake. That has to mean something." Shannon was reaching for straws, but he knew the pregnancy changed everything.

"Hero?" Edgar almost snorted, but as always he held back. "I'm no hero, brother. You don't know what I've done. You couldn't imagine the things I've done. Nobody could." Some painful memory or memories was pulling at him, but he seemed to have it subdued or maybe he had simply come to terms with it very recently. "The only one that knows what I did overseas, truly

288

knows, is my Maker and I think he's decided its time to settle up…Besides, they ain't going to take no chance on me being part of some big trial with national attention. They can't have me talking, brother."

Shannon was completely lost.

"What are you talking about, Edgar? Who are they? The military? This has nothing to do with you being a soldier, Edgar. We aren't at war. You're home. Remember? People can't go around killing people here."

Just then lights appeared in the pale night and a car pulled up along the curb on the far side of the street. Shannon stood to look as the vehicle cut its lights.

"I have to go now brother." Edgar stood and moved away from the window. He walked just past his brother and then turned and faced him eye to eye. "You don't tell them nothing that's going to ruin your career you hear me? You don't tell them one word that will hurt this family's name.

"That name is all we got. What you've accomplished with your life has brought that name more pride and more honor than anything that could possibly come out of this.

"You have a chance to change things, brother, but you got to be strong and you can't ever forget anything that's happened." They stood inches apart and Shannon could smell the bourbon and stale smoke on his brother's breath. Edgar stood steady as steel. "If you tell them anything we could lose everything you fought for. Everything *we* fought for. And we might never get any of it back."

He reached for Shannon's hand and grabbed it tight. "You be strong for us. You be strong for our children, for our family."

"If I do," Shannon choked. "Promise me you'll leave. Leave all this bullshit behind and go away. Run. Run away and don't ever look back."

"I would if I could brother, but it's too late for that now, and we can never go back. There are only two ways out now, and I swore long ago to the brothers I watched die, I'd never swallow a hollow, never save the last round for a solo toast. So really there is only one way this ends."

It was the most Edgar had said to his brother in many years, and it was followed by a moment that seemed to hang heavy and silent over them, the silence that had been there with them their whole lives and it was the silence that had been the entire world long before the living came to be.

"I guess we really are cursed then?" Shannon asked. "Our family?"

"There's no such thing as curses, brother. You know that as well as I do. This is just how we are – how things turned out. "Hell, it's probably how things have always been. But the fact remains that we both bred children and the Drummond line won't end with us and that means we can't possibly be cursed. "That's all that matters."

There was a firm knock at the door and Shannon instinctively grabbed his brother and hugged him tight, fighting back tears.

"Slip out the back and jump the fence off the south corner of the porch. Don't take the alley. They'll be watching it at either end…I'll miss you."

As the embrace loosened, they looked each other in the eyes once more and Shannon set his hand upon his brother's cheek; his only brother; his baby brother.

"You too brother. You make sure my kid's raised up right."

"Stop talking like that. Everything is going to work out. You'll raise your own child and have more children."

And as Edgar slipped from the room toward the back hall, he stopped and without turning fully around spoke,

"You know I've always been proud of you brother. Dad would be too."

And as the swift knocking struck the door a second time, a muffled voice ended the most emotional moment Drummond men had ever shared and Shannon wiped his eyes and took a breath and collected himself, then walked slowly toward the entryway without ever looking back. He took one deep breath at the door and then opened it to find three somber, well-dressed men standing in the cold beneath the porch light.

"Shannon Drummond." The man in the middle asked. He was older than either man flanking him by a decade. Shannon guessed him to be in his fifties. They were each stern and emotionless.

"Yes." Shannon replied flatly.

The man held out a laminated identification card for Shannon to see.

"My name is Ran Frickle and these are corporals Cornwall and Weststaff. We were wondering if you wouldn't mind taking a little ride with us this evening."

"Wait a minute, are you guys with the FBI? I told the officer…was his name Reese? I told him that I would call him first thing in the morning."

"We understand that sir. That's why were here. We'd like to speak with you before you speak with other agents."

"What is this? Who are you?"

"We'll explain all that in the car, sir. We just need you to come with us."

"I don't suppose I have any choice?"

Frickle shook his head. "That's a negative, sir."

"You do know I'm the Attorney General for the State of Montana, correct?"

"Yes sir. You're not in any kind of trouble, sir. Our goal is simply to intercept and retrieve your brother before anyone else gets hurt. We hate to show up at your house without calling, but we hope you can understand the urgent nature of the matter, sir."

"Alright, let me grab my jacket."

Chapter 31

Sunday morning. The final day of a week's stay at camp. It was an hour before first light and the tarps and the sleeping bags were already rolled up and ready to go. The garbage was piled beside the tent and everything was cleaned off and packed up aside from the stove and the provisions left for one last breakfast. The boys planned to take a short morning hunt and return to camp and eat, then take down the tent and start the first of however many trips it took to get everything out. What little meat remained would be left for the bears. They would leave no signs of life behind except the fire pit and a cache of weather proof supplies stashed beneath a couple old slabs of plywood in a thick stand of the young lodgepole a quarter mile away.

291

The morning was bitter cold but the wind had died and the limbs of the conifers hung quietly without a whisper. The darkest of blues was spreading in the sky but a million stars remained out amidst the sparse clouds that bobbed above like docked ships in a bay, their outlines lit by the moon. The air was clear and the snow glowed, and the details of the small, familiar meadow were almost visible, though the shadows and the distance played tricks upon the cones of the human retina. The world was quiet and calm and felt ancient and unmolested. The winter had arrived in the high mountains and would stay through much of May, possibly June. Returning to town would be like traveling back in time.

The boys each took a turn outdoors tending to their business then returned to the tent and sat fully dressed and waiting. The lantern had run out of fuel and the flashlights' beams were growing faint as well. The only light was that provided from the fire of the open stove. In the shifting glow, Shannon sipped his second cup of coffee, checking his watch periodically and staring at the white-hot flames. He looked terrible, gaunt and exhausted, as did Edgar, who sat to his right and swallowed and yawned and rubbed his eyes and scratched at his greasy mop, waiting with a newly acquired patience.

They were prepared for one more hunt, but it had been a long week and neither held much hope for success. They were beaten both physically and mentally and rose from habit and obligation, unable to sleep or stand lying there alone in the dark with their own thoughts. Still, they had done it. They had continued the camp's tradition in the absence of their father.

Shannon's young face showed his loss of determination as clearly as the whiskers of his inadequate beard. The day prior they had returned from Black Bear Mountain in the early afternoon, and he had sat in camp and sulked. An hour before sunset they had ridden the bikes to a park just off the trail above camp where they sat on the edge of the timber until twenty minutes before dark. They had been in bed an hour later. The disappointment in their hearts had consumed them. But they would see the trip through to its conclusion. There was no question of that. They would hunt that final hunt. Then they would go home and return to their lives and time would march on the same as it always had. For the rest of the season they would hunt on weekends or take evening drives on

Shannon's rare nights off. And hopefully if things worked out and enough sacrifices were made, they would return again the following fall for a week or five days or three days, whatever the situation might allow.

Finally, the time came and Shannon checked his watch one last time and rose and stretched and grabbed his stuff and closed the iron latch on the stove without bothering to adjust the damper and exited the tent with his brother close behind. They walked to the bikes, their boots crunching atop the hard frozen snow. Then Edgar faced his brother, drew what courage remained and spoke.

"I'm going to Windy Ridge." He said. It was the first words either had spoken since well before dark the prior evening. "You should come with me."

These were not the words of a fifteen year old, and Shannon knew his brother was right. He should go. He felt a hunch tugging at him. It wasn't right to stay away from such sacred ground. But he was stubborn and his mind was already made up. He wanted to write his own story, and he didn't want that story to mirror his father's failures. It was all nonsense really. He knew it. But what more was there to life than one's perception of it?

"I'll let you take it." He conceded rather casually, despite the fact that his brother had been lost on the same hunt just days earlier. "Ride out the trail and hunt up onto the ridge from the west. I'll come down through the low saddle above the Split and check those parks down in Six Point. If there are elk hiding in there, one of us should end up pushing them toward the other."

Edgar listened. Then he nodded.
"Don't get way down in that bowl. But don't give up too early either. Walk down and check out the parks and come right back up. I'll either meet you on the trail or see you back at camp. Take your time. This is our last chance. There's no hurry."

Then the two of them just stood there a second and took it all in. The vapors of their breathing froze the air between them. Whatever answers or questions they awaited went unsaid and the world paid them little mind. So they climbed on their bikes and pulled their hats down low and rode off without witness to finish obligations to self and each other and to men dead and gone.

As they traveled, so did the sun. It was nearing the horizon now and there was just enough light to see without the aid of the headlight as Edgar crested the Main Ridge and started down beyond his destination. When the timber cleared he cut the light and coasted down the hill until he found a suitable spot to leave the bike. Then he killed the engine and the silence engulfed all at once. The dark overhead had grown a drab gray and the stars had vanished and only the clouds forecast the changing colors with hints of extended visibility. Edgar squeezed his gloved hands and registered the cold then turned his thoughts to the comfort of a hot shower in the coming hours. The sensations of cold and discomfort had grown so familiar on his nose, lips, fingers and toes that week that he couldn't imagine the absence of it. His runny nose in particular had grown raw and chapped from near constant wiping.

As he checked his rifle and scope in the dull light his thoughts were activated and his body went through the motions as the dread of being lost revisited him with renewed clarity. But he wasn't afraid and he started off optimistic that it was morning, the beginning and not the end. Still, elk were the furthest thing from his mind. He had thought less and less of that purpose as the week had progressed, and the past few days his thoughts had been little more than drifting images and startling ideas half-clairvoyant in nature. His ability to differentiate between dream and reality was irrelevant as both states of consciousness found him aimlessly wandering around through endless expanses of cold, snow-covered wilderness in search of something that he knew wasn't what he was truly after, but rather only a metaphor for the true, unknown objective – which almost certainly did not exist.

It took him less than twenty minutes to crest the ridge and as he started down a blinding glare shone from the southeast to his left. The rising sun lit the sky in pale blue and haloed the farthest horizons in all direction. It was a different world from his previous visit only a few days prior. This time he never stopped. He simply continued on at the same pace as the snow vanished and was replaced by lifeless leaning grass amidst gravel and broken rock and he found himself upon the rocky ledge climbing toward the park beyond the high, desolate knob. He saw the place where he had sat in the fog and contemplated his life and it seemed so long ago, like a different existence entirely. He barely remembered her face, her voice, their shared touch.

Then he was upon the exposed face and the wind greeted him instantly, albeit rather placidly for this location and time of year. Almost like it felt pity for him. Yet the cold was bitter. His body was drained of its natural defenses, and the wind caused his eyes to water then dry out. He was forced to duck his head against the gust which cut through his layers with ease. His bones ached and his ears burned hot beneath his cap.

He could have easily turned around here, told his brother he had found the parks empty yet again. No one would ever question it. But this never crossed his mind and he continued on another five minutes until he had crested the knob and looked down upon the wind drifted park where three bull elk were feeding away from him down the ridge toward the timber on his right hand side.

When he saw them he was standing in the open fully exposed on the rock ledge, unprepared and silhouetted by the new day's sun. But the wind was coming up the ridge from the gulch, and the elk were moving in the direction from which it blew. The critters fed with their heads down, twenty yards between each, and the closest one to the edge of the park still had a hundred yards to the safety of the timber.

There was a bare, snarled dead protruding from the granite some thirty yards uphill from where Edgar stood. But he didn't move for it. He didn't look for a lean or lie prone as his father had taught him. He didn't even size up the animals' antlers. He didn't think at all. He simply raised the rifle to his shoulder and found the closest bull in his scope. He estimated the distance quickly at about two hundred yards, and as he located it in the crosshairs, the bull raised its head and looked around cautiously. It sniffed at the air. Edgar tried to steady the intersecting crosshairs on the critter's shoulder, but his pulse was pounding and he had a difficult time holding the rifle still free handed. Afraid the bull had detected his presence he exhaled his breath and squeezed the trigger.

As the shot rang out, and the recoil kicked him hard in the shoulder, he lowered the rifle and looked at the scene again with his naked eyes. The first thing he acknowledged were the elk thundering for the timber and he slid the bolt back and flung the still smoking shell to the earth and cocked in a second shell and raised the rifle once more.

It took him what felt like too long to find hide again and when he did he had no idea if it was even the same bull he had previously fired on. The animal was nearing the timber and the contrast in the early light made distinguishing hide from background more difficult. The last thing he saw in his shaky, narrowed field of vision was the white of the critter's ass. He squeezed the trigger.

As he lowered the weapon a second time, he caught a flash of movement as something vanished into the timber. From the distance he stood, he couldn't hear any movement, only the wind and his labored breathing and his heart pounding in his chest. He didn't give chase. He stood there a moment gathering his thoughts for the first time. He considered what had just taken place trying desperately to think if he had hit the animal, but he couldn't convince himself either way. His legs were shaking and he squatted down on his haunches and set there until his adrenaline slowed and he had caught his breath. He was excited and angry with himself and anxious and confused all at once. Instinctively, he reached for a chew before remembering he was out. It took a few minutes for time to return to a manageable pace and still he reached no definitive decision. He just set there watching the timber where the elk had entered as if he half expected the elk to come running back out, wishing in his heart for a chance to do the whole thing over.

Finally, he grew calm enough to realize how cold he was and he looked around him at the surrounding horizons off in the distance. The sun had risen fully over the mountains and there were few sparse clouds expanding low overhead. There was little sign that the day would warm much, if any. He stood and he listened a moment longer and then he started down into the park on wobbly legs toward the place where the bull had stood when he first shot.

When he reached the general proximity he began searching the ground for blood. The grass stood nearly to his knee in places and the earth was spotted with rock and crusted, windblown snow and ice all around. Everything looked the same and after several minutes of unsuccessful examination, he looked back up the ridge to where he had stood and tried to decide if he was in the right area. Again his mind was indecisive and soon the self-doubt began to spread. He thought about the things he should have done differently. But he refused to accept failure and continued to slowly expand his perimeter.

Then he found it; red. A spray of blood upon a clump of frozen earth. Then a few feet later another messy splattering across the snow and base of the grass. It wasn't much but it was something.

He slung his rifle on his shoulder then unslung it and jammed in two shells from his pocket and cocked one in the chamber and thought a moment longer before clicking the safety on and reslinging it. He crept slowly in the direction the blood took toward the timber and found more sign every few steps. Some spots were almost insignificant. Others were splatters the size of his hand. He didn't think the wound looked fatal, but he had already decided he would find his prey even if he had to follow it to the ends of the earth.

He reached the edge of the timber and as the terrain changed the snow returned with consistency and depth, and the tracks became easier to follow. He took his time and inched along a few steps at a time, stopping now and again to examine his surroundings. Every ten feet another splatter. Then the tracks ran together and it appeared as if a herd of elk had passed through. The tracks zigged and zagged crisscrossing each other. Once or twice he had to backtrack to stay on the wounded bull. He lost track of time. He was a quarter mile down the hill when the trail turned hard and vanished into a thicket of willows that sprang up from a hidden spring and he saw no choice but to follow. There was no way to track blood in the thick brush. The leaves rattled and the thin branches whipped and snapped as he pushed his way through. Every step caused a real racket.

Then he heard a commotion up ahead and he stopped. A hundred yards ahead in the timber he saw the bull's antlers raise as it struggled to stand. It looked back toward the six to eight foot brush and he locked eyes with it before it turned to run. Its eyes were dark orbs void of emotion.

He unslung his rifle as he fought through the last of the vine-like willows. By the time he was clear of the thicket the bull was moving downhill and he raced behind it. He couldn't see the critter but he knew from the sound of its movement that it was dragging a limb. He listened as he ran and sought shooting lanes in the bull's direction. The timber was sparse and mature fir for long stretches below him where it would eventually cease and the parks along the base of the bowl would open. He reached that timber and slowed his pace and looked all around. His heart pounded, though he had no perception of this. The elk stumbled, sliding into view to his left then turned and ran below him. He didn't want to lose it, for he knew it might not bed down again.

As he stopped and leaned the barrel of the rifle against a tree, it too stopped momentarily and looked back again. He took aim, but he had failed to dial his scope down and when the critter appeared it was a blur of fur in the crosshairs. He pulled the trigger and loaded another shell as he ran forward twisting the setting on the scope without looking. He found the animal quickly where it had fallen and he stopped and checked the scope to be sure he had dialed it in the right direction.

The bull was trying to stand again but couldn't. It had been fatally wounded and Edgar closed within thirty yards of the animal at a gentle pace. As it looked back at him he saw black matted hide where blood spilled from its hind quarter. He could hear its uneven panting as it labored for its final breaths. Only then did he notice the size of its antlers, dark majestic horns with sharpened white tips that stood out in the dim timber. The horns turned as its body writhed and kicked.

The boy raised the rifle and shot the animal in the head and it slumped to the snow and kicked once with great fury and a second time hardly noticeable. Then it died. Its large black eyes left open.

He leaned against a tree never taking his eyes off the great creature as he heaved for air. This was the greatest achievement in his young life and he stood there and examined the bull for a long time taking it all in. The excitement caught up to him quickly and he swore aloud and pumped his fist as shivers of joy climbed his spine. Then he set down in the snow and listened to the morning warbles of the chickadees and the finches and the nuthatches. He had never felt such emotion and his ears rang as his thoughts came through in incomplete pulses.

He was sweating. He leaned the rifle against a nearby tree and removed his gloves and his hat and set them near where the stock sat in the snow. It was still cold, but the air was calm in the shaded timber and he felt nothing but overwhelming joy. He didn't revel overly long. Despite not knowing where to start, he grabbed the animal by the base of the antlers and twisted its neck, doing his best to roll the animal over. The body was massive and sturdy and still warm and the work required phases. Once he had it on its side he opened its legs and removed his jacket and pulled out his knife and cut in just above the anus and worked around the penis and up along the pelvis. He had gutted and skinned deer, and the work was familiar though on a much larger scale. The maneuvering was also more difficult due to the mass of the animal. He made it as far as the ribcage and then wiped the sweat from his brow with his shoulder and took rope from his pack and tied one of the back legs to a nearby tree as he had seen his father do. Then he rolled his sleeves past his elbows and unsheathed his pack saw and cut through the brisket and removed the guts, throwing the entrails down the hill away from the carcass. After he had pulled out the windpipe and cut it and cut away any remaining waste and tipped the carcass and drained the remaining blood, he braced the ribcage open with a large branch and examined his work.

One hindquarter was damaged from where he had shot the animal in the ass and there was a second wound where a bullet had hit the animal in the guts quartering away and just missed the lungs and front shoulder. He wasn't sure if this had been his first or third shot.

He tossed snow into the open cavity and used the slush surrounding his work to clean his dulled blade, leaving bits of meat and blood that he couldn't get at drying along the hilt of the tool. Then he cleaned his hands and forearms and searched his fanny for his tag and cut the date out using tiny triangles and taped the tag to the antlers using orange flagging tape. Then he searched for a chew before again remembering he was out. So he squatted and examined the animal a little longer and debated his next move.

It was a nice six point bull, not huge but mature and symmetrical and beautiful. He had hunted hard and nothing about the moment felt underserved or bittersweet. It was a well earned kill. He was a warrior now, and that distinction changed him and could never be taken away.

He remembered the ivories and broke the bottom jaw and pried both out with the point of his blade. He couldn't wait to show his brother. If Shannon was on the Split or down in Six Point he should have heard the shots. If he wasn't already headed in Edgar's direction, he would be soon. Edgar wondered what his brother would have to say about his accomplishment. He envisioned the pride in his face and the moment they would share and the bond that was growing between them. He thought of how none of this could have ever happened without his brother. He pictured the embrace. He smiled and reflected on all the hard work and struggles they had faced in the past week as he looked around him and up through the dense canopy of the giant firs at the blue sky overhead. Such a long and tireless week. What a way for it to end.

He didn't know how they would get this animal out on the bikes. But he wasn't worried about that. Shannon would know. Besides it was cold and if they had to borrow horses and come back the animal should be ok. Maybe they would skin it or quarter it and pack it out piece by piece. Whatever had to be done, his brother would guide him.

He grabbed his jacket and hat and gloves and put them on and grabbed the rifle and cocked out the spent cartridge and held it in his hand and blew across the empty shell making it whistle. Then he placed the shell in his pocket and started back up the hill in the direction from which he had come. He would wait for his brother on the park atop the ridge.

As he started up the hill his hunger and thirst and fatigue registered. He hoped there was time for breakfast before they went to work. He was starving. But he knew they had a long day ahead, and he wouldn't complain or make requests. He would let his brother decide what was to be done, and he would follow his instructions. He couldn't wait to see his brother's face. Shannon would be so proud of him.

Chapter 32

...This just in, two more have been found dead in Montana. While the latest fatalities have not been confirmed or officially identified, this reporter has been told that one of the individuals is a long time suspected local crime lord by the name of Robert Grisham...

...Allegedly Mr. Grisham had replaced former area mob boss, Zeke Franklin, after Mr. Franklin died of a heart attack while serving a ten year sentence in the Montana State Prison for racketeering and prostitution charges in the late seventies. CNN research finds that Franklin had also been linked to at least three murders in the decades leading up to his conviction and tried on charges in two subsequent instances, being found not guilty of a list of crimes on both occasions. County records show that Mr. Grisham was previously convicted of a felony count of assault with a deadly weapon some thirty plus years ago, but hasn't had any charges against him since. It is alleged that Grisham took over as mob boss either directly following Franklin's death or possibly after some unidentified intermediary. Of course all of this remains speculative. But, again, several local sources who have come forward in the matter suggest Mr. Grisham was at the top of a powerful, highly-sophisticated, criminal organization running a large scale extortion, prostitution and drug syndicate in central Montana. A few opinions are even suggesting that local authorities were either directly or indirectly involved with Grisham's activities, which were run through a pub he owned, and for which he maintained day-to-day managerial responsibilities. Still others maintain that Mr. Grisham was an upstanding citizen and generous member of the community and are adamant of his innocence. So far, local authorities are not commenting on any link between these deaths, or any criminal organization, and the violence two nights ago that left another two men dead, a century-old apartment in ashes and a local couple missing. But again, numerous sources are coming forward and reporting the existence of a deep- rooted, decades-old, large scale illegal mob in Montana that was led by the man pictured on the left, tavern owner Robert

Grisham. We'll have more on this story as events unfold and more facts are brought to light...

...Authorities are now confirming that the victims found this morning were that of Robert Grisham and his associate and believed bodyguard Austin Connors, both originally of Butte, Montana. The bodies were found at Mr. Grisham's pub and were believed to have been killed in the early morning hours either shortly after the bar had closed or long before it was scheduled to reopen at one that afternoon. We are being told that the body of Mr. Connors was found with a knife wound in the upper thigh, but it is being reported that the cause of death was in fact blunt trauma to the head. Connors was found in the hallway outside of an office in the back of the building. Apparently, Mr. Grisham's body was found beside a sawed off shotgun inside the office. It is speculated that Mr. Grisham was using this weapon to defend himself, as I'm being told the office door had several large holes fired through it and the hallway wall was riddled with buckshot...

...No images are being released of the body, but the corner has confirmed that the only wound sustained by Mr. Grisham was a fatal gunshot to his forehead, believed to have been made by a single shot from a .44 caliber handgun held very near or even against the victim's skin. This would seem to confirm the execution style killing we had early speculated ...

...Authorities in Lewis and Clark County are confirming six deaths in yesterday afternoon's shootout in the Missouri River Canyon. A spokesman for the Sheriff's Department has confirmed the deaths, along with one man in critical condition, bringing the total body count to thirteen confirmed fatalities in what is now being labeled as the Montana Massacre, a seventy-two hour spree of violence and death that began with a bombing at the apartment of a former marine and his new wife and ended with a mid-day shootout at a secluded, rural barn that is being linked to illegal high stakes gambling, prostitution and arms trafficking as well as connections to the Hell's Angels. The conflict is the bloodiest civilian incident in Montana history and may go down as one of the country's deadliest three day periods...

... We are told that the barn was the location of a weekend bordello and high stakes illegal gambling outfit that is believed to have been run by decorated retired marine officer Staff Sergeant Edgar Drummond, brother of Montana State Attorney General Shannon Drummond. Speculators are suggesting that an unknown dispute between the former marine and a local crime syndicate is responsible for setting off the violence that has left in its wake fourteen confirmed deaths including former Staff Sergeant Drummond and a powerful suspected crime boss named Robert Grisham. There is only speculation so far on Attorney General Drummond's involvement in the bordello or any of the other events...

...the bodies were found by local and federal authorities when a tip phoned in by an unidentified source led a small army of law enforcement officers and state SWAT teams to a secluded barn off a private drive atop the canyon bluff. Seven bodies were found strewn about in the aftermath of a shootout that one officer called "a graphic war scene with automatic weapons and spent shells everywhere..."

...It has now been nearly forty-eight hours since the last report of bloodshed in central Montana where a gruesome assault on a rural barn ended a seventy-two hour rampage of violence and death unmatched by anything the Big Sky state has ever witnessed. A total of fourteen men have been confirmed dead with one critically wounded and a local Sheriff missing. Current theories suggest that the violence stemmed from a mob war of sorts. But no one is certain yet what set off the bloodshed...

...The only survivor from this week's violence in Montana that left at least fifteen dead and local Sheriff Brad Gale missing has been identified as Quinn O'Leary, an active member of the Army Reserve and childhood friend and classmate of retired Staff Sergeant Edgar Drummond, who of course is the decorated marine that seems to be at the center of this whole traumatic incident. O'Leary remains listed as being unconscious and in critical

303

condition and we will keep you updated on any updates in this story...

...While it has been widely speculated that Drummond was running a bordello that rivaled Grisham's, and that his interests were protected by his brother, the State Attorney General. This station is reporting that several sources, that will remain nameless on the grounds of anonymity, have now come forward denying such allegations and claiming that Staff Sergeant Drummond's role in the massacre was one of vigilante-style justice, and that the elder Drummond was naïve to the entire ordeal and has always been an upstanding civil servant of the community. Adding to the mystery of the story, the US Federal Government is providing few details in response to new rumors of highly covert operations performed during the military career of Staff Sergeant Drummond...

...Shannon Drummond has just left the court house here in Helena where he addressed the media, saying that he is faithful in his belief that his brother never ran a bordello or any other criminal enterprise of any kind. He was adamant that his brother had simply been in the wrong place at the wrong time, owing money to the wrong kind of people and suggested that his brother was merely acting in self-defense to protect his community, his pregnant wife and his unborn child. Attorney General Drummond looked rather gaunt and pale, and in my opinion overall unwell, but stated that "these were the exact kinds of thugs and criminals he swore to protect his state from" and that he still planned to finish out his term. Still few details have been confirmed on his brother's military career. Sources are suggesting that Edgar Drummond definitely played some role in covert operations both in Eastern Europe and throughout Asia, yet nothing specific has been nailed down. The questions of course were raised when the initial investigation into his career was greatly deterred and all of the information deemed classified. The details only grew murkier after the release of his military transcripts stated that Staff Sergeant Drummond had served two tours in Afghanistan with the 2nd Battalion, 11th Marines, which was then immediately disputed by other members of the close-knit unit ...

304

Chapter 32

The reporters were everywhere. Like vultures. They came in packs and droves from every airport between Spokane and Billings. For ten days there wasn't a vacant room to be found in Butte or Helena. Great Falls ran out of cars to rent. They filled the restaurants and businesses downtown, and a local could hardly turn around without some gal from New York or Los Angeles in a full length designer pea coat with perfect hair and hard makeup sticking a tape recorder or microphone in his face, searching for a scoop; any secret the others lacked.

They picked at the wound, kept it infected and freshly bleeding. But they would never solve this one. It was a tight lipped town to begin with and the whole situation grew old pretty quickly. Still most people were too shocked and dumbfounded at how any of it could possibly be real to mount any significant resistance. The police didn't want to talk. The Sheriff's Department was completely embarrassed. They circled the wagons best they could.

The kid's brother did his best to remain hospitable and was fairly cordial, all things considered.

Oliver couldn't handle any of it. He was too old and too feeble for such a blow. He fell ill amidst the commotion, and reality just started fading away. It was sad. But he remained noble and faced it with honor. At first, he tried to keep up appearances. He went to the gym twice. But his light had gone dim overnight, and he saw only indifference in their hurried questions and emotionless faces. He never said one word to them. Then again, what was there to say? He was as in the dark as anyone else regarding the true scale of this whole thing.

He did talk to Sil on a couple occasions. Tried to open up. Get whatever it was out. But it wasn't a conflict to be resolved. Like a snakebite, it was done and gone the second it hit him, and the venom left a hole in him that couldn't possibly be refilled so late in life. He continued going to mass every morning and most nights. Otherwise he sat at home in the quiet of his empty house and reflected on life and all the loss and the hardship that existed out there. Wondering why. He wondered how the kingdom he cherished could be so blunt and brutal, and if the devil wasn't winning that ancient war.

The kid's brother called him one afternoon and they spoke for a short time though never directly on the subject. He told Oliver he would like to come and visit him sometime when all of this had passed. Oliver told him that such things never pass. Such things only build on other experiences and outcomes and help to shape a man's view of life. Shannon never responded to this, but the old man knew he understood. If anyone understood, it was this man. Before hanging up, he asked the old man about training his brother in those final years.

"He was true to himself," Oliver replied. "I'll say that for damn sure."

Everything else slowed to a crawl. Without a purpose, lonesomeness reclaimed him and each time he hobbled up the great stone steps and entered the vast and ornate cathedral and found his usual spot, in the quiet rush before the sermon as the pews filled around him, he found himself half expecting the boy to show up smiling and sit beside him in that somber silence of his. He had invited him many times. And the boy never seemed against the offer. The old man always imagined he might show.

But then the organ would cease and mass would begin and he would be reminded that the boy would never return to the land of the living, and he would see him in violent scenes as those final minutes of his life must have unfolded as the cold, dead flame burned out his soul. Then he would turn his thoughts to Heaven and pray that God find a place for such a boy. But there was doubt in his soul that fractured his poise and bled the faith from him. For the Bible had taught him that acts such as the kid had committed were unredeemable and he could no longer convince himself of God's existence in a world where boys like Edgar could be led so far astray, lost to such violence and desperation. This battle waged within him constantly, and would continue to for the remainder of his life.

Chapter 33

Shannon parked the truck and rolled down the window and grabbed the binoculars that sat on the seat beside him and glassed the hills to the north. He heard the kid open the passenger door as he stepped out and leaned over the hood glassing the areas farther east. To the west, the black scars ran up toward the old camp.

A lightening storm had started a wildfire in Pickett's Gulch two summers past and the black stood out along Camp Ridge beyond the foothills. It remained an eyesore. But grass was beginning to grow amidst the black trunks of the needle-less trees and the ache had eased in Shannon's heart. He knew it could have been much worse, and he had learned from a life long lived to find slivers of optimism amidst sorrowful events.

The blaze had spread for just four days before the winds shifted and turned the fire back on itself extinguishing it long before it ever reached the trenches dug by Forest Service firefighters a few miles away. Prevention was the policy, but for fires so remote amidst such rugged terrain, suppression and protection of property was the only option. Years of drought and the recent bark beetle epidemic had created endless landscapes of fuel all across the Rockies. The land was as scorched and dry as the people and stood on the brink of the same surrender. Resources had to be conserved for economic loss and human welfare. With this fire, the closest houses were the ranches far down in the valley beyond the foothills. The cows that summered in the mountains were all further north on the high plains at the base of Black Bear or east of Camp Ridge in the opposite direction from which the fire headed. There were cabins but not anywhere close. In the end, not an ounce of water nor retardant was dropped. All anyone could do was stand back and watch it burn and hope that it was regulated by the fickle will of the nature that caused it. The smoke clogged the skies over town for a week and anyone that stepped out of their house could smell it and feel it in their eyes.

In the aftermath of the flames, he had ridden his four-wheeler out the ridge to camp and made a perimeter of the charred remains. It had torched every inch of every acre from Camp Ridge down through the gulch and up over the Split before it bottlenecked itself by racing both up and down Six Point Gulch simultaneously. The barren walls and sheer relief of Windy Ridge were too steep to feed it oxygen fast enough, and as the wind shifted the ferocious flames suffocated itself in the blind haste to consume more. It was a sad sight to see and to smell, and it amazed him how anything could change a place so quickly and in such a lasting way. Even the earth was burnt and the heat and the smoke lingered about in the wretched black long after. Not a critter moved nor a bird sang. All he could do was shake his head at the size and brutality of the wound left behind. But he knew that in coniferous habitat fire served a purpose. It brought opportunity, decreasing the density of vegetation and cleansing the forests of the deadfall and underbrush that stifled new life. The resilient evergreens would reclaim the area in due time and the critters would return. The mosses and mushrooms were already hard at work, and the primary species were starting to reappear. There was grass growing in patches already, and it was green and vigorous, unafraid amidst the black. In the decades to come, new growth would spread quickly across the nutrient rich soil. In his lifetime, the kid would hunt those haloed grounds beneath mature fir and lodgepole as three generations of Drummond had done before him. That knowledge gave him some reprieve.

But that was yet to come. For the time being, Shannon had moved the camp to the opposite side of the Main Ridge, along the eastern base of the mountain, a stone's throw from where he had led his brother up toward the peak in desperate haste on a frigid morning all those years ago. Sometimes it felt like another lifetime. Other times it felt like only yesterday. The nightmares had never left him.

This would be his third fall at the new location, yet the camp still felt foreign. It probably always would. A man grew accustomed to the way things were and valued ritual and tradition, more as he aged. Yet even at the lower relief the solitude was the same, and he was finding new places to hunt and still learning. Always learning. He had learned to hunt smarter rather than harder and to avoid the long hard hikes up out of the God forsaken depths of those steep gulches. He enjoyed the vast distances of open terrain of the high plain on the northern side of the ridge. He saw a lot more hunters these days. But he was learning to accept that too. What other choice was there?

This year he would bring the boy along for the full week's stay. He was ten now. Hard to believe. Soon he would be old enough to carry a rifle. He was already shooting the old Savage with consistent accuracy at two hundred yards. He was a fast learner; a tough boy for his age. He had an easier-going disposition than his father. But that same trademark intensity still showed itself from time to time. He talked more than his father ever did, but Shannon liked that and figured his brother would have too.

His face was the mirror image of his father and grandfather before him, and it was a face Shannon caught himself getting lost in from time to time as the boy grew. His mother had never remarried, hardly dated, but she was tough too and she had carried on courageously despite all that happened. She lived for that boy and that boy alone. And Shannon helped as much as he could and had done his best to raise the boy as if he were his own. As he had promised his brother he would do. He and Krystle rarely spoke of his brother in specifics after those first few months of mourning. Despite everything that had happened in his life, those had been his hardest days and he could only imagine what she went through.

How much she told the boy he couldn't be sure. But he knew his father had died before he was ever born, and Shannon expected this would play some role in the shaping of his identity. A boy needed a father. He needed an example to follow and emulate, words of encouragement and occasional advice. Besides that, people talked, he would hear things, probably already had, and eventually he would read the stories on the internet and in old newspaper clippings. It wouldn't be easy. Being a Drummond never was.

He was ten years old and the time had come for his initiation. A right of passage. An interaction between predator and prey that was older than man, perhaps older than the mountains. There was much to teach, and he was ready to learn. The fire had certainly changed things. But it wasn't just the fire or the drought or the beetles. Everything was changing, as things had always changed.

The Big Sky State's population was closing in on a million people, and each fall seemed to bring more and more hunters

309

deeper into the hills. Four-wheelers were the norm now, as common as trucks had once been along the rugged, dirt roads and trails of Montana's wilderness areas. Few hunted by horse and even fewer by motorcycle.

Not only were there more hunters but other competition as well. Wolves had been reintroduced in the Yellowstone Park ecosystem and that age-old adversary of hunters and ranchers had branched out and started packs throughout the state. Mountain lion and grizzly numbers were up and the elk numbers way down. Plus the planet was warming and had the liberals up in arms. He heard it said that the environmentalists and activists growing voice would mean the end of big game hunting forever.

But he didn't believe it. It was all cyclical. The elk were still out there. A guy just hand to hunt a little harder and a little smarter to find them. Besides, wolves and mountain lions could be shot too.

He scanned the hills up to the high distant peaks still white with snow. Then he looked back at the prairies dry and rocky below. The water from Fir Creek ran out toward a larger creek and then dumped into the Missouri and eventually the ocean somewhere far off and unimaginable. It was early summer and already the water ran low far below the cut-bank where it turned and headed north and east following the contours of the earth. He had read somewhere that the mountains had long protected the inhabitants of higher elevations from outside invasions but also isolated them from wider influences of culture. But he knew the people that braved those high mountain passes and the harsh climate and wildlife and the long work days had mostly been running away from that culture to begin with. The rest were mostly running away from the law or otherwise out of options.

It had been almost a decade since he had lost his bid for the Democratic nomination for governor. He was working as a public defender now and he enjoyed the work. Lately there had been much talk of his becoming a judge, and he was open to such aspirations, although he knew his past would come under greater inspection. But he didn't worry about these things like he once had. There was more to life. His girls' basketball and volleyball and softball games for one. A charity organization for at-risk youth that he ran. He had even taken up fly-fishing. Plus he enjoyed

310

taking two weeks off every hunting season and never having to stress about it. It was a good life. A life he was finally content with.

He had never won Jill back, his first and only true love. She had eventually remarried, a doctor by the name of Stolker – a man of Dutch descent, from Eastern Montana; probably a whitetail deer hunter if a hunter at all. It had been a few years now. He couldn't remember how long exactly. But he and his ex-wife were on amiable terms, and they raised their daughters with very unstructured and equal custody. He had never been able to forgive her fully, or Zowiky. But that too had long since passed, and he was finally at peace with who he was and his place in the world. Of course there were moments of regret; days of gloom and doubt and struggle. Days where all he saw was his fifteen-year-old brother catching him in the embrace of his young girlfriend. But he faced those days and those harmful thoughts with grace, convinced he had learned all he could from his past, and he would never again let such guilt dictate his life.

"Uncle Shannon," the boy shouted. "I see them! They are on the open hillside way over there."

He looked out through the windshield toward the boy who was pointing to the east at a forty-five degree angle to the passenger side mirror. What looked like shrubs dotted a distant, grassy slope. He stepped out of the truck and looked in that direction. Sure enough, a large herd covered an open hillside more than a thousand yards away. With the naked eye they were indistinguishable at that distance even upon closer scrutiny, yet he knew they were undeniably elk before he ever raised his glasses.

"Good spot, Thomas." He commended as he raised his binoculars for a closer look. There were close to a hundred head dotted along from a low draw to the horizon. All but a few were lying down with their heads raised. The bulls should be growing their antlers again, but at that distance Shannon was unable to distinguish them from the cows. They looked peaceful and at ease at such great distance, lying that way in the open in such large numbers. Such evident disregard for furtiveness would be short lived though. Soon the antlers would grow and the velvet would itch and everything would start to change. In the dying days of summer the bulls would rut and one would chase all the others off

311

until the work of breeding and fending off challengers exhausted him and he wandered off by himself or with a few fellow bachelors and found a secluded place to hide deep in the dark forest where he could feed and replenish and wait out yet another winter. If he was careful enough and his luck held out, he might survive to repeat the whole cycle the following spring. If not, a new bull would replace him and the cycle would continue all the same. It was a bizarre existence, but such was life.

"How many do you think there are?" the boy asked. The excitement in his voice was infectious.

"I would say close to a hundred. Wouldn't you?"

"Yeah." The boy beamed. "Do you think they'll still be there when we come out to hunt?"

"Hard to say if they'll even be there tomorrow."

The boy's face showed disappointment, and his mind worked as he watched his uncle watch the elk.

"Would you shoot any of the bulls that are up there?"

"You bet I would."

"Me too. I can't wait until I get to shoot one."

"I know it. I'm excited for you to keep me company this year."

"Yeah. Me too."

It was late afternoon by the time they headed back to town. The sun hung low in the sky before them and Shannon had the visors down and his sunglasses on. It was a warm, gorgeous evening with very little wind and the boy had his window down as the truck coasted down through the foothills toward the highway. The radio was off and the only sounds in the truck were of the tires rolling across the gravel. The sky was just starting to color and the land was bathed in gold all around.

"Uncle Shannon, do you think that me and you will ever shoot bulls together like you and my dad did?"

"I sure hope so."

"I do too." The boy nodded. He wore a grey hooded sweatshirt with the sleeves extended out over his hands and he whipped the air with them as he spoke. His cowlick looked blond where it stood like an approaching wave on the left side of his scalp. "But first I have to learn to be a good hunter, huh?"

"There is a lot to learn. I still learn new things every year."

312

"Really?"

"Sure."

"Like what?"

"Well, like where elk like to hang out and how they behave. Things about the land and how the wind shifts and which parks are better for morning hunts and which are better to approach in the afternoon. Mostly, I learn to respect and enjoy the wilderness and the hunt more and to worry less about the harvest."

"Yeah, that will take me a long time." The boy said, his gaze drifting toward his window. They had turned onto the highway now and the air whistled through the open window as the truck gathered speed. "Good thing I have you to teach me about hunting huh?"

"I'll sure try and teach you what I know." There was moment of quiet and Shannon asked the boy if he wouldn't mind rolling up his window, which the boy did.

"Sometimes, I wish my dad was around to teach me stuff too." The boy said, but the words were spoken very matter-of-factly and there was little sorrow in the statement.

"Me too." Shannon swallowed keeping his eyes on the road ahead.

"Do you ever miss him?"

"Everyday." Shannon answered, and as he did he looked at the great Widow Makers stretched out along the distant horizon far beyond the gravelly range, the shapes and shadows and vegetation of the valley so familiar after all these years. He looked at those mountains so vast and ageless and in that fleeting moment, eyes hidden behind the lenses of his dark glasses, glare shining in from the sinking sun, he considered the insignificance of a human lifetime against the age of the world and for once it felt fair and just and curses seemed something only possible in the imaginings of man, and he was glad for the opportunity of this time he had been given to do with as he saw fit and to be part of things he believed in and strived for and couldn't possibly ignore, both chaotic and beautiful in this great mountain region along the southern border of the world's last frontier. He thought about hunting and about family and about the past and the future, violence and unstoppable change. He thought about the winter and the cold and the way the contours of the earth seem to flatten out

313

when viewed from the top of a high mountain peak. He thought of these things and other things for several minutes, and the boy had already moved on to thinking of something else when Shannon spoke again in the vacuum of that Ford pickup cab.

"I miss your dad every day."

The End

36942605R00180

Made in the USA
San Bernardino, CA
06 August 2016